PRAISE FOR HANNAH SUNDERLAND:

'Told with huge warmth and heart from start to finish'
Miranda Dickinson, author of *Our Story*

'A love story with a difference . . . uplifting and unusual'
Gillian McAllister, author of *How to Disappear*

'A delightfully romantic and endlessly enjoyable love story'
Isabelle Broom, author of *Hello, Again*

'Beautiful – I am a tiny bit broken'
Lisa Hall, author of *The Perfect Couple*

'Real and raw – I struggled to put it down'
Anna Bell, author of *We Just Clicked*

Also by Hannah Sunderland:

Very Nearly Normal

Hannah Sunderland was born and bred in Sutton Coldfield, north of Birmingham, where she still lives with her partner, several thousand books and a Swiss cheese plant named Wallace. She has a BA Hons degree in Fine Art from the University of Derby and now runs her own business, a company that makes props for crime scene reconstruction. The writing bug set in when someone handed her a notebook and she realised that she could create a world within it. She was a debut author during the Covid-19 lockdown and during this time discovered that a writer's life is not so different from self-isolation anyway. Her claim to fame is playing Tree #4 in her Year One school play.

You can follow @hjsunderland143 on Twitter.

At First Sight

Hannah Sunderland

avon.

Published by AVON
A division of HarperCollins*Publishers* Ltd
1 London Bridge Street
London SE1 9GF

www.harpercollins.co.uk

HarperCollins*Publishers*
1st Floor, Watermarque Building, Ringsend Road
Dublin 4, Ireland

A Paperback Original 2021

First published in Great Britain by HarperCollins*Publishers* 2021

Copyright © Hannah Sunderland 2021

Hannah Sunderland asserts the moral right to be
identified as the author of this work.

A catalogue copy of this book is available from the British Library.

ISBN: 978-0-00-836572-1

Typeset in Minion by Palimpsest Book Production Limited, Falkirk, Stirlingshire
Printed and bound in UK by CPI Group (UK) Ltd, Croydon CR0 4YY

MIX
Paper from
responsible sources
FSC™ C007454

This book is produced from independently certified FSC™ paper
to ensure responsible forest management.

For more information visit: www.harpercollins.co.uk/green

Author's Note

This book deals with loss, grief, depression and suicide. If any of these subjects are sensitive for you then please approach with care. I hope I have dealt with these important issues delicately.

This book is for Matt, Mom, Dad and for all of those whose light at the end of the tunnel has ever seemed dim.

Chapter One

Is there any time more stressful than your lunch break? That small span of time that evaporates so quickly while you're standing in a queue behind someone loitering at the till, who chooses their coffee at snail's pace while you bob, impatiently, on the balls of your feet. All I wanted from life was a sandwich and to not receive a disparaging look from my manager when I returned to the office, sweaty and red-faced.

I stood, fourth in line, in a queue that hadn't moved in over three minutes. The person on the till was clearly new and, while I sympathised with his wide-eyed and panicked expression, my patience was running low. I jostled my packet of crisps and paper-wrapped hummus and red pepper sandwich around in my arms until I managed to get a hand free to check my phone. I shuffled a little closer to the till as the woman at the front of the queue received her coffee and trotted off to a seat. The café was filling up quickly and if this rookie employee didn't hurry the hell up, I wasn't going to get a seat.

I caught the eye of the newbie's supervisor who stood behind him, patiently watching, although I could see that his patience was wearing thin too, and he nodded a look of recognition my way. We'd never really spoken more than the usual niceties. I didn't even know his name, his badge simply bearing the word 'supervisor' in worn black print, but I'd been coming in here for years and so we knew each other by sight. He had a shaved head, although the stubble that was always trying to creep through showed that his baldness was a choice and not a curse, and he wore thick-rimmed glasses, held in place by a silver nose stud.

There was one table free in the corner over by the window and three people in front of me. The man at the front of the queue had a plastic KeepCup ready in his hands for the barista to fill, so it was fair to say that he wasn't sticking around. The man in front of me already had a seat because the woman who was with him had darted off when a seat had become free a minute or two ago. So that left one other person, my rival for that one remaining seat. This café was my place to come for lunch, had been for years. But ever since they'd been featured in that issue of *The Birmingham Mail* a few months ago, it'd been getting busier and busier until there was no longer room for loyal customers like me who'd stuck with them through their experimental turmeric latte and chai tea scones phases.

KeepCup man took his freshly replenished cup back from the dazed-looking employee and headed for the door. My one remaining rival for that coveted final seat ordered his drink, paid and stood to the side as the man before me moved to the till and ordered two teas. I gave a little inward whoop as he said it. Tea was easy, quick. I might just have a chance at that chair. As I'd predicted, his teas were served quickly and he turned away to the table claimed earlier by the woman I assumed was his wife. I quickly ordered my Americano, a swift and simple choice, and tapped my card against the reader. I sent the poor overwhelmed boy a cheerfully sympathetic smile before stepping to the side and standing beside my rival.

I could see the barista in the background, putting the final sickly drizzle of caramel sauce on to whatever bastardised coffee monstrosity my rival had ordered and willed the girl beside her, who was just about done with my Americano, to move a little quicker. They turned at the same moment and presented the finished drinks. I nipped forward and grabbed my coffee, my fingers twinging at the heat that permeated through the cup as I clutched it, and turned to my table. Ha-ha! Victory was mine.

But as my eyes landed on the table that I'd been about to dive in the direction of, I saw that a couple were already sat there, perusing a menu and hanging their coats on the backs of the chairs that should have been mine. I tossed my head back and groaned. My rival with the diabetic coma in a cup turned on the ball of his foot and headed for the door. Turns out he was never a rival in the first place.

I looked around, searching for anywhere to sit, at this point an upturned box would do just fine. I pushed the sandwich up so that it was wedged between my less than generous chest and my forearm, the crisps from my meal deal gripped in my elbow, coffee in my left hand. I reached down with my free right hand and got out my phone. Twenty-seven minutes of freedom remained and I intended to spend that time sitting down. Over by the window was one of those annoying communal tables. It was rectangular and had several separate groups of people sitting at it. There wasn't much room, but just there on the end was one space, next to a lone dark-haired man, his back to me, his shoulders hunched over towards the table. I clutched everything tightly and set off towards my last hope of a seat.

I hated situations like the one I would shortly find myself in, where I had to share an enclosed, intimate space with strangers whom I felt like I should talk to, out of politeness, but whom I knew had absolutely no interest in talking to me, nor me in talking to them. My mother hadn't tried to force many traits upon me when I was younger, but politeness had been something she had been stern about. She always tried to encourage me to smile at strangers who passed me by and strike up small talk with people in lifts. I had very little control over it, as if the politeness that had been drummed into me as a child took physical form and began overriding my ability to stay quiet. It happened all the time in taxis. One minute I'd be sitting, quite happily minding my own business and trying to distract myself with my phone, the next I'd ask the question that every cabby must hear a thousand times a day: 'So, have you been busy?'

Before the ride was over, I would know all about them: their name, every single one of their past employers, their children's names and where they went to school. I'd leave feeling like me and old Mahmood were childhood friends and then we'd part, never to set eyes on each other again.

I arrived at the table as my sandwich began slipping from my arm and I bowed to speak to the hunched man. 'Excuse me.' He jumped a little and turned to me with cornflower blue, darkly lashed eyes. It looked as though I'd interrupted

4

a deep thought, which was lingering like fog on a wet autumn morning. 'Do you mind if I sit here?' Before he could answer, the sandwich made its escape and slipped from my grasp. I jerked my arm upwards, clocking it with my elbow and sending it careening up into the air. It tumbled, rather more gracefully than I would have imagined, before falling downwards in the direction of the lone man's head. I gasped inwardly as the sandwich slapped into the side of his face with a wet thud, flopping into his lap before dropping through his knees and thumping onto the floor.

We stared at each other for a silent moment, the other people around the table sheepishly looking on or sniggering behind hands. I wasn't quite sure if he was about to shout at me, or burst into laughter. 'Ha-ha.' I spoke it rather than laughed. 'Guess hu-mussed the catch on that one? I guess that joke only works if you know that there's hummus in the sandwich, which you didn't and the joke wasn't any good anyway.' Oh, shut up, Nell. He pressed his lips together suppressing laughter or embarrassment, bent down and picked it up. He placed the sandwich down on the table in front of the empty seat and shrugged his trendily unruly eyebrows.

'Be my guest,' he mumbled.

'Thank you.' I sat, arranging my things on the table. I already felt awkward as I peeled back the wrapping on my slightly misshapen sandwich and raised it inelegantly to my mouth. I hated eating in public when I felt as though I was being watched. I was not what anyone would call a graceful eater. I was one of those people who go into some sort of food-induced trance, where I become completely unreachable until the food is gone. I have no idea what I must look like when I do this. I have mental images of Henry VIII chomping down on a turkey leg, or a snake when a frozen mouse is dropped into its paths and it has to unhinge its jaws around it. It's something that I've been trying to work on, ever since I became old enough to be embarrassed by it. It's still a work in progress, much like the not speaking to strangers thing.

The man beside me had resumed the position he'd held when I'd stormed in to ruin his calm, sitting with his head hunched over his mug of tea. The bag was still floating in the cup, secured by a white string that was folded over the handle. The liquid it was bobbing in looked to have gone cold. I wondered if he too was on his lunch break. I doubted it. He looked far too relaxed. He didn't look dressed for work either, unless he was one of those arty types who work as graphic designers and their bosses don't care about how they dress. It could be an office thing like dress-down Fridays, but it was Wednesday. Maybe he worked somewhere hipster? Wasn't every day a dressed-down day for a hipster?

He wore black jeans, purposefully ripped at the knees, and a dark grey shirt that was slightly too large for him. It had several tiny holes in it and faded artwork on the front – some sort of zombie film poster from the Sixties or Seventies. Over the shirt sat a stonewashed denim jacket that looked as old as he was, the sleeves rolled up to reveal pale forearms with a covering of dark hair. Despite all of the strategic sartorial distressing, he managed to not look like he'd just had a fight with a porcupine or had been living on the streets, which I applauded him for.

He looked creative, as if he could also be an artist or a sculptor or something. Whatever his job was, he certainly didn't look as if he worked in an office like the one I'd just left. I swallowed my bite of sandwich and took a sip of coffee, the liquid scalding me slightly as it passed over my tongue. I swallowed that too and I made the mistake of not filling my mouth with something before the words began to try and push themselves out of it. I made a strange 'ku' sound before jamming the sandwich back into my mouth and smearing hummus over my right cheek. He looked up from under his tousled dark fringe and observed my awkwardness for a moment, before going back to nursing his cold tea, staring down at the surface as if he was trying to read the tea leaves.

The hand that clutched his cup wasn't covered in paint or ink or clay and so I threw my guess about him being an artist out the window. I noticed a burst of hairline scars that crackled over the knuckles of his right hand, which lay balled into a fist on the surface of the table, the scars taking the pattern of forked lightning. A further glance caused me to notice that the nails of his scarred hand were slightly longer than those on his left and the ends of his fingers on his left hand were calloused. Musician – that was it. He played guitar.

My mouth opened again to ask him what sort of music he played but, again, I stopped myself. *Just eat your sandwich and shut up,* I chastised myself. *You don't need to speak to him. You can bet a million pounds that he does not, under any circumstances, want to talk to you.*

'So, what are they saying?' For God's sake!

He looked up at my question with that same fog lingering in his eyes.

'I'm sorry?' he asked in an accent that I didn't quite catch.

I awkwardly gestured to his cup and said it again, cringing inwardly as I did. 'Your tea leaves, what are they saying?' Why could I not just sit still and be quiet?

He looked down at his used-up teabag and prodded it

with the end of his finger. It bobbed pathetically in the milky water before settling again. He huffed a laugh that was so subtle it simply sounded like a heavy breath.

'Not very much, to tell yer the truth,' he replied and this time I heard his Irish accent loud and clear. 'I don't think they tell yer too much when they're still in the bag.'

'Ah,' I said, 'that must be where I've been going wrong.'

We smiled at each other as the rest of the people around the table retracted themselves a little further from the conversation, as if they feared being pulled into its gravitational field. He unfurled his scarred hand and I noticed that he was holding something small and orange. I got a better look at it as he rolled what seemed to be a misshapen marble between two fingers.

'Wildly underappreciated game,' I said, almost raising a hand to my face and slapping myself silent.

He turned to me with a questioning frown.

'Marbles.' I pointed to the one in his hand. 'Used to play it with my uncle.'

'Uh-huh,' he said, slipping the marble back into his pocket.

'You play guitar?' I nodded towards his hands, only then realising how creepy my observations were.

'That's right – among other things.' Although he was frowning, his mouth was pulled up on the one side by a wry smile. 'How'd yer know that?'

'Fingernails. My ex used to play. I'd recognise the cause of those callouses anywhere.' I blushed. Had I just inadvertently flirted with this man by casually dropping into conversation that I was single? I wasn't usually this bold. It had taken me a year to even imply to my ex-boyfriend that I fancied him.

8

The guy beside me was attractive, in that very specific musician kind of way, with large blue eyes lined with dark lashes and a chin dappled with dark stubble, which was interspersed at intervals with flecks of red.

'Sorry.' I nervously sipped my coffee and swallowed the bitter liquid. 'I know it's not the done thing to talk to strangers anymore, but I can't seem to keep my mouth shut.'

'So, this is somewhat of a chronic problem for yer then?' His smile grew a little until it was almost a full-blown grin and my stomach lurched like I'd just driven fast over the brow of a steep hill.

'Oh yes, since birth. In fact, I left the womb plying the midwife with small talk.' I laughed in that moronic way I did when I found something surprisingly funny. He countered with a laugh more musical than I would ever be able to muster.

'Well, no need to worry, I don't mind talking. Although, I don't know how much I'll have to say or how interesting it'll be. I've never been what'cha'd call chatty.'

'No problem. I'll probably just talk at you until you die of boredom. So, if you're okay with that then I'll chat away.'

'I can't think of a better way to go.'

I shuffled a little closer to the table, my knee bumping his and making me all flustered. 'Sorry. Sorry.' I giggled girlishly and then shook my head at myself. 'Sorry.'

'It's only a knee. I've got another one,' he quipped.

I shuffled backwards again and pulled the crust away from the remaining half of my sandwich, placing it down on the greaseproof wrapping.

'So, erm . . . are you on your lunch break?' I asked.

'No, I, err, I actually quit my job at Aldi yesterday.' He

rubbed the back of his neck with his hand and a spark of something filled his eyes for a moment as he stared forward out of the window at the brick wall across the street. He looked intense, as if he'd remembered something imperative that he should have done, which had completely slipped his mind until now.

'Congratulations. Were you there long?'

'A few years longer than I should have been,' he answered as he looked back at me, the intensity beginning to filter away.

'What about you?' he asked. 'You've the panicked look of someone trying to get the most out of their lunch hour.'

'Well deduced,' I replied. 'Yeah, it's not that I'm desperate to get away, I think I'm one of the very few people who actually enjoy their job. But I'm a messy eater, you see, and so I have to factor in clean-up time.' Why did I just say that? I was making myself sound like I had the motor functions of a toddler.

He chuckled. 'Well, I haven't had to duck and cover for a second time yet, so I think you'll be back in time.' He looked into my eyes, his grin pulling wide again, and something about it sent a lead weight toppling into my stomach.

My own face pulled into a smile and I worried that I had red pepper in my teeth, but he didn't look disgusted so I guessed I was all right, or maybe he just had a kink for women who wore their food instead of ate it. If he did then who was I – his dream, food-clad woman – to kink-shame him?

I moved my legs nervously, my toe hitting something hard under the table that rocked backwards and forwards in an attempt to stay upright, making a hollow sound against the aged oak floorboards as it moved.

I looked down under the table and found a brown paper bag with the logo of the fancy liquor shop in the old Victorian arcade around the corner. I looked back up to find him looking mildly embarrassed.

'A breaking up with your work present to yourself?' I asked, trying to lighten the sudden shift in mood.

His smile was soon back in place. 'Something like that, yeah.'

'So, what are you doing here? I think I've managed to deduce that you're not a native Brummie.'

'Really?' He raised his eyebrows in mock admiration, his accent thickening comically. 'Well, I'll be damned. What a keen ear yer have.'

We both laughed.

I was shocked at how well this was going. Was I successfully hitting on a man, a very good-looking, nice-seeming, sane-appearing, charming, stomach-butterfly-inducing man? And to top it all off, he was Irish and everyone knew that an Irish accent made a person about eighty per cent more attractive.

Maybe this was my meet-cute. Maybe this was the moment I met the man I was going to marry and we'd look back in ten years with our children around us and we'd both thank that couple for taking up the last empty table.

'So, err, I moved away from home at eighteen and then to London for a while before eventually ending up here.'

'Was the call of Birmingham just too much to resist?' I asked sarcastically.

'Hey, don't talk yourself down. This place is all right, once yer get past the funny accent.'

'You're one to talk.' I chuckled and when my laughter died

down, I became aware that he was staring at me, his mouth curled up in a crooked smile. It made my insides turn to putty. God damn it, he was pretty. But the longer he looked, the more I began to worry that he was staring at something I'd unwittingly adhered to my face. I raised a hand and patted my cheeks worriedly.

'What?' I asked, feeling myself blush.

'Nothin'.' He inhaled a deep breath and looked back down at the surface of his tea. 'You've a lovely smile, is all.'

My heart felt tight, like it might burst. Was I having a heart attack or indigestion? Or was I simply not used to these feelings? The minutes ticked by and, gradually, our time ran out. How dare my job interfere with this moment where everything was seeming to fall into place.

I was cutting it fine, with a five- or six-minute walk back to the office and only four to spare. I could jog, I supposed. I hated being late. It filled me with an unspeakable anxiety left over from when I turned up late for school and ended up having to stand at the front of assembly facing the whole school until it was over.

'I just realised that I've been so busy talking that I haven't even asked your name,' I said, leaning in a little.

He looked up from his tea, stroking the rim of the cup with his index finger. 'Charlie.'

'Nell.'

His eyes softened. 'Nice to meet you, Nell.'

Ask for his number. Just do it. You've been speaking to him for ages now – just ask for his number. If he wasn't single then he wouldn't have kept the conversation up and if he wasn't interested then he'd have left ages ago. It's not like his cold tea was keeping him here.

12

'Well, Charlie,' I said, testing this new name out on my tongue to see how it felt. It felt pretty right to me. 'I'd better be getting back to work.'

He held out his hand and I don't know if it was just wishful thinking, but I think I saw a hint of disappointment in his kind eyes.

'It's been really nice talking to you,' I added. *Ask for his number! If you only listen to the voices inside your head just once in your whole, entire existence then let it be now. Let this be the moment!* I reached out and took his hand, shaking it slowly, lingering as our skin touched for the first time. Maybe there would be other times too? But only if I stopped being a coward and asked for his number.

'You too, Nell. I think I needed a chat with someone like you today.'

'Me too,' I replied.

He loosened his grip on my hand and I felt my stomach lurch as our hands parted ways.

'It's been great to meet you,' I said, realising that I was stalling while I worked up the guts to ask.

Do it!

I stood up and pulled my bag strap over my shoulder. Gathered my rubbish and empty mug.

DO IT!

'You too,' he replied.

Do it, you loser!

I exhaled loudly, the words on my tongue but unwilling to fall out of my mouth. I was scared. I was a stupid scared little coward. I wasn't used to this. It had been so long since I'd asked someone out and, even then, I'd got a friend to do it for me.

13

I sighed at myself and dithered a little on the balls of my feet. 'Well . . . see ya.' I lifted my rubbish-filled hand in a small wave and turned away.

I tugged open the door, more furious with myself than I had ever been before. I'd been so confident up until that last second. Shit! What was wrong with me? You couldn't shut me up when it came to my lifelong bout of verbal diarrhoea, but when the moment was right, when the words really mattered, I became mute.

The soles of my trainers slapped against the pavement angrily as I stormed past people who eyed me with suspicion.

I was almost back at the office, the dismal grey building looming over me like a dystopian skyline, when I stopped, the momentum of my angry walk making me sway as I halted. You would never guess, from the outside, how much good happened inside that building.

When was this ever going to happen again? When was I going to have an accidental run-in with a good-looking Irishman? When did things like that ever happen in real life? Never! That's when and I'd just wasted the moment of a lifetime.

I spun on my heel and began running back to the café, the courage to do what needed to be done burbling in my stomach along with my hastily eaten lunch.

Come on, Nell, you can do this. I held my bag tight against my hip as I ran. I hadn't run in years, not since school and the dreaded bleep test. My legs cried out in anguish, as if asking, 'What did we do to deserve this?'

I turned the corner, almost ploughing into a woman with a pram. I shouted a hasty apology before lowering my chin to my chest and sprinting the rest of the way. By the time I reached the café, I was panting so hard that I thought I might pass out. Sweat beaded on my brow and I just knew that my make-up would be a mess now, sliding down my face like a custard pie.

I opened the door and looked over at the bench but the space where he'd been was empty.

My shoulders sagged with the knowledge that I would probably never see him again and I felt like crying. This had been my one opportunity and I'd thrown it away.

I bit down hard on my bottom lip and turned around, walking back to work slowly, the journey harder this time because of my aching legs and the weight of crushing disappointment that I was carrying.

There was absolutely no way I was going to be on time now.

Chapter Two

I woke with that sickening feeling that I always got when I found a weight in the bed beside me and the sound of another person's slumberous breaths on the pillow a few inches away from my face.

I opened one eye, squinting as if letting in less of the image would stop me from seeing what I knew I was about to see. There, his head half sunken into the memory foam pillow, was the face I'd woken up to thousands of times before. His unruly, finely kinked hair was a cloud around his head, tousled to disarray by the way he tossed and turned in his sleep.

Joel and I had broken up two years ago, after seven and a half years together. Things had been going south for a while prior to that and so when the time came to call a time of death, I did. It had been hard; breaking up always is, especially after so long. You grow to depend on the other person, settle into a routine and then all of a sudden, you have to picture your day without them and all the things that being with someone entails.

I'd been thinking about being on my own for a while, craving the solitude that came with not having someone else to think about all the time, but things had become startlingly clear to me almost two years before we broke up when I'd found myself in the self-service queue in Boots waiting to buy a pregnancy test. My period had been a week and a half late and the panic had been building up inside me since that little notification had popped up on my phone from my period tracking app, telling me that I was late.

I'd cried as I'd waited for my future to be spelled out in little pink lines and thought about what a baby would mean for us. I couldn't raise a baby alone. I didn't have the money, we didn't have the space and I couldn't imagine a young life being shaped in that horrid little hovel that we'd shared at the time. Thankfully there had been no baby and, even though it would take me a good long while to be able to act on the feelings of discontent I had towards our relationship, that was the moment I knew that the forever that Joel and I had promised ourselves at the start wouldn't be as long as we'd both thought.

Us ending was for the best. There wasn't a person alive or dead who would argue with that. We were happier apart. We functioned better, got along better too and we respected each other way more than we had done over half of the duration of our relationship. But over the last six months, to the chagrin and dismay of the few who knew, we'd started to become each other's cushion against the harsh world that we hadn't had to engage with before.

We were both in the same terrifying, unfamiliar boat and so it only seemed logical that we would run back to each other for solace.

It all started when Joel's dad had died. He'd been at working at the builders' merchant, where he'd been for over fifteen years, walking between the stacks to help a customer find something. A forklift on the other side of the stack was getting a pallet of cement bags from one of the high shelves when the whole stack collapsed. Joel's dad and the customer had died instantly and Joel had been devastated. He'd comforted his mum, but one night as she slept off the tranquiliser that the doctor had given her, he'd gone out walking and ended up at my front door.

Ned, my housemate, best friend and colleague (it's a long story), was not a fan of Joel, to put it lightly. He thought he was a waste of space who'd wronged me far too many times to be excused, but Joel had been the first and only love of my life and there's a bond there that you can't deny will always exist. I'd let him in, shed a tear or two along with him and he'd ended up staying the night. Now, I didn't sleep with him out of pity. I don't want anyone thinking that I'm some sort of compassionate hooker, paid in sad stories. He was lonely and I was too. I think we needed each other with a kind of mutual loneliness that could only be solved in one way.

After that, Joel and I spent quite a bit of time together. I had been close with his mother and brothers and so I had helped them with the funeral arrangements and been there with my friendly, absorbent shoulder when they needed it. His father's side of the family came from Nigeria and so I had never met them before. His grandmother was so old that she reminded me of when you burn paper and the ash retains its shape. I feared that one touch might damage her deep brown, creped skin and turn her to dust. We'd talked on the phone and I'd been on the front of every Christmas card that the family had sent to her for the last six years. So, no one had the heart to tell her that we'd broken up. I'm pretty sure she'd have gone into cardiac arrest right there and then if we'd told her. We'd kept up the charade for ten days, until the family went back home and Joel and I parted awkwardly at the door.

We'd slept together about fifteen times since then, which was fifteen more times than we had over the last eighteen months of our relationship.

These nights of weakness usually came when one of us was upset or lonely, when one of us had had a bad day or if we were simply bored.

Ned told me that I was being reckless, but I reminded him that if his ex-wife showed up, the last thing he'd do was turn her away.

I sighed into the bunched-up duvet that I'd pulled over my face and slipped out of bed as soundlessly as possible. I took Joel's faded red Bob Dylan T-shirt from the floor and pulled it over my head before easing open the door and running to the bathroom.

I jumped into the shower and turned the heat right up in an attempt to scald away my shame. I'd felt awful last night, my stomach churning with regret at not having the balls to ask Charlie for his number. When I'd called Joel and invited him over, I'd wanted to be calling someone else. When I'd plied him with beer and kissed him in the kitchen, I'd imagined he was Charlie. When I was leading him upstairs, I don't know what I was thinking, but my head wasn't filled with what I know Joel wished it was. I sanded off a layer of skin with an exfoliating mitt and dabbed myself dry with a fluffy towel before going and standing by the mirror and taking a long, hard, literal look at myself. I looked the same as I had yesterday; perpetually tanned skin – courtesy of my father as my mother was as pale as Casper – same long chestnut-coloured hair, same large unruly eyebrows sitting above even larger brown eyes. But added on to that familiar image of myself were dark bags beneath my eyes, weighed down with all of the self-hatred that I felt towards myself right now.

I knew how this encounter would end. It would be the same as all the other times and I didn't know if I could have that conversation again. I combed out my hair, brushed my teeth, heaved a great sigh and made my way back to my room. Just as I reached the door, Ned stepped out onto the landing and tilted his head in judgement.

'Don't,' I said quietly, with the hope that I could get dressed and slip out to work without Joel waking. It was a coward's way out, but I had never pretended to be brave. 'I already hate myself enough.'

I slipped into the room and my heart sank when I found Joel, half dressed, his red-rimmed glasses, which I'd picked out for him, perched on the bridge of his nose, and searching for his T-shirt. 'Ah, there it is,' he said with a wide, cheerful grin when he saw me. 'I've been looking for that.' He walked over and placed a hand on my shoulder. 'Looks far better on you though.' He leaned forward and tried to kiss me. I don't know why he did this. Why he always thought that things were going to change, that this time would be different.

'Joel, you know what I'm going to say,' I said, quietly, feeling like the worst person in the world. When we initiated these encounters/booty calls, we would always start off on

20

the same page. Sex, that's all this was. A tumble in the sheets to alleviate the boredom and loneliness of our otherwise socially barren lives, but in the mornings, he would always think that things had changed, that wounds had been repaired, that I loved him again like I once had.

'Come on, Nell. There has to be a reason why we keep coming back to each other. I know we let things slip a bit at the end, but we're meant to be together. I know you feel it.'

I walked over to my chest of drawers, just so he'd stop looking into my eyes like Kaa from *The Jungle Book*, trying to hypnotise me into loving him again. I found some underwear and awkwardly put it on while keeping Joel's shirt firmly over the parts that I didn't want him seeing again.

'We agreed,' I almost snapped then tried to soften my voice a little. 'We agreed that sex was all this was. You agreed to that too, remember?' I hated who Joel turned me into. I hadn't been a nice person during our last couple of years together. I could see that now in retrospect and I never wanted to be that version of me again. Bitter and depressed with a volatile anger that needed little to ignite, but the more time I spent with Joel, the more I felt her coming back.

'I do remember – but, Nell, we've been doing this for half a year now. Surely that's got to tell you something.'

My anger was building by the millisecond. He always made me feel like the villain; it was his specialty. He knew full well that he'd agreed to this. Smash and dash. Moment of weakness. Tryst. One-night stand. Ill-advised mistake. Whatever you wanted to call it, that's what it was.

'No, Joel.' I pulled off his T-shirt, now that everything was hidden behind the appropriate underwear, and held it out to him as I stared firmly into his eyes.

'Just because we have sex every so often doesn't mean that things have changed. It doesn't mean that we've fixed anything that was broken. All this does is plaster over the cracks for a while. If we got back together things would turn out the same as they did the first time.' He took the shirt from me, his eyes wide like a child on the verge of a crying fit. 'I think that this should be the last time this happens.' I know that I'd said this before, that I'd meant it all the other times too. Not that I was the only one to blame for this toxic thing we had going, but I couldn't do this anymore. I couldn't see the disappointment in his eyes when his plan to reunite us failed for the umpteenth time. It wasn't fair on him and his manipulation, making me feel bad about myself for days afterwards, wasn't fair on me either.

He pulled the Bob Dylan shirt over his head and sniffed. I turned away and went over to the mirror to tackle the task of making myself look presentable for the day.

'I'll be seeing you then,' he said, coming up to the mirror and sliding his hands around my waist. He pulled me backward, pressing his body to mine and kissed me gently on the cheek. Damn him.

I didn't turn around and watch him leave. This was it. This was the final time.

It had to be.

Chapter Three

The big fat pigeon sitting outside the window taunted me with its freedom and cooed at me through the glass, its beady little eyes goading me into distress. I'd been watching it and it had been watching me, in some sort of wild-west-style stare-off, ever since I returned from the bathroom a few minutes ago. It strutted about on the windowsill, more compact than your regular crumb scavenger that hangs around outside Greggs awaiting a morsel of pastry from a sausage and bean melt. No one in the office probably knew that this taunting little bird was a tumbler pigeon, if they'd even noticed it at all. I only knew what it was because my uncle had been a pigeon fancier and had kept several different types over the years.

I'd always found the term pigeon fancier a little disconcerting, giving me mental images of fully-grown men looking at pigeons the way Bob Hoskins looks at Jessica Rabbit.

The pigeon turned away from me, as if its daily quota of interest in my life had run dry and I didn't blame it. How that mistake at the café yesterday and the subsequent Joel-based mistake had haunted me like a bad odour ever since, turning everything sour. The pigeon stepped from the sill, unfurling its wings and taking off into the dusk sky, disappearing before I had chance to see it show off its moves.

I'd seen them before, flying completely normally until, all of a sudden, they stop, as if shot from the sky. They tumble over themselves, spinning their way through the air towards the ground until you think that their time here is up, their ticket punched, their bucket kicked. But then, they right themselves, returning to the flock and carrying on as if nothing has happened. My uncle had told me once that it's a survival tactic that domestic pigeons have developed over centuries but it seems strange to me, that a method of survival should look so much like the opposite.

I heaved a sigh, dug my heels into the pale blue carpet tile below my desk, threadbare from years of wear, and pulled myself closer to the desk. I replaced my headset, the plastic band returning to the notch it always created in the skin behind my ear.

I looked at my screen and saw that there were three calls waiting to be answered. I clicked a call, accepted it and sat back in my chair, taking a breath before speaking. 'Hello, you're through to Healthy Minds. Can I ask who's calling please?'

'Hey, is that Nell?' The familiar voice came on the line.

'Hey, Jackson,' I replied. 'How's it going today?'

Jackson had been a regular caller, almost once a week, for the past five years. In fact, his first call to the helpline had been during my first shift and so I felt a sort of affinity with him. He was bipolar and had severe social anxiety that he tried to fight at every opportunity. Some of those fights were more successful than others. During my time helping him on calls, we'd managed to find him an appropriate doctor, the right meds and he was doing better now than he ever had before. Things had been going well until his mother had died last year, making matters worse.

'I'm okay,' he said as if trying to reassure himself. 'Better than last week, but worse than I'll be after I hear your voice for a few more minutes.'

I smiled and relaxed a little. Jackson always set me at ease because it was like talking to an old friend. I often found it strange that if I passed him in the street I would have no idea who he was. But I knew more about the inner workings of his mind than anyone else on the planet, other than his doctor. Whenever he got through to another operator, he would ask to be patched through to me, no matter how long he had to wait.

I hadn't thought about this as a career choice when I was younger. I'd wanted to be a counsellor or support worker because I liked to help people, enjoyed seeing a smile at the end of the tears. But uni had been daunting for me and I'd found myself sinking in a sea of people who seemed to be far surer about everything than I was. I hadn't known what I'd missed, if there was a book I'd failed to read or a class I'd somehow not attended, but everyone else seemed to know far more than I did and, in the end, I'd decided to leave that confusing world behind.

I kept in touch with my friends who were still at uni, doing the drinking and partying part of student life in lieu of the actual student part. That's how I met Joel. I worked in cafés for a while, a carpet shop for a little bit, but after working for years in jobs that made nothing but money and did nothing of greater value for the world, I decided to volunteer at the Healthy Minds helpline. I had only planned on staying for a couple of months, but six months later I was still there and the office manager had offered me one of the very few paid positions. I'd snapped up the offer in a millisecond.

I loved helping people. I loved putting the phone down and knowing that the person who'd called was freer and happier than they had been when I'd picked up. But the job wasn't always so rosy. I could usually tell within thirty seconds if a call was going to be a suicidal one or not and whenever those dreaded calls came in, my stomach would bunch up in knots and my heart would hammer in my chest. Not that they happened as often as people might think. But when they did all moisture would leave my mouth and I would find myself calm and reassuring on the outside, but inside a maelstrom of anxiety was raging. Because all it takes to tip someone over from thinking about it to actually doing it, is one badly constructed sentence, one thoughtlessly uttered phrase – and that's a lot of pressure.

You could always tell when Ned'd had a suicidal call. We referred to them as hard calls, because that's exactly what they were. Hard for them, hard for us.

He'd had a particularly bad one a couple of years ago and it just so happened that that call happened on his birthday. He'd been happy for the majority of the day, which was odd for him because he usually detested his birthday. Barry, the office manager, had presented him with a cake and we'd all sung to him. Then he'd got back to work and answered the call that would put a stop to his birthday joviality. He never knew what happened to the person on the other end of the line and, in some ways, that's even worse than knowing the truth, because ambiguity allows for hope and there is no crueller thing in this world than hope.

Jackson had been a hard call on a few occasions, but not today. Today all he wanted to do was chat and talk about his day at work and how he'd been feeling. The doctor was trying him on a new course of anti-anxiety medication and he said that, so far, it was working a treat. We talked about how he was ordering himself a curry, and how he'd be setting up the first season of *Game of Thrones*, ready to watch once the delivery man arrived.

It was fifteen minutes before he signed off with his usual 'Ta-ra, Bab' and then he was gone.

I sat back in my chair, seeing that all of the other calls were being handled at the moment, and I looked out of the window again. The light outside was turning from dusk to darkness and I caught sight of my reflection in the glass. My hair was no longer holding the delicate beachy wave, which I'd attempted with great success this morning when Joel had left, after watching a YouTube tutorial on ten different uses for flat irons. It had now fallen both flat and frizzy, which I didn't even think was possible. I grabbed one of the decade-old bobbles from beside my monitor and twisted my unruly locks into a topknot.

I saw Ned in the reflection of the window as he made his way over, coming back in from a meeting with Barry.

'If you're quite done admiring yourself, Barry's got a favour to ask,' he said when he reached his cubicle and leaned one elbow nonchalantly on the partition between our desks. Barry was the single least inspiring person I'd ever encountered. Even the resigned timbre of his voice was enough to sap the enthusiasm from any conversation. And yet, he was such a good counsellor that he'd started as a volunteer and worked his way up to manager over the eight years he'd been here.

'Admiring wouldn't be the right word,' I replied. 'Loathing would be a good alternative, berating maybe.'

'What do I keep telling you? You need to leave Joel behind. He's no good for you,' he said with an air of I told you so about him.

'I know.' I sighed. 'Now what is it that Barry wants me to do?'

'That new volunteer, Caleb, he's stuck in traffic and will be a tad late. Do you mind covering until he arrives?'

'Fine. Anything to take my mind off how much of a tit I am.' I sent a smile his way.

He glanced around to check that no one was paying us any attention and whispered, 'I got some mince on my lunch break. You up for spag bol and a marathon of *Cold Case Files*?'

'Sounds like perfection,' I whispered back before turning to the screen and readjusting my headset. Ned eyeballed Beryl, the volunteer opposite me, and slid back into his cubicle as if he'd just successfully pulled off a covert op.

Ned and I had got along well ever since I started here five years ago. He'd been here a little longer than me and was one of the others who were paid for their time here. We sat in the far back corner, a coveted spot that we'd earned from years of consistently moving along a desk when someone left until we finally got our chosen seats. He was in his forties, although I didn't know where exactly as he was always very vague on the subject. He was shorter than average with a longer than average neck, which I am sure is trying to make

28

up for the deficit in leg length. He has large brown eyes and his hair is short, dark and unremarkable. He is, in almost every way, very plain. But he possesses that thing that some people have, that glimmer of something that shines out and puts a glow over everything else. I know that a lot of the women in the office fancy him but he's always just been good old platonic Ned to me.

Ned and his wife had separated several years ago and I think that she'd messed him around for much longer than any decent woman should have. He lived alone in a huge Victorian detached house on one of the most sought-after suburban roads in town and I think that he was just as lonely as I was. When I'd started at the helpline, I'd been living in a shitty little flat above a kebab shop on a road that, let's just say was in a less desirable postcode. Joel and I had moved in there together a year after leaving university and three weeks after moving in, there was a drive-by shooting at the end of the road, but luckily the only victim had been the driver's side door of a Peugeot 206.

Joel and I lived crammed together in the tiny little hovel for years, before our relationship fell apart and he left to go back home and live with his parents. I'd struggled to keep up the payments alone, not that Joel had contributed much towards rent when he lived there anyway, and the air inside the flat always smelled like three-day-old doner meat and mint yogurt, which after surprisingly little time of living there, had put me off kebabs for life.

Ned and I had quickly become good friends after I'd had an emotional breakdown in the toilets at work, during a particularly bitchy phone call from my landlady, and Ned had heard me crying from the hallway. He'd taken me out for a cheer-up Chinese and asked me if I wanted to move in with him as a lodger. It made sense – he had that huge empty house and I hated my horrid little flat. He only wanted half the amount of rent that I was already paying and he said it would be nice to have someone around to watch true crime documentaries with in the evenings and that having someone else there would make him feel less guilty about putting the heating on.

I waited out the month in my flat and moved in with Ned within the fortnight, leaving the kebab-scented sofa behind.

Twenty minutes into my overtime and Caleb still hadn't shown. Ned wasn't done for another hour, so I was in no rush to get home, mind. I didn't want any spare time to ponder on missed opportunities with handsome Irishmen and opportunities that I wished had been missed with ex-boyfriends.

The beep of a new call sounded through the headset and I straightened myself in my chair. I took a breath, donned my calm and reassuring tone and accepted the call.

'Hello, you're through to Healthy Minds. Can I ask your name?'

The only response that came was a slight whoosh of wind as it brushed against the mouthpiece. I waited a second or two before trying again.

'Hello? Are you there?' I heard someone inhale. 'Hello?'

'Hi.' The voice came from the other end of the line.

'Hi there. How are you doing?' It was a regular question, one that was asked every day out in the world and very rarely was it answered truthfully. But here, in this office and all the other offices like it, the prescribed answer wasn't necessary. Here we always strived to get the truth.

30

The line crackled, the connection fizzing in and out of clarity.

'I-I don't —ow —ed.'

'I'm having trouble hearing you. Is it possible to move around a little to see if we can get a better connection?' I scrunched up my face, as if this would somehow help, and pressed my earphones against my ears.

I heard movement and a moment later the voice came through clear.

'Hi, can you hear me now?' he asked and something landed in my stomach like a lead weight.

'Yeah, I can hear you,' I replied. 'How are you feeling this evening?'

'I've had better days I'm not gonna lie to yer,' the man answered, his Irish accent sending a shiver through me. Could it really be him? No, surely not. There had to be more than one Irishman living in Birmingham, hadn't there? But he sounded so very like him.

What was I supposed to do? I couldn't let him unload his woes onto me without letting him know who I was, could I?

'Your name wouldn't happen to be Charlie, would it?' my mouth asked before my brain had signed off on it.

'Erm . . . yeah,' he responded, nonplussed. 'Do I, err, do I know yer?'

'I think I may have thrown my lunch at you yesterday.' I chuckled through my words nervously.

'Nell?' he asked. 'From the café?'

I laughed through a nervous breath, a little chuffed that he'd remembered my name, and nodded even though he couldn't see it. 'What a small world, hey? Although, we both do live in the same city and only ran into each other yesterday, so maybe not so small and, for the love of God, I should stop talking and let you say what you rang to say. That's if you even want to talk to me. I could put you on to someone who doesn't have an aggressive sandwich-based history with you, if you'd like.'

'Jesus, you really weren't lyin' about that verbal diarrhoea, were yer?'

'Not even slightly, no.' I chuckled nervously again. 'So, what made you call today?'

'Erm . . .' He took a deep breath and the sound of his feet pacing found my ears. 'I feel like an eejit doing this, but I just called because I'm worried about my uncle. He's been a bit weird lately.'

'Weird how?' I questioned, my brain quickly switching from giggly flirtation to serious counsellor.

'Oh, you know, gettin' distant, closed off, that kind of thing. He used to talk so much that you'd be offering him money to stop, but lately it's been nothin' but one-word answers.'

'What's your uncle's name?' I asked.

'Carrick.'

'Has he spoken to you about this or are you just picking up on his behaviour?'

'They're just observations,' he replied. 'Thing is, I'm terrible at this kind of thing. I'd probably just end up makin' it worse, so that's why I called yer.'

I opened my mouth to ask if Carrick might consider talking to me and agree to a call with both of us, but before I could get the words out, Charlie was speaking again. He scoffed in disbelief. 'I-I just don't believe this,' he said, sounding slightly embarrassed. 'What are the odds that it's you who picks up my call?'

'I know.' I'd spent all day cursing myself for not being brave enough to ask for his number and I felt like I couldn't let a second chance slip away from me without at least trying. I looked around, checking that Ned was on a call before pulling myself right up against the edge of my desk, lowering my head to the surface and hushing my voice to an almost whisper.

'This is gonna sound a little . . . odd. But, what would you say if I suggested that we carry on this conversation . . . not over the phone?'

'I'm listening.' I thought I heard the inclination of a smile in his voice.

'Well, I should be finishing work within the next half hour and I wondered if you wanted to, you know, carry on this chat in person? Feel free to say no and to forget that I ever spoke, because I'm pretty sure I could get fired for asking you this, but I really enjoyed speaking with you yesterday and I'm getting kinda hungry and I know you wouldn't want to miss an opportunity to see me eat again.'

'How could I possibly pass up that opportunity. Where shall I meet yer?'

'Really?' I asked, astonished. 'That was easy.'

'Hey now,' he said suavely. 'I won't have yer running all over town tellin' everyone I'm easy, okay? I've an untarnished reputation to uphold. So, shall I meet yer at work?'

'Sure,' I said and gave him the address, my face so close to the desk to avoid being overheard that the heat of my breath bounced back onto my face.

'I'll see yer soon then, Nell.' The sound of my name on his voice made me grin from ear to ear.

'See you soon.' The line went dead and I breathed an excited laugh into the desk.

'What's got you going all giggly?' Ned's accusatory voice made me jump and I flung myself around in my chair so fast that I rolled all the way to the window, my knee bouncing against the floor-to-ceiling glass pane as I came to a stop.

'Nothing,' I said rather unconvincingly. 'Change of plan. I'm going out after work, so I'm gonna have to take a rain check on spag bol and true crime.'

'Please tell me that you're not going with Joel.' He pouted and tilted his head.

'It will be a Joel-free evening.' From the corner of my eye, I saw the flustered mess of who I assumed was now a very late Caleb come crashing through the door, his lanyard twisted around his neck and looped under his arm as if he'd put it on while flying around in one of those skydiving simulators. 'And I think that's my cue.' I signed off the computer, grabbed my notes and made my way to Barry's office, with excitement zinging in my stomach like popping candy.

Chapter Four

I sighed into the smudged mirror of the poorly maintained bathroom and wondered what tricks I could pull out of my sleeve to make myself look a little less like I'd been dragged through a hedge backwards. My hair had begun to break free of the elastic that held it in a topknot. The messy bun slowly sliding down the right side of my head like an ice cream, slipping from its cone on a hot day. I tucked my finger under the bobble and pulled it free, my hair knotting around it and sending a sharp pain down into my scalp as it tugged against the roots. I hissed and untangled the strands before letting my hair fall down in a curtain of chestnut mess. I combed it with my fingers and scrunched the ends to try and make it presentable before wiping the eyeliner from beneath my eyes and pinching my cheeks to give them a tiny bit of colour.

The sound of loud, tuneless music drummed through the door and into my skull and I wondered how people possibly enjoyed this type of noise. I could cope with there being no words, it was the lack of anything other than a bassline that made me question its validity as music.

I turned away from the mirror and opened the door, the music assaulting me with its loudness as I stepped back into the bar.

The Street Food Market was somewhat crowded, for a Thursday night, and the air hung with the mingling smells that drifted in from the various food trucks outside. The trucks collected in a courtyard three days a week, decorated with fairy lights and neon signs, selling everything from pimped-up brownies to Indian fish and chips, a miasma of all the combined foods making one delicious odour. Aside from the street food, there were also three bars, each boasting a different theme. I'd been here a few times before and tried them all at least once, but this time we'd opted to try the bar at the far end, a 1920s-themed one with pied floor tiles and plush red seating.

I weaved my way through the crowd back to where I'd left Charlie at the bar, perched on a tall stool and picking unen-thusiastically at some jerk chicken with a wooden fork. He smiled goofily as I pulled myself up onto the stool beside him. The man who'd sold it to us had, I think, been border-line insane and, when Charlie had asked how spicy the food was, he had replied, 'It'll slap you in the face and take you shopping.' Neither of us had known exactly what that meant and if it was even a good thing to say about what you were going to put in your mouth. He'd been such a born salesman that we hadn't been able to turn away without parting with what seemed like a great deal of money for such a small portion.

'How's the food?' I asked, catching the eye of the barmaid

and signalling for a refill of our empty beer glasses. 'Did it slap you in the face and take you shopping?'

'Not exactly how I'd describe it. It's more like eating napalm,' he said, touching the fork to his tongue and wincing a few moments later when the heat hit him.

'That's the mild one.' I chuckled, reaching over, taking a piece with my fingers and popping it into my mouth. The heat was most certainly there, though it didn't make me turn puce like Charlie. He let the fork slump back into the cardboard tray and pushed it towards me.

'Be my guest. My poor Irish tongue can't handle it.' The bartender brought over two frothing pints, one of which Charlie grabbed and glugged until it quelled the burning in his mouth. I tapped my card to the card reader and the bartender sent me a wink.

I picked up the wooden fork and ate the rest of our 'shared' meal in what I expect was a matter of seconds. When I looked up, he was watching me with fondness. I blushed and quickly wiped at my mouth with my sleeve.

'Sorry. I tend to forget that the rest of the world exists when I eat. I'm sure it's horrifying to witness.'

'Not at all,' he countered.

I pushed away the empty tray and reached for my beer.

I had a surprisingly high tolerance for alcohol for someone of my size and so two beers were nothing to worry about. I sipped at the cold beer and felt it mingle with the spice on my tongue, the bubbles aggravating it before the coolness calmed it again.

'So, tell me about Carrick,' I said and his body language changed instantly. He looked at me through dark, fanning lashes but didn't reply. I shrugged my eyebrows and tilted my head. I could tell that he didn't really want to talk about it, that pushing away whatever it was that was playing on his mind was his way of dealing with his worry, but it was my job to extract the unextractable.

'We don't have to.' He exhaled loudly through his nose and looked back to his beer. 'You've finished work for the day. You don't want to be talking to me about this kinda stuff now.'

'I met you before you called today. This isn't work, this is me helping a friend.' I tentatively threw the idea out there. Sure, we hadn't known each other for very long and I felt my heart go a little haywire whenever he met my eyes, but why couldn't we be friends?

'A friend?' he asked, his crooked smile bringing a cheeky look to his face. 'Do you even know my last name?'

'No. But you only really need to know last names if you're going to be sleeping together, don't you?' My cheeks burned as I realised what I'd just said. 'I . . . I mean, isn't that the rule?'

He laughed under his breath but his face was blushing a little too. 'Don't get ahead of yourself; you'll have to buy me a drink first.' He looked from me to the beer in his hand with mock surprise. 'Well, would yer look at that.' His eyes were playful as he sipped from his glass and looked at me over the rim. 'It's Stone, by the way,' he uttered after swallowing. 'My last name.'

'That's a good last name,' I babbled. 'Strong. Both in the sense of how it sounds and, you know, stone.' *Oh God, shut up!* I looked down at my hands lying limply in my lap and prayed that no more words would fall out of my mouth. After a few moments of awkward silence, I thought of something to say and opened my mouth to ask him a question, but before the sound could find its way out of my mouth, he was already speaking.

'So, Carrick is this upbeat, annoying, in yer face kinda guy. I think that maybe he was meant to be a twin and, in the womb, he absorbed enough personality for two people.'

'And he's changed?'

He nodded solemnly.

'Any reason?' I asked. I noticed how my demeanour had changed, my voice got lower, more authoritative but not too much to be off-putting. My brow took on a pensive furrow and my hands clasped in my lap.

'Heartbreak, feelin' lost in life, the whole shebang really.'

'Do you think he'd talk to me?'

He shook his head with certainty. 'No, I highly doubt it. But I can ask.'

'Please do. Sometimes the most unlikely of people are just waiting for someone to ask them how they are. Think of it like a bottle of champagne. The cork is always jammed right in there, keeping it all inside, but all it takes is a little shake and it all comes spewing out.'

He chuckled. 'I've never heard anyone speak like you before.'

I looked at him from under furrowed brows. 'Is that a good thing?'

'I think so.' His mouth curled into a one-sided smile and it did things to me that I never thought a smile could do. 'So, tell me about yerself. Seeing as we're now wholly committed to this friend business. What's your family lookin' like?'

'My family is a little bit unconventional.'

'Right, that sounds like a gold mine of conversation. Start from the beginning.' He leaned forward a touch, holding his beer with one hand, while the other messed, idly, with a loose thread on the hem of his shirt.

'Erm, okay, well, my mum is this really intelligent, beautiful woman. She went to uni in London and became a geologist. She's one of the people who find the best places to build off-shore wind farms. But when she was twenty-one, she had the first, and only, irresponsible night of her entire existence with a man that she didn't recall the next day. Nine months later, I arrived, hence no brothers and sisters.'

'Firstly—' he held up a finger and leaned forward a little more '—that sounds like an awesome job. Secondly, you don't know who your dad is?'

'No idea. Neither does she.'

'Does that bother you?'

'Not really. It did when I was younger and I saw my friends with their dads, but I had my uncle to fill that role. I lived with him when my mum was off working, but he died when I was sixteen and so it was just me and her after that.'

'Sorry to hear that.' He looked a little saddened.

'It's fine . . . now,' I said as he took a swig of his beer. 'Then there's Ned, the guy I live with.' I don't know if it was just wishful thinking on my part, but I think I saw his shoulders sag. 'We work together, that's how we met, and when I broke up with Joel, I moved in as a lodger.'

A sudden loud cough came as Charlie seemed to choke on some of his drink, cleared his throat several times and lifted a balled fist to his mouth to cover it. 'You live and work with this guy? This Ned?' he asked with furrows forming on his brow.

40

'Uh-huh,' I replied.

'So, yer live with this man, but you've never . . . yer know?'

I scrunched up my face, horrified by the mere thought of it. 'Absolutely not! He's old enough to be my dad. He *could* be my dad for all I know. Oh God, what a distressing thought.'

'Okay, so no nookie with the co-worker. And you're not married or betrothed?' he checked. I shook my head. 'No boyfriends that are gonna come up and start a fight with me for having a drink with their girl?' he carried on.

'Nope, not anymore.'

'Sounds like there's a story there.'

'Not really. There's only ever been the aforementioned Joel.'

'And who is Joel?'

Wow, we were really getting the exes conversation out of the way straight out of the gate, weren't we?

'Met at uni. I was with him for seven and a half years. Now I'm not, but he's eager to get back together,' I said simply, leaving out the occasional booty call part that made me ashamed of myself.

'Who broke up with who?'

'Me with him.'

'Why was that?'

'He quit his job and ploughed all of his money, and a great deal of mine, into his online web-building company. He also gambled a lot online, which I knew nothing about until I finally read one of my bank statements instead of throwing it in the kitchen drawer and saw that he'd spent over two hundred pounds that month on Betfred. By the end of the second year of living together, we were so broke that

41

we almost got evicted.' I sighed and felt the ache of remembered anxiety. 'We started shouting instead of talking and the only time we ever touched was when we passed in the hallway and when I handed him his dinner. In the end I was so miserable that I decided I'd rather be on my own than with him. Funny, isn't it, how eighteen months of misery can obliterate years of happiness?'

'It's a shame.'

I waved a passive hand. 'That was almost two years ago now though. I'm over it,' I said, although that wasn't one hundred per cent true. 'What about you? Someone like you must have left a trail of broken hearts trailing across the Irish Sea.' I sipped my beer, realising that my glass was already half empty, although I didn't remember drinking it.

'Not really.' He glugged down the rest of his beer and turned to the bar. 'Do you want another drink?' I took the hint that this was a touchy subject for him and decided to move on.

'I'm okay, thanks.' I held up my glass to show how much I had left. He signalled the bartender and ordered another pint. 'So, seeing as we've tackled my family, what's the story with yours? Tell me more about Carrick.'

'Erm, nothin' too interestin'. My parents still live in Westport, County Mayo, with Carrick, who's my dad's brother. He's quite a bit younger than my dad and only twelve years older than me and so he was sort of like a brother.'

'What's he like?'

Charlie laughed at a memory that I could almost see as it played out inside his head. 'He's unpredictable and loud, forgetful, obnoxious and tactless. But he's kind and good. He only acts out because he's lonely, I guess.

42

'He drives my mam up the wall sometimes. Him and my da run the family business and my parents live in this little house with panoramic views of Clew Bay. There's this mountain called Croagh Patrick on the opposite side of the water. Pilgrims travel to it every last Sunday in July and climb it. Some of them do it barefoot, some on their knees and you have a great view of the mountain from my parents' place.'

'They climb a mountain on their knees?' I asked, astounded. 'How tall is this mountain?'

'About two and a half thousand feet.'

'Holy crap,' I said, then worried that I might have offended him. He was Irish after all, and I was only now realising how much I blasphemed in everyday life. 'Sorry.'

'For what?' he asked, frowning.

'Taking the Lord's name in vain, or whatever.'

'Ah, cuss away. It matters nothin' to me.' He smiled, his fingers stroking the beads of condensation on the outside of his glass, as his eyes stayed locked on to mine. 'I like a person who says what they're thinking.'

I'd never had a moment like this, where everything else bleeds away and you know exactly what the other is thinking, simply by the look in their eyes. I came over all hot and flustered, running a hand through my hair and forcing myself to look away from him before I gave too much away.

'So . . .' I cleared my throat, my voice strangely breathy. 'You were saying about Carrick?'

'Yeah, erm . . .' He looked down too, drawing a hand through his stubble and pressing his knuckles to his lips for a moment before carrying on. 'Carrick has this big house high up on the hill in Knockranny, not far from my parents'

43

house. It's big and it's filled with all that fancy shite he likes, but he barely spends any time there. He's always at my parents' place, livin' in the summerhouse out back.'

'Why's that?' I asked as his next drink was delivered.

'He can't stand his own company. He's funny that way.'

I smiled. 'He definitely sounds like he's got a lot on his mind. Is there someone over there he can talk to?'

He shook his head. 'Na, Mammy would lose her mind with the shame of it.'

'There's nothing to be ashamed of.'

'I know that.' He took his new pint in hand and started on that one. 'But family . . . it's complicated, yer know.'

'Sure is.'

He held my gaze for a moment or two before speaking again. 'There doesn't seem to be many people in your life. Yer seem a little lonely. Is that right?'

'Maybe, I haven't given it much thought,' I lied.

'I don't think it's somethin' yer give much thought to. I think it's one of those things that you wake up one day and it's just there.'

'Are you speaking from experience?' I asked.

'Maybe.' He smirked. 'I haven't given it much thought either.'

By the time the taxi pulled up on the kerb outside home, Charlie was needing a little more propping up than he had before. He'd gradually slid over from his side of the car to mine, his weight pressing against my shoulder as he stared, blankly, out the window. 'This is me,' I said, feeling a tug-of-war inside my stomach. On one end of the rope was my bed, warm and soft and awaiting me with open sheets; on the other was Charlie and how much I didn't want to just go inside the house and possibly never see him again.

'I'll get out here too.' He slurred a little as he spoke and unbuckled his seatbelt. I thanked the driver, Ahmed (his children were called Pritika and Arnab and they'd both gone to uni to study law).

'You don't have to,' I replied. 'I'm sure I can make it to the door without being attacked.'

But he was already out of the car.

I got out and the car swiftly disappeared. I joined Charlie on the pavement, looking up at the large Victorian house, dark except for a warm yellow light behind the curtain of Ned's room.

'Nice place,' he muttered.

'Yeah, it's not too shabby, maybe a little run-down.'

He slowly turned to face me, his eyelids hanging at half-mast over his eyes.

'This evening didn't turn out like I thought it would,' he said as fine rain began to dust us both.

'Me neither.' I smiled at the soft, drunk look in his eyes. I tucked my hair behind my ear, pulling it away from where the rain was beginning to flatten it to my forehead. He reached out a hand towards my chest. For a moment, I didn't know what he would do and I drew in an uncertain breath. He picked up the small fraying plait that I'd absentmindedly braided during a call earlier on in my shift and stroked it between the pads of his thumb and index finger.

My heart rate quickened at the physical contact that I couldn't even feel and I watched his faraway eyes as they watched what his fingers were doing, as if he had no control over them and was interested to see what they would do next.

His brow drew into a frown and his mouth quirked as if he was in mild pain. He said something through lips that barely moved and it was so quiet that I didn't know if I'd imagined it or not.

'Sorry?' I bowed my head and tried to bring myself into his gaze. 'What was that?'

He looked up and the moment his eyes met mine, I was struck by the expression in them. I couldn't place it because I didn't think I'd ever seen it before.

'I said, thank you,' he said a little clearer.

'For what?'

'For talking to me in the café.'

'No problem.' I smiled softly. My confidence soared from the positive vibes I was getting from him and the alcohol that was coursing through my veins. I knew I must be more drunk than I thought I was because of what I said next. 'It's not every lunch break that you find yourself sitting next to a pretty Irishman, so I thought I'd try and make the most of it.'

His mouth drew into a wide smile and lines carved their way into his cheeks, partially hidden behind that stubble that I kept imagining scratching its way across my chin. 'Pretty? Is that what I am?'

I blushed, but didn't look away, the alcohol making me braver than I could remember being in recent memory. 'There it is,' he said, placing his crooked finger beneath my chin. 'That smile.'

'I've been smiling all night,' I said nervously.

'No, that's your show smile. This here, this is the real one. It's like sunshine.'

'Okay, now I know you've had too much to drink.'

My grin grew wider as I tried to not let the feel of his skin on mine, no matter how little skin that was, turn me into a giggling, babbling moron.

I felt like all of the social rules about personal space had already evaporated. Like if I wanted to reach out and touch him, I could, and it wouldn't be weird. I wondered if this, if Charlie, would turn out to be my first one-night stand. I'd never liked the idea of them – maybe because I was conceived during one – but the idea of being naked and vulnerable with a near-stranger seemed like something I'd need a hell of a lot more alcohol for than this.

He stepped closer, my thin piece of braided hair still in his hand and his eyes on mine. I felt a swell of nerves in my chest and found myself wanting him to kiss me more than I had ever wanted anything in my whole life.

Were you meant to kiss on the first date? Would doing that make me easy or was that only a rule in Noughties sitcoms? And who was even policing these rules? Was there a board of people waiting in the conifer hedge to leap out and call me a whore?

'Do . . . you . . . erm . . .' I mumbled as his face drew a little closer and mine mirrored his movement until I could feel his breath dancing across my lips, smell the detergent drifting up from his clothes, feel the heat seeping through the fabric of his T-shirt and into the sliver of air between our chests. 'Do . . . you want to come in?'

I had no idea how I was being so brazen, but the idea of not kissing him before the night was out was too much of a tragedy to contemplate. I moved a little closer, my lips pouting out to meet his. My top lip grazed his and I felt the stubble of his upper lip, wiry and sharp against the soft skin of my face.

His lips parted and his body moved against mine, his chest firm and warm. All of a sudden, I felt like we were both wearing far too many clothes. I laced my fingers through the hand that hung at his side.

'I . . .' he began. We were so close that we were sharing breaths, the air leaving my lungs and falling straight into his. 'I can't do this.'

I exhaled a disappointed breath as he swiftly stepped away and my heart fell into my stomach. 'Oh.'

He walked away a few paces and dragged rigid fingers through his hair. 'What the feck am I doing?' he said quietly, almost to himself.

'What's wrong?' I asked, reaching out to touch the sleeve of his jacket, but he shook my hand away. I stepped back, my pride smarting.

He turned around halfway, but didn't meet my eye. 'I just can't do this. Okay?' His words were clipped and almost angry.

'What happened? Everything was fine a minute ago,' I said taking a step closer. He countered with a step back.

'I need to go.' He spun on the ball of his foot and began marching away.

'Shall I call you?' I shouted after him.

'No. No. Just . . .' he replied '. . . don't.'

Then he was off, walking into the darkness and leaving me confused on the driveway.

I would be lying if I said that I didn't go straight upstairs, get into a shower that was too hot to be physically safe, and cry a little into the scalding water. The heart is like a rattle-snake in the way that if you leave it alone and don't provoke it, it won't hurt you. It'll just carry on doing its thing, while you carry on doing yours. But once it senses danger, it begins preparations to protect itself. It remembers all the hurts that came before, the ones that almost destroyed it, and it knows that it can't let that happen again. I'd provoked my heart again, letting it run away with itself on the childish idea that meeting a man in a café would be my happily ever after. But that was not how life worked in the real world. Maybe in the choruses of Eighties ballads or in the finale of TV shows, but life never came out that cleanly.

I turned my face up to the deluge of water that was almost too hot to bear and let it drum against my skin. I didn't know what had happened to make him change so suddenly. It was as if he'd had a crisis of conscience, but I had no idea what had provoked it. What had that sudden guilt been about?

I hit the button on the shower and the water ceased to fall. I stood in the glass box for a minute or two, the water dripping from me like my whole body was crying.

A little over twenty-four hours ago, I hadn't even known Charlie Stone, so why was I so upset?

I stepped out of the shower and wrapped myself in my fuchsia pink towel. A good sleep – that was probably all I needed and, in the morning, this would all be forgotten. I hoped.

Chapter Five

I had been wrong. A single sleep could not cheer me up, not even slightly. I sat on the sofa in my pyjamas after a poor night's sleep, with my feet propped up on the coffee table and my bowl of Cheerios balanced on my boobs. I was knackered and had just wanted to stay in bed, but after waking up at the crack of dawn, I'd struggled to do anything other than lie there, staring up at my ceiling and getting gradually more annoyed at my sustained wakefulness.

I clicked the remote with my lazy left hand and found some mindless, colourful cartoon to numb my brain for twenty minutes.

'You're up early.' Ned's voice drifted into the room a moment or two before he appeared in the doorway. I spotted him in my peripheral vision, but didn't turn. That would have been far too much effort. He walked over to the sofa and I looked up and found him eyeing me expectantly, his dark green tie lying limp and unknotted around his neck. 'Go on then, what's he like?'

I shoved a heaped spoon of cereal into my mouth and chewed down on the soggy little rings. 'He's like Prince Charming, but during a bad-boy phase where he joins a band and starts wearing jewellery.'

'Okay, that was strangely specific.'

'Yeah. Strange is the word I'd use too.'

'Why?' He paused but I didn't answer. I didn't know quite how to explain what had happened. 'Well, at least give me a name. What did you do? How did it end?' I didn't need to look at him to know he'd sent a wink my way.

'His name is Charlie and . . .' I stopped and looked up at him with narrowed eyes. 'We went to a bar, we almost kissed and then he ruined it all.'

'What happened?'

'Nothing happened. It was all going well and sparks were, you know, flying and whatnot. But then, abruptly he closed off, got kind of angry and then told me not to call him.'

'Oh, and you have no idea what made him change his mind?'

I shook my head.

'Did you eat in front of him? Because that would be enough to put any man off,' he said in a vain attempt to lighten the mood.

'Shut up.' I managed a pathetic smile.

'What did he get angry about?'

'I have no idea. It was like he felt guilty about almost kissing me.'

Ned tilted his head in thought. 'He's not married, is he?'

I let out a long sigh and closed my eyes. 'Shit. I can't believe I didn't think of that.' I scoffed at my own stupidity. 'He's married, isn't he?'

51

'Did he mention a wife or girlfriend?' He perched himself on the sofa arm and fiddled with the ends of his tie.

I smacked my forehead with my palm. 'No, but when I brought that up in conversation, he quickly changed the subject.'

'It's looking like you might have dropped the ball on this one, Nell.'

'I'm a homewrecker. A skanky little homewrecker.' I groaned in frustration. How had I even thought for one second that a man like that was single?

'Don't beat yourself up. If he is married then he's the one who should be feeling stupid.'

'He wasn't wearing a ring.' I thought back to the café when I'd seen the guitar callouses on his fingers. No, I don't think I saw a ring. My hope flared.

'Neither did I. Not every person does,' he replied.

Hope, dashed.

My shoulders sagged.

'Well,' Ned said as he took hold of his tie and began knotting it, 'even if he's hitched, it was nice to see you getting out again. You've spent long enough doing whatever it is that you're doing with that idiot, Joel.' It was no secret that Ned didn't think highly of Joel, not after those first few months when he'd show up outside the house. This one time he'd thrown pebbles at my window, only it wasn't my window, it was Ned's, and the pebbles he was throwing proved a little too large when one found its way on to Ned's bedroom floor surrounded by tiny shards of glass.

In the past I'd fought Joel's corner when people talked poorly of him, but I was slowly coming to realise that sticking up for him wasn't my job anymore.

'How long are you going to stay mad about that window?' I asked. 'Joel could have been worse, I guess. He didn't have a secret wife, like Charlie probably has, and he didn't run off with someone else like Connie did.' I saw him flinch a little at the mention of his ex-wife's name, but he was becoming more immune to her as time went on. 'He could have done much worse to me.'

'Yeah, he could have done much better too.' Ned sighed and fiddled with the knot of his tie until it sat, smartly, against his collar. 'Let's just agree that we are both terrible at picking partners for ourselves.' Ned shook his head in frustration. 'You gonna be okay?' he asked, reaching down a hand to squeeze my shoulder.

I sucked my teeth in response.

'Well, text me if there are any developments. I'm off, but I'll see you in a bit. Don't forget we have that meeting with the project manager at two.'

'I hadn't forgotten,' I lied.

He walked to the door but stopped at the last second, holding the doorframe with both hands and peering around it. 'Oh, are we doing shitty film night tonight?'

I looked at him over my shoulder. 'It's not like I have any other plans. My boyfriend's busy with his wife.' I sighed and reassumed the position of lazing on the sofa. I watched as several computer-animated dogs in various work uniforms jumped clumsily across the screen. I sighed as I heard the sound of the front door closing. Alone again. I shoved another spoonful of cereal into my mouth and chewed angrily.

No one would have guessed, by how I handled myself at work, that I was completely distracted by thoughts of the night before and by the time the end of my shift rolled around I was feeling exhausted from faking a cheerful façade all day. That afternoon, Ned and I left work together and headed to Tesco to buy dinner and to peruse the bargain DVD shelves for our Friday night tradition of shitty film, beer and pizza. The rules were that the film had to be under five pounds and the pizza had to have garlic and herb dip; other than those two stipulations, we were pretty flexible.

I was reading the back of an early Noughties' horror film, with a screaming, blood-spattered, scantily clad woman on the front, when my phone began buzzing in my pocket. I pulled it out and saw my mum's face beaming at me from the screen. I accepted the video call and held the phone up.

'*Guten Abend*,' she said when her beaming face appeared. She looked beautiful, as always, her blonde hair coiffed to perfection, her green eyes twinkling in the muted lighting. Her phone was propped up on a crisp white tablecloth, so I got to see the whole envy-inducing image of her lounging in a warmly lit corner of a bustling restaurant.

'Good evening to you too,' I responded and tossed the film into my basket. 'How's Germany?' I wished I could have been more specific but she moved around so much and with so little notice that if she hadn't just greeted me in German, I would have completely forgotten where she was. It never used to bother me too much when I saw her off in all of these places that I had never even come close to, because I always thought that I'd be having my own adventure when the time was right. I'd thought that, eventually, my crippling fear of flying would subside and I'd be able to jet off wherever I wanted when the time came. But time had been and gone and I still hadn't set foot very far outside the UK. So now, whenever she called from Germany or China or Denmark, I got a pang of FOMO in my gut that set me off kilter for a moment or two.

'Cold,' she answered. 'Nothing much more to report. We're wrapping up here and so I'm going to have some free time in the next month. Wondered if I could come and see you and crash in a spare bed?'

I sucked my teeth as I pretended to ponder the question and shook my head. 'Oh, I don't think that's going to be possible.'

'Damn it, the gutter it is then.' We both chuckled and the sound of wine sloshing into a glass could be heard down the line.

'Sounds like you're enjoying yourself.' I turned at the end of the aisle and made my way to the pizza section where Ned would, no doubt, be facing his weekly conundrum: four cheese or ham and mushroom.

'I'm just out for drinks with a couple of co-workers.' She picked up the phone and turned it to show me the other five people chatting animatedly at the table. I recognised one of them as Piero. She'd had a casual romance with him ever since they met on a job in Italy a few years ago. I'd never met him and I doubted I ever would. She liked him, but my mother's true love was her work and no man was ever going to get between those two. She placed the phone back on the table and reclined in her chair. Her cream silk dress clinging to a body that a woman who never set foot in a gym had absolutely no right in having.

'How are things with you? How's Ned?' she asked as she lifted a glass of red to her lips and sipped.

'Ned's fine. We're just getting dinner.' I didn't carry on but something about the look on my face must have betrayed me.

'What aren't you telling me?'

I sighed and lowered my voice as I spoke. 'I did something I shouldn't have.'

'Oh God, please tell me you didn't. Not with Ned.' Her eyes widened with genuine fear and she lowered her head into her free hand. She looked sickened. 'Nelly. No.'

'Ew, Mum, no,' I said. Why was sex with Ned always the first place people's minds went to? 'It's nothing to do with Ned at all. I kind of went on a date with a man I met over the phone at work.'

She almost choked on her second sip of wine. 'You did what, Nelly?'

My mother was the only person on the planet that I allowed to call me Nelly and that was simply because she'd gone through the agony of birthing me. I'd escaped from school pretty unscathed in terms of bullies, but I think I'd been referred to as Nelly the Elephant about twenty thousand times between the ages of five and sixteen.

'It's a long story that didn't end up going anywhere, so I'll just fill you in when you get here. When will that be, exactly?'

'You'll know as soon as I do.' Her eyes filled with pity. 'Did you like this man, the one you went out with?'

I scrunched up my face and my voice turned to a whine. 'I did.'

'Well, I'm sorry it didn't turn out how you wanted it to, but, Nelly, it's so nice to know you're back out there.'

'God! Is everyone just waiting with bated breath for me to start dating again?' Everyone was acting as if I'd just

56

renounced my vow of chastity. I mean, she didn't know about me and Joel restarting the physical side of things, but even so, it hadn't been that long since I'd gone on that Tinder date with that overly handsy radiographer who kept tutting every time I neglected my coaster. But then again, maybe it was for the best that no one remembered that particular lapse in judgement.

'Nelly, it's been two years. You'll be thirty soon and I just don't want you ending up alone.'

'You don't mind being alone, neither do I,' I argued.

'I do mind, very much so. It's just that my job and all the travelling don't allow for that kind of thing.' She sipped her wine again and gracefully tucked her hair behind her ear. 'Anyway, I'll let you know when I'll be heading back to you.' She tutted. 'And, Nelly, don't be sad about him. He's an idiot if he didn't fall head over heels for you, but maybe this was just the start of you stepping out again.'

'Stepping out? Which era is that term from, exactly?' I asked as I turned up the pizza aisle and, as expected, found Ned looking at two pizzas as if his life depended on the choice he had to make. I walked over and stood beside him. 'Maybe you're right. I could get back on Tinder and see what prime specimens are out there?'

'Don't do that,' Ned said without looking up. 'You'll end up with another gropey X-ray technician.' Shit, I guess not everyone had forgotten. 'You'd be much better off going on Bumble.'

'That's right, listen to Ned,' Mum said through the phone and he looked up at the mention of his name.

'Oh, hi, Cassie.' Ned stepped into the frame of the camera, waving at her enthusiastically.

She lifted a hand and returned the greeting. 'Oh, nice dress.'

I sent him a warning glare. 'Look.' I turned my attention back to her. 'I'll try and be successfully ensconced with someone by the time you arrive, but don't hold your breath.' I was getting exasperated with the conversation.

'Ooo, she's coming to stay?' he asked me, then turned to the phone screen again. 'You're coming to stay?'

'Yes, I'll see you soon,' she answered. 'If that's all right.'

'More than all right,' he said enthusiastically.

I held the phone to my chest and covered the microphone. 'Okay, down boy,' I chided. 'Remember that she's my mother.'

He grinned cheekily, looking back to his pizza conundrum, while I turned my attention back to the call. 'Right, Mum, I need to go before Ned blows a gasket over trying to pick a pizza. Enjoy your evening and tell Piero I said hi.' I threw that last bit in to annoy Ned.

'Will do. Bye, sweetie.' She blew a kiss and hung up.

'Erg, Piero,' Ned said, tossing the four-cheese pizza back on the shelf and placing the ham and mushroom one into the basket.

That evening, as we watched the film that we'd known would be bad, but surpassed even our low expectations, I thought about the strangeness that had occurred over the last two days. Yes, I was disappointed about my rom-com moment not playing out like I'd hoped it would, but I was more annoyed about the fact that he'd just left, without explanation. Was Ned right about him being married? Or was the moment I moved closer to him the same moment that he realised that I wasn't worth his time?

I picked up my phone and began typing out a message to him:

Hey, how are you?

But after a few moments, I deleted it.

I shook my head, and slouched a little further into the sofa as I tried to get back into the film. I felt a weight drop onto my shoulder and I turned to see Ned's steady hand there. He patted me, reassuringly, before his hand returned to his beer.

'Cheer up, kid.' He pointed to the half-naked, surgically enhanced woman on the screen who was being chased through a dark corridor, her ginormous breasts jiggling in the seedy lighting. 'I'm pretty sure this idiot's gonna get skewered any second.'

Chapter Six

'So, she walks into the fire and you're thinking that there's no way she's coming out of this alive. I was bummed out; I'll tell you that. But then the fire dies down and there she is, sat in the ashes with these three baby dragons clutching on to her,' Jackson said, his tone enthusiastic as it travelled through my headset.

'It sounds really exciting,' I responded, pretending that I hadn't already watched what he was talking about several years ago.

'It's really worth a watch,' he said again.

'So, apart from watching an entire two seasons of *Game of Thrones* since we last spoke, how has everything else been?' I asked, directing the question back to him. He sniffed loudly and the enthusiasm in his voice waned.

'I'm all right when I have something to take my mind away from . . . all of that stuff. It's when I'm left with my own thoughts that things get bad.'

'A lot of people say that taking up a hobby is very helpful

for quieting the mind. Something like knitting or reading or writing, even. I'm sure you'd benefit greatly from writing your thoughts down.'

'I don't know if the knitting life is for me, although I've enough balls of wool left over from Mum.' I heard his tone shift when he started talking about his mother.

'No, I'm not a knitter either. My mother tried to teach me once but she's left-handed and I'm not, so my scarf came out looking like a four-year-old had done it,' I said. Jackson chuckled.

'I like the idea of writing though. Maybe I'll pen the next great memoir?'

'You never know.'

'Okay, well, thanks for the chat, Nell. I'll speak to you again soon.'

'See you Jackson.' I took off my headset for the day. I sighed heavily, exhaling the tension that had built up over the last eight hours and feeling it linger in the form of a tension headache, like a rubber band across my brow.

'Everything okay, Nell?' Barry droned as he sauntered over to me from his glass-doored office.

'I'm okay, just signing off for the day. You?'

'Had a hard call this morning.' He looked down.

I sighed an empathetic, yet unhelpful sigh. There was nothing I could do to help; there was nothing anyone could do. 'I'm sure you did a brilliant job, as usual.' I gnawed at my lip and then smiled his way before standing and placing a supportive hand on his shoulder. 'Do you wanna talk about it?'

He looked, for a moment, as if he might accept my offer, but ended up shaking his head.

'Okay,' I said, knowing that sometimes talking about it

only made you feel more like you did something wrong, or realise that you could have done more. 'I'm sure Ned will be free for a drink later, if you change your mind.' It had been Ned's day off today, but he could never say no to a person in need of delving into the depths of their emotions.

'Okay. Thanks, Nell.' His mouth gave the impression of a smile as I turned and walked towards the cloakroom.

I arrived home as the sky was on the verge of night and the street lamps burst into life as I passed along the road. A warm welcoming light glowed from the hallway as I slipped my key into the lock and pushed the door with my shoulder. It stuck a little, as it often did in winter when the wood of the door swelled in its frame, but a few short, sharp thrusts of using my body like a battering ram and it fell open with a quiet squeal.

I took off my coat and hung it over the balustrade, slinging my bag onto the Victorian tiles that I was pretty sure were original to the house. This building was always so quiet, even with both of us milling around inside it. The walls were thick, the ceilings high, the rooms large and impossible to heat to a comfortable temperature during the depths of winter. It had a large unmaintained garden in the rear and a huge kitchen that I often felt sorry for because it was never used to the grand standards it was so clearly equipped for.

Ned had lived in this house with Connie, his ex-wife, whom he had been trying to win back for over six years, but who, as far as I was concerned, was an example of the worst of humankind and should be ashamed of how she'd treated him. She'd run off with a colleague named Richard, after having an eighteen-month affair with him, but had played Ned like a cello, making sure she got as much of his money as she possibly could. Ned had been wealthy once, family money, but not so much anymore.

The house was too big for two people really. Ned and I had spent a drunken evening in the back garden last summer, musing on our lives, and he'd told me then that he really would have loved to have children, but that his time for that had probably passed him by now. When he'd told me this, I'd decided that Ned needed something to care for. He was a carer, a lover, and he needed something to focus that care and love upon. I didn't count because I could take care of myself and a pet seemed like a big commitment to just spring on someone. And so, one day, I brought home Lola and introduced him to the world of succulent ownership. She'd been with us for six months now, sitting in her little yellow pot on her own shelf (which Ned had put up especially for her) in the kitchen above the kettle. Sometimes, in the morning I could hear Ned talking to her.

It seemed wholly unfair to me that a good man like Ned should end up losing his money, living in an empty home with all of his paternal instincts focused on a houseplant, whereas Connie – mistress of Beelzebub – got everything she wanted. I'd tried to brighten the place up and make it more homely for him by bringing in colourful blankets, lavender bubble bath and Lola, of course. The place had been pretty stark when I got here, after Connie had stripped the place of what she wanted and left Ned to live like a poverty-sworn monk. I was still in the process of trying to make the house more homely but I was bringing in the changes slowly so it didn't look like I was dictating the decor. We faced a lot of darkness in our line of work, it only made sense that our home life should be filled with colour.

I became aware of the soft sounds of Eighties soft rock coming from the kitchen and followed it to where I found Ned sitting at the kitchen table, chocolate Hobnob hovering over a cup of steaming tea, nose buried in this month's issue of his beloved *History Today* magazine, the silky tones of 'I Want to Know What Love Is' drifting from the speaker by the kettle.

'Feeling emotionally vulnerable?' I asked as I pulled out a chair and sat down beside him. He looked up from his article about the Aztecs just as his soggy Hobnob disintegrated, falling away from the main biscuit and disappearing into the milky tea.

'I wasn't until I lost my biscuit,' he replied, fishing out the crumbly mess with a teaspoon, his brow furrowed with disappointment. He deposited the soggy crumbs onto the plate of Hobnobs beside him and I reached over and grabbed one before the liquid could reach them.

'I'm out tonight,' he said, looking less than thrilled by the prospect.

'Oh yeah? Got a date?' I ate the Hobnob in two bites and instantly wanted another, although I resisted.

'Oh yeah. With a sexy little minx called Barry,' he countered.

'Hot,' I jested. 'He had a rough day today.'

I wouldn't go as far to say that Ned and Barry were friends, more like co-workers bonded over a mutual love of the job. Barry was about as exciting as a bowl of unsweetened almond milk porridge and he rarely had a word to say about anything. Yet they still went out together about once a month. What they did during these outings, I had no idea. I had visions of them sat, stoic, in one of those old-man pubs, not sharing a single word until they said goodbye. But maybe they both saved their wild sides for each other and what they were actually doing was going to street races and karaoke bars.

'Oh, those came for you. They were on the porch when I got back from shopping today.' Ned roused me from my mental images of Barry and Ned duetting to 'Don't Go Breaking My Heart' and pointed over his shoulder with his thumb to a bunch of flowers standing in a cardboard container on the countertop.

'For me?' I asked. 'From who?'

'I didn't open the card,' he answered. 'But they're pungent. They'll be setting my hay fever off before too long.'

My chest buzzed with excitement as I got up and walked over to them. The scent found my nose when I was still several paces away and as I got nearer, I saw the eucalyptus leaves, nestled between yellow tulips and purple hyacinths. They looked expensive, like the kind you get from an actual florist and not from those big black buckets in Aldi. At the edge was a plastic holder and in it a little envelope. I took the envelope and pulled out a tiny card, which had so much writing on it I had to squint to read the words.

Nell,

I'm sorry about how we left things the other night. I know that I was rude before I left.

I wanted to send you something, as a way of apologising and also for the chance to tell you that I'm not the person I made myself out to be.

65

I hope you like the flowers. It's the first time I've ever been into a florist and so I didn't really know what I was doing. I must have looked like a right eejit.

She said that the purple ones are meant to mean 'sorry' and the yellow ones are just there to make it look cheerful, I think.

Anyway, I totally understand if you don't want to, but I'll be at our café tonight – you know, the one where we met. I'll wait for you until it closes, but in case you don't show, thank you for everything.

Hope to see you soon,

Charlie xxx

My heart thumped in my chest, making the card shake in my hands as I reread it and then placed it against my chest, pressing it hard into my sternum as if I could absorb it into myself. No one had ever bought me flowers before.

'They're from Charlie. He says he wants to meet me again,' I said, walking back over to the chair, taking the flowers with me and setting them down on the table. Ned stopped reading his magazine again and looked up at them.

'The married one?' He leaned back in his chair, looking almost fearfully at the bouquet and the inevitable congestion they would bring.

'We don't know that he's married,' I snapped, clinging on to my one last shred of hope.

'You gonna meet him?' he asked, rubbing his nose with his palm, his voice turning nasal.

'I don't know. What do you think I should do?'

He shrugged. 'Don't ask me.'

'Ned!' I chastised. 'What good is it, me living with a counsellor, if I don't get to reap any of the benefits?'

He sat forward in his chair and clasped his hands together on the tabletop, striking his therapist's pose. 'Yes, you have a lot to lose here in terms of how emotionally invested I can see you getting in this guy, but what else are you going to do with your evening? Come to the pub with me and Barry?'

'Oh, God no.' I grimaced at the thought. 'I was thinking about going to buy some scatter cushions to brighten up the living room.'

'Sod the scatter cushions, Nell. Do you like this man?'

'Yes.'

'Do you think that he's married?'

'Possibly.'

'Is that a problem for you?'

'I think so, yes,' I replied.

'But we don't know whether that's the case yet.'

'We don't.'

'Then, what would you say to taking chances?'

I narrowed my eyes and thought for a moment. 'Ned, did you just use Celine Dion lyrics to advise me in my love life?'

'I believe I did, Nell, yes. Whatever problems you're facing in life, I guarantee that Celine has a piece of advice for it and on the rare occasion that Celine can't help, there's always Michael Bolton.'

I sighed and slumped back into the chair. 'Is that how you handle your calls, just feed them lyrics by ballad-singing icons?' I whined.

'It hasn't failed me yet.' Ned looked at me with raised brows and waited for me to give him my decision.

I thought about my options for a moment before sitting up. 'Can I borrow the car?'

I stood, a few paces away from the café door, still undecided as to whether I would be walking through it or not. I hadn't checked to see if he was inside and the large blackboard by the door showed that they'd be closing in half an hour. The bitterness from Charlie's strange sort of rejection made me want to flee the scene before he had any chance of seeing me, but those bastarding little butterflies, those deceitful little skips in my heartbeat made me take a few steps forward, before my mother's voice came back into my head and I stopped walking.

'Never let anyone make you work for something that makes you feel like less than you are.' She'd said that one night, her voice travelling the seven hundred or so miles from Denmark to my tear-stained phone after I'd had a particularly mentally destroying evening with Joel a few years ago.

Something about Charlie made me nervous. Why had he decided to send those flowers and rekindle something that could quite easily have fallen into obscurity? I took a tentative step closer and peered through the fogged glass. Sure enough, my eyes found the hunched shoulders of Charlie Stone, sat in the same place he'd been sitting when I'd thrown my sandwich at him and set this whole thing in motion.

I wondered if Ned would have been so eager for me to go out and take a risk on Charlie, if he knew the whole story about me meeting him after he'd called in? Probably not, but that wasn't worth worrying about now. This could be the chance that I lived to regret in a few days, or maybe it could be the one that paid off.

Celine Dion crept into my brain again and I hated that Ned was right; she did give good advice.

I pushed the door, the palm of my hand chilling in seconds against the condensation-obscured glass.

I nodded a nervous hello to the supervisor as I stepped through the door. He held up a tattoo-adorned arm and waved. 'You're welcome to a drink, but we're closing soon,' he called out over the sound of the newbie employee – who had miraculously lived to work another day – clanking metal jugs together.

'It's okay. I'm just coming to meet someone.' I sent him a kind smile and turned my attention back to Charlie and found that he'd twisted in his chair, his eyes staring my way, his eyebrows raised and his lips curled in happy surprise. I cleared my throat and walked over to the table, keeping my eyes downcast until the last second. I looked up and made a deal with myself that I would not be won over by blue eyes and Irish charm. I was a grown-ass woman and my protective walls would not be brought down that easily.

'You came,' he said with quiet shock.

'To thank you for the flowers, that's all,' I shot back, although that wasn't completely true.

'I'm glad yer liked them.' His eyes shifted awkwardly and he pointed towards the chair beside him. 'D'yer wanna sit?'

'No,' I said matter-of-factly.

'Okay,' he said, disappointed.

I stood for a few seconds longer, the tension thickening,

before shrugging my eyebrows and trying to keep my impartial expression intact as I sat. I slung my keys onto the table where they landed with a jingling clatter.

He leaned forward, crossing his arms loosely and leaning them on the edge of the table. He rearranged them several more times until he gave up and lowered his fidgeting hands to his lap.

'I'm . . . erm, I'm sorry, about storming off the other night.'

He looked to me for a reply, but I gave none.

'The beer just got into my brain and made it all screwy. It was nothin' you did. I'm sorry I was rude. I didn't wanna upset yer.'

'Are you married?' I blurted.

He looked taken aback by my question, his eyes glazing for a moment before he answered. 'No, I'm not.'

'You sure about that?'

'I think I'd be aware of it if I was.'

'And you're not lying to me? You have no pre-existing romantic connection that would mean that we couldn't be . . . friends?'

'None at all. In fact, you're the first woman I've talked to in . . . well, I don't truly remember the last time.'

I watched him warily and when I didn't reply, he shifted uncomfortably in his seat. 'I blew it, didn't I?' He looked at me again and it was like fricking kryptonite to my stone-cold resolve. I could feel the mortar between the bricks of my wall beginning to crumble and fall.

'Maybe,' I allowed, making him stew a little longer. 'But they do say it's all in the recovery.'

'I was a complete eejit – there's no denyin' that. Any chance of starting over?' When I didn't answer straight away, he lowered his head like a guilty puppy and looked up at me through his lashes. 'I did so very like havin' a friend.'

I tried to force the corners of my mouth to stay down, but a small, treacherous smile found its way onto my lips. God damn it! That accent was to me what soft pipe music was to snakes in baskets.

I rolled my eyes and that was it: the bricks came tumbling down and crashed into nothingness. 'You're a pain in the arse, do you know that?'

'Of course. It's the only thing I've been sure of my whole life. My mother told me so very often when I was young.' He cocked his head to the side. 'And when I was older, in fact.'

'She's a smart woman, your mother.'

'Aye. At least I got a smile outta yer though.'

I pulled my smile wider. 'Which smile is it? My show one or my sunshine smile?'

'What?'

'It's what you said before. That my real smile was like sunshine,' I said, enjoying how much he squirmed.

'Ah, God. Did I say that? Smile like sunshine?' He grimaced. 'Never let me drink again. There's no call for me to start getting all poetic.'

Despite everything I chuckled and looked down at the table, annoyed with myself for not being harder to crack. I'd thought that I would be like granite but I'd ended up being Play-Doh.

He clenched his teeth together and sent me a toothy grin, complete with hopefully raised eyebrows, and nudged me with his elbow.

I shook my head and exhaled loudly, sitting back and

71

dragging my keys from the table to my lap. The staff began to close in around us, placing chairs on tables and dragging crumb-filled brooms across the floor, the subtle go-home signals not so subtle anymore.

'What are you doing now?'

He shrugged and smiled a crooked, cheeky smile. 'Talkin' to a pretty girl. How about you?'

I rolled my eyes. 'I'm going shopping.'

'Oh, okay.' He looked down at his hands in his lap.

'I could use your help though, if you wanted to come.'

He looked up again, hope back in his eyes. 'Ah.' He sighed. 'I was so hopin' yer'd say that.'

Chapter Seven

The distant sound of 'Islands in the Stream' played from speakers, suspended high up in the corrugated metal ceiling of the homeware superstore. Charlie and I stood before a wall of scatter cushions that was so extensive it stretched from one end of the shop to the other and had every shape, size and colour that any human could ever need.

'Well, you've certainly come to the right place for scatter cushions,' Charlie said as he grabbed a royal blue one and began feeling the velvet with subconscious strokes of his fingers.

'Okay, so we're going for anything cheerful.' I took down a yellow cushion and tossed it into the trolley behind us.

'How many do you want?' he asked, holding up the blue velvet one. I nodded and he threw it in too.

'I don't know. Let's just choose the ones we like and we can whittle it down later,' I replied.

He walked a little way down the aisle, pulling out a bright orange one and holding it out in the air in front of him at arm's length, like he was inspecting a work of art.

73

I took an oblong violet cushion from the bottom shelf and playfully swung it to meet with the back of his knees. He lost his balance for a moment and took my arm in his hand for support.

'Don't think for a second that I'm goin' to have a pillow fight with you in the middle of this shop and certainly not in my underwear,' he said.

'I'm sorry to be the one to have to tell you this, but women don't really do that.'

'You mean . . . it was all a lie?' His arms fell to his sides in mock disappointment. 'Ah well, another day, another crushed dream.'

'I'm sorry, but someone had to tell you eventually.'

He turned back to the shelf and slid the orange cushion into the space it'd come from.

I winced a little as the figure popped up on the screen of the horridly out-of-date till and the cashier motioned towards the card reader. We'd run away with ourselves a little and had failed to whittle down the amount by more than a few. We'd spent a good hour in the shop, walking the aisles with our trolley of cushions and sharing small talk. The whole time, I found myself trying to supress the glimmer of excitement that refused to leave me alone whenever he was in view, or out of view for that matter.

I'd lost Charlie to the pick 'n' mix stand at one point and he'd rejoined me in the queue after several minutes of shovelling sweets into a clear plastic bag. I'd looked down at it and seen that it was filled with nothing other than hundreds of gummy bears, their stubby little limbs pressing against the bag as if they were begging to be set free. The cashier looked at me from beneath her under-pruned brows as she tried to decide what two people could want with seventeen scatter cushions and a kilogram of pure uncut gummy bears. By the look of confusion that lingered on her face as we left, I doubted that she'd come to a conclusion.

We made our way to the car, where we proceeded to stuff every available space with our purchases. We raced each other to the trolley park and back and were out of breath by the time we slumped into the seats.

I leaned back against the headrest and angled my head towards the windscreen, although I was watching him from the corner of my eye. He breathed heavily as he sat there in the passenger seat, little puffs of steam whisping from his lips, and he drew a hand through his shaggy dark hair. His lips sat in an almost smile, although the set of his jaw looked tense, as though he was worried about something.

'I came back, you know,' I said out of nowhere.

He looked up at me with a question in his eyes.

'When we met at the café, after I left. I got all the way back to work before I turned around and came back, but you were gone.'

'Oh yeah. Why d'ya do that, then?' he asked, his cheeky expression showing me that he knew exactly why.

'Because I wanted to see you again and I thought that that would never happen if I didn't get your number.'

'That's right, is it?' He was smiling and, of course, that meant I was too.

'I just knew, the moment that I saw you, that . . .' I paused for dramatic effect '. . . that you'd be the only one that I ever wanted to go scatter cushion shopping with.'

75

He chuckled and pulled on his seatbelt, sat forward and clapped his hands together. 'So, where to next?'

'Home.' I sat up and pushed the key into the ignition. 'Do you want me to drop you at yours?'

'I wouldn't mind helping you take all of this into the house.' He gestured over his shoulder at the mountain of pillows behind him. 'You know, somethin' people don't get about pillows, is that they're just so . . . heavy. I wouldn't want you strainin' yourself.'

'Oh, and you're just the big strong man to help me, are you?'

'Yeah. I mean, I've seen the guns on yer and all. But I'm just sayin' that yer might, y'know, want the help.'

'Okay.' I grinned and clipped in my seatbelt. Charlie reached over and pushed the button for the radio.

'Oh, the radio doesn't work. Hasn't for years since Ned took his ex-wife to the safari park and the aerial got torn off by a particularly spiteful macaque.'

He stared at me for a moment, waiting for me to indicate that I was joking, but I wasn't.

'There might be some CDs in there,' I said, pointing to the glove box.

He leaned forward and pulled it open. 'You can tell a lot about a person by what's in their glove box,' he said, bending double in the seat to rifle through it.

'Well, it's Ned's glove box, so you won't learn anything about me from in there.' He pulled out a decrepit old A to Z, a pair of woolly gloves that looked as if the moths had been at them, a packet of tissues and three CDs, held together with the sticky, decade-old glue of a melted boiled sweet.

'Delightful,' he said, pulling on the cases until he prised

them apart with a sound like a wax strip being torn from a thigh. 'Is this guy for real?' He turned to me with lowered brows.

'What do you mean?'

'The man's radio doesn't work, the only alternative he has is the CD player and these are all he can bring to the table?' He held out the options. A sun-faded audiobook of *The Hobbit*, the soundtrack to *Phantom of the Opera* and *The Best of Michael Bolton*.

'Hey, don't knock Bolton,' I said, taking the CD from him and turning it over to see the track list.

'Oh, please don't tell me you're a fan or I might have to rethink this whole "friendship" thing.'

I turned in my seat to face him, holding up the image of peak Nineties Michael Bolton, his face slightly concealed by gooey red sugar. 'This man's voice has both the raw masculine power of an Eighties wrestler, whilst also being as silky smooth as caramel. There's no one else like him.'

'You mean to say that his voice is like Hulk Hogan covered in butterscotch?'

'No, caramel,' I repeated. 'Have you even listened to him or is this like when people say they don't like a food they've never tried?'

'He's the "Lean on Me" guy isn't he?'

'Oh, Charlie.' I chortled through my words. 'Charlie, Charlie, Charlie. He's so much more than that.' I took the slightly sticky disk from the case and slid it into the player. The first soulful bars of 'Time, Love and Tenderness' played out into the car and I balled a fist and drew it slowly down through the air in front of my face as I sang. I got so into the song that I almost forgot that Charlie was in the car and when I opened my eyes, I found him leaning back against the inside of the door, his eyebrows raised.

'Sorry,' I said, regaining my composure. I turned the volume down a touch and placed my hands on the wheel. 'I can't be held responsible for anything I do while that golden-haired, gravel-voiced man is singing.'

'Clearly.' The smile was still tugging at his mouth. 'I apologise. I was wrong about him.'

'You bet your ass you were,' I responded as I checked behind me and pulled out of the space.

The headlights dazzled against the wall of the house as I pulled up onto the inclined drive and shut off the engine just as the first tinkling notes of 'How Am I Supposed to Live Without You' came on. I turned to Charlie, who was still eyeing me with wariness, and expelled a sigh full of a contentment that only musical nostalgia can bring. I was raised on Bolton, moulded by him. Like Bane only more likely to seduce you than kill you.

'So,' I said, 'have I changed your perspective on the great man himself?'

'How could you not with passion like that?' He breathed a laugh and reached for the door handle.

We piled all of the cushions onto the living room floor, between the sofa and the rarely used fireplace, the floor becoming an uneven rainbow patchwork. As I stood at the edge of the ocean of pillows, Charlie munching gracelessly on his bag of gummy bears beside me, I thought to myself that I may have gone slightly overboard. Did we even have enough places to put all of these?

'Well, there's only one thing for it now,' Charlie said,

scrunching the top of his gummy bear bag, turning around and lowering himself back onto the cushions. He wriggled around for a moment, the pillows shifting into place beneath him. After a few seconds he let out a long, contented sigh and closed his eyes, his arms splayed out at either side of him. 'You comin' in? The water's great.'

I knelt down and crawled to a spot that was an acceptable distance from him, turned over and lay down. I settled into position the cushions rising between us and popping out from under my body like when you stand on a pool float that slips from under your feet. The cushions formed a small barricade between us and I was glad of it, because at least this physical divide would absorb some of the sexual tension I felt towards him. I often found it a struggle to look away from him. The feelings zipping and chiming in my chest when he caught me with that intense blue stare.

The room held the damp chill that old houses always do, the subtle blast of evening heating that I could still feel lingering in the air, unable to chase away all of the cold. The ceiling, high above us, held hairline cracks, again just a product of age, that ran across the whole span of it, disappearing behind the ornate plaster ceiling rose.

'Do you miss it?' I asked, my voice sounding quiet in the large room.

'Do I miss what?' His voice was dreamy, content.

'Home. Ireland. Your family.'

'Yes and no. I miss the place, obviously. It's beautiful. Have yer ever been?'

'I haven't, but well done on that particular attempt at conversational misdirection. Almost seamless. What about your family?' I probed further.

'Touché. Erm, some of them. I highly doubt they miss me though.'

'Why is that?' I pressed a little more, hoping that I wasn't pushing my luck.

He sighed. 'I did something real shitty a couple of years back.'

I shifted a little, the zip of one of the cushion coverings digging into my side. 'What did you do?'

'Technically it's more of what I didn't do.' He paused, his voice thick with something I couldn't quite decipher.

'Do you want to talk about it?'

'No,' he replied. 'At some point, but not now.'

We lay in the silence for a while, the air thick with our own individual trains of thought. It was a while before either of us made a sound and when that sound came, it came in the form of a rustling plastic bag. A moment or two after the rustling, a hand appeared over the barricade of soft furnishings, clutching a fist full of gummy bears.

I reached up and touched my hand gently to his. His fist unfurled and a rainbow of bears fell into my open palm. 'Thanks.'

'No worries,' I heard him utter in a dreamlike way as he retracted his arm. I tossed one into my mouth, without taking notice of the colour as all gummy bears tasted the same to me, and the sound of my chewing was so loud in my ears that I stuffed them all into my mouth and got rid of them in one go.

I felt something uncomfortable behind my back and reached around, pulling out a blue cushion, covered with brown patches of atlas print. I ran my fingers over the soft surface of the cushion, mentally counting the places Mum had been to and lived in over the years. So many different places, filled with new people and cultures. And where had I been? Cowering in a corner, making excuses not to visit her because I was afraid of flying.

I saw movement over the wine-red pillow of the barricade and I watched as his fingers began to set up a line of gummy bears, all looking over into my section. I narrowed my eyes and looked at the bears a little more closely, lined up as if they were about to begin a goose step, and all of them had had their heads removed, the vacant space filled with a head of a different colour.

I leaned up on my elbows and looked at the line of bears in horror. 'Erm . . . are you doing some weird gummy bear head transplant surgery over there?'

He placed another bear in the line, red with a green head. 'Yeah, with this one I was goin' for a festive Christmas sort of vibe.' I still couldn't see his face, only his right shoulder leaning against the blue velvet cushion he'd picked out himself.

'Isn't the first sign of a serial killer when they start butchering poor defenceless animals?' I asked.

'I don't think gelatine bears count.'

I blew a laugh through my nose and sent one of them over into his section with a flick of my finger.

'Hey!' he called with somewhat genuine annoyance. 'What'ya doin' to young Frankenstein there?' A moment later, delicate fingers picked him up and placed him back in line.

'Sorry, I didn't know you'd grown so attached to them.' I saw the dark hair of his head, bobbing over the partition as he constructed more poor unfortunate monstrosities. 'You do know that the monster wasn't actually called Frankenstein though, right?' I said, throwing a piece of utterly useless knowledge out there.

'Yes, he was,' he argued as he placed his eighth creation, a clear head on a yellow body, in line.

'No, the doctor was called Victor Frankenstein; the creature didn't have a name. He's referred to as Adam at one point, because he's the first of his kind, but it's not his official name.'

'Are'ya serious?' he asked, sitting up and finally coming back into view. 'Yer tellin' me I've been gettin' that wrong me whole life?' He stared at me with pinched brows and a mouth hanging crookedly open in question.

'The whole theme of the book is abandonment and the fact that he refuses to give the creature a name reflects the theme,' I said, reiterating something that my mother had once told me.

'Where d'ya keep it all?' he asked, looking impressed.

'What, the useless information? I store it in the spaces reserved for actual useful knowledge, like where the Isle of Man is or how to change a fuse.'

The overhead light emitted a warm glow that made shadows of the strands of his dark hair, which hung down over his eyes, and the straight bridge of his nose.

He picked up the 'festive' gummy bear and raised it to his lips.

'No,' I gasped comically, 'you can't.'

'Oh, I can and, shortly, you'll see that I will.' He opened his mouth and held it just inside.

'But you brought them into this world!'

He dropped it onto his tongue, closed his mouth and chewed.

'You monster!' I exclaimed.

A forced, evil cackle rolled from his lips. 'Mwahaha!' He snatched the rest of them up and piled them onto his tongue and, just like that, he put an end to his creations.

We both laughed and I was filled with the same kind of foolish, simple joy that fills you in your teenage years when you're doing something stupid with someone you have a crush on.

'What time is it?' he asked abruptly.

I checked my phone and was shocked to see how late it had got. 'It's eight forty-five.'

'Damn it, I'd better get goin',' he said and something inside me deflated. He pushed himself up and I followed, my feet slipping as I padded over the cushions in sock-covered feet. I met him on solid flooring and readjusted my loose jumper from where it had ridden up in all the wrong places.

'Hey, what's that?' He gestured to the top of my shoulder blade where the small greyish black blades of a wind turbine tattoo poked out from under my clothes.

'Oh, that,' I said, pulling my hair over my opposite shoulder and tugging the back of my jumper down a little. I turned to the side so it could be seen more clearly, about the size of a fifty-pence piece, the bottom of it disappearing into waves. 'I'd always wanted a tattoo but couldn't think of anything to get and then one day when my mum came back from one of her work trips, we both went and got the same tattoo, so that we will always be linked, no matter how far apart we are.'

I looked over my shoulder as he raised a hand and ran his fingers over the skin of my tattoo. I closed my eyes and exhaled a shaky breath as his thumb moved in gentle circles and I felt goose bumps over every inch of my skin. 'Do you . . . erm . . . d-do you have any?'

'Huh?' he said quietly, not really listening.

'T-tattoos? Do you have any?'

'No, I don't.' His voice seemed far away. 'I'm glad that we're, you know, friends again.'

'Me too.'

But we were not friends. I didn't lie in bed at night thinking about friends like I did about Charlie. I didn't go over every word I'd said to them, slapping my pillow with frustrated hands when I remembered a moment where I'd embarrassed myself. My breathing became heavy as I turned around to face him and I looked at his lips, surrounded by stubble that was on the verge of becoming a beard. He moved a little closer. He was so close that I could smell the sweet scent of gummy bears on his breath and I wondered if he'd taste like them too, when his lips finally reached mine. He moved closer still, the heat of his body radiating out to mine through the unforgivably cold air of this big old house. His hand moved up to my face and a tender fingertip ran along the line of my jaw. I closed my eyes and almost shivered at the touch and when I opened my eyes again, I found him even closer than he had been before.

I prepared myself for what I imagined would be an end-credits kiss, the big one that happens to swelling orchestral music and where doves take off and circle above us as the camera pans out and fades to black, a cheerful pop song taking over from the orchestra as the names roll by. I could practically hear the conductor readying the ensemble as Charlie looked down at my lips.

This was going to be it. A second chance at the moment he'd screwed up before.

He moved closer, his lips barely an inch from mine and then, just as my eyes fell closed, he stopped.

'I'll . . . erm . . .' He cleared his throat and stepped away, so very far away. The conductor in my brain threw his baton in frustration, the orchestra disassembling in disappointment. He stepped away, grabbed his shoes from by the door and left, disappearing once again.

Chapter Eight

My mum had always been a fan of those who-done-it murder mystery adaptations that always come on around Christmas, where you spend the whole time trying to work out who it is that killed old Viscount Mulberry with the cyanide in the parlour. I wasn't ever much of a fan of those; I didn't have the patience for them. So, the real-life, walking (but not so much talking) mystery, otherwise known as Charlie Stone, was proving to be one of the most frustrating people I had ever attempted to wrap my head around. It had been thirteen days now, almost an entire two weeks, since Charlie and I had shared a moment of pure, erotica-level sexual tension, quickly followed by a hurried, wordless goodbye. Almost two weeks since he took his second chance and used it to sexually frustrate me once more with almost kisses and I hadn't heard a peep from him since.

Meanwhile, I'd been going through the full spectrum of emotions. Denial, waiting up for an hour or two after he left to see if he might come back and explain himself. Anger, where I lay in bed, staring at the ceiling, seething with a concentrated fury that I hadn't felt in years. Bargaining, sitting between calls at work and thinking that maybe there was a reason for his running away. That was where I was stuck right now, coming up with endless excuses and reasons why. Maybe he'd suddenly found himself feeling ill or remembered he'd left the stove on. Maybe something had happened with Carrick and he'd had to go home to Ireland? I'd worried that he hadn't taken my number down right, that he'd missed a digit or that the phone masts were down, but we usually got bulletins about problems with the phone lines at work and I hadn't heard of any recently.

I then went back to the much more believable theory of him being married. I could think of no reason more fitting for the guilty look that'd arrived on his face after the first of the two almost kisses. Just because he'd told me that he wasn't married, didn't mean that that was the case. I'd had several moments over the last two weeks when all I'd been seeing in my mind's eye were stills of him with his beautiful, Victoria's Secret model wife who'd have a name like Cara, their two perfect children playing on the carpet with the Labrador beside the log fire. Charlie smiling as he withdrew a roast from the Aga and placed it on the perfectly laid, polished oak table.

Another option was that he was dead. What if he'd never made it home after that night of butchered gummy bears and tentative touches? What if he was lying, unidentified, in a morgue somewhere, heading for nothing but years as a John Doe in a freezer, ice crystals forming on those thick dark lashes? All of these theories were plausible, if not likely, but all of them had one single purpose: to not allow myself to think about the most probable reason for it all. What if he just didn't want to talk to me? I'd gone onto Facebook and searched for him after four days of radio silence, but his profile was private and I didn't want to dignify his ghosting, if that was what this was, with any sign that it was bothering me.

His profile picture was one of him standing on a hill, bathed in sunshine. He looked so different, slightly heavier than he was now, his stubble and long hair stripped away in favour of a clean shave and slickly styled quiff. He beamed into the camera with a cocky look of excitement in his eyes, one that I hadn't seen there in my time of knowing him, which, granted, had not been that long. The only other picture I could see was one of him and a group of friends. They looked like your typical yuppy bankers with ostentatiously sized watches and slip-on loafers over sockless feet. Charlie, although looking a little out of place, seemed to be enjoying himself. His smile wide, his eyes bright. He looked like a stranger.

'Well, which do you think it is?' I asked, pushing my head through the hole of a turtleneck jumper, like I was being born all over again, and pulling my hair out from inside the collar. It was instantly hit by that static frizz that is impossible to get rid of once it happens and I quickly checked the damage in the camera of my phone. 'Dead, married or ghosting me?'

'Honestly, Nelly, I don't know,' Mum said through the screen. 'I don't know which one you want me to say.' She was in her office, typing something into her computer with rapid fingers, not even glancing down at the keyboard.

'The one that you think is the truth,' I replied a little tetchily.

She sighed, but didn't stop typing. 'Honestly, love, I think it might be that he's just a prick. One of those . . . what do you young people call them these days? Fuckboys. That's it.'

'Mum!' I exclaimed.

'What? You asked what I think and that's what it is. I think he tried his luck with you and then when you didn't hand it out on the first night or the second, he gave up on it and I'm proud of you for that. The Coleman women are anything but easy.' She stopped typing and scrunched up her nose. 'Well, apart from that one, single, solitary time, when you were conceived. Apart from that, we are chaste women.'

'That's honestly not what it was like, Mum.'

'Well, maybe he's just a little bit unhinged then? You did meet him via a mental health phone line.'

'That doesn't mean he's crazy, Mum. People who feel over-whelmed at times aren't all sitting in the corners of rooms, rocking back and forth in straitjackets, you know? And anyway, he was calling to talk about his uncle, not himself.'

She sighed. 'Look, you gave him a chance, two even. I'd call it quits now.'

'But I really liked him.' I groaned. 'He's just so flaky. He said he'd text me soon, he promised. It's been two weeks.'

'Well, have you tried to contact him? It's the twenty-first century, you know. Women aren't expected to wait for the men anymore.'

'I've texted him three times and sent him a couple of memes and he's ignored every single one of my messages. He's read them – I can see that – he just doesn't bother to respond.'

She sucked her teeth and looked thoughtful for a moment. 'Well, I suppose that two weeks isn't that long in the grand scheme of things.'

'It is when you don't have a job and you've already disappeared once already. Being ghosted has genuine detrimental psychological effects, you know. There's been articles on it.'

'He doesn't have a job?'

'He's between jobs,' I said, looking away from the camera to hide from her withering stare. Why was I defending him? What was wrong with me?

'And what is his profession?' she asked. She folded her arms and leaned back in her chair.

'He's a make-up artist.'

'A make-up artist? Like the ones in MAC? Because you know that they tend to, more often than not, be . . .'

'He's not gay, Mum, but way to stereotype. No, he's not one of those make-up artists anyway. He's one of the ones that make fake noses out of silicone or make you look like your arm's just been sawn off.' I grabbed a brush from my makeshift vanity table – a spare plank of laminate flooring propped up with books at either end – and gently combed it through my hair to try and undo the damage the statically charged jumper had done.

'What a charming job.' Her nostrils flared a little before she spoke again. 'Is he any good?'

'I have no idea. That would involve him actually divulging some personal information, wouldn't it, and that's not something he seems capable of doing.' I carried on dragging the brush through my hair, harder and harder, until my scalp began to ache. 'I just don't understand him. One minute he's saying that he's in desperate need of a friend and that I *am* that friend and that he wants to know more about me and then he's looking at me with those big, I want to kiss you eyes and then poof, he's gone again.' I could feel the brush snapping through hair when the bristles encountered tiny knots but I couldn't stop; the brushing, and subsequent pain, was cathartic.

'Darling, darling. You'll have no hair left.' She held her hand up to the camera, begging me to stop. 'You know your grandmother had trouble holding on to her hair. Let's not help the genes on their way.'

I dropped the brush down onto the 'table' like it'd turned white hot and surveyed the number of hairs lying in the bristles. Not too many – I wouldn't be going bald just yet.

'Seems to me like he's messing you around and you're better off following Ned's advice and getting yourself on Bumble.' She resumed her typing, although each hammer of the key was a little louder this time.

'I don't want to go on Bumble, but I agree with you about the messing me around thing. I'm giving him one last day. He has until the stroke of midnight to text me and if he doesn't, then I guess he goes back to being a pumpkin.'

'Good plan, Nelly. Let me know how it goes. No word on when I'll be back just yet, but it'll be soon, I promise.' She picked up the phone and drew it towards her face.

'Uh-huh. A lot of people keep making me promises at the moment.' I sighed.

'Nelly, I am your mother. If you can't trust me to keep a promise then who can you trust?' She blew a kiss into the camera. I caught it and returned one of my own before hanging up and turning to the mirror.

I was wearing my hair straight today, parted in the middle like a Seventies hippy. I applied some hair oil to my hand and dragged it through my unruly locks in a last-ditch attempt to calm the frizz. I had done very little with my day so far. My only real objective had been to go into town to buy a film and some pizza for me and Ned tonight. I'd thought about calling around to my ever-evaporating pool of friends but in the end, I decided that I'd much rather wander around town on my own. It had been an empty, boring kind of day where you can't wait for night to come so you have an excuse to sit around and be lazy.

I caught the bus into town, due to the sudden shower of rain that disappeared as quickly as it came, but gave its all while it was here. I vowed to walk my way home and attempt to get to at least four digits on the pedometer.

I tried to clear my mind and enjoy my day, but there was a quiet anger that bubbled away in the background, turning my smallest of actions into expressions of frustration. I'd slapped my card down so forcefully onto the reader when I entered the bus that the driver recoiled a little. I knew that the annoyed, proud part of me, the part that'd been raised on tales of Boudica and Pocahontas, wanted to be strong and cut my losses with Charlie Stone now, before that treacherous warmth in my chest grew to be something that I'd carry with me in various forms of damaging behaviour for the rest of my life. I was a strong, capable woman and I didn't need a man to complete me. I would, however, like to have someone to sleep beside or kiss me when I left for work. I had Ned for all my platonic needs but it would be nice to have the romantic needs covered too.

I went into HMV and bought a bargain-bin romantic drama with an embracing couple on the cover. Ned was a sucker for this type of film and he'd be overjoyed to curl up in our mountain of scatter cushions and use one of them to hide his moistening eyes when the credits rolled. God forbid we had a tear-stained repeat of the *A Walk to Remember* debacle of 2019.

I grabbed two pizzas and a couple of four-packs of Peroni and began heading back home. It took about twenty minutes to walk and that would give me enough time to think a little more about the Charlie situation, before putting it all to rest. It must have been somewhere near five o'clock, so that gave him seven hours to text and if he didn't, then I would do what I should have done a week ago and step away.

The walk home seemed long and arduous and I thought about turning around and heading to the bus station, but I had promised myself that I would get at least some exercise. Caffeine was what I needed, a little boost to see me through.

I turned in the direction of caffeine and approached Cool Beans Café. I shamelessly walked in through the glass door, turned opaque with condensation, and scoured the room for him, like I'd done every lunchtime these past two weeks, and came up with nothing. I walked up to the counter and ordered a coffee from the rookie employee as I continued to scour the place with increasingly frustrated eyes.

'Americano,' the boy said and handed me my drink. I thanked him and was about to walk away when I turned back to him and glanced down at his name tag.

'Sorry, erm, Russel?' I asked. Russel turned back to me, worried that he'd cocked up my order. 'Can I just ask if that Irishman with the dark hair has been coming in recently?' A magenta-lipped woman in the queue sucked her teeth in my direction. I had become the very thing I hated the most, someone who holds up the line.

'Oh, you mean cold tea guy?' he asked, his eyes momentarily widening, and then he quickly checked over his shoulder to make sure no one had heard him. 'Sorry, we're not supposed to refer to regulars by the nicknames we give them.'

'Nicknames? Do I have one?' I asked, getting a little distracted.

He grinned. 'Yeah. You're smiley girl.' He leaned in and whispered, 'But if anyone asks, I didn't tell you that.' He resumed his position and cleared his throat. 'So, it's him you're looking for? The one who always leaves his tea?'

'That's the one,' I replied.

'Yeah, he was in here not too long ago.'

'As in . . . today?' I asked.

'As in, like, five minutes ago. He took a tea and some banana bread.' He grinned, terribly pleased with himself that he could remember the order.

'Did you see which way he went?' I asked, even though I could feel the impatient eyes of every person in the queue boring into me.

He scrunched up his face as if his usefulness was coming to an end and began to shake his head. 'Erm, well,' his face unscrunched and his eyebrows rose a little higher. 'Isn't that him there?' He pointed out the window to one of the few tables put out front for smokers and in one of those cold, rain-spattered chairs, was the melancholy outline of Charlie Stone.

I turned back to Russel and nodded my thanks, taking all the change I had out of my pocket, which amounted to about three pounds, and cast it into the tips jar. 'Thank you. You're doing a great job here, Russ. Keep it up.' He straightened a little, infused with pride, as I turned on my heel and walked back along the queue of staring people.

I walked to the door and stepped outside, wondering what I was meant to do now that I had this information. Maybe he'd lost his phone or maybe he had that daily amnesia like Drew Barrymore in *50 First Dates*. Unlikely, but maybe.

A far more likely and far more upsetting explanation was that I was just another person getting ghosted by their crush.

I took a deep breath, attempted to slow the beat of my heart back to usual human levels and turned in his direction. A sad, rain-spotted brown paper bag lay on the table, dripped upon by the leaky awning. The remnants of his banana bread lay scattered around the tabletop in the form of crumbs and a discarded, unused serviette. He looked up when I was a couple of paces away, doing a double take and looking back up the second time with an expression of horror on his face.

'Nell, err, how are yer?'

'Great,' I said a little too enthusiastically and with a definite edge of suppressed anger. 'You been busy?'

He shrugged. 'Not really. You?'

Not really? Was that really all he had to say? My anger started to simmer in my stomach and I felt like I might say something too telling, something too much for this stage in the . . . I was going to say relationship but that probably wasn't what this was.

'Did you find someone to get your phone fixed?' I asked, tilting my head passive-aggressively to the side.

'My phone?' Confusion found his face. 'It's not brok— ohh.' Realisation hit. 'I see what yer did there.'

'Are you injured? Hurt? Did you run away with the circus

95

or get hit by a car and die in a ditch? Am I talking to your ghost right now?' I snapped.

'I'm sorry I didn't reply.'

I didn't acknowledge his apology. I was too angry. I should probably have tried to calm down, but rational Nell was lost beneath hurt Nell.

'All I wanted to do was get to know you a little more, help you out and be the friend that you say you so desperately need. But apparently you can't quite decide what it is you want. I even thought I had a little crush on you there for a minute too.' Understatement of the century right there.

'I do want to be your friend.' He stood from the table, picking up his takeaway cup of probably untouched tea and warming his hands around the cardboard. 'I've just had quite a lot going on this week.'

'But you just said you hadn't been busy.' I lifted my coffee to my lips and took a confident swig through the little plastic lid, the liquid coming out too hot and scalding my lip, but I didn't react. He would not see weakness from me.

'Look, Nell, I—'

I held up my hand and cut him off. 'No need. I totally understand.' I stared coldly into his eyes with what I hoped was an unreadably deadpan face. He slid his hand into mine and I shook it forcefully, trying not to acknowledge the twinge in my chest that felt like it might implode at any second. 'It was nice to meet you, Charlie Stone. I hope you have a very nice rest of your life.'

'Nell, I didn't mean to—'

'Don't worry about it.' I smiled a clearly meaningless smile, dropped his hand, turned around and called, 'See you,' over my shoulder.

I walked quickly, so quickly that I must have looked ridiculous.

I felt like crying but I wasn't going to give him the satisfaction of making me cry. I only cried at things that mattered like Instagram videos about abandoned dogs or episodes of Dolly Parton's *Heartstrings* on Netflix. Charlie Stone didn't matter to me and so I wasn't going to cry about him. Why should he matter to me when I so clearly wasn't even worth a text after all I'd done for him? No, my time spent thinking about brooding Irishmen was over.

I thought back to how embarrassingly sentimental I'd been about that first meeting in the coffee shop that I used to love, but would now only associate with Charlie Bloody Stone. How excited I'd been during that first meeting, how hopeful that Charlie and me were only at the beginning of what I'd hoped would be a long story. But it had turned out to be less of a tome and more of a novella, maybe even a haiku or perhaps a limerick was more fitting in this case.

I took a left and walked a little way up the steep hill towards home, moving on autopilot while a barrage of self-inflicted insults bounced their way around my brain, ricocheting back and forth like hurtful little squash balls. I'd instinctively taken the shortest way home past the town hall and I looked up at the face of the clock tower, high up at the end of the long Victorian building. Ned would be home by now, but the bags were hurting my hands, so I walked over to the war memorial, a bronze statue of a soldier surrounded by wreaths of plastic red poppies left over from last November. I slumped down on the surrounding wall, letting my bags of shopping slide onto the ground.

I pulled my phone from my pocket and saw that I had two messages, one from Charlie and one from Joel. Great, this day just kept getting better. I didn't bother reading either. My time for caring what either of them had to say was over, so I swiped the texts away.

I don't know how long I sat there, but it was growing dark by the time I got up and began the rest of the journey home. On the way, curiosity got the better of me and I opened up Joel's message. All the words were the same as the last several hundred texts he'd sent, just in a different order.

Hey You, How's things? I really think we need to talk. Sort out what we're feeling and stuff. Could I come by at some point? J xxx

P.S. I found a box of some of your stuff and so I'll bring that over too.

The 'I've just happened upon some of your possessions' excuse was one of Joel's favourites. I think he'd actually found all of my stuff within a few weeks of us breaking up and had divided it up into little groups that he was systematically bringing back to me in dribs and drabs.

I couldn't deal with Joel and whatever it was he wanted to talk about right now. So, I pushed my phone into my pocket and tried to forget about both of the troublesome men in my life.

When I eventually got home, I let myself into the house and was met by the sound of the radio playing softly in the kitchen. The bag handles had begun to dig into the fleshy pads of my fingers and I couldn't wait to put them all down. I made a mental note to, in future, walk into town and catch the bus home instead. I walked into the kitchen and heaved the bags up onto the counter, sighing with relief when my hands were finally free.

'Nell, I was wondering where you were,' Ned said.

'I got caught up in the farce that is my love life, but I'm back now and I come bearing Meat Medley Pizza and Channing Tatum.'

When I turned to show him the film cover, I found his eyes wide and staring.

'What?' I asked a little haughtily.

'I'm making tea for us. Would you like some too?' I frowned at him as he stared meaningfully into my eyes and used his pupils to point over in the direction of the table. I looked over and saw what I hadn't when I walked in. Sitting at the table with a pained smile on his face was Charlie. He was peering out from behind what was left of the flowers he'd sent, which must have obscured him from my vision when I'd walked in. The eucalyptus was still holding up well, but the tulips had long since drooped and found their way into the bin. Ned, unable to stand the smell, was desperate to throw them out, but, even though the sentiment of the bouquet now made me grit my teeth, I still couldn't throw them out just yet. I could hardly condemn the flowers to an early grave, simply because the person who sent them to me was an insensitive arsehole. That odd, sad look was in Charlie's eyes again and I heaved a sigh of frustration. For God's sake. Here we go again.

'No, to the tea – thanks, Ned. There's something slightly stronger in the bag that I have a feeling I'm going to be needing shortly,' I said, my eyes glued to Charlie's.

'I asked Charlie to stay for pizza and a film. I hope that's okay?' he asked, meddling away.

I sighed. 'What did you go and do that for?' A series of annoyed tuts left my mouth before I turned back to Charlie. I must have been shooting daggers at him because he looked genuinely afraid. 'Charlie, can I talk to you in the other room for a moment, please?'

'Err, sure.' He rose worriedly from the table and looked to Ned as if he might need to call in backup at any moment. He was dressed in that annoying cool way he always did, in the same black ripped jeans that he'd worn every single time I'd seen him, slightly pointy-toed shoes and a cable-knit jumper that was rolled up at the sleeves. I looked him over for what I hoped wasn't a long time, turned abruptly and walked towards the living room. I slapped the light on with an overly aggressive hand, marched over to the far wall, turned with the dexterity of an Olympic swimmer and by the time I had folded my arms across my chest, he was tentatively making his way through the door.

'What about our earlier conversation made it seem like I'd invited you round for tea?' I asked.

He stood for a moment, looking unsure as his mouth opened and closed over and over again. Then without warning he stepped forward and flung his arms around me. His chin tucked itself into the curve of my neck and his hot breath danced through my hair. Whatever words I'd planned on saying next were pushed from my lungs in the form of a quiet wheeze as he squeezed me tightly. My arms unfolded and I managed to slide them out from between us. They fell to my sides and dangled there while Charlie hugged me. I felt my heart stutter a little and I was appalled with myself. Why was I so bloody forgiving? And what was it about this man that made me feel like doing it so easily?

'Charlie?'

'Yeah?'

'Can you get off me, please?'

'Sure. Sure,' he said, taking his time in unhooking his arms and stepping back a few paces.

'I didn't write back because I've been dealing with some stuff. I know that's not an excuse and I was wrong to ignore you, especially after we, yer know, left things. But I really do want us to be friends. I'm sorry.'

'Is Carrick okay?' I asked.

'He's fine.' That guilty look crept back onto his face.

'All of this has been on your terms,' I said, surprised at how angry my voice came out. 'Frankly, Charlie, that's not how friendships work.' I crossed my arms over my chest. 'Meeting with you after you called could have landed me in real trouble with work – a job that I love. We talk, we flirt, you make sure I get home safely. Then you try to kiss me but end up shouting at me instead. Eventually, you come back and I feel like that was the one excusable mess-up. I was sort of pleased because I thought that it meant that you'd got it out of the way early. But then you ghost me, again. You couldn't even be bothered to send an emoji in response?'

'I know, I know. I suck.'

'I'm almost thirty, I don't have time for this school-kid shit. You come in here and act like . . .' I paused, unsure how to put this into words. 'You act like you want me, as a friend and sometimes way more than that. But at the slightest sign of anything happening between us, you turn into frigging Houdini.'

'Nell, look. I have absolutely no idea what I'm doin' at the moment. Life is runnin' away from me a little and meetin'' you, well, it's made me think about what I should do,' he said, his eyes finding mine and, once again, I was struck by their blue intensity.

'What do you mean?'

'I mean that I was changin' things. I quit my job, made a plan and thought that I had everythin' set out and then I met you and . . . you sorta cast a new filter over everythin.'

I frowned with confusion. What did any of this even mean?

'Look, Charlie. I know you're dealing with some heavy stuff with your uncle at the moment and I want to help you with it, but I can't do that if you don't talk to me.'

'I know, I know and I do want to tell yer, I just . . . I know I've been an arse and the last thing I want yer to do is think badly of me.'

'Well, I do think badly of you. I'm a person, with feelings. Feelings that you don't seem to give a shit about.'

He winced as if he knew he was onto a loser. 'I do give a shit about your feelin's.'

'Shall I pop the pizzas in?' Ned called from the other room.

'Yeah!' I shouted back.

'Nell—' Charlie uttered.

I held up my hand to stop him. 'My mum always said to forgive, but only to forget if I was certain that the person asking for forgiveness wouldn't end up needing forgiveness again and, so far, you've needed it twice.'

'Charlie, beer?' Ned called again.

'Ned!' I shouted back. 'Can't you hear that we're having an argument here?'

'Sorry!' he said and I heard the soft shutting of the kitchen door.

102

'If yer don't want to forgive me, then please don't. I deserve no less. But, if it's okay with yer, I'd like to stay for pizza.'

I hated myself for wanting him to stay.

'Fine. But you're Ned's guest, not mine.'

The door creaked and I knew Ned was eavesdropping, even before he appeared and stepped into the room. He was holding his hands up like a white flag as he stepped into the battlefield that was the living room.

'I'm sorry, I know I shouldn't have been listening, but you weren't exactly whispering.' He came to a stop between us.

'What do you want, Ned?' I snapped.

He sighed and looked from me to Charlie. They spoke without words as they looked at each other, Charlie seeming to come to an unspoken understanding with Ned. It was almost as if . . . no.

'Wait, do you two know each other?' I asked, my eyes scrunched, my brows lowered.

Ned raised his brows at Charlie and nodded gently. 'I think you need to tell her.'

Charlie looked panicked, his eyes darting to me and then back to Ned as he squirmed on the spot.

'Look, Charlie, I know Nell and if you don't explain yourself now, you're never going to get her to trust you and you certainly won't get her to stop asking questions until she knows everything.'

I took a step forward, frustration making me seethe.

'Do you know each other?' I said a little more firmly.

'Yes. We know each other,' Charlie said, his hands flailing as if he had no idea what to do with them or where to place them.

'How?'

I looked to Charlie for an answer, but it was Ned who did. 'Do you remember, two years ago when I got that hard call on my birthday? The jumper?'

'Yeah, of course I do. It upset you for weeks.'

'I didn't know if the person who called had gone through with it, because they hung up before I was able to get them to come down from the tower. I scoured the obituaries and the news but I had very little to go on. I didn't even know his name. All I knew was that he was from Birmingham and that he was Irish.'

It took a moment for Ned's words to make sense, like liquid slowly seeping through sand. I gasped and held a hand to my mouth, my eyes turning to Charlie. 'It was you?'

Charlie was looking down at the floor, almost embarrassed.

'You wanted to kill yourself?' I asked, panicking at the thought of a world without Charlie in it.

He looked up, eyes reddened and slick with moisture. 'I did.'

'Why?' I asked.

'Let's tackle one thing at a time,' Ned said, holding up a protective hand.

'I couldn't cope. Something really bad had happened and I didn't know what to do to make it any better. The only thing I remember thinking was that if I couldn't stop myself from feeling the bad things, that I'd just have to stop myself feeling anything at all, forever. So, I went to the clock tower and I was about to jump, when I chickened out and threw myself backwards instead. I landed on the floor and that's when I saw the sticker.'

'The clock tower at the town hall? What sticker?' I paused and took a breath, my lungs burning in my chest.

'Yeah. There's this sticker at the top with the number for the helpline on. I took it as a sign and called it and that's how I met Ned.'

'I had no idea it was him until Charlie mentioned the helpline when we were chatting in the kitchen and I put two and two together,' Ned said.

'So, it was never about your uncle at all?' I asked.

He shook his head.

'And when you called me,' I said, taking a step closer to Charlie. 'Were you planning on trying a second time?'

He met my eyes and, slowly, he nodded.

He wiped at his eyes with the sleeve of his jumper and sniffled loudly. 'So, do yer think I'm a nutjob now? Shall I let myself out?'

My breaths whistled in and out of my nose at rapid speed, my heart beating so fast that it sounded like a rocket ship about to take off. My feet were moving forward before I even thought to move them and in a second, I had reached him, my arms wrapping around him and pulling him to my chest.

I felt him sob once or twice, then stop himself, as if he was frightened to show this much emotion.

'That's why I've been all over the place. I'm sorry I dragged yer into it.' He sniffed into the curve of my neck. 'I'd put everythin' in order; I'd made peace with it. I was ninety-nine per cent sure that it was what I wanted, then I met yer and I felt something that I thought I'd never feel again. It gave me hope, I guess, and then I wasn't so sure anymore.'

'Why didn't you tell me?' I asked.

'It's not like it's good date talk, Nell. No one talks about this kinda thing until it's already happened and I didn't want yer thinkin' I was mental.'

'Charlie.' I pulled away and held him at arm's length. 'This doesn't make you crazy. Being sad doesn't make you crazy. I work at a fricking mental health charity, you idiot. I'm pretty much the most understanding person you could have chosen.'

He chuckled, though his tears were still falling.

'Just because it's not talked about, doesn't meant that it shouldn't be.'

'See, I told you she'd understand.' Ned's voice made me jump. I'd forgotten he was there in all the drama.

I suddenly understood Charlie's skittish behaviour, his rapid changes in mood, his disappearing acts.

'How're you feeling now?' I asked nervously.

'Don't worry, I'm not gonna stick my head in yer oven or smother myself with scatter cushions.'

'That is very good to hear,' I said, moving toward him and pulling him into another hug. I wanted him close with my protective arms around him to keep him safe.

He cleared his throat of emotion, the sound loud in my ear. 'Ned said this thing to me when I called him a couple of years back and it's stuck with me ever since.'

I felt Ned bristle with pride beside me. 'Oh yeah and what was that particular pearl of wisdom?' I asked.

'He said "it's the moment you think you can't, that you realise you can" and right now, I feel like I can.'

I felt the weight of an arm land on my shoulder as Ned joined the hug.

'Ned?' I asked.

'Uh-huh?'

'That wouldn't happen to be a Celine Dion quote, would it?'

'Yes, Nell. Yes, it would.'

I closed the oven door and stood with my back resting against the counter, paused as my brain tried to catch up with everything.

It was awful to even contemplate, but I couldn't help wonder how different things would have gone if I'd taken a packed lunch that day instead of going to the café or if Caleb hadn't been late and I'd gone home on time instead of being forced to stay longer to cover him.

I guess it was flattering, knowing that someone had spent twenty minutes talking with me and he'd decided to stay alive because of it, because I'd given him hope of something beyond his sadness. But there was a pressure in my chest now that hadn't been there before. What if I didn't live up to the hope? What if I bored him and he decided that falling face first into concrete from a great height was a more appealing option than talking to me for a moment longer?

What if I was only postponing the inevitable and setting myself up for a hurt like no other? I just knew that from now on I was going to be the girlfriend equivalent of a helicopter parent, but I wasn't even his girlfriend. Oh God this was all so confusing and I was already nervous, even with him only in the next room.

The sound of the doorbell ringing cut through my thoughts.

'Ned, could you get that?' I called down the hall, as I popped the cap from my second bottle of Peroni and grabbed two for the others. I flung all of the caps at the bin, managing to get one of them in, the others clanging to the floor as the doorbell rang a second time. I tutted, grabbing the bottles as I went to answer the door myself.

I stepped out of the kitchen, the cool bottles chinking in my hands, just in time to see that Charlie was standing at the door, the Yale lock already unlatched in his hand. I glanced through the frosted window pane and the bottom fell out of my stomach as I recognised the silhouette of the person on the other side.

'Charlie, no,' I whisper-shouted and moved towards him at what felt like quarter speed. But he didn't hear me and before I could move more than three steps, the door was open and the two men were staring at each other awkwardly.

I heard a small whimper leave my throat. There was no hiding. I was in plain view, so I slapped on a smile and pretended that this wasn't going to be the world's most awkward encounter. 'Joel. Hi.' I forced my feet to move towards him, even though my body was urging me to turn and run in the opposite direction. I'd be able to scale the back fence if I really needed to, right?

'Hi,' Joel said, his voice small, shocked. He looked from me to Charlie and then to the box sitting in his hands.

There was a moment of crippling, writhing silence where not one single member of our Mexican stand-off had any idea what to do.

Eventually Charlie outstretched his hand in Joel's direction.

'Hi, I'm Charlie Stone,' he said with a hastily slapped-on cheerfulness that I had seen so many times, but only this time did I see through it. Joel looked down at his hand as if he suspected it rigged with explosives, before taking it and shaking it firmly.

'Joel. Oni.'

I don't know why they were being so formal, acting like this was a job interview.

'Nice t'meet yer,' Charlie uttered.

'You too,' Joel mumbled unconvincingly before looking at me with boiling eyes. 'Erm . . .' He dithered in that aggressively awkward way that he always did and stepped forward, holding the box out to me. From here I could already see the pitiful array of things inside. An old toothbrush, the bristles way past the point of usability, a rechargeable camera battery for a camera I no longer owned, some out-of-date blush, in a garishly bright pink, from about five years ago, and a strategically placed photograph of the two of us at a family barbecue with his parents. This was by far the weakest of the boxes he'd presented to me. He must have been running out of things to fill them with by now. 'I don't know if you still need any of it, but I thought you'd want them all the same.'

'Thank you,' I said, handing Charlie the beers and taking the box from Joel.

Joel's hand brushed mine, accidentally on purpose, as I took it from him. I placed the box down in the hallway, successfully hiding the wave of nostalgia that crashed over me like a tsunami when I looked at the photograph of us that sat in the box. I remembered that day well; it was one of my favourite memories with Joel.

'How are you doing?' I asked, turning back to him.

'Fine. Fine. I'm fine.' He looked from Charlie to me, wounded. 'Thriving, one might say.'

We both frowned at his strange choice of words and obvious lie.

Don't do it, I said to myself inside my head. *Don't you dare say it, Nell. Keep your mouth shut and do not let those words in your brain come out of your mouth.* 'You can come in if you like.' I hated myself!

Please refuse. Please, please refuse.

'No, I don't think that would be good for anyone involved.' He looked up at Charlie, jealousy-fuelled hatred all over his face.

'Okay, well thank you,' I said. 'For the box.'

'You're welcome. Enjoy your evening,' he said through gritted teeth, gave Charlie one last long stare, turned and walked away.

As I watched his figure disappear, the one that had once caused me to pulse with excitement whenever I saw it coming towards me, I felt a deep chasm of sadness open up inside me. How easy it actually was for inseparable people to separate, for lovers to drift to strangers, before becoming nothing at all.

I sat on the sofa beside Ned, with Charlie sitting on a mound of scatter cushions on the floor, his shoulder leaning against my leg as he watched the film with wide, interested eyes.

Needless to say, I didn't pay much attention. It's hard to do so when you find out that the man you have a crush on had planned to kill himself less than a month earlier.

The thought of him not being here, of me never knowing him, was too upsetting for me to even contemplate and that only added to the fear that whatever had overwhelmed him twice before, may well overwhelm him again.

It wasn't until the second half of the film until I felt his fingertips snake under the hem of my jeans. He didn't venture far, but the heat of his skin on mine, no matter how little skin that was, made me forget how to breathe. His fingers moved in circles, etching rings of goose bumps on my flesh, and I wondered how it might be to feel those goose bumps elsewhere, to have them cover me from head to toe.

It was almost half ten before Charlie and I found ourselves stood on either side of the open front door, the frigid air seeping in and raising the hairs on my legs that I probably needed to start doing something about.

'Thank you,' he said, his hands shoved into his pockets against the cold and, I suspected, out of nerves. He was fully exposed to me now, his pains an open wound for me to see and all I wanted to do was help him heal them.

The impatient part of me begged my mouth to ask the question that my brain was screaming. What was it that made you feel that way? And can I help? But I knew not to push him.

'No worries,' I replied with a reassuring smile. 'Thank you for telling me . . . what you told me. I know that couldn't have been easy.'

'It was time for me t'tell yer. I should've known yer'd be all right with it anyway, with what you do.'

'If you need to talk or even if you just need someone to distract you, then you know where I am.'

He looked down at his foot and kicked at the ground with the toe of his scuffed black boot.

'You're a good friend, Nell.'

The word 'friend' smarted a little after everything. I'm

pretty sure friends didn't fondle each other's ankles during film time, but now was not the time to raise this point.

'You can totally stay here, if you want. We have a spare room.' *And you're always welcome in my bed,* I added, but only in thought. Also, *I'm scared that if I say goodbye, it might be the last time I ever say it.*

'Thanks, but I'll be fine.' He looked back up and I could tell from the slight strain between his brows that he was embarrassed when he had no need to be. 'Say, what are you doin' right now?' he asked, suddenly imbued with some sort of enthusiasm.

'Probably gonna head to a rave, take some drugs, an orgy or two. You know, just a regular Friday night.'

'Damn it.' He sighed overdramatically, playing into the joke. 'So, you wouldn't be at all interested in coming for a quick walk with me?'

'Now?'

'Yeah. There's somethin' I wanna show yer.'

112

Chapter Nine

The halo of light pollution floated above the town responsible for it like a radioactive cloud, the street lamps and warmly lit windows nothing but tiny dots of light from the top of the clock tower. Charlie had let us in through a back door that he had a key to because he'd once worked on a show here and had 'forgotten' to give it back. He'd reassured me that he was only bringing me here to show me something, but still, climbing to the top of the tower from which he'd planned to never come down alive, made me feel on edge.

We'd climbed the seemingly endless metal steps to the top, the sounds and light of the clock mechanics whirring above us and creating the perfect atmosphere for a horror film murder scene. I had thought twice about walking into a strange, dark building with him, so I'd sent Ned a text to tell him where I was and I felt comforted that, if in the unlikely event that Charlie turned out to be a serial killer, I had a purple belt in taekwondo to lean back on. Mum had bought me lessons for my birthday that year I'd had my bag snatched on the way home from work, but I thankfully hadn't had to utilise my skills yet.

When we'd arrived at the top of the tower, Charlie had walked out on to the bird-mess-spattered, softly lit paving stones, surrounded by a half wall, and crouched down in a corner that the diffused light from the clockface didn't reach. I watched him closely and he stood a moment or two later with a bottle of whisky in his hand. I recognised it as the fancy bottle I'd kicked under the table when I'd first met him.

'No one else comes up here then, huh?' I asked, hugging my arms around myself.

'Only the odd maintenance person, but other than that, it's just me,' he said, walking towards the edge and sitting on the low half wall. Seeing him that close to the edge made my stomach flip but he just pulled the cork from the bottle and held it out to me. 'Come and join me.'

I took a steadying breath and went to join him at the edge. My fear of flying was simply a by-product of my acrophobia and as I looked down at the distant pavement below, I felt my head begin to swim and my knees go all hot, as if they might collapse underneath me.

'Erm, I'm good over here, thanks.'

'Yer scared of heights?' he asked.

'Just a smidge.'

'Come on. I won't let yer fall,' he replied.

'Na, I'm good.'

He chuckled and held the bottle out to me where I stood. I'd never swigged whisky from a bottle before. Everyone who did it on TV always had a certain roguish ease that made them look cool doing it. I, however, swigged too much resulting in rivulets of whisky running down my cheek and neck before disappearing under the collar of my shirt.

'Smoothly done.' Charlie chuckled again and took the bottle. He lifted it to his lips and swigged cleanly. 'So, what do you think? Pretty cool, huh?' He nodded in the direction of the clockface. It was strange seeing it this close. The sheer hugeness of it, coupled with the whirring from the gears and cogs working inside, made it feel ominous, almost like you were watching your life tick away before your eyes.

'I come up here when I need everything to be a little quieter, to get away from all the noise down there,' he said, looking back over his shoulder at the town below us.

'It's nice. Would be nicer if it was lower down though.'

He stood and walked over to me and I felt my breaths coming easier with each step he took away from the edge.

I felt a sudden, gentle warmth in my hand and a moment later, his fingers laced through mine. I turned to look at him, the rush of hormones doing nothing to stop the world from spinning beneath me.

'I won't let you fall,' he said with a sad smile. 'I've got you.'

My heart fizzed in my chest as his eyes steadied mine and, all of a sudden, I wasn't as frightened anymore.

'So, I want you to picture the scene,' Charlie said, his voice calm and far away. 'This is my place where I come to think, to get away from everythin' and one day, when it all gets a little too noisy down there and somethin' bad happens that changes my life forever, I walk up those stairs and . . . well, yer know what I was planning to do; yer don't need the details.' He slid his free hand into his pocket and withdrew the orange marble that I'd seen him messing with in the café

115

when we first met. But now, on closer inspection, I realised that it wasn't a marble at all. It was frosted and misshapen into an almost oval and looked more like a glass pebble than anything. He didn't mention it, just rolled it between his fingers like a worry bead. I was going to ask him about it, but I didn't want to interrupt his story.

'After hours of sittin' up here until my fingers were numb from the cold, I decided that it was time. But I couldn't do it, I was too afraid, and so I threw myself backwards instead and landed on the floor, right there.' He pointed to the ground. 'I lay there for a while, tryin' to figure out what to do next, when a pigeon landed on the wall. I rolled my head to the side to look at it and that's when I saw this.' He unlaced his fingers from mine and walked back over to the ledge, crouching down and pointing to the wall that he'd just been sitting on. I moved to his side and knelt down beside him, following the tip of his finger to just below the lip of the wall. I hadn't noticed it before, but from where I crouched, I saw the sticker for the helpline. It sat there, orange and white with patches where the weather had eroded it away to show the brick beneath. I read it and noticed a spelling mistake. 'Caring for your mental heath.'

Around the edges, someone had written something in Sharpie pen, the letters still there but hard to read.

'The sun will come up tomorrow, and who knows what the tide will bring along?' Charlie said dreamily.

'It's beautiful. Is it a poem?' I asked.

He shook his head. 'No, it's Tom Hanks. It's something he says in *Castaway*, which is my favourite film. So, I'm lyin' here, lookin' at a sticker for a mental health helpline that I've never noticed before, despite the fact that I've been spending

116

a lot of time up here, and that sticker just so happens to have a reference to my favourite film written in pen around the edge. Funny, don't yer think?'

'Seems almost like . . .' I didn't want to end the sentence, for fear of sounding like an idiot.

'Fate?'

I nodded. 'Like the universe wanted to make sure you stuck around.'

'Do you have any idea who put it here?' he asked. 'I mean, it looked pretty battered when I saw it two years ago, so it must have been up a while.'

'No,' I answered. 'I've never seen us use stickers like this.'

'That's a shame.' His shoulders sagged a little as he spoke.

Charlie ducked back inside the tower and tinkered around with a switch on the wall until the light from behind the clockface died down and he returned with an ancient-looking blanket, which he shook out and laid on the floor.

'What did you turn the light out for?' I asked.

'To give our eyes time to adjust. You can't see the stars with that thing on,' he said, lying down on the blanket and folding his arms behind his head. I sat down beside him and lay back, mirroring his pose. He was right about this place being quiet, removed. From here the lights of the town were duller, the sounds muffled and unobtrusive. It hadn't taken me long to start to feel the cold deep inside my bones and when Charlie saw me shivering, he shuffled closer, pressing his side to mine to share his warmth. The more my eyes adjusted to the darkness, the more stars became visible and before long, the sky was littered with thousands of glittering specks.

'So,' I said, breaking the silence and rolling my head to the side. 'Not only did that sticker lead you to Ned, who spoke with you the first time, but also to me, who helped you the second time. And it just so happens that us two live together.'

'Uh-huh,' Charlie said, rolling his head to face me. 'Improbable, huh?'

'Seems to me that someone up there really cares about you, Charlie Stone,' I said, still trying to comprehend it all. He turned back to the sky and swallowed what looked like a lump in his throat. 'And someone down here does too,' I added.

The slightest of smiles flickered across his face and his hand fell into mine. Something quite like butterflies, but bigger, albatrosses maybe, took flight inside my stomach at the feel of his skin on mine.

'That's nice to know.'

This felt like the moment, the one where I might lean over and kiss him. Everything was out in the open now, all secrets revealed. There was, hopefully, nothing else holding him back. But just as I was contemplating making a move, a sound so loud that I felt it in my bones made my heart falter and I sat bolt upright.

It took me a moment or two to realise that the sound wasn't the police arriving to arrest us for trespassing or a bomb going off, but simply the clock behind us, tolling the arrival of midnight.

Charlie's laughter could be heard through the pauses between chimes as he rolled around on the blanket beside me.

'You bastard, you knew that was coming,' I shouted above the din.

118

He sat up, once his fit of hysteria had ended, and placed a hand on my face. 'I'm sorry, I meant to mention it.' His thumb stroked the soft skin over my cheekbone as he looked into my panic-stricken eyes. 'It must have slipped my mind.' He chuckled and before long I was laughing along with him.

Chapter Ten

There are moments in life when you stop for a moment and simply have to ask yourself, how the hell did I end up here? And as I sat in the uncomfortably itchy folding cinema seat with my prosthetic latex nose slowly detaching from my skin and dangling precariously over the bucket of mixed popcorn in my lap, I decided that this was most definitely one of those moments.

The Day of the Marathon was on over in Worcester, a one-day film festival showing all the George Romero zombie films. My heart had sunk at the thought of it. Not only would it be zombie films, but ancient ones, the kind that have niche, cult followings of men with untamed facial hair whose staple diet is Mountain Dew and Wotsits and still live in their parents' basements at the age of forty-five. Nonetheless, I had accepted, simply because it meant several uninterrupted hours of time spent with Charlie. It wasn't until I had sworn myself into this event, that he'd added a caveat.

I picked up a puffed kernel of corn and chucked it in the general direction of my mouth with a sassy and seemingly putrefying hand. Soft sniggering came from the seat beside me and I cast a pissed-off look his way. I'd agreed for him to come to mine a couple of hours before we had to leave so that he'd have time to transform me into one of the undead, on the promise that everyone would be doing it and that there would be a prize for the best cosplay.

I'd been reluctant at first but he'd looked at me with downturned corners of his mouth and pinched lines between his brows and I'd come to the conclusion that this whole thing was happening in Worcester, where I knew no one. It would be fine; I'd just take the back routes to the motorway, so I didn't drive past anyone I knew, not that they'd even recognise me with blacked-out eyes and half a rotten face.

So, I'd sat there at the kitchen table and let him do his worst. He'd gently rested the crook of his wrist on my cheek and worked carefully, with a concentrative tongue pinched between pursed lips. After a few seconds I'd realised that having him paint my face was the perfect excuse for me to do what I'd wanted to do since I'd first met him, sit and stare at his face from close proximity, but in a way that wouldn't make me look like a creep. As time ticked by and he delicately augmented the blood spatter above my top lip, I took in the fine lines that had begun to take up permanent residence in the skin around his eyes, the deep russet reds that sprung up at intervals throughout the otherwise dark hair of his chin and the subtle scars scattered over his cheeks, which must have been left over from teenage acne.

A strand of hair, which had escaped the claw clip holding

my hair back from the array of sticky things being applied to my face, trembled with every aggressive thump of my heart. He looked good. Putting his mind to things, using his skill. I had wondered, in those minutes when he hovered a few inches away from me, what would happen if I leaned over and kissed him. Would he lean into it, or turn on his heel and run for the door again? I'd thought about it and come to the conclusion that, as far as I knew, he wasn't into necrophilia and so, me lunging in with zombie face probably wasn't the best turn-on.

'You've never looked more beautiful,' he said, and even though I knew it was a joke, the albatrosses took flight inside my stomach again.

Three and a half hours later, the glue that he'd used to adhere my fake rotting nose to my real, thankfully un-rotting, nose was beginning to itch and it was taking all the resolve I had to not tear it from my skin and throw it across the crowded theatre. The rows were filled with all kinds of people of all ages and all walks of life, not just the type of people I'd thought would be here. But whoever they all were, none of them, I repeat none, were made up like zombies and the second I'd realised this, I'd almost got straight back in the car and driven home without him. He seemed unaffected by the strange and amused looks that we sparked when we walked into the foyer, as if he didn't care a bit that he appeared to have a gaping hole in his cheek, through which fake blackened teeth could be seen.

As we walked through to the screen, I saw a timetable on the wall, detailing how the movies would play. My heart sank when I saw the extensive list of films, but Charlie reassured me that we were only staying for the first three as, according to him, they were the only three worth watching and that we could leave if I got too bored.

The first film flew by in a blur of popcorn and screaming and I'd enjoyed it more than I thought I would, or more than I'd openly admit to Charlie. There was one person behind us, a right Chatty Cathy, who was sitting about two rows back and had whisper-talked throughout the whole thing. She needed to recalibrate her whisper to talking ratio because I could hear every single one of the passive-aggressive comments she handed out to her husband throughout the film. I only knew that he was her husband because at one point she'd muttered into her plastic, foil-topped glass of rosé, 'I can't believe I married someone who's into all of this shite.'

Now, I wasn't the biggest fan of anything zombie-related, but even so, I'd rather have added another three films to this marathon, than hear her whinging commentary for a moment longer about how the special effects in *The Walking Dead* were so much better.

The final grainy black and white shots of the film played out and the house lights came up. I shuffled, self-consciously, down in my seat and shoved another handful of what seemed to be never-ending popcorn into my black-lipped mouth.

Charlie let out a satisfied sigh and turned to look down at me from where he sat, upright and confidently unfazed, in his seat.

'Jesus, are yer still embarrassed?' He chuckled. 'How do yer think anyone is going to recognise yer with all that crap on your face?' He reached over and took a handful of popcorn. 'Go on, I know that signature smile is still under there somewhere.'

'I don't know,' I replied haughtily. 'But it'll be just my luck to meet someone I haven't seen in years when I'm here looking like an idiot.'

'An idiot? I'll have yer know that you've about fifty quids' worth of make-up on your face. If anythin', yer look like a movie-quality badass,' he said, proudly. 'Did yer at least enjoy the film?'

'It was . . . okay.' I allowed. His brows arched into an exaggerated look of distress. 'I never claimed to be a zombie fan. Never have I ever claimed to like this stuff. However, here I am, looking like a complete loser in itchy make-up and sitting through a six-hour zombie film marathon to make you happy.'

'And I thank yer for it.' He sniggered and scratched at his own zombie nose, the entirety of his prosthetic moving a few millimetres with every unsatisfying scratch of his nail.

'Yer heard from yer fella since the other night?' he asked.

'He's not *my* fella. He's just *a* fella. And fella really is a bad word to describe him. He's not someone you'd look at and the word fella would spring to mind.' He rolled his eyes at my babbling and waited for me to actually answer his question. 'No, he hasn't been in touch. Why'd you ask?'

He micro-shrugged. 'I just wondered if he was okay. Couldn't have been easy for him to open the door and see such a strappin' young man with his girl.'

'Oh, don't worry. He's seen Ned before,' I jested.

'Oh, aren't yer just hilarious,' he said sarcastically and chuckled to himself as he started picking pieces of popcorn from where it sat in various places around his person.

How I'd left things with Joel had been sitting awkwardly in my stomach ever since he'd turned up at the house and I didn't quite know how to handle it. Was I supposed to ignore him? I guess, ignoring him would be the most compassionate way to handle it – just leave him to do whatever he wanted with the information he had. And anyway, if I did text him, what would I say? Sorry?

I wasn't sorry that I'd called quits on us. It was time, and I was exhausted by carrying the ten-ton corpse of our relationship around with me all the time. I wasn't sorry that I'd met Charlie either. Yes, Charlie was not the most straightforward of people to have a second try at love with, but I was feeling something again and I wasn't going to apologise for that.

I'd known from about six months in that Joel loved me more than I would ever love him, but nonetheless, I did – love him that is.

'He still loves yer, that's plain to see,' Charlie said.

'I know.' I sighed and leaned back heavily in my chair. 'But he needs to sort himself out. Figure out what he wants to do with his life and then do it. If that boy completed one thing in his whole life, it would be a bloody miracle. He used to argue that da Vinci never finished anything. But I always found it hard to believe that when da Vinci decided not to continue with something, it wasn't because he'd much rather be sat around in five-day-old boxer shorts, watching *Storage Wars* and drinking soup out of a mug.'

'We all have our moments where we lose sight of what's important. It's easier if yer don't care about things, but after a while the carin' catches up with yer.'

'Do you speak from experience?' I asked.

'Maybe a little.' He blew a laugh through his nose. 'Would yer take him back – Joel?'

'No. I didn't like who I was with him.'

'I understand that.' He seemed a little nervous, the skin around his eyes scrunching into little crow's feet that remained etched into his face paint even when he moved his face. 'Who I was, up until as recently as a couple of years ago, I don't know if you'd have liked him.'

'Why?' I asked, worried. How different could he have been? My brain instantly started concocting tons of terrible scenarios in which he was a drug addict, shooting up in alleyways outside nightclubs, or some sex-crazed womaniser, who owned his own sex swing and who would probably be bored to tears by anything I had to offer.

'I was just a bit of a fake, yer know? Cocky, sure of himself. Come t'think of it, I was just like my uncle, just without his likable charm.'

'You? Without charm? Don't pretend like that's even slightly possible. You're a textbook brooding rom-com charmer. There's no fighting it; it's just who you are.'

He looked at me from the corners of his eyes and smiled, revealing white teeth and causing those half-moon lines to crease his cheek behind all the grey make-up.

'You think too well of people,' he said as people around us began to settle back in for the second film.

'I'm an optimist. I see the best in people, even if they're reluctant to show it.'

He looked up fully now, his eyes once more agleam with mischief. 'I'm not sayin' that I kicked puppies or talked in the cinema.' He said the last point a little louder than the rest, directing the comment towards the Chatty Cathy two rows behind us.

'Good.' I responded equally loudly and equally sarcastically. 'Because there's a special place in hell for those people!'

I think I heard a small harrumph from her but that was the end of it.

'I was just a bit of a tosspot and not a very nice person. I was one of those men who speak fluent banter and think that spending twelve hours straight on *Call of Duty* is an acceptable use of time. I'd only have the latest phones and watches, even though I only ever wore them to show off to people. I'd drink in the fanciest of bars and I'd always be the first to buy a round to give them all the impression that I was doing better than I actually was. I once spent almost my whole month's paycheque in one night out so that I wouldn't have people knowing that I wasn't gettin' any theatre work. I had to take out a loan, which whooped my ass for a good few months until Carrick paid it off for me.

'I used to look down on people who stayed home in Westport – the ones who settled there and didn't move away. I thought that they were all small-town losers, missing out on what I thought life was about, but they're all happy now and I'm not. So, I'm the one who got it wrong.'

'Sounds to me like a bad person wouldn't be sitting here confessing all of this to me in the hopes of being absolved,' I said. 'Yeah, it sounds like maybe you were a bit of a tosspot, but I think everyone has been someone they're ashamed of at some point in their life. If you're susceptible to peer pressure, it can force you into becoming someone you never anticipated yourself being – someone you don't like.'

'I bet no one's ever peer-pressured you a day in your life.' He chuckled. His eyes were filled with such affection as they caressed my face from afar, that I found I had a small lump lodged in my throat. I swallowed it down and heard the audible gulp as it fell away.

'You'd be surprised.' I thought back to the rides I'd been talked on to at theme parks, the nights out in my teen years when I'd wanted to go home, but had stayed out to appease someone else. The boy's hands I'd let stray further than I was comfortable with because I didn't want to be perceived as a prude. I thought of that one and only time I'd smoked a cigarette and then thrown up in a nearby bush when I found my mouth tasting like I'd just licked a barbecue. And I thought of Joel and all the times I'd let him pressure me into making decisions, into investing money in his business, into staying with him longer than I should have. Into rekindling long-dead flames that should have stayed extinguished.

'I don't think so.' His eyes drifted down to my lips for a split second, before looking back up into my eyes. 'I think you're the most real person I've ever met.'

'My mother's brain is like this Aladdin's cave of useless facts and fridge magnet metaphors and this one time she found me in her bedroom when I was only about twelve, slapping make-up all over my face and crying because some girls at school had called me ugly. She got a wipe and helped me get rid of the mess I'd made of myself. She said that pretending to be someone you aren't was like wearing one of those big rubber Halloween masks. You can hide behind it for as long as you like, but eventually you're going to get uncomfortable and you'll need to take a breath and the only thing you can do in order to breathe, is take it off. If only she could see me now.' I pointed to my rotting face.

'Yer miss her a lot, don't yer?'

128

'Yeah,' I said, my voice quiet. I was somewhat unnerved by how much sadness filled me up when I thought about her and it was happening more and more recently.

'She sounds like one of those wise women, yer know, all knowin' and whatnot.' He frowned again, struggling, I think, to convey what he meant. After a moment, his frown unfurled and his eyebrows rose. 'Like Rafiki.'

'Rafiki?' I laughed. 'The mandrill from *The Lion King*.'

'Isn't he a baboon?'

'Common mistake. But that's a useless fact for another time.' I batted away the mental detour. 'Just promise me one thing, Charlie?' I said, placing my hand on his arm, which lounged lazily on our shared armrest. 'If you enjoy living, then please, never say that she reminds you of Rafiki to her face.'

'Noted.' He chuckled. 'So, does that mean I'm gonna be around long enough to meet her?'

I blushed, but didn't look away. 'If you behave yourself,' I said through a smile.

There it was again, that intense look that filled his eyes and made my stomach feel like I'd swallowed hundreds of squirming little worms. The insanity of falling for someone was so ridiculous, so nonsensical and against all self-preservation instincts, that I wasn't surprised that so many people sang and wrote and centred their lives on it.

I wondered if he felt what I felt. The rush of blood that whooshed in my ears and thundered in my temples and the prickling of anticipation on my skin.

I'd tried not to get pulled into it, but there had simply been nothing I could do. My heart was working independently to my head and logic no longer had a say in the matter of whether I could keep myself safe from falling in love with Charlie Stone. I thought about leaning over and kissing him, of finally knowing what it would feel like, after so many missed opportunities, to be that close to him. But just as I was moulding the thought in my brain, his expression changed from one of temptation to one of amused puzzlement.

'What is it?' I asked, confused and a little breathless.

'It's just . . . yer nose.' He sniggered.

I frowned, lifted my phone to my face and turned on the forward-facing camera.

'Oh God,' I said, instantly holding up my hand to hide the fact that my latex nose was detaching itself from my face. 'Can you fix it?' I asked.

'Let me see?' he said through a suppressed laugh. I took my hand away and, as I did, there was a thud, followed by a rustling, as the glue completely disconnected and my fake nose dropped into the bucket of popcorn on my lap.

I pressed my lips together, hard, before looking back up to Charlie, whose fingers were now covering his mouth. I reached up and touched my sweaty, air-deprived nose, covered in tiny ribbons of dried glue, and before I could do anything to stop it, a chortle barged its way through my newly human nose. Charlie followed suit, laughing until tears filled his eyes. I fished out the nose and pressed it back to my face but the glue had all dried up.

'This is just the universe sayin' that yer too damn pretty to be hidden behind all that make-up,' he said through his laughter and reached a hand up to my face. His fingertips rested on my cheek while his thumb ran over my nose, taking the dried glue off in gentle strokes.

'It was criminal to hide yer away behind all of this,' he said quietly.

He carried on stroking my nose until I was pretty sure that all of the glue was gone. '*Álainn*,' he said under his breath, so quietly that I almost didn't hear it.

Just as I was about to ask what he'd just said, the lights dropped, sending the theatre into darkness and the ominous music of *Dawn of the Dead* began playing out into a room. He gave me one last meaningful glance before sitting far back until he was almost lying down in his seat, grabbing a handful of popcorn and piling it onto his chest, where he picked at it like a grazing pigeon.

A sleeping woman, apparently having a bad dream, came up on the screen, beginning the second leg of this marathon. I turned away and pulled my phone from my pocket, hiding it down the side of my leg in the aisle, away from Charlie, and dimming the screen. I tried to type what he'd just said into Google, but I had no idea how to spell it and after receiving an angry tut from a man opposite, I tucked the phone away.

The little plastic bobble-head zombie jiggled on the dashboard as I pulled up outside Charlie's flat. He'd told me to park around the corner because the one-way system around where he lived was confusing, so I didn't actually see the flat, just the general area. It was nice, not as good as where Ned's and mine was but also nowhere near the depths of despair that my old kebab-scented flat had been.

'Thank yer for coming with me,' he said with one hand on the passenger-side door. 'I've always wanted to go to one of those.'

He looked so funny under the light of the LED street lamp that drifted through the rain-speckled windscreen. He too had had enough of his itchy fake nose by the end of the second film and had pulled it off like that famous scene in *Poltergeist*, where the man tears off his face in the bathroom mirror. He'd purposefully done it in plain view of Chatty Cathy from a few rows back, whom I was sure would be seeking out therapy sometime soon by the look of horror on her face. His real nose poked through the ruined make-up, a nice little reminder that his handsome face still existed beneath it all.

'Don't forget your prize,' I said, reaching for the bobblehead. It was a prize that didn't really justify the amount of effort that Charlie had put into it, but there was a charm to its mediocrity. It'd been unceremoniously handed to us by an usher who could not have cared less and, somehow, looked more like a zombie than we did. We'd decided to call the bobblehead George in honour of the George Romero marathon and we'd both become ridiculously attached to him very quickly.

'Can you take care of him for now?' he asked, tapping George's head and making it jiggle with a quiet creak of its springs.

'Of course. My lawyers will be in touch with your lawyers about custody.' I chuckled and placed George back on the dashboard. 'So,' I said, turning back to him as he opened the door. 'I'll see you soon?' It was a question that asked so much more than what the actual words meant.

'Don't worry, Nell. I'm not goin' anywhere. I swear on George's life.' He leaned over the handbrake and pressed his lips to my cheek. They lingered there for a moment or two before he pulled away, sent me one last smile and got out of the car.

I watched him until he disappeared around a corner with one final wave and I felt a tugging in my stomach.

Why was it that every time he walked away, it felt so final, as if I'd never see him again?

Chapter Eleven

February transitioned into March with a chorus of birdsong that had been absent the day before. It was as if the birds had been waiting for the frigid winds of February to pass before coming out and darting around the windows of the office, ecstatic to feel the warmth of spring.

'I like him,' Ned said, his feet crossed at the ankles and resting on the corner of his desk as he ate a coronation chicken sandwich with the grace of a refuse truck. When I started commenting on people's messy eating, you knew there was a problem. He'd prepared for the onslaught of yellow sauce that now sat on his chest, pre-empting any stains by cutting open the liner from his waste bin and laying it between the sandwich and his shirt. Needless to say, it wasn't an elegant sight. 'Charlie – I think he's good for you and you're good for him.'

'You think?' I asked, my mouth forming a happy grin.

'Well, I don't think I've ever seen you smile as much as the last couple of weeks. Granted, not when he was messing you around, but the rest of the time, you can't seem to keep that grin off your face.'

I bit into my own sandwich, laying the wrapping down with as much care as I would an injured kitten. It had arrived about twenty minutes earlier in the hands of a volunteer I'd never met before, who hadn't known who I was so had ended up just shouting my name out into the room until my head popped up, whack-a-mole style, from my cubicle. He'd handed me a hot cup of coffee, along with a paper bag containing a hummus and pepper sandwich from Cool Beans, with a note scribbled on the paper.

Try not to fling this one at any unsuspecting Irishmen.
Dinner tonight? Let me know and I'll meet you from work if you want to.
But until then, this is to tide you over.
Charlie

My face had blushed bright red as I read the note and had turned radioactive when Ned had called from his cubicle in a high-pitched voice, 'Ooo, Nell got a love note.'

The rest of the office had turned to look at me and I had quickly hurried back to my seat before I could spontaneously combust from embarrassment.

'If you don't stop smiling your face is going to split in half,' Ned slurred around his lunch.

'Shut up, Old Man,' I jibed.

He sighed. 'Oh, to be young and in love.'

'You're just jealous because you had to make your own sandwich,' I replied, taking an overzealous bite and almost choking on it.

Hours passed by so unbelievably slowly that I wondered at one point if Ned had remotely reset the clock on my screen to mess with me and the longer time took to pass, the more nervous I'd got. I flicked the head of George the bobblehead zombie, the springs inside his head letting out a quiet squeak. He'd been sitting on my computer every shift since we'd won him. I'd always slip him into my bag when I was headed home though, as I couldn't stand the thought of leaving him alone overnight.

I knew I'd done things with Charlie before, but this was the first thing that felt like a date, with the romantic note and the surprise offer of dinner. I had a short but positive call from Jackson where he told me that he'd somehow managed to finish off the entirety of *Game of Thrones* since I'd last spoken to him and then listened to a fifteen-minute rant on how he'd have preferred it to end. It was good to hear him so enthusiastic about something again. The drugs that the doctor had put him on were working better than anything he'd tried before and he was hopeful that he'd soon be anxiety-free enough to ask out the girl at work that he'd had his eyes on. This was a huge step for him. When we first started talking, he could barely talk to the postman and now he was contemplating dating.

I'd signed off feeling like Jackson would be just fine and it gave me an extra spring in my step. People often saw anti-depressants and anti-anxiety meds as giving in to weakness but that couldn't be further from the truth. Having the guts to ask for help was a strength that all too many people didn't possess and the social stigma around anxiety, depression or other mental health issues often deprives people of that final ounce of courage to seek the help they need.

* * *

Ned descended the stairs beside me at the end of our shift with the enthusiasm that came of knowing that a fresh pot of Ben and Jerry's and a newly purchased box set of *Cold Case Files* awaited him at home. We'd been trying to get more adventurous with our ice cream flavours, graduating from Chocolate Fudge Brownie to Cherry Garcia to what awaited us now, Birthday Cake flavoured ice cream. It could go one of two ways, but no matter if he loved it or hated it, history dictated that it would be gone in less than thirty minutes and I wouldn't even get a look-in.

My enthusiasm, as I almost skipped down the stairs beside him, was for a completely different reason. I craned my neck as we neared the last landing, scanning through the glass doors to steal a glance at him, but his brooding silhouette didn't fall into view. I'd ducked into the bathroom before leaving just to drag a brush through my hair and apply a revitalising layer of mascara. I'd taken a long hard look at my reflection in the water-stained bathroom mirror and given myself a pep talk.

'Now,' I'd said to myself with seriousness, 'there is no need to be nervous. Everything is fine. You will chew your food with care and under no circumstances will you order the salad, because everyone knows that there is no graceful way to eat a salad. You don't need the food working against you. You will think before you speak and limit yourself to make sure that he gets a word in edgeways. Do you understand me, Nell Coleman?'

It was at this point that I'd heard the flush of a toilet and one of the cubicle doors had opened. Striding out of it had been someone wearing a lanyard from the homeless charity across the hall. I'd felt my cheeks begin to radiate heat strong enough to give someone sunburn as I'd tried to quickly gather up my make-up and hairbrush, somehow managing to fling them further out of reach. I'd almost yelped a little when I looked up to find the girl staring at me in the reflection of the mirror.

'You'll do great. I believe in you,' she'd said. 'And you are right, there is no graceful way to eat a salad.'

'Th-thank you,' I'd said glancing down at her lanyard, 'Kathy.'

'No worries.' And with that she'd disappeared out into the hall.

Ned was complaining about something that the new volunteer, Maddie, had said whilst he'd been waiting for the filter coffee to dribble into the communal pot. But I wasn't really listening, overcome with a brand-new sense of infectious confidence, as we stepped through the automatic door. The air was still as cold as it had been in January, the spring air harshened by an icy blast of lingering winter. Just outside the building, leaning with one shoulder against the sign that bore the names of Healthy Minds and all the other companies that shared our building, was the figure I'd been waiting to see. I recognised the brooding slant of his shoulders, the nonchalant way that he crossed one leg behind the other, balancing on the sole of one hefty black boot like a grungy flamingo. His hand was up beside his face, holding his phone to his ear. I could hear the tinny voice of the other person from here, their words distorted by a bad connection. I held a finger to my lips, hushing Ned, and pointed Charlie out before sneaking up behind him.

'Boo!' I said, loudly into his ear.

'Feck me!' Charlie cried out, clutching a hand to his chest and spinning around in surprise.

'Not here, surely?' I jested.

His phone fell away from his ear and the screen burst back into light. The voice on the other end of the line said something in distorted, garbled sounds and I glanced at it long enough to see that the number wasn't saved into his phone. He quickly ended the call and shoved it into his back pocket.

'Yer tryin' to kill me, woman? 'Cause I could have done with yer a couple of years ago if that's the case.' He pretended to be annoyed but I could see the worried smile trying to break through his forcibly sullen face.

'Not funny,' I said loudly, the information too new to be mentioned flippantly.

'Shame. And we put so much work into plotting your demise,' Ned said, deadpan. He held out a hand for Charlie to shake and it felt very formal for two people who'd, less than a week ago, seen each other tear up over Channing Tatum.

Charlie shook his hand and then pushed both fists down into the fraying pockets of his denim jacket. He was wearing a red beanie hat that squeezed his hair down over his eyes and made it look twice as long with the way it flicked out from under the hem.

'So, have you decided where you want to eat? It's ladies' choice,' he asked.

'I don't mind. Anywhere is good, although I am craving garlic bread,' I replied.

'Italian it is then.' He smiled, lighting up his eyes, which I swear got a deeper shade of blue every time I saw them. 'You can come too, Ned, if you want to.'

I turned to Ned with wide eyes that did all the talking for me. They said, *don't you dare. This is my chance, Ned. My*

chance at being more than a counsellor to that beautiful man.
Go home and eat your ice cream and watch some decade-old
crimes being solved.

Ned looked at me as if to say, *as if I'd want to come and
watch you mentally undressing him over the table.* 'Thanks for
the offer, but I've got a date with a spoon and two men right
now. And besides that, I've seen her eating spaghetti before
and I still have PTSD about it.' He leaned over and kissed
the side of my forehead. I looked up and caught his eye. He
sent me a wink, hailed his goodbye and strode off down the
path.

'Two men, one spoon?' Charlie asked once Ned was out
of earshot.

'Ben and Jerry,' I explained.

'Oh, thank God.' He sighed. 'For a moment there, I thought
he'd found himself some very niche porn.'

We watched him disappear into the darkness as the
beginning-of-date awkwardness began to thicken the air
between us.

He looked at me from under his eyebrows and a smile
tugged at one corner of his lips. 'You'll have to lead the way.
I haven't been out for a proper sit-down meal in so long that
I don't even know where the restaurants are anymore.'

I lifted a hand and pointed in the vague direction of
Giorgio's, the only Italian worth going to around here, and
we set off at a slow ramble. I copied his stance by pushing
my hands into the pockets of my coat. I wished I'd known
this morning that this would be happening – that way I might
have dressed a little less office chic and a little more daringly.
Compared to Charlie's easy style, I looked like I might be his
accountant or parole officer.

'So, have you got over Channing Tatum yet?' I asked, deeming the actor safe grounds for conversation.

'Can anyone ever truly get over Channing Tatum?' he said moving beside me and jutting out his elbow. I fidgeted for a moment, stunned a little by the sudden invitation for physical contact, then slid my arm through his. The coarse fabric of his sleeve brushed against the material of my coat, making little swishing sounds as we walked.

'Well, there's something I feel like I should tell you.' I looked up into his eyes with feigned concern. His brows knitted with worry. 'There's an alternate ending on the DVD extras. I found Ned watching it last night when I got in. So, I'm pretty sure we're going to have to watch it all over again and play the other ending instead.'

His brow softened and his smile returned. 'I don't know if my heart can take it.' He chuckled.

He stiffened a little and moved his hand around to his back pocket, pulling out his phone and frowning at the same unknown number.

'You avoiding someone?' I asked, that sense of dread creeping back to me like it did so often around him. Was the persistent person on the other end something to do with the things he'd told me about? Or was it a whole other can of worms that we hadn't even found the right tin opener for yet?

He scrunched up his nose and shook his head. 'It's not important.' He pushed the phone back into his pocket and turned to me with a forced smile. 'You sloppily eating spaghetti is all I want to be thinking about right now. I'm imagining something like the Ood from *Doctor Who*, with the mouth tentacles.'

'I know who the Ood are; you can't hold the monopoly on being a nerd you know. And be careful what you wish for, because I've been told that I make an uncanny resemblance.'

'Oh good,' he said with mock excitement. 'Because I always found the Ood the sexiest of all the *Doctor Who* creatures.'

As we settled into the window booth of Giorgio's Italian, with a smiling waiter pouring iced water into our glasses, I began to think that this was a bit of a heavy place for me to have chosen. The ceiling hung with obviously fake, but aesthetically pleasing vines that trailed down around large columns and mock frescos sat on faux-aged walls. I clutched my menu with nervous fingers as Charlie pulled off his hat and ruffled a hand through his unruly hair.

Violin music played through the speakers and the subdued lighting made it the perfect brightness for all of the couples. The waiter withdrew a lighter from his pocket, clicked it on and lit a candle between us, smiling manically, as if years of hearing this same violin music over and over again had driven him into the realms of insanity. Charlie seemed unfazed by the enforced levels of romance as he checked his phone again and pushed it underneath his hat, which lay on the table next to an unnecessarily large pepper grinder.

Who knew, maybe this was exactly the sort of setting he'd been after when he'd asked me to choose a place to eat, or maybe he was just being too polite to show his discomfort at the couple at the table closest to us who were hand feeding each other chocolate-dipped strawberries. The woman lifted a fondue fork, stabbed a square of waffle and dipped it into the bubbling cauldron of chocolate, before lifting it to her partner's mouth. He didn't get to it in time, the chocolate dribbling down his chin and onto the napkin waiting on his lap. They giggled and he wiped it from his chin with a playful finger, offering it up to her. I watched on in horror as she raised his finger to her mouth, placed it inside and licked the chocolate from his skin.

I looked back at Charlie but he hadn't seen a thing.

I wondered if Charlie and I would ever get to those sickening levels of cliché where you don't even care that you're a cliché anymore, because the endorphins are making you feel all ridiculous and fuzzy inside?

I looked back at Charlie who was frowning at the menu like it'd just insulted him. He was wearing a red lumberjack shirt, open over that same *Night of the Living Dead* T-shirt he'd been wearing when I'd first met him and I found myself smiling at his charming boyishness and the memory of us two lone zombies, sat side by side in a cinema of regular-looking people. He had an air of nervous energy tonight, his aura pulsing with anxiety.

'You okay?' I asked.

He glanced up from his menu, not maintaining eye contact for long and then looking back down. 'Grand. Yerself?'

'Uh-huh,' I replied, unconvinced. 'So, what is this in aid of?'

He looked up and sat back in his chair. 'Well, I thought, seeing as, so far, I've caused yer to violate rules at work, been a bastard, ghosted yer and dropped the bombshell that is my mental health, I'd give yer somethin' nice for a change.' He sipped his water and crunched through an ice cube with careless, clearly unsensitive teeth. 'Yer deserve things like this after what you do for everyone else all day.'

I grinned as the waiter arrived and took our order.

I ordered a glass of red wine, which Charlie upgraded to a bottle. We got olives to start and eventually, he decided on a pepperoni pizza. I decided to go for ravioli, because it seemed the most graceful to eat of the foods on offer. I did glance down at my pale blue shirt when I read the words 'rich tomato sauce' and uttered a silent apology to my later self, the one with a nail brush and a tub of Oxi Action. I added on the garlic bread that I'd been craving and the waiter congratulated us hyperbolically.

He sashayed away, humming as he went, and returned almost immediately with a pot of olives on a saucer, tooth-picks in little paper sleeves sitting around it in a circle.

'I'll pay for my half,' I said, unprompted. I was always uncomfortable when other people paid for stuff for me. This was probably due to Joel never paying for anything. In seven and a half years I could count on one hand the number of times he'd taken me out for a meal and paid. I could, however, count on several thousand hands the number of times he'd 'forgotten' his wallet or his card had been 'surprisingly' declined and I'd ended up having to foot the bill.

'If yer want to pay then that's fine, don't want to offend, but I did ask yer here and so I'm more than happy to pay. Think of it as a thank you for puttin' in the overtime with me.'

He reached over to the olive bowl and unsheathed a tooth-pick from the surrounding saucer, twiddling it between his fingers.

'I enjoy it,' I said. 'My job, I mean. It's not like I feel that I'm owed anything for helping people.'

'And that is why you're a significantly better person than

the rest of us.' He smiled and ran a hand through his hair. 'You've enough patience for ten people. You're a good egg.'

A good egg? Sexy, I thought.

'I have this one caller. I've been talking to him for years and whenever he calls, he only ever wants to talk to me.'

'Well, I can certainly understand that.' He gave me a subtle smile and an intensely blue stare that made my chest flutter. The neck of his T-shirt was stretched from overwear, the deep curve of it hanging lower than normal and showing the smattering of dark hair that sat on his sternum. I paused for a moment while I regained control of my thoughts, dragging them out of the gutter and back to the moment in hand.

'He's my favourite caller,' I said when I finally found my voice.

'I'll try not to get offended by that.'

'Present company excluded, obviously.'

'Do yer think you'll do it your whole life, or is this just a steppin' stone?'

'I never planned on staying this long,' I admitted. 'I feel like there's so much more I want to do, but I worry about what would happen if I left.'

'What do yer mean?' He leaned forward and crossed his arms, resting them on the edge of the table.

I stopped twiddling the toothpick and stabbed a green olive, as the black ones always tasted as if they were going off to me. 'I wanted to work with people, not phone lines. Like with Jac—' I stopped talking, realising just in time that I was about to violate Jackson's confidentiality. 'Like with my favourite caller. I know him so intimately and I'd go as far to class him as a buddy, yet I've never met him. I've helped him so much over the years, all from the other end of a phone. Imagine what I could have done had we been in the same room.'

He nodded understandingly.

'And lately I've kinda been thinking . . .' I stopped and looked down at my hands, not knowing if what I was about to say was going to sound stupid or not. 'I've been thinking about going back to uni and finishing the course I started.'

'I think that's a great idea. Why did you quit in the first place?' he asked.

I flinched at the word 'quit'. It sounded so aggressively final. 'I don't think I was ready. I had no idea what I was doing and I saw my friends from school having the quintessential university experience and that's just not what was happening for me. But I feel like the pressure to go out and get drunk and act like an idiot wouldn't apply to me now that I'm older. I actually think I might enjoy learning again. But I don't know if I can leave.'

'Why is that?'

'Because what happens to my callers if I go? What happens to Ned?'

'Ned's a big boy. He'll cope. Granted, the caller situation is a tough one, but couldn't you keep in touch?'

'It's not really allowed – not that I haven't broken the rules before.' I smirked his way, placed the olive into my mouth and rolled the bitter little ovoid around on my tongue. 'Anyway, that's enough talk about work. Switch off, Nell,' I said, the olive still clutched between my molars.

The waiter returned with our bottle of wine and two glasses. He poured a small amount into my glass, stopped and looked at me expectantly. I looked worriedly at Charlie,

146

lifted the glass, took a sip and then looked at the expectant waiter's face with slight panic. I nodded. 'Yep, that's wine.'

'Eccellente.' He chuckled. I did wonder if this man was actually Italian or if he was required as part of the job description to pretend. Was he really Luca from Sicily, as his name tag and accent suggested, or was he something far less impressive, like Kyle from Small Heath?

'Luca' grinned from ear to ear and topped up my glass before pouring Charlie's and trotting off to the kitchen.

'What shall we toast to?' I asked, holding my glass ceremoniously up in the air.

He looked a frown my way as he thought, before he too raised his glass up to join mine. 'To whoever slapped that sticker on the clock tower,' he said.

I winced a little at the thought of what would have happened if that sticker hadn't been there and he hadn't had easy access to our number. It was a miracle really that it was there. The person who'd put it there was the one who'd really saved Charlie's life. 'To the phantom sticker slapper,' I said, chinking my glass to his.

Charlie raised the glass to his lips and took a large swig, his pupils upturned to the ceiling as if he was nervous. 'You okay?' I asked, taking a sip myself and washing the bitter olive flavour from my tongue.

'Mmm-hmm.' He swallowed and placed the glass down on the table, but held on to it with delicate, nervous fingers.

'What is it?' I asked, sitting forward.

'See.' He sighed. 'Part of the reason I wanted to bring yer here tonight was to tell yer what yer want to know, about why I was at the tower that night and the time before, but now I feel like a jackass because we're havin' a nice time and

147

this is a nice place and I don't want yer to forever think of this place as the place that I told yer that my wife died.' I felt a weight drop into my stomach. 'Ah feck!'

'You had a wife and she . . .?' I managed to say before my voice failed me.

'Died, yes.'

'W-what? When?' was all I managed to say.

'Two years ago, next Saturday.' He raised a black olive, slick with oil and herbs to his mouth and took it from the cocktail stick with his teeth.

'Oh my God, Charlie. I'm so sorry.'

He winced and held his hand up. 'Please, don't.' He swallowed and looked up, meeting my eye again, but his gaze was harder this time. 'When . . . it happened, that's all people ever said to me. After a week or two, the pity got unbearable.'

I was still so shocked that I didn't know what to say. Everything I'd learned over the years about how to talk to someone who was grieving left my head and I felt completely unequipped for the conversation. 'I'd had a lot of friends, before, but they filtered away pretty damn sharp when I turned out to not be as fun as I used to be. It seems that people givin' a shit about what you're goin' through has an expiry date.' He stabbed another olive with a little more anger than the last and ate that one too. 'They all said things like "time heals all wounds" and "she's in a better place now". Fecking bullshit, all of it. Time's done sod all and, I'll never tell my mother this, but I don't believe in all that heaven stuff.'

'I'm sure they just wanted to reassure you, make you feel better,' I said.

'Well, it didn't help.'

He picked up his glass and took a large swig.

'How did it happen?' I asked. I realised that I was leaning across the table now, waiting with bated breath for what he would say next.

He winced again. 'Can't yet.'

'Okay, no rush.'

'But can I ask her name?'

He cleared his throat loudly. 'Abi.'

'Abi,' I repeated.

He sat forward, his elbows leaning against the surface of the table. 'I don't want you to think that I'm lookin' for sympathy or anythin' like that. I just wanted yer to know what it was that had me feelin' like shite the day I called yer.'

'I know that must have been hard. Thank you for telling me,' I said. 'How long were you together?'

He frowned as he tried to calculate it, those deep furrows etching themselves into his brow. 'Married twelve years, together twenty-one, on and off.'

My eyes widened even more. 'Wow, that's a long time. You must have been so young when you got together.'

'Fourteen,' he told me. 'She used to joke and say that we only got together because we lived in such a small town and there weren't any other options. That wasn't the truth of it though.' He smiled a sad smile and sipped at his wine again.

I couldn't imagine loving someone for that long. Seven and a half years had felt like a struggle, but I guess that was because Joel and I weren't meant to be together. Maybe we'd had that kind of love, once, but it hadn't been long-lived.

'When . . . if you want to talk about it, then I'm happy to listen,' I said.

His nervous fingers stopped fidgeting around the slender

149

stem of the wine glass. 'That wouldn't be weird for yer?' he asked, with narrowed eyes.

'Why . . . why would it be weird for me?' I asked, but, in truth, there was no way it wouldn't be weird for me to sit there while he recounted tales of how much he had and still loved another woman.

'No reason,' he said, staring meaningfully at me.

'This is what I do for a living and besides that, I . . . care about you. If I can help, then of course I'll listen.'

We ate our food to the tune of a different topic of conversation, but my mind was nothing but a swirling mess of new information. The food went fast and the wine even faster and Charlie got us a second bottle.

'How do you do that?' I asked as Luca brought the bill over, the tray beneath it bearing little jelly babies.

'Do what?' Charlie asked.

'Tell me something like you just told me and then just have a normal conversation and eat a meal.'

He thought for a moment and tossed his card onto the receipt. 'Most of the time I'm okay. The pain is there and it aches, but it's so constant that I can almost forget about it. But then something happens, and it can be something tiny and insignificant, like an orange scatter cushion that reminds me of Abi's hair or the smell of bacon that reminds me of Sunday mornings, and the pain flares again.

'And I hate how the pain feels, but it's the only thing she left me with and I've felt it for so long that I feel almost empty when I don't feel it. So, sometimes I'll find myself actively triggering it, like prodding a bad tooth, so that I can feel it again. It's not always there, but when it is, it's like the oxygen has been pumped from the room and replaced with burning gas.'

'Oh.' I wasn't really sure what to say after that, because I knew the feeling he was talking about – not to the extent that he did, but I knew it.

Charlie paid, although I offered several times, and we were sent on our way by Luca shouting 'Ciao' from the doorway. We walked aimlessly along the road with the half bottle of wine that was left, pushed into my bag.

'Yer see, the thing with modern zombie films is that they completely miss the point of what the zombie was meant to represent in the first place.' He'd been talking about zombie films for a while, as if sitting through a marathon of movies on the subject wasn't torture enough. As it turned out, he was even more passionate on the subject than I'd thought he was.

'And what was that?' I asked, my head feeling so very heavy after the barrage of Montepulciano D'abruzzo that I'd just provided it with.

'Zombies are slow. They walk, they don't run, because they symbolise death followin' yer. The idea is that no matter how slowly it's comin' for yer, it's always gonna catch up in the end.'

Was that how he really felt? Like those two nights on the clock tower were always there, in the fog of the horizon, on their way to get him?

I hummed a sleepy sigh and lay my head down on his shoulder, as he went on about something else zombie-related. I tried to keep up but my brain had turned to mush and my eyelids were slipping down over my tired eyes. I don't know how long I zoned out on his shoulder for, my legs moving on autopilot as I snoozed, but I was roused by the jarring sound of an ambulance siren in the near distance and opened my eyes to find that we were somewhere I didn't recognise.

'Where are we?' I asked, blinking the sleepiness from my eyes.

We stopped walking and he looked up, as if he had no idea either. 'Ah, sorry. I was too busy dronin' on that I walked us to my house instead to yours.'

'Uh-huh.' I stepped back and put my hands on my hips. 'If you wanted me to come over then all you had to do was ask,' I jibed.

'Oh, I know,' he said, stepping closer, his own eyes semi closed with drunkenness. 'What woman, or man for that matter, could resist an adorable emotionally crippled, unemployed widower like this?' He gestured to himself and nodded in a feigned cocky sort of way.

I chuckled quietly and stepped a little closer. The collar of his shirt was bent the wrong way and poking out over the collar of his jacket.

I reached up a hand and tucked it back inside, my fingers lingering there, where the fabric sung with the retained warmth of his skin.

'Don't put yourself down. You've a lot of very appealing qualities that a girl, such as myself, but not specifically me, would find . . . you know . . . attractive.'

'Oh yeah? And what are these qualities you speak of?' His hand landed on my arm and I wasn't sure if it was through affection or the need to stop himself from falling down.

'Well, you're not hideous and your accent is pretty appealing, some would even say sexy – not me though, I much prefer the dulcet tones of a thoroughbred Brummie.'

'Is that so?' he asked through a flirtatious smirk. 'Do go on.'

'Erm, let's see. Well you have a skill, which is more than can be said for the majority of the population and you have your own place. All positives.'

'Yeah, well I don't think that my place is anythin' to get excited about.'

I looked up at the apartment block that I hadn't been able to see when I dropped him off the other night. I tried to remember how I'd got home from here, but my addled brain was struggling with keeping me upright, without throwing orienteering into the mix. I squinted until my eyes started co-operating with my brain. The apartment block wasn't fancy but wasn't one of those horrid concrete structures either. It wasn't tall, only three storeys of warm red brick and each apartment seemed to have French doors that opened to an immediate metal fence that ran along the length of the windows. I bet that in the brochures they label them as balconies, but they were about as little like a balcony as you could get, while still using the word to describe it.

'Why is that?'

'Er, because it's an absolute tip and I'm ashamed to call it mine. You'll probably die on entrance from inhaling spores, which haven't killed me, simply because I've grown immune to them over time.'

'It can't be that bad and, anyway, I don't mind messy houses or messy people for that matter.'

'Explains why you like me then.' He looked up at a window that I assumed was his and then back at me with apprehension tugging at the muscles in his face.

'It really is just truly an appalling mess.'

'Charlie, I don't care.'

He sighed melodramatically and slowly began walking towards the building. 'All right, but don't you dare judge me.'

Charlie's flat was on the second floor, so we climbed the stairs with the sluggish speed of two people with too much wine running through their veins. Passing the door of number two brought with it the lingering smell of curry and spices that had made me feel equally as likely to knock on the door and ask for a doggy bag or throw up into the tall plastic ficus that sat beside their door. Whoever lived at number three had clearly had a good evening because the smell of rose-scented candles crept under the door along with the sultry, sexy sounds of D'Angelo playing, muffled through the walls. Charlie was a little way ahead of me, ignoring all of the things I was finding interest in. He climbed the last set of stairs and came to a stop on the top floor, next to a pale blue door that bore the number six in dulled silver. He glanced at me as I came to a stop at his side, muted panic in his eyes.

'Now remember your promise. No judgement.'

I held up three fingers and clapped my heels. 'Scouts honour.'

He shook his head at me, although I saw his smile before he had chance to hide it, and he turned back to the door, slid in the key and gave it a push. The door fell open with a squeal that suggested WD-40 was in order and came to a premature stop as it hit something behind it. He reached inside and flicked on the light before slipping into the apartment with a sense of nervous tension keeping his shoulders rigid.

I followed him in and tried my best to keep my eyebrows from raising when I took a look around. I imagined the voiceover from one of the true crime documentaries that Ned and I watched. The scene was not all that different from the ones shown in grainy, darkened footage at the beginning of every episode before someone finds a dismembered body in the bathtub.

The flat followed the blue theme set by the front door, although the shade was a little darker in the open-plan living room and kitchenette. I closed the door behind me and tried not to look with horror at the pile of unopened letters on the mat that sat like a snowdrift against the skirting board. Bowls and pans were stacked high in the sink and a pile of clothes lay on the floor in front of the washing machine, with a soggy load turning musty in the drum. Stacks of books and an incomprehensible number of remotes and game controllers lay over the coffee table that sat between a sofa and the large wall-mounted TV and a pillow and duvet were lying in disarray on the sofa cushions, showing that he'd slept there recently.

A bottle of whisky lay empty on the floor beside the sofa, next to a wilting Swiss cheese plant, its leaves drooping sadly down towards the gunmetal grey carpet.

'Well, you weren't lying,' I said, feeling more impressed than anything that he was capable of living functionally in all of this.

'Thank you. The upkeep is almost a full-time job,' he jested. 'D'yer know how difficult it is to stack bowls that high?' He picked up a few things and nervously fondled them while looking for somewhere else to put them. 'I don't tend to have visitors anymore. Not since . . . yer know.' He glanced towards a door off the living room that sat ajar. He paused, looking truly uncomfortable for a moment or two before he turned around to the sink and began tipping water from soaking pans.

Self-neglect. The progressive lack of care about one's own levels of personal hygiene and/or the cleanliness of living areas. This had been the topic for one of the few papers I wrote for my first year of uni. It all comes from the idea that the person thinks themselves unimportant, unworthy and therefore, combing their hair or doing the dishes doesn't seem necessary. It's strange how the human brain can sabotage itself sometimes. I hoped that if Charlie hadn't told me about his depression, that I'd have known when I'd walked in here tonight. But then again, I'd been pretty useless at noticing hints up until now.

'You don't need to tidy on my account,' I said, walking over to the sofa covered in Charlie's bedding. On the wall to my left, there were around eight or nine small photo frames, all a different bright colour and in a mock baroque style that could have come off as tacky, but seemed to look good here. Each frame sat empty, the wall showing through where the photograph should have sat and I wondered if this was just a quirky interior design choice, or if the photos had been removed by Charlie after Abi's death. I wondered what she'd think of me being here, or me in general. It's hard to imagine the feelings you might have for the person that comes after you. Would she be happy that he was finally beginning to move on, or would she want to try and cross back over from the afterlife, just to gouge my eyes out with her bare ghostly hands? How would I feel towards the person Joel found next? I guess only time would tell.

I moved aside an empty Starburst packet and sat down on the grey corduroy sofa. 'You got any clean glasses?' I asked, pulling the unfinished bottle of wine from my bag.

'Probably not, but I'll see if I can remember how to wash them up.' I leaned back my head and awarded myself the luxury of closing my eyes for a moment or two, the soft hands of sleep beckoning me to it. I felt the weight of Charlie drop onto the sofa beside me and my moment of sleepiness was over.

I saw that he was sitting uncomfortably rigid, staring forward at the plastic beaker on the table in front of him that sat beside one of those enormous Sports Direct mugs.

'You okay?' I heaved myself up to a more acceptable, yet less comfortable, sitting position and put the bottle of wine on the coffee table.

'I will be. It feels a bit odd, is all.' He seemed to be finding it hard to make eye contact. 'There's not been a woman in this apartment since her.'

'I understand,' I said, although that wasn't wholly true.

'Shall we finish this?' He motioned to the wine and shuffled forward in his seat. He poured what was left of the wine into the two cups and handed me the Sports Direct one. '*Sláinte*.'

I assumed that meant cheers in Irish and repeated it, clinking my mug to his plastic beaker. He pretty much downed what was in it and placed it back on the table, beside a stack of books.

I felt a strange feeling churn in my stomach that I couldn't quite put a name to. It felt kind of like when you eat ice cream and then wash it down with a glass of Coke and you can feel it curdling in your gut.

'Has there been anyone else, since Abi?' I asked, without really thinking.

He visibly flinched and glanced at me from the corner of his eye.

'Not really.' His eyes glazed a little as a memory entered his mind. 'About a year ago, most of my friends had fecked off already, but Jamie was still stickin' around at that point. He came to get me for a lads' night out.' He chuckled and looked down at his wringing hands. 'There was this packet of pork mince in the back of the fridge that I hadn't found the energy to throw out yet. It was what, almost four weeks out of date? And I seriously considered eating it raw to get out of lads' night. Food poisonin' was more appealin' to me than goin' out with Jamie and his friends whose brains hadn't developed any further than their fourteenth year. Jamie was married to one of Abi's closest friends, Una, and Jamie and I had kinda been shoved together and forced to be friends. In the end, I didn't try to poison myself and went out with them instead. There was a group of about ten of us, all leering, cocky little bastards, the lot of 'em. We went to this nightclub in town, the one with the big gold sign. You know it?' he asked looking up.

I nodded and then scrunched up my nose. 'I went there once when I was eighteen.'

He continued. 'So, I'm in this club and hating every moment of it. The lights were too bright, the music was deafening and the people – sweet Jesus. I need to tell my mammy to stop praying for the youth of today because she's fighting a losing battle on that one. But, anyway, Jamie sends this girl my way. She couldn't have been older than twenty and had left the house without ninety per cent of her clothes.

I didn't want to talk to her, doubt I could even hear a word she said over the noise, but I held out my hand and said hi. This girl grabbed my hand and put it straight on her boob then she just pulled me in and kissed me.'

A twang in my chest. The feeling of curdled ice cream got a little stronger.

'I try to push her away but she's on me like a limpet,' he carries on. 'So, in the end I just roll with it. Try to pretend it's Abi. But it wasn't like any kisses I'd ever had with Abi. Kisses with someone you love are emotional, intimate – you know this – but that kiss was like . . . it was purely about sex and her trying to check if I still had tonsils with her tongue. I eventually got her off of me and went to the bathroom where I ended up gettin' so frustrated with myself that I punched the reflection of myself in the mirror and cut up my hand.' He flashed his hand to me and, once again, I saw the hairline scars that I'd noticed on that first day I'd met him, running over his knuckles like fractals of ice. 'I wrapped my hand up in toilet paper and went out to find Jamie to tell him I'd better take myself out before I was kicked out and what did I find?'

'I dread to think what you'd find in there.'

'I find Jamie in the smoking area with some girl pressed up against the wall.' He gritted his teeth together and shook his head. 'There I was, attempting to forget that my wife was dead by attempting to have a "good time" and there was Jamie, making a fool of his own wife by stickin' it wherever would take it.'

'Oh my God. What did you do?' I asked, shocked.

'I started screamin' at him. His pupils were the size of golf balls and he kept tellin' me to calm down. Needless to say, I didn't.

'He ended up lampin' me round the head when I said that he needed to show Una some respect and tell her. So, I punched him right back. It looked ten times worse than it was because of the blood from the mirror, but they threw me out anyway and I never spoke to Jamie again after that.' He took a deep breath. 'And that is the story of the only person who has been anywhere near me, since Abi and also about how I earned a lifetime ban from that club.'

There was an uncomfortable silence for a moment or two.

'I didn't know you were a felon,' I jested to try and ease the tension.

'I resigned myself to the monk's way of life after that. Hell, I'm not even sure if everything still works down there.'

Would you like me to check? I thought and then instantly started chastising myself.

'I didn't think it would happen again.'

'What?' I asked.

'Feelin' things for someone. I thought all of that was done with . . .' he turned and looked me directly in the eyes '. . . until you threw a sandwich at me.'

A pregnant pause. A flickering of eyelids, unsure whether to look away or not.

'You know, I've heard this before,' I said, just to fill the aching silence. 'Most men do find me irresistible, especially the way I eat like a starving bloodhound. It's kind of like a fetish.'

'That's it!' He held up a finger in the air between us. 'That's what yer looked like at dinner.'

We both chuckled.

'Nell,' Charlie uttered quietly and I looked up. Before my brain had time to even compute the fact that his finger was under my chin and his face was moving closer, he already had his lips pressed to mine and I was holding a startled breath in my chest.

His lips were warm and soft, a stark contrast to the stubble that grated against my face as his lips moved over mine. Gentle knuckles moved along the line of my jaw, his fingers unfurling and sliding into my hair as he pulled me closer to him. My blood thundered through my ears, blocking out the sounds of my heavy breaths, the smack of lip upon lip.

Was this wrong? Should this be happening now, after he'd just told me about Abi? Or was that the last bit of withheld information, the final obstacle to overcome, before allowing himself to do this?

I had never really settled on a decision as to whether I believed in any sort of afterlife, but if there was one and ghosts were real, what would Abi have to say about this?

I had no idea what she looked like but I could imagine her there, a faceless blur in my periphery staring daggers at me while I made out with her husband.

Well, seems as though it IS all still in working order down there, she'd be saying, or something equally as snarky.

I think that our minds must have had the same thought at the same time, because just as I was about to pull away, Charlie broke the connection and leaned back.

For a moment we just looked at each other, our lips still pursed, stuck in kiss face as our eyes narrowed at each other.

I cleared my throat. 'Thank you,' I said, awkwardly.

'You're welcome,' he replied, formally, withdrawing his hands to his lap. 'And, thank you, too.'

He reached for his wine, sipped at the last straggling drop

161

and bounced his legs up and down, making the sofa shake as he did.

'So . . . erm . . .' I fidgeted awkwardly as I tried to think of how to word it. 'How exactly does something like this work?'

'You tell me. You're the one with all the advice.' He chortled nervously.

'Seems I've drawn a blank on this one. Although I'm not sure that kissing someone in the same evening as telling them about your dead wife is best,' I said.

'I don't know. It seemed to make me forget for a moment or two.'

I wondered what advice Ned, or rather Celine Dion via Ned, would have for me now.

'Sometimes it feels like it was ten minutes ago and other times it feels as if it didn't happen to me at all. The idea of doin' anythin' with someone other than her is gonna take some gettin' used to.'

'I understand.' I nodded. The air of romance sapped from the room and a new awkwardness hung in the air like the strange smell coming from the sink. 'I should get going.' I pulled my phone from my bag and was beginning to summon an Uber when he spoke again.

'Yer don't have to. Yer can sleep on the sofa if you want. I know you're tired.'

He was right: I was so very tired and the idea of even travelling to the bathroom seemed like too much.

'You sure?'

'Yeah. There's a pillow and duvet there,' he said, motioning to the sofa.

'Okay.'

He stood and walked towards one of the two doors leading off from the room. 'I'll get the light for yer.'

He waited for me to settle under the blanket.

'Safely in bed,' I called to him.

He sent me a smile and switched off the light. 'Night, Nell.'

'Night,' I said, my eyes already falling closed.

I was so tired that I instantly felt myself slipping, but the room was spinning. The only consolation being that I wouldn't have to endure a hungover day at work tomorrow and could spend the day slowly coming back to life at my own speed.

My lips still tingled where his had touched mine, the skin around them tender from his facial hair. I hoped that, in the morning, things wouldn't be different, awkward. That one drunken kiss on a sofa wasn't going to ruin everything.

The situation was delicate. Charlie was delicate and I guessed that, to an extent, so was I. Even when I had known that I was in love with Joel, I didn't feel vulnerable, as if my heart was in any way at risk by handing it to him. But maybe that was because I never handed Joel the whole thing?

Chapter Twelve

I woke with a feeling like someone had parked a tank on top of my head. Wine was not my friend. How many times did I have to do this to myself to remember that fact?

I peeled open my eyes, one by one, and was surprised I didn't hear a sound like Velcro being pulled apart. It took me a moment to realise where I was and when I did, my stomach tossed and tumbled like a shoe in a washing machine. Charlie was nowhere to be seen, but images of what had happened last night on this sofa, a kiss shared in wine-soaked curiosity, made my heart begin to thump in my ears. I shifted onto my elbows, pushing myself up with a groan, as if every inch of me now weighed ten times as much as it had done when I'd fallen asleep. I wiped my face with my hand. Yesterday's make-up flaking away against my palm.

My legs felt as if they'd fused into position and I groaned as I eased them straight, but as I did, I became aware of a weight on my stomach. I looked down and was met with a pair of large yellow eyes. After a brief moment of shock where a small gasp escaped my lips, I reached out a hand and tentatively ran it over the fluffy ginger head of the cat sitting in my lap. It was one of those cats that need grooming almost every day due to their long, fine hair to stop knotted clumps from forming, but clearly, Charlie hadn't been keeping up with the grooming schedule, if this was indeed Charlie's cat and not a street urchin who'd somehow found a way in. It had a stub nose and a perpetual grimace that made it look like he should be living in a dustbin on *Sesame Street*.

'Hello there,' I said. The cat opened its mouth and made a soft, high-pitched warbling noise that I could only assume was a greeting, before curling itself back up and tucking its face away from view.

I sat for a while, weighing up the pros and cons of moving. My bladder ached, but as anyone who has ever been chosen as the spot for a cat's nap will know, disturbing them seems like the worst thing you'll ever do in your entire existence. Eventually I simply had to go and gently placed the mass of ginger fur down on the ground before scurrying off to the toilet. There were two doors branching off from the living room – one leading to an indescribably messy bedroom, the duvet sliding limply down the side of the mattress onto the floor and the pillows lying in disarray. I glanced around for Charlie but didn't find him, noticing a speckling of fine glass shards on the floor a few feet inside, before I turned to the other door where, thankfully, I found the toilet.

I rushed over and took care of business and as I made my way over to the sink, I noticed the sound of quiet breathing coming from somewhere in the room.

I looked around, puzzled, trying to find the serial killer lurking in the corner, ready for me to catch a spooky glance

165

of him in the mirror behind me, but didn't find him. Instead, my eyes travelled to the bathtub, where I peeled back the shower curtain a little way, to find Charlie, sleeping peacefully amongst a mass of blankets and towels. He clearly must have been more drunk than I'd thought to end up sleeping there, rather than the perfectly fine bed in the next room.

I made my way out quietly and closed the door behind me, wondering what I was meant to do now. Did I just hang around until he woke up or sneak out quickly? No, this wasn't a sleazy one-night stand; I would stay and be waiting with a soothing cup of coffee when he woke. That's if I could find the coffee amongst the mess.

I walked over to the kitchen and started looking around for any form of coffee. Finding a jar of Nescafé in the cupboard and then moving on to the next obstacle that lay between me and caffeine. Mugs.

I moved over to the sink and washed up two mugs, running away with myself a little and ending up doing the whole lot and scouring the apartment for elusive cups on tables and behind curtains.

The cat jumped up on the counter and watched every move I made as if it was learning for future use.

I took my phone from my pocket and saw a couple of text messages on my screen, both from Ned, both from last night. One asked me if I planned on coming home and the second one extended his hopes that I was safe and wasn't lying in a shallow grave in open farmland. He'd be up for work by now and so I texted him back, apologising for ignoring him and assuring him that I was, in fact, still living, even if it didn't feel like it. I made myself a coffee in the giant Sports Direct mug, and drank it down, feeling the caffeine chipping away at my hangover, and when I felt a little less like I was about to keel over, I turned my attention to the rest of the flat. Seeing as I was here with nothing to do, I might as well make myself useful.

I straightened the piles of books, watered the Swiss cheese plant – which I imagined sighed in relief at finally getting some liquid – and cleaned down the coffee table, clicking on the kettle for further caffeine fuel, before I turned my attention to the pile of letters behind the door. I sat down on the mat, sorting them into levels of scariness with the brown ones from the tax office at the top and the flyers from takeaways on the bottom. I made a separate pile of the handwritten envelopes, of which there were many. Some in plain envelopes with blue airmail stickers on them and others in those envelopes with red and blue stripes around the edge. The handwriting looked the same on all of them and so I stacked them all together and put them on the counter by the empty bread bin. The handwriting was sloppy and untidy, but legible, and up in the top left-hand corner of every envelope sat a return address and a name, Carrick Stone.

Charlie's uncle – the one he'd concocted a story about when he first me. Why would Carrick be writing actual letters to his nephew and not texts or emails, let alone in such volume? There had to be around ten, all from Carrick, all unopened, and I'd seen more of them when I was tidying, thrust into a drawer in the kitchen. I opened the drawer again and pulled out a further four letters from amongst the detritus of the drawer.

At the bottom, peeping out from under what looked like a less than pleasant letter from the landlord, was a photograph, glossy-surfaced and dog-eared at the corners. I reached in and pulled it from between the papers, holding it gently by the edges as I'd always been told to and looking at the image of Charlie and a woman who must have been Abi. In the photo they sat together in a booth at what looked like a bar. They were both wearing everyday clothes, except for the cheap-looking veil affixed to a plastic headband that sat atop Abi's hair and the sash that she wore across her chest that read *Just Married*. Charlie was looking at her like he couldn't believe he'd got her, his arms around her tiny waist. Abi stared at the camera, her tongue sticking out and her right eye scrunched up in a wink like young girls do in pictures. She was slender and tall, with pale skin to match Charlie's and auburn-coloured freckles that dusted the bridge of her nose and the undersides of her eyes. Her hair was long and straight, parted in the middle and the colour of fallen autumn leaves. She was dainty and ethereal-looking, like she wouldn't look out of place dancing around a pixie's fire with clothes made from petals.

Okay, Nancy Drew, snoop time's over. The suddenness of the thought that I almost heard, made me jump.

There she was again, like she had been last night, only now I had a face to put to the voice of my conscience disguised as Abi. I could just imagine her, full of sass leaning against the counter with her long arms crossed over her chest. I pushed the picture back under the letters and closed the drawer. I went back to my trusty Sports Direct mug, spooned in three teaspoons of granules before pouring boiling water up to the halfway point.

Someone's making herself at home, isn't she? Even got yerself a favourite mug.

'Shut up,' I murmured to myself, fully aware of how mental I would look, if there was anyone around to see me, other

168

than a passive-aggressive cat of course. I made my way to the sofa and sat down, setting the coffee aside to cool as the cat came over and plonked himself back down on my knee.

I grabbed a remote and turned the TV on and the volume down. I stroked the soft head of the cat and quiet purrs arose as I closed my eyes. I wasn't going to sleep, just resting for a moment.

Next thing I knew I was woken by the feeling of someone's weight falling onto the sofa beside me. 'Well, that's a miracle if ever I saw one.' Charlie's voice made me jump and I turned, bleary-eyed, to find him next to me as an extremely unattractive, mildly terrified groan escaped my lips. I glanced towards the TV and saw that the ten o'clock news was on.

'What is?' I asked, quickly checking for dribble and smoothing down my hair.

'Magnus, sitting on you, being pleasant. That's not how he rolls, not with me anyway.'

'Magnus?' I asked.

'The cat.' He pointed at what looked like a melted pile of ginger hair in my lap and frowned. 'He was Abi's. Little fecker hates the air I breathe. I think he's sexist, personally.'

He swigged at his coffee and motioned towards a full cup of steaming coffee sitting on the table. 'I made you another one. The last one went cold. Thank you for cleanin' up by the way; you didn't have to. I feel kinda bad about it to be honest.'

'Don't be. I was only planning to wash up, but it was helping my hangover to focus on something other than my building urge to throw up and then I ran away with it a little.'

'I've needed to do something about it for ages, but the

task was so overwhelming that I didn't know where to start.'

I reached forward and took my mug, sipping at the liquid and feeling the caffeine hit me almost instantly. I sighed and settled back into the doughy sofa cushion. I sent him a sideways glance as he reached over and attempted to stroke the cat's head. Magnus looked up before he even made contact, hissed violently, swiped with razor-sharp claws and then stared Charlie down until he withdrew his hand.

'See? I wasn't lyin'.'

'Oh, before I forget,' I said. 'There's some broken glass in the bedroom. I was going to sweep it up but I couldn't find a dustpan and brush.'

'Oh, I know about that. It's fine, leave it,' he replied, looking down at the coffee cup in his hands. He ran his thumb along the edge of the rim, his lashes downcast over his eyes.

'What are they, the jars?' I probed.

'Sea glass,' he said, reaching into the pocket of his jeans, which were rumpled and creased from sleeping all cramped up in the tub, and pulled out the small rounded lump of orange glass. It was a strange shape, like the shape of a bubble that's still clinging on to the wand.

'She collected it.' He shook his head and sighed. 'The number of hours I've lost trawling beaches for these little bastards.' He handed it to me, the almost weightless glass rolling on the skin of my palm. I took it between my thumb and finger and held it up to the light where it was set aflame like a burning ember.

'I've never seen orange sea glass before,' I said, recalling all of the times I'd gone beachcombing with my mum over the years. I'd seen green and clear, the odd brown but never orange.

'It's really rare. She'd got red ones and turquoise too. She

170

filled those jars with the stuff so that they'd catch the light when it came through the window.'

I handed the glass back to him and he pushed it back into his pocket. On the TV, the local newsreader handed over to the weatherman, Nathaniel Croome, a tall, perfect-teethed man in the world's tightest suit trousers. He was somewhat of a local celebrity and a heart-throb amongst mums of the West Midlands.

'Who do yer think's fathered more children: this weatherman or Michael Bolton?' Charlie asked, completely changing the topic of conversation.

'Oh, this guy definitely,' I said, gesturing to Croome, who made love to the camera with every glance. 'I saw him, from a distance, at the opening of the German Market last year and I'm pretty sure that every woman within a two-metre radius of him got pregnant that day, just by looking at him. Now if you asked the question of how many children have been conceived whilst listening to Michael Bolton, then I don't think there's a man alive who could beat that record.'

I looked over to where he watched me with a quirked eyebrow. 'Sometimes I worry about yer.'

'Me too, Charlie, me too.' I chuckled.

He observed me for a good long moment, before reaching a hand over and placing it on my knee, the one that wasn't guarded by Magnus, and squeezing.

'Are you feeling okay?' I asked.

'Yeah, a little hungover.'

'Did you throw up? Is that why you slept in the bath?'

'No.' He retracted his hand from my knee and went back to his cup. He took a deep, steady breath and bit his top lip, hard, before speaking again. 'I think I'm ready,' he said, gripping his knees with fingers that quickly turned white-knuckled.

'Ready for what?'

'To tell you what happened. If you want to hear it that is.' He shrugged, looking suddenly nervous.

'Of course,' I said, shifting around in my seat to face him. 'You sure you're ready?'

He nodded firmly and then pushed himself up from the sofa. 'Come.' He held out his hand, his eyes staring into mine with an intensity that made me forget how to breathe. I lay mine in his and he pulled me up, Magnus dropping to the floor with a harrumph.

He looked at me, swallowed hard and, still looking in my eyes, led me to the bedroom door.

Chapter Thirteen

I stood beside the unmade bed, my arms fidgeting nervously at my sides.

Charlie stood frozen on the other side of the door, as if he was afraid to step over the threshold.

'I've never told anyone this, so bear with me.' He exhaled a heavy breath, his top lip clenched between his front teeth.

'My mammy came home from her knittin' circle one day when I was fourteen and told me that the ladies had been sayin' that Siobhan Murphy needed some help,' he began, his eyes downcast as he talked. 'Her husband had died about six months back and she was havin' trouble keepin' up with the garden and so Mammy had volunteered my services. I wasn't too happy about it. I was a teenager. The idea of work eatin' into my band practice time disgusted me, but she told me that I needed to be a good Catholic boy, and go help that poor widowed lady. Patrick, her husband, had had a stroke. He'd come in from the garden after mowing the lawn, sat down in his chair with a glass of beer gettin' warm on the end table beside him. Next anyone knew he was dead.

'The kids had been sayin' things ever since Siobhan had holed herself up in her house. Callin' her a witch and a madwoman. I didn't join in with the name-callin' but I must admit, I felt a little nervous goin' to that house. When she answered the door, I thought I'd got the wrong place. She'd always been a looker, Mrs Murphy. My Uncle Carrick always said so and stared at her arse when he spotted her around town. But in the six months since Mr Murphy had passed, she'd aged about ten years. Her hair used to be this bright red, the colour of flames on a bonfire, but it'd started to turn white and she'd wrapped herself up in these shawls and scarves like bandages, as if she was tryin' to hold herself together with them.

'She did her best to act normally with me, although I could tell that her brain wasn't really there with me in that kitchen. She told me where I could find the mower and the rest of Patrick's gardenin' tools and at the mention of his name, she began to well up. I can't handle it when people cry in front of me – I get all teary m'self and I need to go do somethin' else before I start bawlin' along with them. I went out to the shed, wadin' through the grass and weeds that were knee-high. The grass was so heavy it was falling down on top of itself under its own weight and mattin' into clumps with all the dead grass underneath. I had no idea where to start. I'd never done any gardenin' in my whole life and this seemed like a baptism of fire into the pastime.

'I found a strimmer in the shed – it was one of the few things that I recognised – and I took it, along with an extension lead, and began hacking away at the grass. It came down easily enough at first, but the thickness of it all was makin' the blade slow and I was less than a quarter of the way through before I stopped making any progress. I remember sitting down on the pile of cut grass I'd made and sighin'. I was wet through with sweat and stinkin' to high heaven. I heard this voice call out to me but I couldn't see where it was coming from. "You don't know what you're doin', do yer?"

"'What gave it away?" I called back into the open air. There was a rustlin' up in the tall sycamore tree on the opposite side of the garden and after a few moments, I saw a figure sittin' in its branches.

"'Because, Charlie Stone, you're making a pig's ear of my father's lawn." I squinted against the sun, the figure nothing but a block of human-shaped shadow. I watched as she fiddled with somethin' in her waistband, grabbed hold of the branch, swung herself around and dropped onto the ground. The sun was so bright that I didn't see her until she slumped down into the grass beside me.

"'So, what do you suggest I do then, Abigale Murphy?" I asked, annoyed and embarrassed that she'd borne witness to my attempt. Abigale Murphy, Siobhan's eldest daughter, was a year below me in school, but she was just as much a looker as her mother had once been. Same red hair, same freckles dashed across her nose.

"'I suggest that you pick the right tool, for a start. You need a scythe."

"'A scythe? Like the grim reaper?" I asked. She grinned and flexed her bushy eyebrows at me, before flingin' herself into a backwards roll and runnin' off to the shed. She emerged a few moments later with a scythe, comically large next to the willowy frame of her, and a rake.

'"If I cut, you can get rid of it." She tossed me a roll of bin bags and pulled a book from her waistband and placed it carefully on the sill of the shed window. It was a beaten-up book that I'd never heard of, the cover all creased and curled, as if it had been read a hundred times over.

'"Well come on then," she said and set to scything the grass like that shirtless guy in that period drama. It was hilarious to see. Tiny, scrawny Abi Murphy cuttin' through that grass as if it were butter. I raked everything that she cut and put it into bag after bag until it was clear, the dead grass underneath opened up to the sun so it could try to thrive again. She handed me a cardboard box of grass seed and we spread it around without talkin'. I watered it with the hose and we ended up having a water fight there on the grass and I'm pretty sure that's the moment I fell in love with her, all red hair, dirty face and freckles.

'It wasn't long after we'd both become soaked through with the hose water that her mammy started callin' her from inside, sayin' her sister needed her. Mrs Murphy had had another baby about three years earlier, you see. They called her Kenna. She was unplanned and now she found herself with a baby she could barely remember to look after, so Abi did most of the carin'. She told me that I could leave and that I should come back the next Saturday to get rid of the thorns by the back fence. And so, I walked home and from that moment on, I thought of little other than her.'

He cleared his throat and glanced over at me as if he'd forgotten that I was here. 'Do you want me to carry on?' he asked. 'I know I'm ramblin'.'

'Go on,' I said, my stomach tingling.

'Okay. I spent every Saturday of the summer there, some

Sundays too and sometimes she read to me from her books while we ate lunch on the lawn that grew through good as new.

'She was always covered in scrapes and bruises, cuts and dents that she never moaned about and I ended up buying a box of plasters every Saturday morning in preparation for the inevitable wound she'd give herself that day. She always insisted that they didn't hurt, although I could tell when they did.

'On that last Saturday, when summer was over and the garden looked as good as if Mr Murphy had done it himself, she kissed me at the side gate and told me that she was almost certain that she was in love with me.

'We started seeing each other from then on and everything was going fine. I stuck around for a year after I finished school so that whatever we were going to do, we could do together. She applied for a course in illustration at Dublin University and I thought everythin' was gonna be fine and I was headin' there too for an apprenticeship. Everything was planned out, until she didn't get into Dublin and got accepted to the National University of Ireland over in Galway instead. I'd already found myself somewhere to live and there just wasn't the same theatre culture in Galway that there is in Dublin. I'd have had nothin' to do there.

'We told ourselves that it would work out but there was almost one hundred and thirty miles between us and it wasn't long until she called it quits on us. I was heartbroken and I dealt with it pretty badly. Turned myself into a bit of a tosser, made some awful decisions with some awful people. We didn't talk for about two years after that, until one day in Dublin, I was leaving the theatre where I was working when

177

I literally walked straight into her. We were both as shocked as each other. We didn't say a word, just stared at each other with these beamin' smiles on our faces. We spent the evenin' in a bar, talkin' about old times and before the night was over, we were deep enough in love again that we got married as soon as we could. We didn't tell anyone because we just wanted to do somethin' low-key.

'When our families found out, they weren't happy. They dragged us back home and made us do the whole thing all over again in the "appropriate Catholic way" as Mammy said. After uni was done, Abi moved to live with me in Dublin until she got a job in London and we moved over there. We lived there for a good long while before we realised that commutin' from Birmingham would cost less than living in London and that's how we ended up here.'

'Did you carry on working in London?' I asked.

He nodded. 'For a time. But it's a hard industry.'

'It's a beautiful story.' I had almost forgotten that I already knew the end to this story and I wanted him to stop there. If he stopped talking now then I could pretend that gangly Abigale Murphy and young stupid Charlie Stone got their happy ending. 'We can stop there if you want to, leave the rest for later.'

He shook his head. I could already see his eyes glistening. 'It's okay. I want to finish it.' He swallowed hard, audibly, and took a deep breath through his nose. 'She had these lumps in her boobs. They'd scared the shite outta us both when they showed up, but she got them checked out and the doctor said that they were just these calcified lumps of tissue that would do her no harm. She didn't have the largest, you know, and so you could see one of them through her skin. I couldn't

178

have cared less about them but she wanted them gone, so she went in for the op and had them taken out.

'The operation went fine and that evening I brought her back here and put her in bed. They'd given her these long, tight stockings to put on, but she said they looked stupid and dug into her knees and so she refused to wear them. There was little you could do when Abi had made her mind up about somethin'. Anyway, when she got into bed, she was in a foul mood. The anaesthetic made her all sassy and we'd had an argument on the way home.' I watched as his face changed, then his voice, as the story got closer to the final conclusion. 'She kissed my cheek as I sat her up in bed on all those pillows.' He motioned to the bed, looking almost fearfully at it. 'She apologised and asked me to give her one of the strong painkillers they'd sent her home with and a cup of tea. I remember saying to her, "Abigale Murphy needin' a painkiller? You've gone soft in your old age."

'She rolled her eyes and said to me, "Oh, piss off and get me my tea, will yer?" So, I did. I put the kettle on and, as I was waitin', I got distracted by something on the news and I ended up staying in the living room. By the time I remembered the tea and the painkiller I was pretty sure Abi was going to murder me, but I took it all into her. When I got there, she was asleep, slumped back in the pillows, so I put the tea on the nightstand and left the pill beside it and went back into the livin' room to watch a film. I didn't wanna disturb her, so I thought it best for me to get outta the way.

'I fell asleep on the sofa and by the time I woke up it was past three in the mornin'. I found my way into the room in the dark so I didn't wake her and got into bed.

'I leaned over to kiss her on the forehead, but somethin' was wrong. She was still in the position she'd been in when I left her to make the tea, slumped back onto those pillows. She hadn't moved at all. I nudged her.' His voice broke a little and I saw a tear teetering on the lower lids of his eyes. 'She was so cold, but the room was warm. I didn't understand it. Not until I looked at her face. She always had such an animated face, even when she was sleepin', but it was just . . . blank.

'I called an ambulance but, we all knew that she was dead, even if no one was saying it. They put her on a trolley and carried her out of here and that was the last time I saw her. One of them backed into one of the jars on the way out, knocking it onto the floor and smashing it. Later on, they told me that she'd died of a huge blood clot in her lung due to the operation and that she'd been dead for hours when they came to get her. That means that she was dead when I brought the tea in. Apparently, the faster you act with pulmonary embolisms, the better the person's chances are. I could have saved her, if I hadn't been distracted by the news.'

'Charlie, I . . .' But what could I say to that?

'I came back in here to get some clothes and a couple of other things and I haven't been in here since. The only one who comes in here is the cat. I think he likes that it still smells of her.' He heaved a deep breath and tears rolled freely down his face, which was frozen in a mask of unimaginably deep grief. 'So, there it is. That's why I called you that night. She's dead, because she was worried about how sexy I'd find her with those lumps on her chest and because I was busy watching the TV.'

'It's not your fault,' I said, going over to him and wrapping my arms around his neck. He leaned into me and I felt the shoulder of my shirt moistening as he cried.

So, that's why he'd slept in the bathtub, because he didn't want to sleep in the bed where the worst event of his life had happened.

'That first night when I walked away from you or the times I disappeared, it was all because, if I let myself hurt, then she's still alive in some way. But having these feelings and acting on them, even for a second, it's like I'm allowing her to be dead.' Just as he was sobbing into the crook of my neck, three loud knocks came from the front door. We both jumped and withdrew from our hug. Charlie wiped his face, readying his macho façade, but his face was blotchy and red, his eyes set in a look of bottomless sadness.

'I'll get it,' I said, squeezing his arm and moving through to the living room. I flipped the lock and let the door fall open, which was much easier now that all of the letters had been moved.

Standing in the doorway was a man, in his late forties with a mass of greying curls, facial hair that reminded me of Zorro, and an almost blinding turquoise scarf.

'Erm, hi,' I said as the man lowered his weather-inappropriate shades and stared at me like I'd just answered the door naked.

'Who the hell's this?' he asked in an accent to match Charlie's and if the accent hadn't done enough to suggest that this man was related to Charlie, then the cornflower blue of his eyes was.

'I'm Nell and I'm guessing you're Carrick.'

He grinned with only half his mouth and held his arms

out, as if presenting himself to me. 'The one and only.' He looked almost flattered. 'Nell – lovely name. It means shining light, don't yer know? Is he in?'

'Erm . . .'

'Charlie boy! You in there? Come out and give yer favourite uncle a big ol' smooch,' he bellowed into the flat.

I glanced to Carrick's side and saw a suitcase, small and ostentatiously fuchsia pink.

'What are yer doin' here?' Charlie asked, less than politely, as he appeared behind me.

'I'm here to haul yer arse back home.'

'Er, no, you're not,' he said bluntly.

'Er,' Carrick imitated, 'you've no choice in the matter, I'm afraid, Boyo.'

'No, Carrick. How many times do I have to tell you that there is absolutely no way I'm going back there?' Charlie protested.

'I'd be willin' to talk to yer more on the subject if you'd let me through the front door, instead of leavin' me out in the corridor like a hotel prostitute.'

'Pfft, good job you're not – you'd have few takers,' Charlie said, turning around and walking back into the flat.

'D'yer think that means I'm allowed in?' Carrick asked, leaning in and whispering to me.

'I have no idea,' I responded, stepping aside.

He nodded his approval at me and walked by, rolling his candy-coloured suitcase behind him before announcing to no one in particular, 'I like her.'

Chapter Fourteen

I stood in the window of the first coffee shop I found after leaving Charlie's house. It was a run-of-the-mill chain place with nondescript music only just noticeable over the screech of steam wands and the groaning of coffee grinders. I'd thought it best to get out of Charlie's flat and let what promised to be an uncomfortable conversation between uncle and nephew go ahead without me lurking in the corner. I wasn't sure if I liked Carrick or if he was someone who would quickly get on my nerves, but the potential for both was there.

I watched the barista as he pushed my three paper cups of coffee down into a recycled paper cup holder and then walked in my direction. He looked down at the receipt and reeled them off. 'One Americano, one flat white and one . . . hot chocolate with a shot of chai and caramel syrup.' He grimaced at the sound of it and I didn't blame him. I stepped forward, took the cups and started the short walk back to Charlie's.

The air was definitely changing, getting milder as the dregs of winter filtered away, but there was still an undeniable nip in the air. I pulled the oversized hoodie tight around my body and held the zip together with my free hand. Before I'd left, I'd discovered that Magnus was asleep on my coat and, not wanting to disturb him for a second time in one morning, I'd asked if I could borrow something. Charlie had thrown me the cleanest hoodie he could find and I'd put it on without really thinking about it. But now, as I absent-mindedly let the zips sag away from each other and lifted the collar up to my nose, I thought about how intimate it was to wear someone else's clothes. This was Charlie's smell, impregnated into the fabric and making it smell like no one else on the planet. It was the same smell I'd breathed in as I'd kissed him last night, the same smell I never wanted to forget.

Gettin' a good whiff there, are yer?

Shit not her again. What was happening to me? Was this really just my conscience taken form or was I having a full-blown mental breakdown?

Nah, I think it's just your guilty conscience.

'I have nothing to feel guilty for,' I said quietly. Did that actually just happen? Did I just talk to someone who I knew wasn't there?

Oh no, absolutely nothin'. Two years. Two feckin' years. You can't even finish uni in two years and yet that seems more than enough time to move on to the next hussy.

A postman, clad in red shorts and with an armful of letters, came out of a driveway and nodded me a good morning. I returned it before turning back to whatever the apparition beside me was and whisper-shouting: 'I am not a hussy.'

The postman frowned at me over his shoulder as I turned the corner back to Charlie's.

Oh no, course you aren't. Desperately hanging around with an emotionally distraught widower whilst also stringin' along the boyfriend that you're never gonna get back with, even though you're fully aware that it's gonna break his heart when you eventually get up the balls to send him on his way.

'Shut up.' I was almost jogging now. Literally running away from my problems.

The drinks sloshed through the holes on the lids of the takeaway cups but I didn't care. I had to get back to people, real people. I reached Charlie's building and pressed the buzzer, panting as I checked behind me. She was gone, nowhere to be found.

Back inside the flat, I handed out the drinks and sat down on the sofa beside Charlie while Carrick sat on the edge of the coffee table, his elbows resting on his skinny knees.

'So, what's going on?' I asked, trying to act oblivious to the tension that was turning the consistency of the air to jelly.

'Ah, nothin',' Carrick said, his bottom lip pouty. 'Young Charlie here was just being an enormous pain in my arse and the cat just took a swipe at my ankles, so I'm feelin' welcome.'

I turned to Charlie, the awkwardness making my body feel rigid. He didn't look up at me, just pressed on the lid of his coffee, causing it to make an annoying, incessant clicking noise.

Click, click, click. It sounded like the ticking of a clock, which was fitting, I guess.

'So, what brings you here, Carrick? Are you staying?' I asked.

'I've come here to haul Charlie's pale, insubordinate arse back to Westport to set some things straight.'

'What things?' I asked. Charlie squirmed in his seat and it became clear that there was more to this story that I hadn't heard yet.

'Can't it just be left alone?' Charlie finally joined in the conversation.

Carrick's face turned bright pink for a second and fury flickered through his blue eyes. 'Listen here, Charlie Boy. You made me a promise – remember that. Time's almost up and when yer were up on that clock—' He stopped, eyeing me suspiciously and his anger seemed to wane a little and turn into shiftiness. 'Yer can't leave anythin' undone or any people without explanations, no matter how shitty those explanations are.'

'Don't worry,' Charlie said in an annoyed tone of voice. 'Nell knows.'

Click, click, click.

'Thank feck for that.' He sighed. 'Look, there's a whole lotta people back there that need closure and you're the only one left who can grant it to them. Hell, maybe you'll find a little yerself when yer see that everyone else is movin' on and healin', unlike you.'

So, Carrick had received a call on that night too. Had Carrick's call been before or after Ned's?

Maybe this would be a good thing for Charlie. For two years he'd been running from anything to do with Abi, content with settling into the quagmire of his grief, but maybe a trip home would coerce him into trying to tackle the pain, facing it head on instead of pretending that it didn't exist.

I turned in my seat to face Charlie and he looked at me with worried eyes. 'Maybe going home isn't such a bad idea,' I said, my voice calm and unconfrontational.

'Not you too, Nell.' He sighed with frustration.

'How long did you plan on bringing him over for?' I asked, turning back to Carrick.

'A few days. Just long enough to go to the memorial and see his poor old mammy,' he replied.

'Well, there you have it. You can't not go to your own wife's memorial service. That would be awful.'

'Yeah.' Carrick scoffed and laughed a humourless laugh. 'It's not like he turned up to the actual funeral or anything and so it seems only right he come to the two-year memorial.'

I turned back to Charlie with shocked confusion on my face. 'You didn't go to Abi's funeral?'

Click, click, click, click, click.

He looked down at his coffee again, the endless clicking sounding like it was ticking down to something, the ticks getting faster and faster. 'I couldn't,' he mumbled quietly. 'I tried, but I didn't even make it onto the plane.'

'Yeah, just left it all to the rest of us, didn't yer?' Carrick spat angrily.

'Hey.' I held up a polite, yet forceful hand at Carrick. 'Attacking him isn't going to help anything,' I said, seeing already how Carrick's words had made Charlie close up. I took a beat, composing myself and thinking about the best way to tackle this. 'I think that this would be good for you,' I eventually said. My voice was soft, reassuring. 'I know you want to see your home again and it's only for a few days. This time next week, it will all be long over.'

He looked up at me, his thumb pausing over the loose

section of the lid and the clicking finally coming to a stop. His eyes were glassy, moist and staring.

'No one can force you to do anything, Charlie, but I really do think that this is a good idea,' I said, placing a comforting hand on his wrist.

He sniffed loudly before speaking. 'I'll go.'

'Hallelujah.' Carrick sighed.

'On one condition,' he said. 'That you come with me.'

'Me?' I felt a jolt of panic. 'Are you planning to go by ferry?'

Carrick shook his head. 'Easier to fly to Knock than to sail to Dublin and then drive all the way to Westport.'

I swallowed audibly, desperately trying to think of an excuse. 'I have work.'

'Then I'm not going,' Charlie said matter-of-factly.

Carrick raised a hand to his forehead and blew air out through pursed lips. 'You're more than welcome, Nell, but I need to know so I can book the tickets. It'll be good fun. No one does a send-off like the Irish.'

Good fun? I thought. Wasn't it a memorial he was talking about?

'Hold on. Hold on,' I said, pulling my phone out of my pocket. 'Let me see what I can do.' I pulled up Barry's number and mentally crafted what I was going to say.

Charlie needed to go home and if me flying was the only way to make that happen, then I guess I'd just have to go, wouldn't I?

Chapter Fifteen

I sat at the kitchen table with a condensation-beaded glass of Coke making a dark wet ring on the surface of the oak table in front of me. My half-eaten bowl of chilli con carne sat, congealing with coolness, a few inches away, my stomach unwilling to make room for food amongst all of the worry in there. I'd finally called a time of death on the flowers that now sat in the bin, the least floppy of the eucalyptus stems peeping over the top, as if sending me a final plea for help as they sank slowly to their demise. Ned was overjoyed and his voice would soon lose that bunged-up nasal tone, now that the pollen was no longer lingering in the kitchen to attack him whenever he fancied a cup of tea. I'd sat here and told Ned about Carrick when I'd got home and recounted everything that had happened since I saw him last in deep, heart-breaking detail.

'Poor guy.'

'I know, right.'

I'd rung Ned – as soon as I'd got the all clear from Barry

about me taking the next few days off – to see if it was okay that Carrick and Charlie stayed over. That way we could all leave together for the airport in the morning. It made sense as we lived closer and there was a spare room here that people could actually sleep in, which was not a tableau of pain in the form of a double bed.

Ned laced his hands together and placed them on the tabletop in front of him, adopting the therapist's position. 'How are you feeling about all of this?' he asked.

I thought for a moment before saying, 'Terrified, completely out of my depth and irrationally jealous. Is that enough for you to work your therapist magic on?'

'They're all very valid feelings.' He often sounded like a stranger when he talked like this, far too professional to be my strange buddy Ned, but I guess that's why he'd been doing this for so long, because it was clearly what he was born for. 'I know you're a wuss when it comes to flying, but it's only a short flight, perfect for breaking you in and it's, like, a one in five million chance that you'll go crashing to your death.'

I gulped. 'Thanks, Ned. You're being really helpful.'

He ignored me and carried on. 'As for Charlie, you know the signs, Nell. If he begins to feel like he's losing control again then you'll be able to see it. You're on the same wavelength now. You know everything, so don't worry that he's going to try and do it again. And you're completely allowed to feel like you don't know what you're doing. These are high-risk, uncharted waters for you, for most people, but your job isn't to fix him, it's to let him know that it is possible to be happy again. As far as jealousy is concerned, you don't need to be jealous because you're not in competition with

Abi. He's not got a notebook with your names in columns, ticking off things that each of you are better at.' He unfurled his hands and reached one over, resting it on my mine. 'This was never going to be easy, Nell. But if anyone can handle it, it's you.'

I stared at him for a moment, a nervous energy making me feel as if I might cry. I swallowed down the tears and squeezed his fingers.

'Damn, you're good. You know that?' I said. He chuckled and retracted his hand.

'You're a badass, Nell. Don't for a second think that you can't do this.'

I picked my spoon back up and stirred my congealing chilli, the next sentence forming in my brain, but my mouth was reluctant to spill it.

'What?' Ned asked. 'I know there's more.'

I looked back up and met his eyes. 'It's nothing. I just had a call the other day and I wanted to ask you about it. It wasn't something I'd heard of before.'

'I don't know how much help I'll be but, sure, fire away.' He sat back in his chair, crossing his arms and listening with interest.

'So, it was this person who was feeling guilty about something and they started seeing . . . things.'

'What kind of things?' he asked.

The chair next to him was suddenly filled with the glaring form of Abigale Murphy, her hair coiffed to ludicrously glamorous standards, her lips glossed and pouting as she rested a nonchalant chin upon a crooked hand. *Yeah, Nell. What kinda things?* she sassed.

I took a deep breath and turned my attention back to

Ned, who was eyeing the chair beside him with a worried frown.

'People that weren't, you know, there.' I looked back down at my chilli and pushed around a particularly huge kidney bean with my spoon.

Ned sighed, racking his brain for a moment before answering, 'Hmm, not sure. Could be that these delusions, for lack of another word, could be a manifestation of their guilt, a way of dealing with it all because they don't otherwise know how to combat it? Things like this usually come down to delusional disorder or psychosis.'

Fantastic, I thought, glancing over at Abi, who was grinning at me manically. 'Yeah, yeah. That's what I thought.' I said.

'The human mind is a complicated place. It'll never stop surprising you.' He stood and went over to the sink where he doused his bowl with water.

I took a deep breath, squeezing my eyes shut and then looking back to the chair that I hoped would be empty, but there she still was, staring at me with malevolent glee. She cackled. *Yer can't get rid of me that easily.*

At seven fifteen, the doorbell rang and I found myself uncommonly nervous. I pulled open the door and found Charlie's deadpan stare, his eyelids half closed in a look of pure exasperation. In his hands he held Carrick's hot pink suitcase, a black backpack of his own and a large carrier bag containing what looked like a plastic box.

'Hey,' I said, checking around us for unwanted apparitions of dead wives and thankfully finding none. 'Where's Carrick?'

'He'll be along. Eejit's just getting the cat out from under the driver's seat,' he replied, stepping into the hallway and dropping his bags down onto the floor.

'I'm sorry, did you just say, the cat?'

I looked down the drive at the taxi that idled against the kerb. The driver gesticulated angrily as Carrick flailed about in the back seat. A few seconds passed as I watched in awe, before Carrick emerged with a disgruntled Magnus in his outstretched hands. Carrick shouted one last insult at the driver who brushed the back of his hand under his chin in a physical insult before driving away.

'Success!' Carrick bellowed as he jogged up the drive, holding the cat at arm's length like an unstable grenade. Ned sauntered into the hall just as Carrick made it to the door.

'Ah!' Carrick exclaimed as he stepped inside. 'You must be Ned.'

'I am,' Ned said, warily. 'And you must be Carrick.' He looked down at the cat with worried brows.

'Right yer are.' Carrick thrust Magnus in his direction. 'Take the beast, will yer? Before I lose a pinkie.'

Ned, ever obedient, did as he was told and held Magnus to his chest. The cat instantly looked more at ease and quickly found his way up to Ned's shoulder, where he curled around the back of his neck and settled down with a quiet purr.

'Would yer look at that, Boyo,' Carrick said over his shoulder to an incensed-looking Charlie. 'We've managed t'find the one man on the planet that the little fecker likes.' Carrick took the plastic bag from Charlie and handed it to Ned. 'Here's some food and a litter tray, complete with brand-new, shite-free litter. Don't say we don't treat yer well.' He winked at Ned and then walked over to his nephew, slapping him affectionately on the shoulder. 'So, that's the cat sorted. Where do you want us?'

Chapter Sixteen

The fear of embarrassing myself in front of Charlie was about the only thing keeping me from hyperventilating as I glanced out the window of the plane. A jolt of panic struck me square in the chest as I saw the cloud-speckled world so very far below me, but I just took a deep breath and reminded myself that it wasn't long until we'd be back on the ground. Although, I tried not to think about the landing part. I hated the landing part. Once I was in the air, I was fine. It was just the going up and coming down that made me want to cry like Ned when presented with a Bridget Jones box set.

My knuckles were still a little achy from when I'd clutched Charlie's hand to a state of blueness against the armrest. Everything this morning had gone surprisingly smoothly. Charlie hadn't suddenly decided not to come, like I thought he might and Carrick had been less hungover than I thought he would be, after finding him and Ned in the kitchen just after midnight, three bottles of wine down and playing a particularly competitive game of Jenga, where Carrick had somehow ended up shirtless, his chest stained with long-since-dried droplets of red wine, and could be heard periodically shouting, 'How about that, Sassenach?'

I leaned forward and looked past a slumbering Charlie to see how Carrick was doing. He'd taken the aisle seat as the altitude 'fecked with his bladder' as he'd so poetically put it. He was sleeping it off now, his head leaning back against the headrest and his sunglasses pulled down over his light-sensitive eyes. I hadn't wanted to sit by the window, but Charlie had said it would be good for me and if I was making him face his fears, then I'd have to face some of my own too.

'Don't worry about him. The man wears a hangover as often as he wears trousers,' Charlie said, his voice making me jump.

'For the sake of everyone in Westport, I hope that means that it's often.'

He chuckled and opened his eyes. 'How're you doin'?' he asked, squeezing my hand.

'Okay. You just might have to keep your hands away from me when we land, unless you want your bones crushing again.'

'Duly noted.' He shifted in his seat and took hold of the tea on his little fold-out tray that, surprise surprise, he'd let go cold.

I thought back to the mug beside the bed in which Abi had died, and something clicked.

Tea. It was the last thing he ever did for her. He'd made her a cup of tea, a cup which she never drank. That's why he never drank his own, because why should he be allowed to when Abi hadn't? Did he buy himself cup after cup of wasted tea because it was his own small way of punishing

196

himself, of making sure he never made the mistake of getting distracted again?

'I wonder how Ned's doin' with the cat?' Charlie asked, breaking my train of thought.

'Oh, I don't think you need to worry there. They're soulmates if ever I saw them,' I replied.

There couldn't be that much longer to go now before we started descending and the closer we got, the more haywire my nerves seemed to be getting. What were people going to think when Charlie showed up with a strange new Englishwoman on his arm? Would people think that he'd brought a date to his wife's funeral? Because I was only there for moral support; it wasn't like we were going to be making out on the buffet table after the service, or making out at all for that matter.

'Hey, Nell?' Charlie asked, shuffling in his seat so that he was facing me as much as he could. 'When I disappeared . . .'

'Which time was this? The first time or the second when you ignored me for two weeks?' I grinned to lessen the sharpness.

'Ha-ha.' He mock laughed. 'The second. There was a reason for it, yer know. I was erm . . . well, I was afraid.'

'Afraid of what?'

'Of you.'

'Me?' I asked, my brows knitting at the mere notion of it. 'I know I've got a little bit of a temper sometimes but I wouldn't say that I was particularly menacing.'

'Not of you as a person, of what I felt . . . for yer.'

My chest felt as if it was filling with pressure, like a balloon pressed beneath the sole of a shoe.

'I felt a lot more than I thought I would ever be able to

197

feel again,' he continued. 'I felt guilty. I want yer to understand that Abi and I never broke up. We never fell out of love or ended up hating each other. She was just there one minute, gone the next and I had, still have, no idea what to do with everything I feel for her. So, when I began feelin' that churnin' in my stomach and wanting to lean in and kiss yer. When I touched that tattoo on yer shoulder and wanted to take yer upstairs, that all felt like cheatin' to me, like I was gonna get home and Abi was gonna be there with a private investigator and a look of murder on her face.

'It wasn't because I didn't like yer, it was because I liked yer too much. And I was always gonna come back and talk to you again, explain myself. Yer just beat me to it.' His hand landed gently on mine, his fingers falling into the spaces between.

Since I'd met Charlie, I had felt something for him that I had never felt for another human being before. It was an unspoken intimacy that felt more real, more connected than any bond I'd ever shared with anyone else. It made everything about us, even these new, timid touches, feel natural, inevitable.

'I understand,' I said, my voice almost a whisper. 'I can't imagine how hard this has all been for you and I don't want you to think that I'm trying to replace her or make you move on faster. This can be done at your own speed.'

He leaned his head forward until his forehead rested against mine and he exhaled a relieved breath.

'I'm so glad I met yer, Nell,' he said quietly, his face so close to mine that his eyes morphed into one in the centre of his forehead. But what a handsome cyclops he made.

I thought of what would have happened if we hadn't met.

An extra space at the café table. One call less on the waiting list. The sound of sirens in the distance that I didn't know the purpose of. A cordoned-off road that added a couple of minutes to my journey. A few more miserable mornings of waking up beside Joel. Loneliness.

I leaned up a little and pressed my lips to his gently, where they rested for a moment before I moved away. 'Me too.'

Chapter Seventeen

There had been many things that I'd seen in my life where I had asked myself the question: 'Who the hell thought that this was a good idea?' But never more so than right now, standing in what looked like a car park full of UPVC huts and staring at what can only be described as a Virgin Mary in a jar full of water, being sold under the guise of a snow globe. Mary stood in the middle, surrounded by trees and a village scene that she dwarfed in size and which was periodically rained down on by glitter and little chips of fake snow.

'Fifteen euro,' said the tiny, withered woman behind the counter, who looked as though she might be as old as Mary herself.

'How much?' I asked in horror but I'd already committed to buying it.

Ned had specifically asked me to bring him back a beautiful souvenir and I was prepared to use that adjective as sarcastically as possible. She raised her eyebrows, or at least I think she did. The hair above her eyes was so sparse that they barely constituted eyebrows at all.

'Fifteen euro. That's holy water in there, so it is,' she said as if that was any consolation for paying thirteen pounds for a jam jar full of water with a plastic figurine and some glitter thrown in for good measure. She held my gaze with her wide, sweet eyes and before I knew what was happening, I'd already tapped my card against the reader and she was thanking me with a polite smile. 'Would yer like a wee bag with that?'

I nodded, wanting to get as much from this transaction as possible.

She wrapped Mary up in a sheet of newspaper and put her in a bag, which was less 'wee' and more regular-sized, and I walked away feeling unsure as to how she'd managed to bamboozle me with her Irish charm and lack of brows.

I walked back out into the . . . I guess market is what you'd call it, and found Charlie exactly where I'd left him. He was standing sullenly, our luggage around his feet, beside a stand advertising large empty plastic bottles to fill with holy water and take home. Carrick had gone to find the car that he'd parked on a friend's drive, leaving Charlie and I to peruse the souvenirs on offer.

Charlie leant against an electricity box, his brows lowered over his eyes, his teeth gnawing on his bottom lip. He pulled off the brooding look so well that I often had trouble deciding if he was angry or not. Was he simmering on a medium heat of fury or had his face simply forgotten how to pull any other expression?

'What d'yer have there?' he asked.

'Something for Ned. I said I'd bring him something back.'

'I never took yer or Ned as religious.' He nodded towards the bag in my hand.

'How do you know that I bought something religious?' I asked, reaching in and taking out the paper-wrapped jam jar.

'This is Knock, Nell; everythin's religious.'

I unwrapped it and gave him a peek.

His eyes widened with what I can only assume was intense jealousy, that I should be the owner of such an exquisite object and he not. 'I'm glad to see you went for the tasteful one rather than the tacky stuff.' He took it from me, shook it a few times and grimaced at the pathetic scattering of glitter snow. 'How much did they rob off yer for this?'

'Fifteen euros.'

'Fifteen euro?!' he exclaimed and then immediately started laughing, violently shaking it around.

'Hey, give it back!' I pushed myself up onto my tiptoes and snatched it back. 'I'll have you know that this is holy water.'

'Oh, well I do beg yer pardon.'

'Yeah, jealous now, aren't you?' I said with a grin.

'I am. I mean, just look at the craftsmanship, the . . . oh, good grief.' He took my wrist in his hand and brought the globe closer to his face. I squinted through the glass and saw the Virgin Mary's eyes staring at me judgementally. When I say eyes, however, I mean the twinkly sky-blue diamantes that had been affixed over her eyes.

'Oh, that's a nice touch.' Charlie chuckled.

The sound of one of those jet-propelled boy-racer cars roared to life in the distance, disturbing the quiet town and causing milling tourists to look up from their purchases.

I'd always found the loud-engined, spoiler-clad, narcissism in car form thing baffling. All it spoke of to me was a larger than average ego and a smaller than average penis. I winced and watched as Charlie raised a hand to his forehead and rubbed calming circles into his skin. I turned in the direction of the roaring as a bright orange BMW skidded around the corner and, within a matter of seconds, screamed to a halt, the tyres bouncing away from the kerb as the car rebounded a few inches. I scoffed and rolled my eyes at Charlie, who looked nothing but overwhelmingly embarrassed. The driver's side window opened and out popped Carrick's beaming face.

'Hop in, kids,' he called.

'They let you have your car back then?' Charlie said as he gathered the bags and smiled apologetically at the tourists looking on judgementally.

'On the condition that I get a silencer fitted,' he called back, his head hanging out the window like a Labrador's.

'Uh-huh and when are you going to get that done?'

'We're on the way to the garage now . . . if anyone asks,' he replied.

'You get travel sick?' Charlie asked me over the low top of the car as I popped the door behind the driver's seat. I shook my head. 'Good. But there's a bag in the back of Carrick's seat if you need one. His driving has been known to bring out the vomit in people.'

'Excellent,' I murmured, sliding into the back seat. Charlie got in beside me and Carrick shifted the passenger seat forward so that Charlie's legs could fit in.

'You not going up front?' I asked.

'Nah, it's safer back here . . . I think.'

'Everyone strapped in?' Carrick asked. I quickly buckled my seatbelt and gave him the thumbs up in the mirror. 'Right then, off we go.'

The car left the kerb at such a speed that I felt like I was back on the plane, being thrust back into my seat by the sheer G-force of Carrick's acceleration. We were off and away, leaving nothing but noise pollution and the smell of burning rubber behind us. Before I even had time to feel embarrassed at the distressed looks of the people milling around the streets, Carrick took a corner like a rally driver and we were quickly out of sight. As my body slid across the leather seat and my shoulder collided with the inside of the door, I was struck by the thought that I hadn't said goodbye to my mother or to Ned. I hadn't even rung him when I got off the plane like I'd promised I would. Hopefully, I wouldn't die here, but I decided to send them both a text, just in case.

I didn't take in much of the surroundings as we zoomed past them at breakneck speed. It wasn't that Carrick was a bad driver, in fact, I would say he was better than most by the way he handled the car at high speed, but I do think that he was on a mission to violate as many traffic laws as he possibly could in one single journey.

We passed a brown sign, which I didn't read due to it being nothing but a brown and white blur, but I assumed that it was the 'Welcome to Westport' sign, because as soon as we passed it, Charlie began fidgeting and looking down into his lap.

The atmosphere inside the car was growing more and more tense the closer we got to Charlie's parents' house. I wondered what they would be like. From what I'd heard so far they weren't the easiest of people to warm to, but maybe I'd be pleasantly surprised.

'Attention, tourists,' Carrick said, clearing his throat before he continued. 'If you look to your right, you'll see the picturesque Clew Bay with its fine examples of sunken drumlins. What is a drumlin? I hear you cry. Well, I'll tell yer. The word "drumlin" is derived from the Gaelic word "*drumin*", meaning mound. So, in other words, they're those fancy little hills that stick outta the water and look like boobies in a bathtub.'

'Have you ever seen boobies in a bathtub?' Charlie asked.

'Oh, far too many to count, Boyo, unlike the drumlins, of which there are three hundred and sixty-five. One for every day of the year.'

'Do you get much work as a tour guide?' I asked, sarcastically.

Carrick sent me a wink in the mirror and continued to tell me about how the bay had been the focus of the seafaring O'Malley family, especially Grace O'Malley, the famous pirate queen who had ruled over the bay and terrorised the sailors going to and from Galway during the reign of Elizabeth I. I didn't know how much of it was true, as with much of what Carrick said, but it took my mind off my potential car-related death and so I was glad of it.

Just as he was finishing up his story, we slowed and he pulled the car over to the kerb. He'd parked us in a bus stop, the butt of the car sticking out into the road. A car horn blared from behind and several old ladies at the bus stop began tutting our way, each and every one of them in plastic rain bonnets, tied beneath their turkey-like chins with white strings.

'And that concludes this portion of the tour. Excuse me, will yer – I just need to pick somethin' up,' Carrick added before unbuckling and quickly hopping out of the car.

As soon as he was gone, Charlie turned to me and sighed. 'I can only apologise. He really is a very good driver when he wants to be.'

'It's okay. I only accepted death about three times.'

'Only the three? Well then, I needn't have worried.'

The bay was beautiful, the type of picturesque view that's always found on postcards and souvenir fudge tins.

'So, how does it feel being back?' I asked, watching the old ladies who were whispering to each other and looking straight at us.

'Oh, fantastic.' He attempted a smile, but there was no truth in it. 'Was that convincing?'

'Needs some work.'

There came a tapping of long, claw-like nails, hardened and yellowed with age, on Charlie's window.

'Christ,' he said under his breath, donning a smile and winding down the window.

'Bless my eyes, is that Charlie Stone I see?' the woman said with a hint of flirtatiousness.

'Mrs Kelly, how're yer?' he replied, on the charm offensive.

'Oh, call me Roisin. Yer not a lad anymore.' She giggled.

'Nice t'see yer, Roisin. Yer lookin' well.'

The woman's face suddenly puckered and I braced myself for what I knew was coming next.

'Terrible business with your Abi.' She tutted and shook her head, crossing herself and looking at him with an expression of pity that I knew he'd hate. 'Is that why yer haven't been back home, so?

Another face appeared in the space beside the first, equally as wrinkled and weathered and with a matching rain bonnet. 'Charlie Stone, you get more handsome every time I see yer. You'd better stop hoggin' all of those good looks, else there'll be none left for the rest of us.' She giggled, holding a hand to her heart, her eyes darting to me. 'And who's this?' All attention turned to me and I pressed myself harder into the inside of the door, hoping to defy science and slip through the metal and out onto the other side.

'This is Nell. She's a friend from England.'

'A friend, is it?' the first of the women said with raised brows.

'Too pretty to be friends with if yer ask me,' said the second.

No one did, I thought. *Now go away.*

'Ah, right yer are, Agnes.'

Carrick reappeared on the pavement with a suit bag in hand and sent the old ladies a wolf whistle as he passed. 'Lookin' good, girls.'

The women both straightened and blushed, chuckling to each other like geese.

'Pickin' up yer suit for the memorial, are yer?' Roisin asked him.

'Right yer are.'

'Well, we'll see yer there, won't we, Agnes?'

'Ah, yer will,' Agnes added.

'It was nice t'see yer both,' Charlie said, his finger poised on the window button, ready to block them out.

'Nice t'see yer and t'meet yer new lady friend.' Agnes sent me a wink and they quickly pottered back to the bus stop.

Carrick got back into the car, tossing the suit bag onto the passenger seat.

'What you got there?' I asked.

Carrick turned to me as if he'd been waiting for someone to ask just that question. 'My suit for tomorrow,' he said with pride, unzipping the bag and pulling back the sides. I raised a hand to my mouth to stifle the gasp that came out of it and my eyes rolled from Carrick to Charlie.

'What the feck's that, yer eejit!' Charlie shouted at Carrick from the back seat.

'My suit,' Carrick replied with pinched brows.

Charlie turned his angry eyes up to mine and sighed loudly. 'Would yer look at the state of it!'

'Don't get thick with me, Boyo. I put a lot of thought and money into this. I just thought I'd try to liven things up a little. We had the funeral and anniversary mass already. It's about time we started celebrating her instead of mourning.'

'What . . . erm . . .' I mumbled, unsure how to word it. 'What colour is that?'

'Oh, I think the lass in there called it chartreuse. Had it specially made, I did. What d'yer think, Nell?'

'I think it's . . . very striking.'

Carrick's chest seemed to puff out a little. 'See! Now that's how yer meant to react when yer uncle makes an effort.'

He zipped the bag back up and haughtily threw it back down onto the seat.

'He doesn't need any encouragement to be an arse,' Charlie whispered to me.

'Neither do you,' I pointed out as the engine roared into life. 'He's only trying to make an effort and if anyone can carry a suit like that off, it's Carrick.'

'Right yer are, Nell,' Carrick said, turning in his seat and sending me a serious look. 'Now, are yer feelin' strong? Because there's no more puttin' this off.'

'Sure.' I said. 'How bad can they be?'

Carrick pulled his top lip between his teeth and looked, shiftily, between Charlie and me. I turned to Charlie and asked the question again in the form of worried brows.

'Just . . . prepare yerself,' Carrick said, patting my knee gently.

Chapter Eighteen

'I think it's best to treat this like a waxing strip,' Carrick said as he got out of the car, his shoes landing on the satisfyingly crunchy gravel of the Stones' drive. 'It's gonna be feckin' painful no matter how you do it, but things will be smoother once it's done.'

I jutted out my bottom lip and nodded, impressed with Carrick's metaphor as I got out to join him. Charlie remained in the back seat, looking through the window at the house like he feared he might get murdered when he stepped through the door and right now, I wasn't sure just how possible that might actually be.

'They know I'm coming, right?' I said, turning to Carrick.

'Yeah.' There was a slight hint of worry in his eye that made my stomach acid writhe. 'They're a little more – how can I put this? – by the book with things than I am. The Good Book, I mean, so don't expect them to be too thrilled that you're "livin' in sin",' he said, air quoting the last few words of his worrying sentence.

'Oh, we're not . . . Charlie and I haven't . . .' I said, shaking my head.

'Uh-huh.' Carrick flexed his brows and rolled his eyes. 'Yer mean, yer haven't yet.'

I flailed in the embarrassment of the conversation, even more nervous now than I was before.

Would they be waiting by the door with pitchforks and torches in hand, ready to slap a red A on my chest? I guessed there was only one way to find out.

I turned back to the car to check on Charlie's progress. He'd managed to take off his seatbelt, but that's as far as he'd got. I popped the car door and bent down. 'How you holding up?' I asked.

'Oh, just terrified with a side of panic, nothin' I can't handle,' he replied, his words coming out too quickly and falling over themselves. 'Just give me a minute to myself and I'll be out.'

'Okay,' I said, closing the door to let him marinate in his own panic until he absolutely had to get out of the car.

I turned back and walked a little closer to the house and took in the place where Charlie had grown up.

The house was average in size and everything else for that matter. Average and pleasing to the eye but not winning any prizes for inventive style. It was painted a bright white that contrasted blindingly against the steel grey sky. The house was surrounded by plants, lovingly tended and flourishing with early spring buds. The front door, which sat inside a UPVC porch, was painted a bright red and a mud-speckled Land Rover sat a little further up the gravel drive near a detached garage. The door to the garage was open and soft classical music floated out into the air.

'Eoin!' Carrick bellowed, the sudden volume of it making me jump. 'Oh, beloved brother! I've some guests for yer.'

The music quietened and a moment later, a stout man, who looked much older than Carrick, stepped out of the garage, wiping his hands with an oil-darkened rag.

He looked over for a moment, pausing as if he wanted nothing more than to stay hidden in his man cave, before reluctantly walking towards us with a look of consternation.

'Nell,' Carrick said when Eoin was close enough for me to see the cornflower blue eyes of the Stone boys and the almost black hair, grey at the temples. 'This is my brother Eoin. Eoin, this is Nell, Charlie's friend from England.'

He observed me for a few daunting moments, before extending his grease-blackened hand to me. 'Welcome, Nell. How was the flight?'

'Good. Thank you. It's nice to meet you,' I said timidly.

'Ah, you too, you too.' He sighed through his nose and went back to wiping his hands. I flexed my fingers against my palm, feeling the oily residue that he'd transferred to me during our shake. Eoin glanced over at the car for a millisecond before looking down at the rag in his hands and shouting in a voice that made me jump again. 'Out yer get, Boyo. Let yer father see what it is yer look like these days.'

The tension in the air was palpable as the car door eventually and tentatively opened. It took a good twenty seconds longer for a sheepish-looking Charlie to step out, keeping his eyes firmly glued to the ground. 'Bring yerself over here,' Eoin said, quieter this time. 'My eyes aren't what they used to be.'

I turned back to Eoin and waited, tension building even more, for the crunch of gravel to stop. Charlie came to a halt

212

beside me and I found myself unable to look at anyone, so I looked down at my feet instead.

'You've got skinny,' Eoin said.

'You haven't,' Charlie retorted.

'Yeah, well. With the way yer mother feeds me up, you'd think she was tryin' to do me in. Does she know you're here?'

'No,' Carrick answered after an uncharacteristically long silence. 'We haven't provoked that particular viper yet.'

Eoin inhaled worriedly and stepped away from his son and towards the house. 'Well, there's no time like the present.'

Ava Stone, Charlie's mother, had a friendly, motherly vibe around her that made me, at first, think that everything the others had been saying about her was hyperbole. But it didn't take long before I realised that my first impression of her was nothing but her lulling me into a false sense of security. She was a little shorter than me, with slender, delicate features that lured you into thinking that she was a gentle soul. Her eyes were darkest brown, verging on black that almost perfectly matched the thick, wiry hair that fell down to her shoulder blades. She wore clothing that was soft in both colour and texture. A slightly fluffy baby blue cardigan, with only the top button done up, the rest of it hanging open over her cream jersey dress that hung down to below her knees, the rounded collar neatly pulled out from under the cardigan and folded into place over a string of pearls.

She'd greeted me with a reserved and slightly judgemental air about her and every time she'd looked at me since, it had been clear that she was studying me like I was a rat in a cage. At any second I expected her to pull out a clipboard and start scribbling down notes. She brought a repressed feeling of terror out of the recesses of my brain, feelings long forgotten of frightening teachers and authoritative bosses. I don't think I was getting the best introduction to her, or her husband, Eoin. The air hung thick with a tension aimed at Charlie and I was simply caught in the crossfire.

We sat in the garden with Ava talking nonstop about the flowers that surrounded the central patch of grass, uttering words that I didn't hear often like 'deciduous' and 'perennial'. I had hoped that it might start raining and we'd have to go in, but the steely sky held on to its raindrops, eager to hear more about how she'd recently started using green tea leaves in the soil. After almost an hour of her barely taking a breath and nattering on about nothing of great import, I was ready for a good half hour shut in a darkened room. She didn't ask any questions about me or why I was there, what my life was like back home, or if I was, in fact, living 'in sin' with her not so darling boy. In fact, she barely acknowledged me after my initial greeting, only to ask if I'd like a cup of tea.

The clock had barely stuck midday by the time we'd been ushered in through the front door and all sat down around the large mahogany table that was so highly polished that I could see the dated brass light fitting with its frosted glass shade reflected in the surface.

Stepping into this house had felt like stepping back in time. It was a house you'd expect more of a grandparent than a parent, with a crucifix or some other piece of religious paraphernalia in every single room (even the downstairs toilet), the heating whacked up to Australian outback levels of unbearableness and little porcelain knick-knacks scattered about the place that ranged from poor taste to downright terrifying. A china Bo-Peep-esque woman peered at me from

214

the tiny black pinpricks she had for eyes, her crook raised above her head and three or four sheep around her feet, which looked like they'd been designed by someone who had never seen a sheep in their life.

The house was quiet, to unnerving levels, as Ava walked around the table with an ancient-looking ceramic pot cradled in her arm like a medieval serving wench. Beside Carrick was an empty seat, not unusual around a table for six when there are only five people, but what I found curious was how Ava had set the table for six. Had she been expecting someone else to show? Was it a sign of respect, setting a place for Abi? Or could she simply not stand the lack of symmetry of an unset place? Ava moved around behind Carrick, spooning a ladle of light brown stew into his bowl before moving around to Eoin, who sat at the head of the table. It was plain to see the Stone family resemblance, with the men who all had the same sculpted look to their faces, as if they were bronze busts brought to life.

It seemed baffling to me that Carrick and Eoin were brothers, regardless of the undeniable resemblance. Where Carrick was comically over the top and flamboyant, Eoin was subdued and stoic. Charlie hadn't said much to me about their upbringing, but from what I could see, their experiences had been very different. Eoin sat, expressionless, rigid-backed and joyless, while Carrick sat there, grinning at nothing, his bright turquoise scarf dangling dangerously close to the surface of his stew as he drummed on the edge of the table with his fingers. It struck me that Eoin had been the one to get the clip around the ear, whereas Carrick hadn't had nearly enough. But then, wasn't that often the way with the oft-spoiled younger sibling? I knew nothing about it personally, but to me it always seemed that the youngest could always get away with murder.

I'd been fighting the urge to talk for going on twenty minutes now, since we'd moved inside and the conversations about border flowers had come to an end. My mouth wasn't used to this. Where there was a silence, I was there to fill it. But the tension in the air that came with unsaid words and unsettled scores was striking me mute and, on top of that, I'd never been around anyone who so much as said 'bless you' when I sneezed, let alone staunch Irish Catholics, and so I was afraid that I'd somehow blaspheme and make a tense afternoon even worse.

Ava reached me and gave me a sweet, if somewhat insincere, smile. 'Looks to me like yer need feedin' up a bit,' she said as she dished out a portion of stew, which slopped into my bowl with a thud. 'Have a wee bit'o bread with it.' She nodded towards a bowl of bread in the centre of the table and I obeyed without pause. She moved on to Charlie who sat beside me, his body becoming more rigid the closer his mother got to him. She served his food silently then took her seat, at the opposite end of the table to her husband.

'Smells great, so it does,' Carrick said, fidgeting with the corner of his napkin, his accent seeming thicker now that he was back amongst the family. 'Ava makes a grand stew,' he added, I think for my benefit, and he took some bread for himself. I took this as an invitation to start so I picked up my spoon and plunged it into the bowl.

Ava cleared her throat and I felt the warmth of Charlie's hand land on my knee. He squeezed my leg tightly in warning and I looked up to see Ava smiling, although it could be mistaken for a grimace.

'Would yer like to lead us in sayin' grace, Nell?' Ava asked, her dark eyes narrowing with relish at my first slip-up. I lowered my spoon to the table, remembering too late that it was covered in gravy and smearing it all over the table.

I mumbled an apology as Carrick gracelessly stood, flicked his scarf over his shoulder, picked up his own fabric serviette and mopped up my mess. 'Let me get that for yer.' I thanked him with my eyes.

'Oh, I err, I don't really know ho—' I began. Why did I suddenly feel like I was back in school, being picked on to give an impromptu answer to a question I hadn't been paying attention to.

'I'll do it,' Charlie butted in, saving me from my embarrassment. He cast me an apologetic sideways glance before bowing his head and clasping his hands together. Everyone around the table followed suit and I played along.

Charlie cleared his throat before speaking and then said the words that I knew he didn't believe. 'Bless us, O Lord, and these, Thy gifts, which we are about to receive from Thy bounty. Through Christ, our Lord. Amen.'

The Colemans, the few of us that there were, had never been a family that pretended to be anything other than what we were. My uncle had been gay; my mother was a workaholic and a feminist. I'd taken a while to discover who I was, but when I'd found out, I'd been accepted for it. Even Joel and his family invited everyone in without question and so this was a new experience for me, to see someone pretending. It felt wrong to me that Charlie should have to put on this show for his parents, who must know the actual truth that he didn't hold much stock in the faith he'd been brought up in, but then I guess every family has its own ways.

The word 'Amen' echoed around the table. I mouthed the words but didn't say them out loud. This wasn't my faith; it felt wrong for me to join in. Everyone crossed themselves, except me and the sound of spoons being picked up made me feel safe in going back to mine.

'So,' Ava began, turning her eyes to me and sparking a firework show of anxiety that crackled in my chest, 'how did you two meet?'

Shit! I hadn't had the forethought to come up with a story. We hadn't corroborated facts or agreed on a convincing lie. I was certain that the Stones weren't a family who would openly discuss their mental health, let alone the fact that I'd gotten to know their son when he called a mental health support line, on the night he planned to kill himself. I purposefully spooned an extra-large spoonful of stew into my mouth and apologised with my eyes as I chewed, under the pretext of not wanting to speak with my mouth full.

'Nell and I met at a café. We got to talking and have been friends ever since,' Charlie came in to the rescue.

'Is that so?' She smiled but her eyes remained wide and judgemental. This woman was the queen of passive-aggressive facial expressions. 'It's so nice for yer to offer your ... friendship. But I'm sure a girl as pretty as you doesn't lack for ... friends.'

Charlie cast a warning look her way and squeezed my knee once more, his hand remaining there comfortingly.

The jibe didn't go unnoticed by me either and I inhaled a steadying breath. It would seem that it was okay to call someone a harlot at the dinner table in this house, as long as it was done on the sly.

I sent a forced smile back her way.

'What is it that a girl like you does for a livin'?' she asked.

A stuffiness came over my ears, like when you get water trapped in there after swimming, and just like that, there she was again. Abi leaned against the wall, wearing the same outfit I'd seen in the photograph of her crammed into a drawer, plastic headband veil and all. *It's nice to see that I'm not the only one that woman can make squirm,* she said, her arms crossed over her chest.

Great! That was all I needed now, a figment of my imagination making this conversation even harder than it already was.

'Nell?' Ava said. 'What's your profession?'

'Sorry,' I apologised and tried to ignore Abi as best I could.

I contemplated replying to her question about my career by saying that I was a woman of the night or that I was head rune priestess in a satanic cult, but the intention to enrage the beast was only fleeting.

'I work at a mental health support line,' I said confidently and by the look on her face, rune priestess would have been a more favourable option.

Oh, she'll love that. Abi chuckled cruelly.

'Is that so?' She tilted her head and leaned in over her dinner. 'Well, that can't be an enjoyable job, but I guess that someone has to do it.'

'Actually, I love my job. I find it rewarding to help people work through things that are causing them distress. We help people who are in financial difficulties, emotional distress, people with mental health issues and people contemplating suicide.' I cleared my throat, seeing Charlie flinch at my last couple of words.

Ava drew a sharp intake of breath and crossed herself. She

scoffed and shook her head. 'Well, the Lord must have blessed yer with the patience of a saint to have to talk to those people without judgement. No doubt a lot of them are drug addicts, homeless.' She tutted and shook her head. 'The idea of wasting the Lord's gift of life is . . . well it's inexcusable.'

I felt anger begin to unfurl in my chest and Charlie shifted uncomfortably. 'So, Mammy, how's Siobhan doin?' he said, trying to change the topic. But I wasn't having any of it. One of my bugbears was unempathetic people and Ava had riled me in just the right way to warrant a response.

'Some of them are addicts or recovering addicts, yes, but we don't judge them at all,' I replied, Charlie's question evaporating as if it had never been uttered. 'There are so many causes for mental illness – physical, environmental and psychological. We don't see these people as wasteful or inexcusable. We see them as people who've experienced things that we haven't, whom we can help and reassure.' I said all of this with a taut smile, although my eyes stared into hers with a strength that I hadn't felt in a long time. 'We even work with a few local churches for those who find comfort in their faith.'

It was clear that Ava Stone was used to dominating everyone in a room, but I wasn't frightened of Ava Stone, nor would I let her think for a moment that I was.

Jesus, you've got some brass knackers, ain't yer? Abi sounded a little impressed, before the pressure in my ears lessened and Abi disappeared back to wherever the hell she kept coming from.

'Siobhan, Ma,' Charlie said with a little more force. 'How is she?'

Ava's eyes lingered on mine for a few moments longer. I

could see the battle waging in her head between not wanting to appear like she was trying to provoke an argument and not wanting to be the first to look away. In the end she turned her eyes to her son and answered his question. I caught sight of Carrick in my peripheral vision as I turned back to my stew, his lips pressed tightly together to stop himself from smiling.

I had wondered why Charlie was so dismissive when it came to talking about his family, but now I knew exactly why he hadn't been home in so long. Charlie wasn't judgemental or spiteful in the way he talked, neither did he veil it behind a pretence of piety. I had nothing against people who found comfort in religion – each to their own. But the inability to see anything from another's point of view and judging them for it? I had a problem with that. How had Charlie managed to come out of this family so cleanly, so open-minded?

I guessed that Charlie's kind manner was down to the influence of someone else, someone who'd taken him away from his parents and shown him the greater world. Carrick would surely have had something to do with it, but there was one other person who must have shaped him into who he was today and *she* was the reason why we were all here.

The sound of the front door opening caused everyone to stop eating and look around as purposeful footsteps grew louder. I glanced towards the empty place, set next to Carrick, and wondered if this might be the guest who hadn't shown. I saw Charlie stiffen from the corner of my eye, his spoon clinking down against his bowl and almost disappearing completely under the surface of his stew. When the woman finally appeared at the threshold of the room and stood in the doorway, I heard myself breathe a quiet gasp. For a few

221

terrifying moments, I thought that it was Abi, standing there with a face like thunder. But the longer I looked at her and her film-star-perfect face, her mass of russet corkscrew curls that dwarfed her in size, I realised that this must be Abi's sister, Kenna.

She scanned the room, eyes seething, as each of us stared with quiet fear. She was tiny. Almost a foot smaller than I was and yet, she commanded the room like a giant. Her eyes travelled over each of us, lingering on me for a few seconds more than was comfortable, before moving on to Charlie. I guessed that Charlie had been who she was looking for, because the moment she saw him, she calmly pushed off with her tiny, child-sized feet and made her way to his side.

Charlie, by this point, looked like a baby rabbit when faced with the snarly, saliva-moistened jaws of a fox, his chest rising and falling quickly with rapid breaths.

She came to a stop facing Charlie side on, her back to Ava who reached up an affectionate hand and patted Kenna's shoulder.

'Hi, Ken,' Charlie said, his voice fragile and afraid. 'How've yer bee—' His sentence was cut short by the dainty palm that was brought with surprising speed and strength across his cheek. The sound of it sang around the room, like the final ring of a bell, the connection of palm to face so exquisitely placed that I had no doubt it would leave a mark.

Kenna sighed, looked up at me, smiled and extended a hand across Charlie as if he wasn't there.

'Kenna Murphy, nice t'meet yer.'

'You too,' I said, fearfully shaking her hand. 'Name is Nell. My! My name is Nell.'

Kenna smiled genuinely and then walked around to the

222

empty space, spooning herself some stew before sitting down, her incredible amount of hair moving a moment or two after she did, as if it was a separate entity that travelled around with her. She brought her hands together in front of her, said grace unceremoniously, and brought a large spoonful to her mouth.

'Mmmm, great stew,' she mumbled through her still-full mouth.

I turned to look at Charlie, who remained frozen, his eyes staring forward at Kenna as if she might leap across the table and assault him again at a moment's notice.

'So,' she said in a cheerful voice, as if nothing at all had happened, 'how's everyone been?'

Chapter Nineteen

Siting in Ava Stone's garden, in what passed for the early afternoon sun in Westport, I held my phone in my hand, dew seeping into the fabric of my leggings.

During the lunch that had proved to be one of the least comfortable of my whole life, I'd felt my phone buzz from where I'd pushed it between my skin and my waistband. I'd waited until everyone had finished their stew and Charlie had stopped telling tall tales about the current state of his life to duck outside and read it. Charlie had failed to tell them that he'd quit his job, but then, they hadn't ever known he'd taken a job at Aldi in the first place, and so there was little point. As far as they knew, Charlie was still working in the theatres of Birmingham, his career and his life, still completely on track. I took comfort in the fact that I wasn't the only one here who knew that he was lying. Carrick had seen what state Abi's death had left him in and yet we'd let Charlie have his tall tales, his fabricated life of work fulfilment and contentment that couldn't be further from the truth of what he actually had.

I looked down at the screen of my phone as the sound of Kenna's angry Irish tones drifted across the garden from where she was 'talking' with Charlie, her arms folded neatly across her generous chest, which looked rather too round to be natural, but I didn't want to be one to make sweeping statements. The text that had come through was from Joel, a sequel to the text I'd got yesterday but had ignored. It had simply read:

So, I guess that the ridiculously attractive guy at yours the other night means you're not interested in talking?

This text was just as to-the-point, short and less than sweet.

You can kid yourself that we're over, Nell. You can prance around with that guy and flaunt him in front of me cruelly, but you know as well as I do, that we are always going to come back to each other. We still love each other and we are meant to be together. xxx

Prance? Flaunt? As far as I could remember, I had done neither of those things. Yes, okay. Maybe I had been slightly cruel in leading him on, in making him think that this relationship was salvageable, but I hadn't been cruel about Charlie; I hadn't even been the one to open the door the night that Joel had shown up. Joel was wrong. We weren't meant to be together. We weren't always destined to return to each other and I did not still love him, not in the way he wanted me to. I flinched at my own thoughts. Something clicked inside my brain and suddenly I felt something like an iron band release around my chest. My lungs felt as if they could expand further, the air entering them, cleaner. I did not love Joel anymore and this wasn't just me being positive and vocalising my wishes. I really, truly, categorically, most certainly did not love him.

I pressed the little phone icon at the top of our chat, wincing at one of my not so subtle booty call texts that I could see, half hidden at the top of the screen as if it too was embarrassed by my past actions. Three rings and then there was a rustling as he manoeuvred the phone to his ear.

'Nell.' He sounded painfully enthusiastic. 'I'm so glad you called. You got my text? I knew you'd come around.'

'Joel.' I stopped him before he said anything else that would shortly come back to bite him in the ass. 'Yes, I got your text, but I'm not calling for the reason you think I am.'

'Oh, are you all right? Did something happen?' His tone was markedly more downtrodden.

'Yes, I'm fine.' Not completely true but not a lie either. 'I'm in Ireland actually.'

I could almost hear the angry repositioning of the phone against his ear to check that he'd heard that correctly. 'Ireland? Wha— erm, what are you doing there?'

'I've come over to meet Charlie's parents.' I left out the part about Abi's memorial.

He exhaled loudly, shakily. 'Moving a bit fast, isn't it?'

'Look, Joel,' I said. 'I'm calling because . . . well, because what we've been doing for the past six months is wrong and stupid and something that we should have known would only end painfully for the both of us.'

'That's not how I saw it. I saw it as us trying again to fix something that we both know is best for us.' I heard his purposeful pacing through the phoneline. He always paced when he got angry.

226

'I'm so very sorry for my part in keeping open the wound that we should have let heal a long time ago, but I'm doing now what I should have done when all of this started and saying no.'

'Nell, think about this for a minute.'

'No,' I said, pressure building behind my eyes.

'You know what's going to happen with this Charlie person, don't you? Men like that are all the same.'

'Men like what?' I spat.

'The good-looking, charming, cocky sort, that's who. He'll be all over you while you're new and interesting. It'll even make him feel good about himself, make him feel more wholesome because you're grounded and funny and normal. But as soon as things calm down, he'll realise that he's bored with you and go straight back to dating hot girls. Ones who eat nothing but kale and wear suspenders for him.'

I physically flinched at his words and held a hand to my chest. My mind was whipped back to something that had happened in our third year as a couple. We were still sleeping together at this point but things had become a little stale. He'd brought me some sexy underwear for my birthday and asked me to try it on for him. I'd stood there in the bedroom, looking at myself in the mirror and feeling ridiculous, cheap. I knew it was empowering for some women to dress this way, but not for me. I felt like I was being forced to become the porn star that every millennial boy grew up thinking girls were.

I took it straight off again and instead, walked out there in my normal underwear. He'd thrown a fit, yelling at me about how expensive it had been and how I didn't really love him because I wouldn't wear what he'd bought. That, I think now, was the beginning of the end. But I stayed for so long after that. Why had I wasted all of that time?

'Well, at least Charlie can bring himself to touch me. He can hold a conversation about something that isn't self-serving and he even cares about how I feel. I didn't even know men could be like him. But then I don't have much experience with *men*, do I?'

He heaved a sigh and a growl escaped the back of his throat. 'You know what? You're tired, Nell. No doubt you got stressed during the flight and it's left you confused. We'll talk when you're back.'

I opened my mouth to say that I would rather rip off all of my toenails, right here on this immaculately mown grass, than ever see his face again, but the line went dead. A few tears escaped my eyes and trickled down my cheeks as I tossed my phone onto the lawn and held my face in my hands.

You tell each other, while you're in a relationship, that you're best friends. That even if you should ever split up, you'll still talk. But is that even possible when the ego is so easily bruised? It is funny how the smallest change in your relationship status can open doors to personality traits that you never knew existed within the person you thought you knew inside out. One moment, hating them seems about as likely as Dwayne Johnson becoming prima ballerina for The Royal Ballet and then suddenly, they're talking differently, acting like someone you never thought they would be and the only cause for this is a case of injured pride.

I heard the door to the house slam shut, the argument clearly over with now.

'Nell? What's wrong?' I heard Charlie's voice nearby and

228

the bitter, empty feeling inside me eased a little. I withdrew my hands from my face, wiping tears away as I did, and found him crouching on the grass in front of me.

'I spoke to Joel,' I replied, my voice a little more fragile than I wished it was.

'Was he a bastard?'

'He was.'

'What did he say?' he asked, his eyes narrowing with an anger I hadn't seen in him yet.

'Oh, nothing much. Just that you're going to get bored of me eventually and go back to the hot girls you're accustomed to. That I'm basically nothing without him and won't survive out here in the big world by myself.'

'Fecker,' he muttered under his breath. 'D'ya want me to hit him? Because I will, if it's what yer want. Or we could go together, each have a swing at him?'

I smiled and sadly chuckled through my words. 'No, I don't want you to hit him.' I quickly checked that there was no one around to see, raised my hand to his face and stroked my thumb gently over his cheek, which was still slightly red from his earlier assault by Kenna. 'Thank you for the offer though.'

His eyes softened as I dared to touch him for a moment longer before letting my hand drop back to my lap. He looked down and, with gentle fingers, lifted my hand back to his face. He leaned into my touch as sparks ricocheted around my chest. How was it that he had fixed my sadness so quickly?

Was it because I knew that Joel was wrong and this wasn't just a fleeting fancy? Was it because I knew that Charlie and me were so much more than that, much more than Joel and I had ever been?

Oh God how I wanted to pull him to me, to kiss him and feel that closeness that I'd longed to feel with him. But this was neither the time nor the place and so, after a few moments longer, I withdrew my hand again and pushed myself up to standing. Charlie followed suit and we slowly began meandering back towards the house.

'So, we heard how my argument went, how was yours?' I asked, nodding in the direction of where he and Kenna had been shouting a few minutes ago.

'Oh, fine. That's how Kenna and I communicate. We love each other really though.'

'It certainly looked like it,' I said sarcastically.

The back of Charlie's hand brushed mine, accidentally on purpose. 'She's a right to be mad at me. After what I did.'

'And what did you do?' I asked, stopping and turning to him. He stopped too, turned to me and pressed his lips together.

'I would tell yer, but it's a long story and right now, I need to introduce yer to Steve.'

More family, yay! I thought.

'Who is Steve?' I asked.

'Steve and I go way back.'

'Is he going to slap you too?'

'I most certainly hope not. We met when I was sixteen and became best friends, although life moved on and we became estranged . . . until today that is.' He turned with a sly smile on his lips and walked towards the drive. I followed on, jogging to keep up. 'He was in a pretty terrible state when we met, but Dad helped me get him back on his feet,' he said as we descended a small set of stone steps beside the house and reached the gravel drive. Charlie walked a little further on and disappeared inside the garage that Eoin had emerged from a few hours earlier. 'Well, when I say feet, I mean tyres really.'

He held his arms aloft and presented to me: Steve.

'Steve's a motorbike?' I asked, somewhat relieved that I didn't have to meet more people with bottled-up anger to throw Charlie's way.

'He's not just a motorbike, Nell. He's a Triumph TR6 Trophy, which I know is a hilariously problematic thing for an Irish person to say, but all great love affairs have obstacles.'

'Why Steve?' I asked.

'This is the same model of bike used in the chase scenes in *The Great Escape*.'

'Ah, Steve McQueen. Gotcha.'

'Very good.' He grinned. I didn't know if it was just wishful thinking, but I felt like I could see a change in him already. It was slight, but noticeable. Coming back here, where Abi and he fell in love, must have been terrifyingly daunting. But being here and seeing that not everyone had let their lives fall apart due to their grief seemed to be reassuring him that life could get better.

'So, the ferry to Clare leaves at three thirty. I wondered if you'd like to travel on Steve with me?' he asked with a boyish grin.

'Clare? Ferry? Huh?' I asked, completely confused. 'Just so I'm clear, is Clare a person or another form of transport?'

'Neither. Clare's an island. It's not far, only about three miles off the coast. We're staying with one of Carrick's friends there. So, you happy to travel by bike? Carrick'll take the bags.'

'Seems safer than travelling with Carrick.' I shrugged, Charlie meeting my words with a chuckle.

'So, why are we staying on an island and not here? Isn't Carrick's place nearby?' I asked as Charlie took two helmets from the wall and dusted off a decade of cobwebs.

'Carrick thought it would be a good idea. Abi never went over to the island and so he thought it might be a trigger-free atmosphere to keep fragile little Charlie in while we wait for the memorial.'

'That was thoughtful of him.'

'Don't go thinking too highly of him,' Charlie said, placing both of the helmets on the shining leather seat. 'It's just an excuse to go and see Orlagh – she owns the hotel on the island.'

I raised my eyebrows.

He nodded. 'It's a long story.'

I looked at him as if to say, I've got all day, and he began telling me the tale.

'So, when we drove into town, did yer see the convenience store called Cornerstone?'

I shook my head. 'No, I was too busy looking at the boobs-in-a-bath hills,' I replied.

'Understandable. Well, my family owns that shop and a few more across the county. Carrick began taking the business over from my grandparents and the first summer he worked there, he met Orlagh McCarthy who'd just got a job to save up some money before she went to college. He was, what, twenty-eight at this point, making me about sixteen. I remember takin' the piss outta him relentlessly about how she was ten years younger and he was a cradle snatcher and all. But they loved each other, no denyin' that. They had three months together, before it ended.'

'What happened?' I asked, yet again pulled into one of the romantic sagas of the Stone men.

232

'She went off to uni and he stayed here. Cut to three years later and Orlagh comes back home with a degree and no idea what to do with it. Carrick gave her job back to her while she sorted things out and within six months they were engaged and married.'

'Carrick's married?' I blurted, shocked that he'd managed to find someone to put up with him.

'Was married. Past tense. Orlagh wanted children and Carrick didn't. So, in the end, even though they really did love each other, they got divorced. Ironic really.'

'Why is that ironic?'

'Ah, yer a bright girl, Nelly. I'm sure you'll understand when we get there. She married again about ten years ago. He's nice. Thick, but nice.'

'But that's so sad,' I protested. 'They love each other still?'

'Ah, that they do.'

'Don't you lot have any stories that end happily?'

'I'll let you know when I get to the end of this one,' he said, looking up at me with eyes that made my chest tighten. 'We'd better get to goin' if we're gonna make the ferry on time. Do you think we can just run away or should we go back and say goodbye?' he asked.

'I think that it'll be safer for you to say goodbye, if the slapping is anything to go by.'

He nodded reluctantly and we made our way back inside.

The wind whipped my hair against my face, my arms wrapped around Charlie's torso, as we travelled through the Irish countryside. Hills and trees and expanses of water lay all around us as we zoomed towards where a ferry waited to take us to Clare Island. But no matter how far we travelled, the spectral ghost of Croagh Patrick loomed over us. It was beautiful here, what I'd always expected Ireland to look like, but I could never have imagined the circumstances that would lead me here.

I pulled my arms a little tighter around him and felt the vibration of a contented laugh reverberate through his chest.

Right now, there was no Joel, no Abi, no sadness. There was just me and him, zooming through the landscape on a motorbike called Steve.

Chapter Twenty

'It's a lighthouse,' I said my mouth curled into an excited grin. 'An actual lighthouse, on a cliff, on an island.'

'That it is,' Carrick replied as we stood next to the taxi out front. 'And if yer think the hotel's beautiful, wait until you see the owner.' Carrick hadn't been able to bring his orange death mobile over on the ferry. We'd been able to bring Steve however, but only because Carrick used to go to school with the ferry owner.

I pulled my bag from the boot of the cab and felt a hand on my lower back as Charlie returned from making sure that Steve was safe beneath an awning.

'You ready to spot the irony?' Charlie whispered into my ear as Carrick made his way towards the door and rang the bell.

'I'll keep my eyes peeled,' I whispered back.

'Oh, there'll be no need for that.'

We followed Carrick and arrived at the door just in time for it to open and an elfin-faced woman with golden blonde hair, pinned back to reveal sharp cheekbones, popped her face through the gap.

'Carrick!' Her mouth drew wide and her palest grey eyes lit up as she threw her slender arms around his neck and pulled him towards her.

'Orlagh.' He sighed her name into her neck.

I felt a little awkward standing there in this intimate moment that wasn't mine.

'It's been too long,' she said, her eyes closed, her fingers gripping the back of his jacket as if she was afraid this was a dream and at any moment he might slip away.

Charlie and I stood, awkwardly, while the hug lasted far longer than was socially acceptable and I took great interest in a small rock several inches from the toe of my shoe.

Eventually, they parted and the woman turned to us.

'Orlagh, this is Nell, Charlie's . . . friend.' Carrick motioned to me and then to Charlie. 'And yer already know this eejit.'

'Nice to see you again, Charlie, and welcome, Nell. I've put you up in the room with the best view. Don't want to waste it on these cretins.' She wrinkled her nose as she smiled, took my bag from my hand and walked into the hallway.

'Oh, I can carry that,' I said, not wanting to make a fuss as I followed her inside to a wide, airy hallway.

'Ah, it's no bother,' she said, waving a hand over her shoulder. 'I'm stronger than I look.'

Good, I thought, because her thin, wiry limbs made her look as if a strong breeze might knock her down.

We walked through a sitting room. The warm yellow light coming from the tall standard lamps filled the room with a happy glow that made me feel instantly at home.

'The other room is taken by guests, so just be aware that they'll be around,' she said, speaking mostly to Carrick.

There came a scuffling sound from nearby and, seemingly from nowhere, a swift shadow moved from one of the sofas, a book slipping from the cushion in its wake and toppling onto the maroon high-pile rug. A moment later, I felt a rush of stirring air against my shins as something zoomed past and crashed into Carrick's legs. He made a loud, feigned sound of agony and whisked the shadow up into his arms. Now that he was still, and not moving at a thousand miles an hour, it was clear to see that the shadow was a small boy. Only six or seven.

'Who is this?' Carrick asked, holding the child aloft and looking over every inch of him.

'It's me, Uncle Rick.' The little boy tittered.

'No, it can't possibly be you, you're far too big.'

'Mammy makes me kale for dinner sometimes. Says it'll make me strong like Popeye.'

'Kale? Well, firstly, yer mammy needs to get her references right because that would be spinach, not kale. And secondly, let me just get child services on the phone right now, because that is nothin' but child abuse.' He pulled the child back into his arms and gave him a firm, affection-filled squeeze.

'Nope, I agree,' Charlie said, coming to Carrick's side and ruffling the child's golden hair. 'Can't possibly be young Darlow.'

'It's me, Charlie.' The little boy giggled again and I found myself smiling with him.

Charlie glanced my way and there was something in his eyes that suggested that I should have noticed something, although I didn't know what.

237

Carrick placed the little boy down and took him by the shoulders, turning him around to face me. 'Darlow, this is Nell. Say hello.'

I let out a quiet gasp, unnoticed, at least I hoped so, by the rest of them as I stared into his eyes.

The little boy turned to me with a bashful smile. 'Hello, Nell,' he said in a high, bashful voice.

'Good lad.' Carrick patted him on the shoulder.

'Nice to meet you, Darlow,' I said, holding out my hand. Darlow looked at my extended fingers, blushed beetroot red and then turned his face into Carrick's leg, his chubby arms wrapping around Carrick's skinny thigh.

'Yer so predictable. Clammin' up the second yer see a pretty girl,' Carrick jested and scooped the boy up into the air, tossing him over his shoulder in a fit of giggles. 'Yer can't disrespect a lady by not shakin' her hand. Orlagh, would yer get the door please? We'll have t'toss him in the sea.'

Darlow began squealing and laughing, his legs kicking as Carrick held him in a fireman's lift. 'Sorry, lad, there's nothin' else for it.'

As the three of them played in a din of pure happiness, I wandered over to Charlie's side and whispered, 'I see what you mean about irony.'

Carrick and Orlagh had divorced because Carrick hadn't wanted children and Orlagh had. She'd married again, this time with a man who wanted the same things as she did and she'd given birth to a child. I looked again at the little boy, now back down on the floor and running around with wide, happy eyes. Blue eyes. Stone eyes.

* * *

The steel grey sky seemed to stretch out for eternity as I sat on a patch of dry grass, looking out at the ocean, which seemed as endless as the sky. Charlie sat beside me, his legs outstretched, his arms propping him up against the relentless wind that made my skin feel beaten and tired.

A couple of thousand miles away, in a straight line across that vast, endless sea, was Canada, the States, South America. Places I had always wanted to go, but hadn't yet. The good thing about having my semi-hermit lifestyle with Ned was that it didn't cost much and so I had the money to go and do things like that. But who would I go with? Ned would come with me, but he'd already done it all before. I'd always felt that there's something sad about doing things with people who've already seen it all. A sense of irrational FOMO that leaves you feeling sadder and more left out than anything else.

Joel had never wanted to leave the sofa that had moulded around his backside, Mum was always too busy to go any further than a short trip and I wasn't confident enough to go on my own. I'd be a quivering wreck by the time I found myself in a bustling metropolis like New York City. I wasn't exactly a yokel but I feared that suburban Birmingham hadn't quite given me the street smarts I needed to not end up meeting a sticky end in some downtown alley.

I turned from the view to Charlie, who was staring out to sea with a stern sense of worry that I hadn't seen in him before. I wondered if Charlie had done any of the things that I wanted to do. Scuba diving in crystal oceans, hiking through national parks, seeing landmarks only ever viewed on TV and which I had never quite accepted as real, simply because I had never seen them through anything other than a screen. Would he be my partner on these adventures, or would they just be replays of ones he'd already had with her?

I pulled my phone from my pocket and checked the time. We had an hour before we said we'd be back to help with dinner, but tearing myself away from this view was going to be hard. We'd taken Steve for a drive, taking in the island on a whistle-stop tour and coming to rest at what had once been a Napoleonic signal tower on the cliffs, where we had sat and failed to move from since. The tower was now nothing more than a historic pile of stones, holding its structure for only a number of feet before crumbling to a jagged top edge.

'Where's her husband?' I said, loudly enough to be heard over the wind.

Charlie turned away from the view, his eyes a little vacant. 'Donal works in Dublin so he's not here for big chunks of time.'

'Does he know, that Darlow is Carrick's?'

'He's never said so to anyone. It's hard to not know when the proof is literally staring right at yer.' He sighed. 'Add to that the fact that the name Darlow literally means "secret love" and it's pretty much the most obvious secret in the world.'

'Why doesn't she leave him and go back to Carrick?' I asked.

'Because she'd lose the lighthouse if she did and because Carrick is a difficult person to love and Donal isn't.'

'Is Donal nice at least?' I asked.

'Ah, he's nice enough. Doesn't deserve to have this goin' on behind his back, that's for sure.'

'Yeah, that hug at the door made it pretty clear that Carrick wouldn't be taking up a guest bed tonight.'

'I know, right. I've told them to be careful. One day Darlow's gonna come out with somethin' and drop 'em right in it. But I guess that if I was in their shoes and that was the only way to have the person I loved, I'd probably be doin' the same thing.'

I felt that gnawing, unpleasant feeling in my stomach again, the one that I'd not been able to pinpoint before.

Green-eyed monster gettin' yer down? Poor Nelly. I heard Abi's voice from somewhere behind me but I didn't react, didn't even flinch, because I knew she'd be coming. Every time I saw her was whenever this feeling began unfolding in my gut, this deep irrational jealousy and feeling of inferiority, all sparked by the woman he had loved, still loved, and all of the things they'd done together that we never would. He probably had memories with her in every corner of his hometown and mine for that matter. Every bench had, at one time, probably been witness to a tender kiss or a late-night fight on the way home from an evening out. Every person in this town knew Charlie as Abi's Charlie, not Nell's, and it would probably stay that way forever.

It's not his fault. Abi's voice came again, closer this time, so loud it sounded as though her lips were pressed to my ear. *I'm pretty hard to forget.*

I swallowed hard and pushed myself up to standing.

'We should probably get going if we're gonna help with dinner.'

He looked back out to the view, sighed and stood up. 'Right yer are.'

As we walked back towards Steve, I thought about asking

him how he was feeling about tomorrow, but I didn't. Tomorrow was the day for mourning, the day he'd been dreading for the last two years, and I didn't need to help bring that pain on a day early.

Back at the lighthouse, we found Carrick rolling pastry while Orlagh fried something delicious on the stove. She quickly set us to work whipping cream and cutting strawberries for the Victoria sponge she'd made.

'The other guests should be back soon. They went out to see the abbey,' she said as she filled the pastry-coated pie dish with whatever was in the pan. My mouth watered with the smell of it.

'There's an abbey here?' I asked Charlie, and I saw him flinch a little at my question. It wasn't until I'd spoken it that I realised that it was the homonym causing the discomfort.

'Yeah, just a wee one,' Carrick replied. 'You remember the pirate queen I told yer about on the way into town?'

I nodded.

'She's buried there and her castle's down by the dock. Charlie can show it to yer before we leave tomorrow.'

The sound of voices in the hallway made us all turn and Orlagh transformed from flirting chef to charming hostess. She wiped her hands on a green and white checked tea towel and moved to the doorway where they shared a muffled greeting and when she returned, she brought the two of them in with her. A woman stepped in behind her. She beamed across at Carrick, her brown hair blown wild by the wind.

'This is my dear friend Carrick, his nephew—'

'Charlie,' she said and suddenly, the stranger was rushing forward and flinging her arms around him.

Charlie reciprocated the hug rigidly and tapped her shoulder awkwardly, the knife he'd been using to chop strawberries still in his hand, until she pulled away. 'How the devil are you?'

'I'm okay. It's been a long time,' he said in a voice that wasn't his. 'Are you here for the memorial?'

She nodded and looked from Charlie to me, confusion on her face.

'Sorry, how rude am I? Who is this?' she asked.

'Nell,' Charlie said.

'Hi, Nell. I'm Una.'

Una, where had I heard that name before? And was that the slightest hint of a Brummie accent I detected? 'Were you a friend of Abi's too?'

'No, she didn't know her,' Charlie said before I had chance to. I'd have been annoyed that he wasn't letting me speak, if I didn't know that it was because he was trying not to say something else. I'd had verbal diarrhoea enough times to know when someone was trying to hold it back. 'Are the girls here?'

She rolled her eyes and grinned from ear to ear. 'They're with my parents,' she said, her pinched lips hinting that there was more to this. 'We thought we'd get away while we still can.' Her hand dropped to her belly.

'Your . . . again?' he asked.

She nodded. 'Twins again, can you believe it?'

'I can't,' Charlie said with vacant eyes.

'Oh,' Una responded unsurely before turning back to Charlie. 'Jamie's gonna be so excited to see you.' She looked over her shoulder and shouted, 'Jamie! Look who's here!'

Jamie, why did I know these names? Why did I know . . .

243

As Jamie stepped through the door, I remembered where I knew them from. Jamie, Charlie's ex-friend who'd forced him out that night and Una, the wife who'd been betrayed against the wall of a nightclub smoking area.

I saw Charlie bristle, his hands fidgeting around the knife in his hand, the blade still stained watery red. I hoped that that shade wouldn't be getting darker in the next few seconds.

Jamie was tall, broad and you could tell that he was ripped just from the way his shirt hung over his body. Beneath his clothes he probably looked like Chris Pratt, only a gross, unfaithful, lecherous, detestable version. His hair was blond and slicked back, although the wind had done its best to cast it into disarray, and he came in wearing a smug smile, as if he was feeding from Charlie's obvious discomfort.

'We tried to contact you a few times, but it seemed like you'd dropped off the map. You're skinny,' Una said, looking him up and down, as Jamie came to her side, slotted his arm around her shoulders and kissed the top of her head.

'It's been a while.' Jamie extended his hand to Charlie and for one horribly tense moment, I thought that Charlie was going to turn away. But he didn't and I exhaled a relieved breath as they shook hands, Jamie's fingers brushing the hairline scars across Charlie's knuckles that had been made on the same night that was the cause of all this awkwardness. Did Una know? Had he confessed and were they working through it? Or was the girl at the club one of many who would never be spoken of?

'Doesn't seem like that long to me,' Charlie said, his eyes holding Jamie's gaze in a look of abject disgust.

'Well, we should probably get changed out of these muddy boots,' Una said, trying to break the tension.

'Dinner won't be long now,' Orlagh chimed in.

'Excellent,' Una said, taking Jamie's hand and leading him back towards the door.

'Good seeing you, Charlie.' Jamie narrowed his eyes. 'We missed you last year and the one before that.' He sent Charlie a grin and then he was gone.

I reached over and took the knife from Charlie's shaking, angry fingers, placing it on the worktop and taking Charlie by the hands.

'Come on, let's get some air,' I said and led him towards what I presumed was the back door.

As far as I could see by the tattered love stories of everyone around the table, love and life were often incompatible things – Darlow excluded, although I'm sure he'd have a story to add to our list of doomed love affairs in around fourteen years. Love was the Disney film of emotions. It was the tender kisses and the sunset dances, the fade to black after happily ever after. But there was no such thing as happily ever after; there was only happily ever now or happily ever then. Love cannot last forever. It's slain by poor decisions, lack of compatibility, selfishness, greed and, eventually, death.

With Joel, love had been fleeting and all-consuming, but looking back now, something had always felt ever so slightly wrong. A canker that grew and grew until the love was overcome by it, gradually turning it to hate.

Abi may have died, but Charlie still loved her, as did Carrick and Kenna and countless other people in the town we'd left behind on a motorbike named Steve. But when Charlie died, so would his love. Which begged the question: is there any point in loving? Yes, it makes you feel good at the time, it gives your day purpose and allows you someone to moan to when you return home from work after a bad day, but eventually that love is going to cause someone pain, if it hasn't already. Even the greatest love has hurt someone. Everyone goes on about the love of Romeo and Juliet, but what about Paris? Does anyone spare a thought for him, cast aside and forgotten in a heartbeat as soon as another floated Juliet's boat?

I knew that Charlie felt something for me, but what was it? And even if it was love, how would it compare to the love he felt for Abi? Would he forever find the love he felt for me lacking in some way, unable to put his finger on the reason why his heart never leapt as high, why his palms never grew to the same levels of clamminess as when he'd been holding her hand?

Charlie raised a forkful of piecrust to his mouth and ate it as Carrick regaled us with a story of when he and Orlagh had been married. How could it be that I was jealous of Abi? Someone who I'd never met and never would. Someone who was no threat to me, because she was literally dead and buried. But death did silly things to people's minds. Even the angriest little shite of a person in the whole world could die and still there would be someone who came out with the phrase you hear at every funeral. 'He was someone who touched many lives and who will be missed by all who knew him.'

No, he wasn't. He was a rodent with small-man syndrome who instilled pure hatred in anyone who knew him. But he died and so now he is put on the pedestal that only death can award.

I'm not saying that Abi was a horrible person. I'd never met her so I couldn't possibly know, but her death had canonised her, raised her up to godly standards that I could never dream of reaching while alive.

Chapter Twenty-One

Sometime after dinner, I found myself sitting on the ledge of the actual lighthouse part of the hotel with Charlie, sipping on whisky and listening to the waves crashing somewhere in the distance. I glanced down at the drop below and my stomach lurched when I wasn't able to see the shadow-blackened ground. I looked down at my feet dangling through the railings and felt a sense of pride inside me at the small victory, even if the lack of solid ground beneath my feet did make me feel a little sick.

'Twins!' Charlie exclaimed, his voice thick with quiet rage. 'Two sets of them.'

'I know, but who needs that many children really?' I sighed in reply. 'As soon as they're born he's going to be living in a constant state of sleep deprival and be perpetually covered in some form of bodily fluid. Is that really what you want from your life?' Charlie swigged from the bottle of bourbon that he'd grabbed on the way out of the kitchen and promised to replace before Donal got back.

'Well, no. Maybe not four children, all under the age of five, all in one sticky, snot-covered go. But one would be nice.' The wind was less here than it had been on the cliffs, but it was still cold enough to leave goose bumps in its wake, strong enough to make its way through my clothes. 'All I'm saying is, what the feck am I doing wrong if a person like him is getting rewarded for being a complete prick?'

'You're not doing anything wrong. Life just isn't fair.'

'You're damn right it's not. He has Una, kids, a distressingly nice house and a sweet job and, what do I have? Feck all, that's what.'

That last comment smarted a little. *You have me,* I thought.

'What is it with you and towers?' I asked to get on to a different topic, my mouth burning from the whisky.

'I like being high up,' he replied. 'Like a cat, but not my cat because my cat sucks.'

'Hey,' I said. 'There is nothing wrong with Magnus. He's just a very good judge of character, that's all.'

'Ouch. You wound me, Nell Coleman.' I could feel him easing a little the further away the conversation got from Jamie.

'How are you feeling about tomorrow?' I asked.

'Tryin' not to think about it,' he said, swigging from the bottle again and passing it to me. The glass was warm from his hand. 'Scared shitless of seein' Siobhan. Think she might try'n flay me on the spot.'

'Don't worry, you'll have Carrick and me to protect you,' I said, although I wasn't half as confident as I sounded.

'Ha! I think yer mean you and only you. Carrick won't want to get blood on his pretty green suit.'

I chuckled and took a swig from the neck of the bottle.

'Why would Siobhan want to flay you anyway?'

He paused before answering while I took another swig and passed the bottle back to him.

'When it happened, I completely shut down. I didn't call anyone and tell them, I just lay on the sofa and spent all of my energy tryin' to continue breathin'. Then, one day, the coroner rang and asked what plans we had for the body.' Charlie shook his head, as if trying to shake off the memory. 'I couldn't talk about it, couldn't even think about Abi being referred to as "the body" so I gave him Siobhan's number and told him that she'd be dealin' with the funeral arrangements and gettin' Abi back to Ireland.' He held a hand to his temple and shook his head. 'The first thing that woman knew about her daughter being dead was a coroner calling, two weeks after it'd happened, asking her where he should send the body of Abigale Murphy.'

'Wow.' I was trying to keep my opinions on the matter from showing up on my face. 'So, that's why they're all so mad at you?'

He nodded. 'That and the fact that I didn't come to the funeral or the memorial mass the year after. They think it's because I couldn't be bothered to make the trip, but that's not it at all.'

'It's because, if you did any of those things, it would force you to admit to yourself that she was really gone and that there was nothing you could do about it?'

He nodded. 'And that's exactly what I'll have to do tomorrow.'

His voice gave way at the end, a shuddering breath that

dislodged sudden tears that ran down his face, collecting in his stubble and sitting there like dewdrops on blades of grass. He pursed his lips and blew a calming breath between them.

'What happened the first time you went to the clock tower?' I asked.

He glanced at me, his face blanched by the sterile moonlight shining from the almost full moon. He took a deep, trembling breath and looked back to the dark view. 'Life just suddenly became so much harder than it'd been before. Breathin' became a conscious thought, not something that happened in the background. I would have panic attacks if I was in the house for too long and I couldn't bring myself to even look at the bed, let alone sleep in it. I couldn't stand the thought of staying with friends because then I'd have to tell them what had happened, so I spent a few nights sleeping on benches around town. This one time, a man brought me a sandwich and put a tenner under the bench while I slept. I found a homeless person when I woke up and gave him the food and the money.'

He took a deep breath to power his next sentence, rolled his neck and continued. 'About a month after she died, I made a decision. I left the spare key where Mrs Finney would find it and put a note through her door, telling her that I was going to be away for a while and asking if she could look after the cat while I was gone. I wrote a letter to my family and put it on the coffee table and I made my way to the clock tower. I sat up on that ledge for four hours, until I was so cold that I felt as if I was frozen to the spot. I don't think I wanted to be dead, I just wanted it all to stop. I didn't want to wake up every morning and have that split second where I didn't remember what had happened, before reality would click and I'd remember that she was gone and that I could have done something to stop it.'

'You can't blame yourself for her death, Charlie. There's no telling that you could have saved her even if you had checked her earlier.' I wanted to reach out and hold his hand, but I didn't know if that was something that he'd want me to do right now. So, I just laid my hand on my knee, ready for him to take hold of if he wanted to.

'But I did blame myself; I do blame myself,' he said, more tears rolling down his cheeks. 'So, there I was standing on the ledge of the clock tower, my heart thunderin' in my ears. I was completely terrified and after a second, I fell back onto the wall, pulled myself over and curled into a ball on the floor in front of the clock face and cried like a little bitch for God knows how long.'

'Crying doesn't make you a little bitch, Charlie,' I chastised him for his man-up attitude. 'Why would you have evolved tear ducts if you weren't meant to use them?'

He took a breath and carried on. 'I saw the sticker on the wall, called and got through to Ned. We spoke for over an hour and he told me that I should call my uncle.'

I felt a hot rush of panic in my chest at the thought of him there, so close to the edge, so close to never setting foot in my life.

'Why wait so long between then and the second time?' I asked, trying not to let the panic run away with itself. It had been so very recently that Charlie had been back there, that he'd been prepared to jump for a second time, the feelings inside him no less than the first.

He cleared his throat as a few more tears gathered in that thick line of dark lashes around his eyes. 'I did what Ned said and called Carrick. I told him about what I'd thought about doing. He came straight over and spent a month livin' in the flat with me on suicide watch. He took the sofa and I had a fold-out IKEA futon on the floor. I forbade him from ever tellin' my parents about what I'd thought about doin', on pain of death, and he said that he promised he wouldn't, if I gave him a year of trying and so I did. Then at the end of that year he asked me to give him one more. He said, take it one hour, one day, one year at a time until breathing get easier. So, I made a sort of routine that helped me keep my promise to Carrick. After the first year I found that, even though it didn't feel possible at the beginning, I'd survived a whole three hundred and sixty-five and a quarter days without her. So, I agreed to another year and I found that, if it didn't hurt too much, if it wasn't unbearable, then I could stick around.'

'What changed then, between it being bearable and the night you called me?' I asked.

He leaned forward a little, looking at the drop to the courtyard below. It wasn't as high as the clock tower, but it still made my stomach lurch.

'It was something so small that it sounds stupid to say it out loud.' He swallowed hard and looked my way. 'I was at work, Aldi, restockin' the naan breads, when someone I'd worked on a few shows with came over and said hi. We'd been good mates back in the day, even gone out to dinner a few times with Abi and his wife June. He was working on *Shrek The Musical* and had a gig lined up on *Cats* after that. He tells me this while I'm standin' there next to a basket of iced buns that need half-price stickers slappin' on them. Then he asks me how Abi is and for some reason I tell him that she's fine and that I'll call soon and the four of us can go out to dinner like we used to.

'After work, I went home and something was different. Everythin' seemed bleak because my career was toes-up and I'd just agreed to a dinner date that could never happen because Abi was dead. I felt like I'd gone back a thousand steps and suddenly, breathing wasn't so easy again.

'I guess I felt kind of at peace with it all, the second time around. I'd given Carrick the time he'd asked for, so I put everythin' in place again. Quit my job, sorted out the cat, bought myself a bottle of whisky, that I'd always wanted to try but never been able to justify the price of, and then went to the clock tower. On the way, I felt my nerve slippin' so I went to get a cuppa tea and have a sit-down for a minute or two.' He turned to look at me, his eyes glistening with tears filled with moonlight. 'Then I met you.' Finally, his hand fell into mine and my fingers wasted no time in wrapping around his. 'But, of course, my brain couldn't let me be happy, could it?' He scoffed. 'I started feeling guilty that not even two full years had passed and, there I was, flirting with someone in a café.'

'Moving on isn't something you need to feel guilty about,' I replied. 'At some point or other, you're going to have to let yourself be happy again. I know it must be incredibly hard, but you can't mourn forever.'

He squeezed my hand a little harder and blinked the last of the tears from his eyes.

'You're probably right. But it sure does feel like I could.'

The sound of the waves crashed on the cliffs somewhere in the dark below us and a question popped into my mind.

'What was it?' I asked. 'What changed your mind that day we met in the café?'

'Your happiness,' he said simply. 'It burst right outta yer.'

'I don't feel like it's bursting out of me right now.'

'But it is. Yer can't help it. Yes, your job is tough sometimes and Joel is an A-grade gobshite, but you still, almost always, have a smile on your face. When you sat next to me in the café, yer made me feel it, some of your happiness, like just bein' close to yer made me, like, absorb some of it.' He lifted his hand to my face, his fingers resting on my jaw while his thumb traced the outline of my lips. 'I hadn't felt happiness in so long that when I finally did feel it, it shocked me. I felt it, even though it didn't belong to me, and I thought that, if I'm still capable of feeling it, the next time it happens, perhaps the happiness might be my own.'

Chapter Twenty-Two

I'd woken with a foggy, heavy head the morning after with little memory of where I was. The ferry left at eight and so I'd peeled myself away from the covers and collected up my things.

I'd found Charlie at the breakfast table pushing corn-flakes around in the milk with the end of his spoon. I'd greeted him with a forced cheerfulness that I was far from experiencing with my blossoming headache and the general sense of ennui that filled the room. But today was about being there for Charlie, about making it as painless as possible. He'd looked up, but hadn't met my eye, made a noise deep down in his throat and turned back to his bowl.

Darlow and Orlagh accompanied us down to the docks and waved us off, after a reluctant goodbye from Carrick. It was clear from the way he lingered beside them and his uncharacteristic subduedness when they faded from view, that there was nowhere in the world he would rather be than there with the woman he loved and the son he could never truly be a father to.

I'd tried to make conversation on the way over to the mainland, but it was clear that no one wanted to talk. Charlie and I were hungover from the whisky we'd shared atop the lighthouse and the dread of the day to come was stealing the words from everyone's lips.

I'd been almost relieved when we'd reached the mainland and climbed aboard Steve, relieving the pressure to fill the void with some hastily thought-up words. We zoomed down the winding roads back towards Westport and Carrick's house. The whole time I kept my arms wrapped around Charlie, happy for the excuse to do so and trying not to worry about the day ahead.

The door to the room burst open as I ungracefully snapped the press studs of my body suit together. I yelped and spun around to find Carrick standing at the doorway, looking at me with utter confusion on his face.

I quickly removed my hands from my groin, smoothed my dress down over it and cleared my throat awkwardly.

'I'm not even gonna ask what the hell yer were just doin',' he said and shook the thought from his head. 'Yer ready?' He opened the door a little more, the light from the window behind me revealing Carrick's newly acquired suit.

'Oh my . . . wow,' I said, squinting as my eyes adjusted to the assault on the corneas that was Carrick. The three-piece chartreuse suit was dazzlingly bright and coupled with a magenta shirt and a pair of turquoise-framed sunglasses, presumably so he didn't blind himself whilst wearing it all.

'Ah, Nell. Yer a vision,' he said, wandering in with his arms aloft.

'Carrick, you wouldn't happen to have a cardigan that could pass for acceptable, would you? It's just . . . this,' I said, turning around and pointing to my tattoo.

'Nell, come on.' He placed a hand on either of my shoulders and held me at arm's length. 'D'yer really think anyone's gonna be lookin' at yer with me beside yer?'

'Good point,' I said. His hands fell and I turned back to the mirror, looking at the delicate bun I'd pulled my hair up into. I sucked my teeth as I thought it over, before pulling out the elastic and fluffing my long hair around my shoulders and, more importantly, over the tattoo. That would have to do.

I grabbed my phone, pushed it down into my bra and followed Carrick out of the room. 'Go check on Charlie, will yer?' he said, a little more carefully than usual. 'I think he might need a gentle voice in his ear.'

I nodded. Today I was Charlie's personal cheerleader, his confidence booster, his shoulder to cry on or anything else he needed me to be. I knocked three times, paused a moment and pushed the door open. He was sitting on the end of the bed in his black suit. His elbows were braced on his knees, his hands out in front of him as his fingers fiddled with the piece of orange sea glass that I knew meant so much to him. 'Hey,' I said, walking into the too-quiet room and crossing to the bed. 'You ready?'

He didn't look up but I could see the slightly shiny remnants of hastily wiped away tears around his eyes.

'I think so,' he replied. He pushed the sea glass into his

258

breast pocket and looked up at me with pink-rimmed eyes. 'Wow. Yer look so pretty.'

I tucked my hair behind my ear and grinned down at my shoes, which I saw now were speckled with gravel dust from outside the crematorium at the last funeral I'd been to. Whose had that been? My uncle's? Or maybe that first cousin once removed whom I couldn't even remember the name of now.

'I'm glad you're here,' he said. 'I couldn't have done this without yer.'

'I'll be with you every step,' I said, leaning in and kissing him gently on the cheek. 'Oh!' I blurted a little too loudly. 'I almost forgot. Stay right there.' I held up a finger and dashed back to my room. I rifled through my bag until I found what I was looking for, hid it behind my back and returned to Charlie's room.

'Now I thought you might need a little extra emotional support today and it just so happens that your weekend of custody falls today, so . . .' I pulled my hand around to the front and held George the bobblehead zombie out to him.

His face cracked into a reluctant smile as he took George and flicked his head, the spring inside vibrating as his head wobbled from side to side.

'Now, as you know, he's lactose intolerant so don't give him ice cream, no matter what he tells you, and he should be in bed by nine. I'll have no zombie son of mine being a dirty stop-out.'

'D'yer doubt my parenting skills?' He chuckled, slipping George into his pocket, his smile fading to something less jovial. 'Just whatever you do today, please don't let me cry too much. Don't want to embarrass meself.'

I shook my head. 'Charlie, if you want to cry, you bloody well cry. I won't be stopping you,' I said, brushing the shoulders of his jacket with my hands, not because they needed dusting or anything, just that it was something I'd seen people do in films and it felt like the right time to do it. 'Shall we do this?'

Chapter Twenty-Three

St Mary's church was located on the mall in the middle of the town, with a river running down the centre of the road. Across the river were several flower-lined bridges, humming with lazy cars that idled along the roads as if time didn't exist. The church itself was a slightly ominous-looking stone building with a large rose window of stained glass that sat, pride of place, in the centre. From here, I couldn't see the colours or even make out the pattern, the dark interior of the church not letting it live up to the beauty it was made for.

Ava had arrived at the door of Carrick's house not long after I'd gifted George to Charlie. She'd been in a tizzy, worrying that we wouldn't be there in time to greet the first person that showed. They'd offered us a ride, but after seeing Carrick's suit they'd seemed more than happy to arrive separately to us. Charlie hadn't spoken since we left the house, not that Carrick's verbal stream of consciousness gave him the opportunity to, as we walked the short journey to town.

I didn't know if he was talking so much because he wanted to take everyone's mind off everything or if he was nervous or if, like me, he sometimes just found that there were too many words that needed saying.

We were walking for about three minutes before my arms started turning numb from the cold, but Carrick quickly whipped off his turquoise scarf and placed it around my shoulders. I pulled it tight around my arms, the cashmere silky against my goose-bumped skin.

We lingered outside the church doors, Charlie kicking nervously at stones and wandering over to the river and back as if trying to run up his step count for the day. Carrick stood out like a chav at Ascot, sitting there on the steps like an impatient child, his suit no doubt visible from the end of the street. Ava and Eoin had got there before us, but were standing far enough away that it wasn't immediately obvious that we were a group, lest they be associated with me and the chartreuse wonder behind me.

It wasn't long until the steps were teeming with people, their eyes shiftily searching for the elusive Charlie as he dithered on the spot beside me, wringing his hands as the time for the inevitable drew closer. Agnes and Roisin arrived, this time wearing matching black headscarves instead of rain bonnets and they nodded me a greeting. Una and Jamie were nowhere to be seen yet and I wondered if Jamie had had second thoughts about letting his wife anywhere near the man who had the information to ruin his marriage.

'Ah feck,' I heard Charlie mutter under his breath and I followed his eyes to the two approaching figures. One of the two women was Kenna, her halo of hair so recognisable even from a distance, and the other, I guessed, was the one

Charlie had been dreading to come face to face with. His whole body tensed and he spun on the ball of his foot.

'I can't,' he said, his head bowed, his forehead almost on my shoulder.

'You can,' I replied firmly without taking my eyes off the women. 'This is why we're here.' Everyone turned and watched as Kenna used the pavement as a catwalk. Her six-inch, platform heels brought her up to regular human height and accentuated every muscle that lay behind the flawless milk-white skin of her legs. Her dress was skin-tight and came down to just below her knees, before flicking out like one of those mermaid dresses that normal people have trouble walking in, but not Kenna. It was cinched in at the ludicrously tiny waist and had short batwing sleeves that made her look like all she needed to do was don a black wig and some heavy eyeliner and she'd be set to take up the role of Morticia Addams. Her hair was, once again, huge, her curls looking an even brighter orange than yesterday and coiffed to a height that Dolly Parton herself would have been proud of. I am sure that Kenna was used to diverting the gaze of everyone she passed. In fact, she was so distracting that as she made her way to Ava and Eoin, I completely forgot about the other woman until she was standing in front of me.

'Well, don't yer look lovely. Are yer a friend of Abigale's?' the woman, who could be no one other than Siobhan, asked.

The genes among the Murphy women seemed to be just as strong as the ones shared among the Stone men, with her white-streaked, deep red hair, which had dulled with age but still had the spark of the vibrancy it once held. Her

263

brown eyes and freckle-dappled nose were the mirror of her daughter's.

'Erm, no, I didn't know her. I'm Nell,' I said, my voice shaky.

'Siobhan, nice to meet yer,' she said, shaking my hand. It was clear to see from the intense depth of pain in her eyes that the welcomes and courteous smiles were all a show. On the inside, this woman was hollowed out.

I heard Charlie's feet scuffle against the ground, as if he was about to make a run for it, but there was nowhere for him to go. I was pinning him in on one side, Carrick the second and Siobhan the third. His only other option was to run straight into the stone wall of the church and probably knock himself out in the process, which I wouldn't put past him right now. Charlie needed to talk to Siobhan. There was no way he could avoid it and so I swallowed hard and bit the proverbial bullet. 'I'm one of Charlie's friends. Isn't that right, Charlie?' I said, turning to Charlie and forcing him into the conversation. I could hear the fearful breaths whistling in and out of his nose as he looked at Siobhan with childlike fear.

There was a moment where everyone held their breaths. I saw Ava, from across the expanse of the church's stone steps, glancing over wide-eyed as she ignored whatever Kenna was saying. It was almost unbearable, waiting for something to happen as the seconds ticked by at agonisingly slow speed.

'Siobhan,' Charlie said in a hitching voice that sounded nothing like his own. 'It's good t'see yer.'

After what seemed like minutes of silent staring, I was ready for her to do anything, scream, slap him, full-on murder, just anything that would relieve this tension.

But they just stared at each other, blue eyes on brown.

Siobhan broke the silence by exhaling loudly, her shaky breath whistling through her nose as she raised her hand into the air. Slap him it is, I thought, and I braced myself to see Charlie assaulted a second time. But to my surprise, her hand rose only to his shoulder where she placed it down gently and she drew her shaking bottom lip into her mouth.

'Yer took your time comin' back to see me,' she said, her voice betraying her outward strength.

Charlie shook his head, the first of the tears shed today filling his eyes, and he murmured the words: 'I'm sorry.'

'Now, now. There'll be none of that.' She attempted a smile. 'I'm just glad yer finally made it.'

Without another word, Charlie fell into her arms like an exhausted child. She cupped a reassuring hand, thin-fingered and running with dark veins, on the back of his head. I could see Charlie's shoulders shuddering and knew that he was sobbing, something he'd wanted more than anything to avoid doing. Tears began to roll down Siobhan's face too, her eyes so used to it by now that she looked rather at peace with it all. I guess that, really, Siobhan and Charlie were the only two people, other than Kenna, who could even come close to understanding each other's grief.

It was a long moment before Charlie stepped back and I noted the embarrassed look on Eoin's face as his son wiped away his tears.

'Get yerself together now, lad. I'll have no more tears from either of us. Understand?' Siobhan said firmly, sniffling and righting his hair with her bony hand. 'Now, this girl here,' she said nodding in my direction but keeping her eyes locked to Charlie's. My heart leapt. 'This yer girlfriend?' she asked bluntly and I looked around nervously at people's reactions.

'Erm, I don't . . . We haven't . . . erm . . .' He turned to me for help but found me as flailing as he was. 'I don't know,' he said.

Siobhan smiled understandingly and turned to me with an outstretched hand. I placed mine in hers, because I was frightened of what would happen if I didn't, and she squeezed my fingers with a strength I hadn't expected. 'Well, aren't yer lovely.' I didn't know if I was supposed to answer or what I'd say if I did. 'You'll have to bring her when yer come back to see me again.' She smiled sadly, lifting one of her hands from mine and taking Charlie's, like we were children being led to the supermarket.

'Now come on,' she said, walking us both up the stone steps. 'We need to get a good seat up the front and what in the name of the sweet baby Jesus are yer wearin', Carrick Stone?'

Inside, the church was all tall ceilings and polished columns. From inside, the rose window that had looked dull from outside, burst into segments of reds, blues and yellows. Filled with so much more life this side than from the other. I guessed that was the same with most things really. The way you look at it makes all the difference. More stained glass lined the walls in hues of purple and blue and the altar stood proudly up at the front, ornate and glistening in gold and reds.

It felt odd, sitting in the front pew. I hadn't known Abi and I suspected that she was turning in her grave even having me in the same building that was about to honour her memory, but Charlie wanted me there and I wouldn't be the world's most dedicated counsellor if I turned tail and ran like I wanted to. Charlie sat with me on one side and Siobhan on the other, her hand in his throughout the service.

It was almost two by the time Charlie had finished making small talk with people he hadn't seen in years, accepting their condolences with gritted teeth. He gave Jamie a wide berth and talked with people as if he wasn't on the verge of tears again, as if what had just happened hadn't made him feel as if he was dying.

I made my way over to the river and leaned against the wall. The water burbled by slowly and the sound was a calming quiet after an hour of talking, prayer and music. *Enjoy that, did yer?*

Oh shit, not her again.

I opened my eyes and there she was, sitting on the wall, her long arms crossed over her chest and her eyes watching the dissipating crowd. 'Not in the way you're insinuating, no,' I replied quietly.

Well, my mother likes yer. Maybe yer can invite her to your wedding for old time's sake.

'Why are you so mean to me?' I asked.

Don't ask me, love, I'm the product of your brain.

'I don't want him to forget you or replace you and I think you know that.'

If you know it, then I do. I'm inside your brain, remember? She smiled and it held the slightest hint of affection.

'I just want him to be happy,' I said, closing my eyes and breathing in the fresh spring air.

I heard shuffling feet behind me and when I opened my eyes again, Abi was gone.

'Who yer talkin' to?' I turned, just in time to see Charlie join me at the flower-strewn wall.

'Oh, no one,' I replied. 'Just myself.' It wasn't a complete lie. 'So, what happens now?'

'They're all going to the Aughaval, but I thought we could walk back to Siobhan's and I could show yer a couple of places in town?'

'Aughaval?' I asked.

He nodded. 'It's the name of the graveyard.'

My brows knitted together in the middle. 'Oh, well in that case, don't you think you should go with them?'

He sighed and looked down at the water. 'I don't know if I can.'

I glanced behind me and made sure that no one was watching us before taking his hand and squeezing his fingers. 'Isn't this why we came? To get closure, to move on?'

'I have closure. It's not like I'm under any illusion that she's alive still, I just don't wanna see the patch of grass above her skeleton is all.'

'That's not what it is. It's her final resting place. It's the place she's going to be for the rest of time and I think you need to see that with your own two eyes. Yes, you saw her after it happened, but, Charlie, you were in shock then. Your brain probably still hasn't processed, I mean really processed, the fact that she isn't coming back and I think that's something you need to see before you can move on.'

He turned from the water and back to me. 'See, I know you're right, but I still don't think I can go.'

'Of course, yer can,' Carrick said as he appeared behind

268

us. 'Come on, yer can sit next to me in the limo. Hopefully it's one of those ones with champagne and disco lights.'

'Oh, yeah. I hear that they always rent the ones with stripper poles out for funerals.' Charlie rolled his eyes.

'Ah, that's good.' Carrick grinned. 'I've been meaning t'brush up on my technique. My fireman knee spin is in definite need of some work.'

We both stared at him for a moment, with scarring mental images playing out in our brains, before I turned back to Charlie, ignoring everything Carrick had just said.

'How about this: you go in the car with Carrick and, if when you get there you think you can, you get out and stand in the graveyard for a little while. And, you know, if that's not too bad then maybe you can walk over and see Abi's grave. How does that sound?'

He thought for a moment, his body ready to turn tail and run, but his head knowing that this was what we came here for. 'Okay,' he replied.

'She's smart,' Carrick said, linking arms with his nephew and tugging him gently in the direction of the car. 'Far too smart for yer.'

'Do yer wanna come too?' Charlie asked.

I shook my head. 'No, I think this is something that you can do without me.'

'What are yer gonna do then?' he asked, worried.

'She can come with me,' Kenna said, appearing behind Carrick and coming to stand beside me.

'I'm not goin' either. Can't stand it there.' She shuddered. 'Walk with me back to the house?'

'See,' I said to Charlie as Carrick struggled to get him towards the car. 'I'll be just fine.'

'Great.' Kenna grinned. 'Yer can help me put out the cocktail sausages.'

I turned to Charlie and shrugged. 'How can I turn down an offer like that?'

The thought of being alone with Kenna was far more terrifying than the reality of actually being alone with her.

'So, what d'yer do over there?' she asked as we wandered through town, over bridges and past brightly painted shops.

'I'm a counsellor, of sorts. I work for a mental health helpline.'

'Yer kiddin'? What a great job.'

'What about you?' I asked as we took a left up to a more residential part of the town.

'Oh, I do a bit of everythin'. I do some modellin' in Dublin and over in London – I gotta place with a couple of other girls that overlooks the Liffey.' Her accent was more genteel than Charlie's and soothing in a way that made me think she had missed her calling for recording audiobooks.

'Impressive,' I said, trying to not let the intimidation flare up again. 'Who do you model for?'

'Anyone who'll have me really.' She sighed. 'I do a lot of foot modelling. I have really nice feet. It's mostly shoe stuff, although it is my foot and lower leg on those blister plaster packets, the ones in the purple box.'

'Very impressive.' I glanced down at her peep-toed, monstrously high-heeled shoes. From what I could see of them, they were very good feet. Although, I didn't know what state they'd be in when we got back to the house, which seemed to be miles away. My shoes, although nowhere near as high-heeled as Kenna's, were higher than my poor arches were used to and that ache, fondly remembered from my late teen years of wearing shoes I had no hope of doing anything other than sitting down in, came back to my feet like an old friend that I'd hoped had cut ties with me.

'I did do some private modelling for a client. They just wanted pictures of my feet standing in things like cakes and custard.'

'What the hell did they want those for?'

'Sometimes it's best not to ask questions,' she answered and we both chuckled. 'So, you and Charlie, huh?' she asked after a short pause.

'Erm, I have no idea, to be honest,' I replied, not really knowing how to talk about this with her.

'Charlie Stone is about as good as they come. Sure, sometimes he's the world's biggest eejit, but he's a good person.'

I looked down at the toes of my shoes and smiled. 'What about you?' I asked, eager to change the subject. 'You must be fighting off men with foot fetishes left, right and centre.'

She laughed, swinging her arms casually by her sides. 'That may well be the case, but I'm not interested in them. Or men at all for that matter. I have a . . . companion in London – Naomi – but we're nothing serious.' She abruptly turned to her right and began walking up a driveway towards a large blue front door beneath a wisteria-draped awning porch. It reminded me of the colour of the door to Charlie's flat and I wondered if Abi had painted it that colour to remind her of home.

'I just want you to know,' I said as she slid her key into the door, turning around at the sound of my voice, 'that what's been happening between Charlie and me, it wasn't easy for him. It still isn't easy.'

She smiled at me with her crimson, Cupid's bow lips and soft brown eyes. 'This is Charlie Stone we're talkin' about. Nothin' with him is ever easy. Now come along, these tiny sausages aren't goin' to arrange themselves around some ketchup.'

Chapter Twenty-Four

I sat on a short set of stone steps and stared out into Siobhan's large garden and imagined the young versions of Abi and Charlie settling down on the grass after their first attempt at taming the wild beast that had once been this now expertly pruned garden. How could they know back then that they would make such an impact on each other's lives? I guess there's no confetti cannons or marching bands when the most important people unwittingly stroll into your life. I placed my half-empty glass of Prosecco down on the low stone wall beside me, and wondered how much longer Charlie and Carrick were going to be. I was starting to get anxious, but I kept telling myself that he needed to take his time with this.

Yer were in town and yer never even popped in to say hello.

I sighed into my palm and saw her, lounging nonchalantly on the steps beside me. Abi was shaking her head in forced disappointment.

'Are you actually here?' I asked, turning to look at her face on and seeing her as clearly as I saw the steps beneath her. 'Or am I having some sort of psychotic break?'

I'm sure I don't know what you're talkin' about.

'Yes, you do. You're inside my brain, as you like to remind me so often. So, tell me, am I really talking to you or am I going insane?'

She exhaled loudly through her nose and looked down the length of the garden. *Who knows? The only thing I'm sure of is that either way, people look at yer funny whenever yer talk to me.*

I heard a clattering of plates and turned towards the kitchen window where Siobhan and Kenna stood at the sink. Siobhan was crying, her face pressed into her daughter's shoulder, her body juddering as sobs racked her.

'Poor woman,' I whispered.

Always the mourner, never the corpse, Abi said sadly. *God knows she wishes we could swap places.*

'If she's back then that must mean that Charlie is too,' I said, my heart leaping a little as I stood. I took my Prosecco flute in hand and began scanning the crowd inside.

Tell my husband that I appreciate the effort, she called, making me stop and look back her way. She was staring down the garden now, her eyes half hooded with what looked like sadness. *He'll be able to let go of it someday and when he does, I'd like it to be with me.* I frowned her way and wondered what the hell she meant. She was inside my head, a manifestation of my prickling conscience; she wasn't meant to say things that I didn't understand.

I walked back into the house and nodded politely to the faces that sent me smiles and greetings, but none of those faces were Charlie's.

274

I walked into the kitchen where Siobhan and Kenna stood at the counter, having some alone time under the guise of making tea for the guests. 'Hi,' I said nervously. Siobhan turned to me with a sad smile and red-ringed eyes, her lower lashes still clumped together with tears. I opened my mouth to ask the questions that people ask at times like this like, 'are you okay?' and 'how did it go?' but those questions seemed silly right now. So instead I asked, 'Are Carrick and Charlie back too?'

'No, love. They decided to walk home. Takes the best part of an hour, so give 'em some time,' she said, her voice soft and wavering with bridled emotion. 'Tea?'

'No, thank you,' I said, holding up the glass of Prosecco.

'Let me get that for yer,' Kenna said, topping up the glass.

Almost an hour and a half passed by and I felt every single second of it like a knife twisting in my gut. I spent the time hovering by the window, drinking glass after nervously drunk glass of Prosecco and nibbling on cooled samosas and triangular ham sandwiches when I began to feel a little light-headed.

Hovering by the buffet table in the front window was a good place to keep watch for Charlie and Carrick's return, but the downside was that I kept being pulled into small talk with grey-haired, round-bellied men who returned to the table every twenty minutes or so to replenish their paper plates with more smoked salmon and miniature quiches. Why is it that all buffet tables smell the same? The miasma of slowly staling bread, margarine and cake frosting that come together to create the same scent, no matter if you're at a funeral or a fifth birthday party.

The fear that something had happened to Charlie, or rather

that Charlie had happened to Charlie, had begun around an hour ago, but I took solace in the knowledge that Carrick was with him.

I pulled my phone out of my bra and checked the screen again: no texts, no responses to the message I'd sent him. I cleared my throat in frustration and emptied what little was left in my glass. I wandered towards the kitchen, the front of my shoes pinching my toes more and more as time wore on. I was almost at the kitchen when I heard a familiar and overtly loud voice. I turned towards it and saw that Carrick was stood in the centre of the room with a slightly drunk look in his eyes and a group of people around him who all seemed to be laughing at something he'd said. I spotted Ava and Eoin over in the corner, looking embarrassed about the attention he was demanding from the whole room.

'You two took your time. Where's Charlie?'

'Dunno, I just got here,' he said.

'You haven't been with him?' I asked, my heart sinking down into my stomach.

'At the graveyard yes, then we walked back to town and went to Matt Malloy's. We had a pint of the black stuff and then I got chattin' to someone. He said he'd be back here.'

'Well he isn't.'

'Ah, he'll be about,' he said flippantly, although I could see a hint of panic in his eyes that hadn't been there a moment before.

'Carrick, you know where I met him. You know what he's planned to do before.' I kept my voice low as pricked ears tried to listen in, especially Ava and Eoin's.

'I know. But he wouldn't do anythin', not today.' He

sounded as if he was trying to convince himself with his own words.

'What, on the day he visits Abi's grave for the first time? On the day he finally has to face up to everything he's been running from? Really, Carrick, of all days, would today not be the one you'd choose?'

'Come on,' he said, placing his drink down and taking my wrist in his hand as he marched towards the door. 'We've only been apart about thirty . . .' he checked the clock on the wall '. . . thirty-five minutes.'

'That's a pretty good head start.'

I placed my empty glass down on a sideboard in the hall and walked out into the front garden. I instantly started thinking of high-up places that I'd seen on my walk through the town. But I didn't know the place well enough.

I raised my palm to my forehead. The skin there was hot to the touch, warmed by fear.

'Where would he go?' I asked, stabbing my thumb into the screen of my phone and dialling Charlie's number. Carrick arrived on the path beside me with his phone in hand too.

'No idea. D'yer know yer way back here if we split up?'

'No,' I said as the call went to voicemail. 'But I have Google maps.' I opened the app, set my current location as home and turned expectantly back to Carrick. 'Where should I go?'

'Erm, you take that way,' he said pointing behind me, 'and I'll go this way. Call me if you find him.'

'Okay, you too,' I replied, before taking off at a run, or as much of a run as I could manage in these shoes.

I tried my best not to panic as I jogged through the streets of a town I didn't know, but the thought of him disappearing off the face of the earth, of him not being around anymore, brought hot, wet tears to my eyes. The sky was swollen with dark, storm-grey clouds and I knew that, before long, it would be sending its wrath down on to me.

I dialled Charlie's number for the ten thousandth time and held it to my ear. Voicemail again. I groaned and began tapping out a text.

Charlie, please let me know you're okay. Just one word will do.

I sent it and waited, watching the screen for little typing bubbles to appear, but nothing came.

I stopped for a moment, my head feeling light with Prosecco and fear. I leant against a wall; my fingers white with the amount of pressure falling on them. I tried to summon Abi with my brain, to ask her where he would have gone, but she didn't appear and I wondered why I seemed to be losing control of my own imaginary friend.

The plinking sound of my xylophone ringtone tinkled out of my phone and into my ears.

My heart leapt as I brought the phone up to my face, almost clocking myself on the nose, and saw Charlie's name on the screen. I answered and held it to my ear.

'Charlie! Thank God, where are you?'

'Nell, have you found him yet?' My heart sank as Carrick's voice came down the line.

I felt tears of false hope roll down my cheeks.

'No. Where did you find his phone?' I asked.

'On the table in the pub. He must'a left it. I'll carry on lookin'.' The line went dead and I felt my knees give way. I sank to a crouch and rested my forehead against the wall in an effort to try and calm myself. I had never felt this level of fear before, this all-encompassing dread. Everything was at stake here, everything. There was a rumbling above me. The sky began to turn dark as if it was reflecting my own tumult back at me.

I twisted on the toes of my shoes and collapsed back against the wall. I opened my phone again and did what I always did when I needed help.

'Nell?' Ned's voice came through the phone.

'Ned,' I blubbered. 'I need your help.' A fat, cold raindrop fell from the sky and landed with a splat on my knee and in seconds it was pouring.

'What's wrong?' His voice took on a worried, fatherly tone and I could hear him stand up in preparation for a classic Ned session of pacing.

'We can't find him – Charlie. He's gone and his phone isn't with him and I'm just really frightened that he's . . . that he's done something.'

'Okay, Nell. Calm down. The mind tends to jump to the worst-case scenario at times like this, but just because you can't find him, doesn't mean that he's . . . well that he's . . .'

'Dead?' I asked, my vision now completely useless for all the tears and rain obstructing it.

'Where are you now?'

'I don't know?' I looked around. At the end of the road I could see the buildings fall away and the open space of the bay open up. 'Me and Carrick split up to look for him.'

'Okay, well you're in no fit state to be alone right now. Get yourself back to Carrick and make sure you stay with him.' My clothes were already soaked, but the fear was keeping me warm.

'But I need to find him,' I said, pushing myself back up to standing and walking to the end of the street.

'I know and you will, but right now I'm worried about *you*.' Something in the sky gave way and all of the rain fell at once.

I pushed myself up and began running to the end of the street looking for shelter against this unrelenting rain. The moody grey clouds were staining the bay's waters the same angry colour. I scanned the scene in front of me, my eyes coming to rest on a line of benches looking out at the water. All were empty, except one.

'Oh my God,' I said into the phone, my feet frozen to the ground. 'I found him.'

'Is he okay, Nell?'

I didn't answer, didn't even hang up. I just ran.

I weaved my way between parked cars and moving ones, my eyes filled with raindrops and tears that made the whole world swim in front of me. Hard pavement gave way to sodden grass as I made my way to him, my heels sinking into the mud.

'Charlie!' I called to the stationary figure sat upright on the bench, but my voice barely crested above the din of the rain. 'Charlie!'

As I neared the bench, I slowed down, my heart thudding away inside me like it was preparing to be irrevocably broken. Why was he so still, sitting in the downpour like this?

I edged around and his face finally came into view.

'Charlie?'

His hand on his knee, the orange sea glass pinched between his fingers, he looked up at me with deep red eyes that held a look of surprise.

'What are yer doin'?' he asked, his voice dreamlike as if still half stuck in whatever thought he was just consumed by. 'You'll freeze to death.' He stood and walked over to me. I saw him slip the orange glass back into his pocket and I thought of Abi's last words to me.

Tell him that he'll be able to let go of it someday and when he does, I'd like it to be with me. Had the sea glass been what she'd meant? And how could she possibly have said that when I didn't even know that he'd taken it with him with the intent of putting it on her grave?

His hands reached up and took my shoulders but I slapped them away.

'What the fuck are you doing, Charlie?'

'What did I do?'

'Leaving your phone places and disappearing, when I know that you've almost thrown yourself off a building, twice!' I found myself almost screaming above the splattering of rain upon the ground. The water of the bay around us boiled like mercury, the rain bringing with it a new chill that sank down deep into my bones.

'I'm sorry. I just couldn't go to the house yet. I needed more time,' he replied. I could hear how sorry he was from the tone of his voice, but I was still filled with angry panic and the only way of getting rid of it was shouting.

'Well I need to know that you're not crumpled on a pavement or full of pills in an alleyway somewhere! You know that I love you! You can't do shit like this to me.' The words tumbled out of me with little co-operation from my brain.

I pressed my eyes closed to get rid of some of the rain and before I could open them again, I was being pulled into his arms. I found myself instantly folding into him, fitting to his form and savouring everything that I had thought lost only a minute earlier. The firmness of him, the strength of his arms that curled me into him, the large scarred and calloused hands that stroked my hair in an attempt to stop me from shaking.

'I'm sorry,' he said quietly into my rain-pooled ear. 'I'm sorry.'

'Please, please don't go,' I said as more tears blended in with the rain. I selfishly wanted him to carry on existing because I wanted him, every piece and part of him, even the broken ones. But I wanted him to live for himself too, to not feel this crushing pain every day; to want to become part of the human race again. I wanted him to want his life.

Chapter Twenty-Five

I called Carrick, who sounded rather teary on the other end when I told him that I'd found Charlie and that he was very much alive and unharmed, although soaked to the bone. I'd found six missed calls from Ned on my phone when I'd gone back to it. I sent him a text and told him that I'd call him when I was capable of forming complete sentences again, in the meantime reassuring him that both Charlie and I were okay.

We walked back to the house in a state of emotional and weather-beaten shock. My body had never felt levels of panic quite like it before and even though it had begun to dissipate, it still lingered in my muscles, aching and tingling, hesitant to leave in case it had to spring back at a moment's notice. I let Charlie lead the way, as I had neither the sense of direction nor the mental capabilities to get us back there, and as the tall house came into view with its white wisteria trailing over the porch, I felt Charlie stiffen beside me. We stood there, looking up at the house that held so many memories for him and I waited, the rain now no more than sheets of moisture, dusting my face.

There were years of memories here, in this house, in this town. Every corner of it was probably plastered with moments shared with Abigale Murphy and I felt like a terrible person for being jealous of that. I wanted moments and memories of my own and hopefully, in time, they would come. But for now, I had to watch as he relived every one of those memories with Abi. There was no rushing, no time limit on grieving and Charlie was about the only person on this planet whom I could imagine being that patient for.

'You ready?' I asked, thinking about taking his hand, but holding my own instead.

'No,' he replied and took a step towards the front door.

I sat on the end of Kenna's bed, squeezing my hair between layers of thick maroon towel, as Kenna riffled through a drawer of clothes.

'Most of my good clothes are in London, but I'm sure there's somethin' that's not hideous in here.' She flung shirts and leggings and dresses across the room like a dog flicking earth with its back paws, the clothes landing in a pile of disarray on the carpet beside the bed. 'Here,' she said, emerging from the wardrobe with a black V-neck jumper and some stretchy jeggings. I appreciated the fact that Kenna wasn't even pretending for a moment that we were the same size. Where she had curves, I had flat edges. Where she was womanly, I was more like a fence post, but the things she picked out fitted me pretty well, if slightly saggy in areas. The deep V of the neckline, which I'm sure made Kenna look like something out of *Playboy*, made me look like a 1950s schoolboy, just missing the white collar poking out from beneath.

'So, how's yer singing voice?' she asked, her eyebrows raising with anticipation.

'Terrible, awful, abominable,' I said, overstressing the words. 'Why?'

'Well, it's gettin' to the drunk portion of the memorial and so there'll be a speech where Mammy will excuse herself and go and cry in the downstairs toilet and then, when everyone is thoroughly depressed, in we come with a few songs. That is the Irish way.'

'I think I'd be best left out of it. I don't think anyone needs to be depressed even further and that's just what will happen if any musical sounds try to escape my throat.'

'Hmm.' She held a curled finger to her lips and looked away for a moment in thought. 'Then, how are yer with tambourines?'

When I re-emerged downstairs, I found the house in a state of disarray that it hadn't been in when I'd left. The majority of the buffet table had been consumed and now all that was left were empty platters, scattered crumbs and discarded glasses with millimetres of liquid sitting in the bottom. I found Charlie loitering on the periphery of an animated conversation with a group of people around his age. They must have been friends from school who'd only ever known Charlie as Abi's and Abi as his. Charlie's smile was crooked and not wholly believable. A crystal cut glass containing one large ice cube and a healthy measure of whisky fell into my view, suspended in front of my face by skinny fingers.

'Here we go,' Carrick said from beside me, nodding in the direction of Kenna who was walking through the room with authority. 'Yer gonna need this.' I took the drink and sipped on the cool, astringent liquid. Carrick copied my action with his own, slightly fuller glass and sighed at the numbing liquid. He'd done a good job of hiding how shaken he'd been, but I could see in his strained eyes that he was kicking himself for losing Charlie in the first place. He was looking rather more dishevelled than he had earlier. His soaked chartreuse jacket had been discarded over the banister and his magenta shirt was now undone to the third button and darkened with rain across the shoulders. His greying hair hung down over his eyes in damp, limp curls as he nervously sipped from his glass again.

Kenna walked up to just in front of the French doors that opened out into the garden, the inside of the doors speckled with droplets from when they had been hastily closed once the rain had set in. In her hand she held a bodhrán, one of those large drums that you always see in folk bands. She raised the double-ended drumstick as she reached the doors and brought it down hard on the taut skin of the drum.

The room needed little encouragement to look Kenna's way. She was like the sun: even when you weren't looking at her, you were always aware of her presence. The conversation quietened before muting completely and everyone turned themselves around to face her as she set the drum down.

'Hello, everyone,' she said, her voice sounding professional and crisp in the crowded room. 'I thought that I might get a speech in before yer all get too drunk to remember why we're even here.' She chuckled and a quiet laugh spread amongst the crowd. She cleared her throat and her smile ebbed a little. 'Abi wasn't like me, she didn't enjoy the spot-light, and so she'd be thoroughly mortified to see all of the fuss we've made over her in the last two years. But it warms our family's heart to see so many people who still hold so much love for my big sister.' Her voice broke a little. She cleared her throat, sniffed and composed herself.

I glanced over at Charlie on the other side of the room. His eyes were glassy, his bottom lip pulled into his mouth. I could see him, monitoring his breathing, taking one breath at a time like Carrick had asked him to. I wanted so much to comfort him but he was too far away, separated from me by bodies and bodhráns.

'On this day two years ago, the world lost a kind, funny, accident-prone, short-tempered, good-hearted woman, who had enough love in her heart for every single person in this room and then some. We lost a daughter, a sister, a friend, a wife.' I looked around the room for Siobhan but couldn't see her and I guessed that she was exactly where Kenna had said she'd be, sobbing into triple ply in the downstairs WC. Kenna wiped a tear from her eye with the flash of a gel-tipped finger, not leaving it there long enough for it to smudge her thick, cat liner. 'So, that's enough of the chatter.' She looked towards the door as two suited men walked in with trays of small whisky-filled glasses. I was offered one, but I turned it down, seeing as I'd barely touched the one Carrick had already given me.

'Take yerself a drink as I enlist the musical talents of my uncle-in-law and we all raise a parting glass to Abi.' Carrick upended his glass, gulped down what was left of the whisky, took another one and walked over to the corner of the room, where a standard piano sat against the wall. Kenna followed him and placed a hand on his shoulder as he opened the lid and ran his fingers over the keys. I hadn't seen Charlie move from where he'd been, but as Carrick pressed down to make the first note, I felt him beside me, his nervous energy almost making the air vibrate around him. The room fell silent as Carrick's fingers played a sombre melody and Kenna began to sing.

'Of all the money that e'er I had,
I spent it in good company,
And of all the harm that e'er I've done
Alas it was to none but me.
For all I've done for want of wit,
To memory now I can't recall,
So, fill to me the parting glass
Goodnight and joy be with you all.'

Her voice rang out like a bell in the silence. Delicate and haunting as she sang the words with such emotion that my skin prickled with goose bumps. I felt an instant lump form in my throat and I found myself having to steady my breathing to stave off the tears.

'Of all the comrades that e'er I had,
They are sorry for my going away,
And of all the sweethearts that e'er I've had,
They would wish me one more day to stay.
But since it falls unto my lot,
That I should rise and you should not,
I'll gently rise and softly call,
Goodnight and joy be with you all.'

The words hit me like hailstones, each perfectly fitting word falling harder than the last. I wiped my eyes with the palm of my hand and looked to Charlie who was watching Kenna with glistening eyes, his teeth clenched. I let my hand fall to my side, my fingers finding his and feeling a tight squeeze in return.

I hadn't understood it completely before, the magnitude of the grief he felt, but after running through the streets of Westport with the panic of losing Charlie thick in my throat, I think that now was the closest I'd ever been to understanding it.

Kenna raised her glass into the air and everyone, except Carrick, whose fingers were still playing the melody, copied her. 'To Abigale Murphy,' she said, before closing her eyes and singing the final sorrowful line.

'Goodnight and joy be with you all.'

'To Abi,' the room spoke as a whole.

'To Abi,' I said, my voice wavering slightly as I raised my glass to my lips.

'Abi,' Charlie said and drank down his drink in one.

There was a moment of quiet, where the final of Carrick's notes reverberated through the room, and the air hung thick with a collective grief.

'Right,' Kenna said, wiping her eyes and putting on a smile. 'I'm gonna need some more band members if we're gonna make this a memorial worth coming to. Nell, I got yer tambourine right here.' My stomach fell down onto the floor as I pulled in my head like a tortoise and attempted to hide. I knew she'd mentioned it, but I didn't remember agreeing.

'I see yer there, Nell,' she said, holding out the tambourine. 'And don't think yer got away from it that easily, Charlie Stone.' Her eyes snapped to Charlie. 'Get yer arse up here.'

'We'd better go,' Charlie said with a sigh. 'She won't give up till we do.'

He gave my hand a little tug and we both walked up to join her. I thought that he'd let go and allow my hand to fall when we emerged from the crowd, but he didn't; he held on until he reached for a guitar beside the piano.

I took the tambourine from Kenna as our audience gave us an encouraging clap. Carrick stood up, disappearing for a moment before returning with a fiddle in hand. What was with all the hidden talents here? What the hell were this family, The Corrs?

'I really don't know what I'm doing. What song are we even playing?' I whispered to Kenna as I was hit by an overwhelming sense of stage fright.

'Ah, just bang the thing. Yer can't go wrong,' she said, retaking up her bodhrán and taking a deep breath.

'The old favourite?' Charlie asked, a glimmer of something that looked like excitement in his eyes.

'Yer know it. Yer all ready?' she asked but didn't wait for an answer. She rolled her wrist, clutching the small drumstick in hand, and beat three times on the skin as Carrick raised the fiddle to his shoulder. They all watched each other. I panicked and started banging the tambourine against my thigh. At first it sounded clunky and out of time, but as I began to recognise the tune as that of 'Galway Girl' by Steve Earle, I found myself falling into step with the others. The tempo lent itself to someone who had no idea what they were doing with a tambourine and before too long I was contemplating leaving my job and going on the road with the three of them. I could see myself as a folk musician; Kenna not so much.

She sang and with every word and every strum of Charlie's guitar, I felt a sliver of my sadness ebb away. I looked up at Charlie and found a smile on his face. He looked so at home with that guitar in his hands, his calloused fingertips once again coming into use to defend against the biting strings.

I tapped the tambourine on my leg until my skin sang with mild pain and the room of mourners turned to smiles. Charlie met my eye and his grin pulled wide. A laugh escaped my lips and I thought back to what Carrick had said when he first tried to convince me to come on this trip and I couldn't help but wholeheartedly agree: the Irish really did know how to do a send-off.

Chapter Twenty-Six

I woke up to the sound of seagulls calling and it instilled me with the excitement of childhood holidays to the seaside. I rolled onto my back and looked up at the ceiling as my swollen eyes adjusted to the light of a new morning. After the spontaneous forming of our new band, the evening had descended into music, drinking and dancing, and even Siobhan had seemed to enjoy herself a little once Kenna had found her and pulled her out of the downstairs loo.

We'd stumbled back to Carrick's with Bambi-like legs, all propping each other up with untrustworthy arms. Charlie hadn't been ready to sleep, or rather to be alone, and so he'd stayed up with Carrick, while I collapsed into my bed for the night. I'd fallen asleep almost instantly after hitting the sheets, but I'd been woken a few times, just enough to register the sound of music being played and glasses being clinked.

I dreaded to think what state they were in.

I showered, brushed the whisky-flavoured layer of fuzz

from my teeth and dressed in a pair of jeans, a mustard-coloured cable-knit jumper and my trusty pumps. I packed up, pushing my pair of mud-smeared heels, which were the cause of today's aching feet, into my bag. I put on the bare minimum make-up and braided my hair into a tight French braid. It tugged on my scalp a little, exacerbating the headache already boiling behind my brows, but it was the only acceptable option when there was no hairdryer to hand. I glugged two paracetamols down with some lukewarm water from the bathroom tap and hoped that it would subside.

Down in the kitchen, sitting at a marble-topped, Pringle-scattered kitchen island, was Carrick. The fact that he'd managed to sleep, face down on the marble countertop, propped up by only a stool, was just short of a miracle. I took a clean glass from the dishwasher, which sat open, and filled it with cold water before going over to Carrick and gently shaking him awake.

'Carrick?' I whispered. 'Are you alive?'

He groaned as he came around and became aware of his thumping head. 'I think so. Unfortunately,' he replied as he sat up, squinting against the dim light that came through the curtains. 'What time is it? Don't want yer to miss yer flight.'

'We've got hours yet,' I said, chuckling at his fragile state.

'Is Charlie up yet?'

'Don't think so. I wondered if you could do something for me?'

'Depends on if the thing you want help with requires much brain function.' He groaned, noticed the water and chugged it down.

'Careful, don't want to make yourself sick,' I cautioned.

'Sick? Ha!' He chortled. 'I haven't been sick since 1993. Now, what is it that yer want?'

'Can you just type the name of the graveyard into my phone?' I said, sliding it across the countertop to him, Maps open on the screen.

'What are yer goin' there for?'

'Just want to . . . pay my respects,' I said.

He shrugged and typed in the name. I rubbed his head affectionately, refilled his water and left him dozing on the countertop as I put on my coat and slipped out of the door.

Aughaval graveyard was a field, hemmed in by bushes and trees, with the ever-present spectre of Croagh Patrick hazed in fog in the background. The graveyard was packed to the rafters, filled with stones of different heights, styles and sizes, and it seemed to stretch on forever. It was easily the biggest graveyard I'd been to, not that I'd visited many in my time, but it was still large by graveyard standards. Mum had sent me pictures last year when she'd gone to Père Lachaise in Paris, which I'm sure dwarfed Aughaval in size. I know she was just trying to share her adventures with me, but I couldn't help but wish that she shared them with me in person and not by proxy. I mean, I wouldn't have even had to fly there.

Just before Carrick had nodded off again, he'd told me where Abi was, nestled into the back right-hand corner by a conifer tree. A black stone with silver writing.

It was so quiet here, with nothing but birdsong and the occasional hum of a passing car to break the silence. I walked amongst the stones, scanning each one and thinking how I might never find her, until suddenly, there she was.

Up until now, Abigale Murphy had been nothing but a

story to me, a well fleshed out, tragically real story. But a story nonetheless. But, as I stood before her tombstone, her name spelled out in silver letters, I finally felt the weight of it hit me.

Bingo. Yer found me. Abi sat with her shoulder and head propped against the stone casually.

'I thought it'd be rude to come all this way and not pay you a visit.' I ran my fingers over the carved lines that spelled out the date of when she'd left this world and for a brief moment, wondered what date they might carve on mine. 'I'm sorry about what happened to you. I really am,' I said. I didn't check around for eavesdroppers or worry what someone might think about me talking to someone who wasn't there. This was a graveyard. If there was anywhere you could talk to inanimate objects and not be judged, it was here.

I'm sure you are, she said sarcastically. *I'm sure there's nothin' you'd like better than to have me still around and in your way.*

I looked up at her and stared for a moment as I thought of what to say. 'You're right. But if you hadn't died then there's no telling that I would have ever met Charlie. We'd have both gone on with our lives, completely ignorant of each other.' A gust of wind blew in between the headstones, making little air tunnels that caused strands of hair to dance around my face. I watched Abi's long russet locks, but the wind didn't touch them. 'I'm jealous of you, you know?' I said, finally voicing what I'd been feeling for a while now. 'I hate that, when I have a moment with him, I can see you in his eyes. It's as if every new moment he's having with me reminds him of one he had with you.'

You're not in competition with me. I'm dead.

'I know, but when it comes to love, things are rarely ever rational.' I took a deep, shaky breath and began picking at the nail varnish on my thumb, just so I wouldn't have to look at her. 'I don't want to erase you from his life; you were a huge part of it. Erasing you would be like erasing part of him.'

My spectral companion looked down at the grass covering her grave, her fingers fidgeting in her lap. *It's not that I don't want him to find someone else. I never wanted him to be alone forever after I died; it's just harder to watch him falling in love with someone else than I anticipated.*

I frowned at her words. Her independence from me, some of the things she said and the ways she said them, made me uneasy. 'It's also hard to love him, knowing that he's always going to be in love with someone else, too,' I said, looking up at her through my lashes.

Her eyes met mine and, for a moment, we just stared at each other, until I felt the corners of my mouth move into a smile and her lips copied mine. She held my gaze a little longer before turning away and pretending that our tender moment hadn't just happened.

What a pair we make. She sighed.

I sat on the grave until my hands were numb with the cold and my cheeks reddened by the wind. I pushed myself up to standing and felt my knees ache as they straightened back into place. My mother had warned me that one day I'd try to get up and it wouldn't be as easy as it used to be. I hadn't thought that that day would be when I was still in my twenties, but there I was, holding on to the headstone while the feeling returned to my toes.

'I'd better get going if I don't want to miss my flight,' I said, Abi still sitting beside the headstone, her eyes far away. 'But I don't suppose that this will be the last time I see you.'

I don't know. I think that maybe the time's comin' for us to part ways, she said with a sad, one-sided smile. *I think that when even I start warmin' to yer, it's time to back away.*

'I don't know if I even want to know the answer to this question, but am I really seeing you? Or is this all inside my head?'

She looked up at me with her big brown eyes and sighed quietly. *I think yer already know the answer to that.*

I felt myself getting rather tearful as I stood in the car park of the airport, with Carrick's arms around me. Charlie and I had done the other goodbyes, bidding farewell for now to his parents, Kenna and Siobhan and an even more emotional goodbye to Steve the motorbike, ending with Charlie whispering a promise into the handlebars that he would come back for him soon.

'Take care of him, will yer?' Carrick said into my ear, quiet enough that Charlie wouldn't be able to hear from where he stood at the back of the orange death mobile, pulling our bags from the boot. 'Don't think that I don't appreciate what you and Ned have done for him, for me. I don't know what I'd do without that boy. He's lucky to have yer lookin' out for him.' He took a deep gulp of air, as if he hadn't taken a breath in minutes and his eyes took on a glazed look. 'It's been so good havin' him back. That wouldn't have happened without yer.' Like Charlie, Carrick was very good at hiding his true feelings, but in that moment, just for a second, I saw a hollow loneliness in the azure of his irises.

I pulled him into a hug and squeezed tightly. 'You're always welcome. Promise that you'll come over and see us again soon? I'm sure Ned would be up for another round of drunk Jenga.'

'Ah, with wine in hand is the only way to play the game.' He sniffed, pulled away and grinned, his true feelings safely masked behind a smile as he made his way to his nephew and slapped him hard on the behind. They shared a moment, their faces and words hidden behind the opened boot. I knew that Carrick felt guilty about letting Charlie slip away from him yesterday, but he'd been fooled – like everyone else – that Charlie's grief was waning, that it was about time to move on and be happy.

Being here had been so good for him. Facing the consequences of how he'd let Siobhan and Kenna find out about Abi's death, coming back to the set of their love story and seeing the ground that held Abi in lieu of him, had all been incredible milestones in combating his grief. But healing didn't work like that. Grief simply lasted as long as it lasted, be that a week or a lifetime. There are no quick fixes, no telling when it will be that waking up isn't the day's first torture and tears the first chore. There was no way of hurrying it along with words about things getting back to normal because normal didn't exist anymore. Normal was as dead as Abi.

I knew that watching Charlie grieve for her would be a long and painful road, for both of us, but I was willing to take it, if he was.

'Hold on to that girl, will yer, Boyo!' Carrick shouted as we walked towards the glass doors. 'She's far too good for yer.'

Charlie breathed a laugh through his nose and glanced at me from the corner of his eyes. I could see that they were clearer than before, less clouded with pain than they had been only a couple of days ago, and it somehow made his eyes even bluer.

'The man's right, yer know,' he said. 'You're far too good for me.'

We had run into a problem at airport security when the guard had reached into my bag and pulled out the snow globe that I'd bought for Ned. The holy water inside sloshed around, making the tiny white flecks dance around in the liquid.

'Yer can't take this on the plane,' she said with a scowl.

'But it's holy water,' I said, frowning at my own words as they left my mouth.

'Needs to go in checked luggage if yer want to take it with yer.'

'I've only got hand luggage,' I said, flustered.

The guard, a portly woman, with a belt so tight that it made her look like a balloon that was being squeezed in the middle, leaned forward, brandishing the snow globe for the whole tutting queue behind to see.

'Just tip the water out and refill it when yer get home,' Charlie said, with a sigh.

'But it's holy water.'

'Come on. D'yer really think Ned's gonna be able to tell the difference?' He raised his brows and quirked his head.

'Fine.' I sighed. 'Can I just tip the water away?'

The guard unscrewed the lid of the jar and tipped the water into a bin underneath the counter, the liquid taking all of the little grains of fake snow with it. She slammed it aggressively down on top of the clothes inside my bag and sent it back through the scanner.

'I was wonderin', Charlie said as we settled into our seats on the plane and the anxiety built up in my stomach. 'When we get back, d'yer mind if I stay with yer for a while? I don't think that I can go back to the apartment just yet.'

'Of course,' I said, my heart leaping a little at the thought of it. 'I'm sure Ned won't mind.'

'Thanks,' he said, sitting back and heaving a sigh. 'You were right: I should have gone back home ages ago. I was just runnin' from it.'

'It's going to take time,' I replied. 'Just be patient and ease will come.'

'Oh, I almost forgot.' Charlie shuffled his bag from between his feet, before rummaging around inside it and pulling George from inside, handing him to me with a smile. 'For luck.'

'I don't think that a bobblehead will have much impact on if the plane goes down or not,' I said, although the little plastic zombie had brought a smile to my face.

The plane door was shut and the flight attendants stood to give the demonstration. I swallowed the lump in my throat and braced myself for another mild panic attack. I clutched George with my free hand, my knuckles turning white around him.

Charlie looked at me, his hand upturned, waiting for mine. 'You got this, Nell,' he said as I slipped my hand into his and squeezed tightly. 'You got this.'

* * *

'And my son, Jeremiah, he's just started working in a Wetherspoons to earn some more money while he studies,' John, the Uber driver said into the rear-view mirror as the sat nav instructed him to pull up and drop me off on the right.

'Good for him,' I said, gathering up my bag and sending Charlie an apologetic smile. 'I hope he enjoys his first year. I hear that Derby's a great place to study.'

The car slowed and I popped the door, trying to leave so I could stop compulsively learning the driver's entire family history. 'Send my love to your wife,' I called before shutting the door and wondering why I'd just said that.

'Jesus, woman.' Charlie sighed. 'Yer ever thought about goin' into interrogation?'

I chuckled as we began walking towards the house.

'So, you've conquered yer fear of flyin', guess that means the world's your oyster now then?'

'Hmm, I wouldn't say conquered, more like, put a dent in. But I guess so. I mean, I'm still going to expect death every time the plane so much as wobbles, but I think it's a good start.' It was true. Knowing that I had been on a plane and not plummeted to my death had suddenly made the world feel a little smaller. Those destinations that I once thought unreachable were now tantalisingly close. Who knew, within no time at all I could become one of those insufferable people who posts pictures of crystal blue waters on Instagram and starts sentences with phrases like: 'What I learned from my time hiking in Antigua was . . .'

I dropped my bag onto the doorstep and unzipped my bag to find my key.

'You know, I didn't think it was possible to make this thing

301

any uglier,' I said, pulling the snowless snow globe out and examining it.

'Just fill it up from the tap and he'll be none the wiser.' Charlie chuckled and came to a stop beside the front door as I slid my key into the lock and pushed it open. The sound of loud power ballads floated through the kitchen door and I assumed that Ned was having an after-work chill-out session to the sounds of the one and only Michael Bolton.

'I've got some body glitter upstairs from a Nineties party I went to a couple of years back. I might chuck that in with the water,' I said, walking up the stairs with Charlie following me up to the landing. I let myself into my room, found the glitter in the back of a drawer and tipped the whole thing into the jar. I moved back out to the landing, making my way to the bathroom to refill it, when I found Charlie dithering on the landing, not knowing which way to go.

I swallowed hard and cradled the jar in my hands. 'You can have the spare room if you like, or if you don't want to be alone you can stay in here with me.' I nodded my head in the direction of my open door and I felt my stomach acid begin to boil. 'No pressure. Go where you want to,' I said, moving off to the bathroom and leaving him to make up his mind.

I filled it up with less than holy water and screwed the lid back on to the newly replenished snow globe. As I made my way down the stairs, I glanced through the banister and saw Charlie taking a seat on my bed. My lips curled into a smile as I descended the rest of the stairs and shuffled towards the kitchen door. I shook the snow globe, checking that it worked and smiling as the glitter rose and fell in an equally tacky manner to the fake snow that now lay in the bottom of a bin on the other side of the Irish Sea.

Sitting down by the door, hidden in shadow, was Magnus. He trilled an affectionate mewling sound as I approached, barely audible above the familiar sounds of 'When a Man Loves a Woman' coming through the door. Magnus moved over to me, rubbing the length of his body against my ankles.

'Hey there, fella,' I said, bending down to pick him up with the hand that wasn't holding the world's most beautiful snow globe.

I turned my attention back to the door and pushed it with my foot, the music getting louder.

I stepped inside the room, my eyes widening as I saw the scene unfolding before me. I stood frozen. The two figures unaware that they were being watched for a few seconds too long.

The snow globe fell from my hand and, incredibly, managed not to smash as it bounced over the kitchen tiles. My newly free hand clapped over the eyes of the innocent little cat in my arms and I pulled him close to my chest to protect him from the horrors I was currently witness to. Ned turned his head in the direction of the sound of glass clattering against floor, his eyes going so wide that he looked like a Hanna-Barbera cartoon. I opened my mouth and gasped as the other person turned to me, their face contracting at the horror of the situation. I inhaled deeply and let out a scream that echoed through the whole house. Frenzied footsteps sounded from upstairs and Charlie ran to my aid, but there was nothing he could do to solve this.

'Oh God. Nelly, close your eyes!' my mother screamed as she dismounted Ned first, then the table, and picked up her clothes from the kitchen floor.

'I can't! I can't!' I screamed. 'I want to but I can't!' Oh

God! So much flesh, so many slapping sounds that would haunt me all the way to a psychiatrist's chair.

I almost heaved as I caught a full-frontal view of Ned's erect penis before he managed to conceal it inside a pair of jogging bottoms. The music was still blaring, Michael's gravelly voice singing on, regardless of the life-altering scene unfolding on the kitchen table.

'Nelly.' My mother held her hand to her forehead as she gathered her clothes to her naked chest with the other. 'Oh God! I'm sorry. I'm sorry.'

'We didn't think you'd be back until much later,' Ned chimed in, frantically pulling on his shirt.

Magnus meowed and wriggled free of my grasp, before doing exactly what I wanted to do and crawling underneath the kitchen counter. Was there room enough for me there too?

Mum moved over to me and laid a hand on my shoulder. I flinched and slapped it away with a shudder. 'Don't touch me, woman! I know where that hand's been!' I cried.

Charlie arrived at my side, just as my mother's clothing failed to hide her modesty and a large pink nipple came into view.

'Jesus, Ned! People eat here,' he exclaimed.

'Close your eyes!' I quickly held up a hand and clamped it over his cornflower blues. I would not have him seeing my mother's breasts before he'd even come close to seeing mine! 'Mother, for the love of God, cover yourself.'

'Wha— This is yer mother?' He cleared his throat and held out his hand. 'Nice t'meet yer, Mrs Coleman.'

She shook his hand awkwardly. 'Call me Cassie. Please.'

I lifted my free hand, my other still clasped tightly over

Charlie's eyes, and slapped their hands until they fell apart. 'Don't touch that!' I shouted at Charlie before I took him by the shoulders, quickly turned him around and walked us both into the living room.

When there were no longer any naked bodies of parental figures in view, I unclasped my hand from Charlie's eyes and fell down onto the sofa, then I thought that the kitchen table might not have been the only surface that Ned desecrated our friendship on and abruptly stood, sitting down again on the floor beside the fireplace.

Charlie placed his hands on his hips and blew air through pursed lips. Nervous footsteps approached and a moment later Ned appeared in the doorway.

'Err, Ned, for yer own safety, I think yer'd better leave her for now,' Charlie said from by the window.

'Sorry you had to see that,' Ned said as he moved towards me. 'Make her a cup of tea, will you?' he said to Charlie. 'Milk and one sugar.'

Charlie disappeared quickly and I hoped that my mother was fully clothed by now, lest he get a second flash of areola.

'Tea won't fix this,' I said, cradling my head in my hands. 'My mother, Ned. My mum!'

'I know. I'm sorry you had to find out this way.'

'Find out? How long has this been going on?' I asked, looking up at his face, a light sheen of sweat coating his brow. He pressed his lips into a hard line. 'Since when, Ned?' He still didn't answer.

'Seven or eight times, over the last year. Ever since she came to stay with us after that work trip of hers and she stopped off for a few days.' I retched and Ned had to stifle a smile. 'We didn't tell you because we knew you'd react this way. We decided to see if it was something we wanted to pursue before telling you but we didn't want you to freak out.'

'So, you decided that a visual example on the kitchen table was the best way to break it to me?!'

Ned sighed and sat down in front of me.

'Nell, when a man loves a woman . . .'

'Don't!' I said, holding up a warning finger. 'Don't you even dare use sweet, beautiful Michael Bolton to get yourself out of this one.'

'Fine. Fine. Sorry. But, Nell, can I just ask you one question?' I looked up in to his eyes, waiting for him to ask me some deeply scarring question like: 'Can you start calling me Dad?' or 'How would you feel about a baby sibling with my nose?' but instead, he just raised his hand, brandishing the snow globe and asked, 'What the fuck is this?'

Chapter Twenty-Seven

I don't know if the snow globe was displayed, pride of place on the kitchen shelf to make me feel better about the fact that I had been both mentally and emotionally scarred by seeing my mother splayed out on the kitchen table like a spatchcock chicken, or if Ned actually found some kind of enjoyment in a tack-tastic, diamante-eyed, Virgin Mary swilling around in a jar of glitter water. Whatever the reason was, the snow globe was there, her eyes boring into me as I attempted to eat the takeaway sushi that Mum had bought in to make me feel a little better.

I knew that I was an adult, an adult who had sex. And because of this, I understood that my mother was also an adult, an extremely attractive adult, who had the same physical needs, but there are some things in life that you can know but never dwell on and there are some sights that you simply cannot come back from. I skewered a salmon nigiri from my plate of untouched food on a chopstick and gave it a healthy soak in the sodium bath of soy sauce, before raising it to my mouth. I had tried to forget about what I had seen, but even the action of skewering the sushi had made me break out in a cold sweat and I fantasised about stabbing chopsticks into my eyes so they could never be harmed again by such heinous sights.

Mum and Charlie were filling the void of silence between Ned and me by talking about her work. I think that Charlie was genuinely interested, but I could see the strained looks behind their eyes. The look in his that said, 'I've seen your nipple, Mrs Coleman,' and the look in hers that replied: 'Please tell no one.'

I stared at Ned over the expanse of the table, my lids lowered, my jaw clenched, as he pretended that he didn't see me, making patterns in his wasabi paste with the end of his chopstick.

How? How exactly could my closest friend possibly go behind my back like this? They had been so discreet and lied to me so seamlessly that I hadn't suspected for a moment. But why would I suspect such treachery from the person who filled the void of best friend and father in one fell swoop. I guess that he was taking that paternal role he'd always filled in my life before to new levels now.

For now, the image of Ned's betrayal was still there inside my brain in glistening 4K ultra HD, but I held out hope that my brain would soon adorn the offending memory with a neat little fig leaf. I chewed the nigiri three times before spitting it back out onto the plate and washing my mouth out with lukewarm water.

It took me a moment before I realised that everyone was watching me.

'Sorry,' I said, looking down at the half-chewed sushi on

my plate and only now realising how gross that would have looked. 'I'm just nursing some PTSD.'

'Joel came by again while you were gone,' Ned said, deftly changing the subject. 'Brought another box.'

'Oh yeah?' I answered, passive-aggressively stabbing a tuna maki roll and dousing it in wasabi. Maybe the burn would take away the memories. 'What was in it this time, a dust bunny he thought I'd grown emotionally attached to or a broken spatula from six years back?'

'Nope. It was just the one thing this time.' He stretched out a leg to the side where an empty Walkers Crisps box sat on the floor by the wall. He kicked it under the table and I looked down between my knees at whatever treasure he'd sent back to me this time. The box was big enough to fit fifteen or so books, but sitting down in the bottom right-hand corner was one tiny thing that made my stomach lurch.

I reached down and picked up the ring – silver with a large black stone set into it and little delicate flowers made of the same silver that kept the stone in place.

I swallowed the lump in my throat and took a deep breath as pressure began to build behind my eyes.

'What is it?' Charlie asked, his comforting hand landing on my knee. The warmth of it snapped me out of my thoughts and I placed the ring onto my finger.

'Just an old trinket,' I said, unconvincingly.

I stood in the bathroom, my chin dripping water into the sink as I stared down at the ring on my hand. Rings were so small, so losable, that I'd just put it there out of fear of mislaying it. But having it there, sitting on my prematurely bony finger, was bringing back all sorts of memories. Not all of them good, but memories nonetheless.

I sighed and stared hard at my reflection. Why was I even thinking about Joel right now when Charlie was in my bedroom, getting ready to jump into the same bed as me?

We'd had a quick debriefing before I'd come to wash my face about what the logistics of sleeping in a bed with someone you would very much like to lick every square inch of, but couldn't out of respect for his grieving process. We'd agreed that there was no pressure from either side to do anything other than sleep. He didn't want to be alone and, to be honest, neither did I. We were two fully grown adults. We were capable of sleeping next to each other without succumbing to hormones, like Ned and my mother seemed incapable of doing.

Three quiet raps came on the door and, without invitation from me, it fell open and Mum's face poked through. Excluding the event that I hoped my mind would soon blank out and the following horrendously awkward dinner, I couldn't remember the last time I'd seen her. 'Hey, Nelly,' she said with a worried smile and slipped into the room.

I took a breath, wiped my face with a towel and made a concerted effort not to remember my own mother's sex face.

'Hi, Mum,' I said as she hugged me. 'How come you didn't tell me you were coming?' I said. I almost added that she probably did it so that her and Ned could have a secret tryst before seeing me, but I let that particular comment die on my tongue.

'I wanted to surprise you and surprise you I did, I suppose.'

'Uh-huh.' I flinched, shifting away from her a little, looking down at my feet and wondering how best to say what I wanted to say. 'You're not playing him around, are you, Mum?'

'What do you mean, love?' she asked, her flawless brow furrowing. She really was a beauty. Her usually pale as milk skin held a slight tan, obviously out of a bottle because her skin was impervious to tanning, and her piercing green eyes were a nice contrast against her honey blonde hair.

'I know this is going to sound like I'm sad about my childhood or something – I'm not, I had a great childhood. But what I feel like I need to say is that, talking as someone who has fallen foul of thinking that you'll stick around for them, I know what it feels like to watch you go, after convincing myself that you won't leave again.'

I saw my words hurt her, but they were true and she needed to hear them. 'Ned's already had one woman string him along and break his heart, so if you're going to be just like Connie, end it now.'

'Honey, what happened between Ned and me—' She stammered her way through the sentence.

I held up a hand. 'I know Ned much better than you do. He's a romantic. He cries at rom-coms and dreams of silver anniversaries. And I know you. You're loving and kind, but everything comes second to work. Other than you, Ned is the only family I have and I won't lose him over a relationship gone wrong.' I stepped closer, placing my hand on her arm to lessen the harshness of my words. 'Please, Mum. I can't imagine my life without Ned. Don't make me have to.'

She looked as if she might cry, raising her palm to press it against my face. 'Of course, sweetie. But just so you know, you have never come second to anything, not since the

311

moment I found out I was going to have you.' She pulled me close and we both tried to disguise the fact that we shed a few tears. 'You know,' she said as we left the bathroom, 'maybe it's time to come home and settle down again.'

'I'll believe it when I see it,' I scoffed, remembering the last few times she'd said this in passing, as if it meant nothing more than suggesting she'd pop out and buy some milk. She didn't know how much it hurt when she then signed up for an eighteen-month assignment to China.

She shrugged her eyebrows and nodded. 'Well, yeah.'

I shook my head and grimaced. 'Ned. I just never thought he'd be your type.'

'Me neither.' She chuckled.

'You know he has a strange affinity with Celine Dion and reads history magazines, right?'

'I do.'

'And that doesn't put you off?'

'Actually, quite the opposite.'

I shuddered and wished I'd never asked.

By the time I got back to my room, Charlie was already in bed and the sight of him there made my insides twist with excitement.

Everything that had happened between Charlie and me, thus far, had happened in such a baptism of fire that I no longer questioned the strength of my feelings towards him. You often hear about love forged in extreme circumstances and how it burns bright and fast, ending in just as much of a cataclysm as it started in. I hoped that we wouldn't fall foul of that same affliction.

I slipped into the room, the tears from my conversation with my mother still moistening my lashes.

'You all right?' he asked, sitting up a little against the headboard.

'Yeah.' I nodded, shutting the door. I suddenly felt very awkward.

'So,' he said, looking down at his hands, which were clasped on his lap atop the duvet. 'The ring that Joel dropped round. What's the story?'

'What makes you think there's a story?' I asked.

''Cause all the blood drained from yer face like yer'd seen a ghost the second you saw what it was.'

I sighed and sat down cross-legged on the bed facing him. I turned the ring around on my finger, remembering the market stall where I'd first seen it a month before it landed on my finger. 'I always said, for the whole time that I was with Joel, that I didn't want to get married. Something about the idea of it made me panic, like I was being trapped. So, I told him one day and it seemed like he was on the same page.'

I turned away from Charlie, looking down at the ring, the stone duller than it had once been. 'One day, about two years into the relationship, we went to this craft market in the middle of town. I saw this ring and really loved it, but neither of us had any money and so I left it there and forgot about it.' I pulled it from my finger and handed it to Charlie, who took it tentatively and looked it over.

'Joel took the woman's card. He emailed her and explained that he wanted to buy it, but would need to get some money together first. She agreed to keep it for him and a month later, when the market came back, he bought it and gave it to me. He said that he understood that I didn't want to marry, but he wanted to give that to me as a sort of promise ring, saying that we'd love each other forever.'

313

'Sounds like he really loved yer,' Charlie said, clearing his throat.

'He still does – that's what makes this so hard.'

'What do yer mean?'

'I mean that . . .' I took a deep breath as I plucked up the courage to say what I had been thinking for years. 'I mean that it was never that I didn't want to get married, it was just that I never wanted to marry Joel.'

'Is that a hint?' He chuckled and handed it back to me.

I laughed nervously and held on to the ring, not wanting to put it back on, but not quite ready to let go of it. 'I just see what you had with Abi.' He looked down, unable to meet my eye while I spoke her name. 'The kind of love you had, still have for her . . .' I'm not going to lie, that last part stung. 'Joel and I never had that. We were never meant to be.'

'Yer know, I never believed in meant to be or destiny or anything like that.' He spoke quietly and reached a hand over to my knee. 'But the way this has happened, finding that sticker up there on the clock tower and leading me to Ned, then to you and meeting you in that café. It all just feels like someone wants us together.'

We had been through so much together already and, in that moment, I finally realised that I loved him too deeply already for this to all be for nothing.

'I know what you mean,' I replied. 'I just can't help but think that maybe this is what was meant to happen and I was meant to love you, but to me the timing . . .'

'. . . feels off?' He finished my sentence for me.

'Exactly.' I sighed and shuffled a little closer to him, the warmth of his hand finding my knee. I leaned in and placed my palm gently on his cheek. His impossibly blue eyes latched on to mine. 'I love you, Charlie Stone.' His mouth broke into a smile and for a heart-jolting moment, I thought he might say it back, but he just swallowed his smile and breathed a shaky sigh.

'I want to kiss you without you thinking of Abi. I want to spend the night with you without you feeling like you're being unfaithful to your wife. You're still grieving, and that's okay.'

He opened his mouth to protest, but the look in his eyes showed me that he agreed with what I was saying. 'You need more time. Time to put your heart back together before you give it away again. I want us to have a chance and if we're going to have that, we need to be patient.'

His eyes were glassy now, his lips puckering as he drew them into his mouth. 'Yer right.' His voice broke and he groaned in frustration. 'Erg! I'm sorry I keep cryin' all the time.'

'Don't apologise.' I placed a hand on his other cheek and angled his face back to mine. 'You need to let yourself feel it. It's like owning a mean old bird.'

He chuckled and dislodged more tears. 'How the hell is this anythin' like owning a mean old bird?'

'Okay, maybe not my best analogy, but hear me out. If you cage it up and lock it away, you're never going to be rid of it. But if you open the cage door and let it out, it'll take off out the window and make room for a nice friendly one to move in.'

'And the nice friendly bird is what exactly?'

'Happiness,' I replied. 'Let yourself hurt, Charlie, and when you're ready, we can see what happens.'

He wiped his tears away and took my hands from his face,

folding them inside his. 'What if everything's changed by the time I'm ready?'

'Then I guess it's not meant to be.'

I pushed myself up off the bed and slipped my feet into the pumps that lay on the floor.

'Where are you going?' he asked.

'There's something I need to do. It's all well and good being the counsellor, but right now, I need to listen to my own advice. You know, practise what you preach and all that.' I pulled on my coat from the hook behind the door and grabbed my phone from the bed, sliding the promise ring back onto my finger.

'Let me walk you – it's dark.'

'Don't worry. I'm not going far,' I said. 'I need to do this on my own.'

'What are you going to do?' he asked, flinging back the duvet and letting one leg fall to the floor.

'Set the bird free.'

Joel was already there when I arrived, sitting with hunched shoulders on the bench outside the park. In the daylight, this small patch of grass was beautiful, with beds of yolk yellow daffodils and violet crocuses that never seemed to stay for long enough. But in the dark the flowers were all in shadow, their colour lost in the night. The only light came from the dim street lamp a few metres away. He hadn't seen me yet, his eyes downturned to the phone in his hands, his face illuminated by the dimmed screen.

When I was a few paces away, he looked up and stood.

'Nell.' He grinned, leaning in and planting a kiss worryingly close to my lips. He lingered there for a moment longer than was necessary and I felt a slight shudder run through me.

'Thanks for coming. Sorry I called so late.' I pulled away from him and sat down on the bench. Joel retook his seat and angled his knees towards me.

'You know I'm a night owl, Nell,' he said, placing his hand on my leg. I thought how different it felt to have Joel's hand there, where Charlie's had been less than half an hour earlier. 'It's nice to see that back on your finger.' He said, taking my hand and moving the ring around with his thumb. 'Back where it belongs.'

'Joel.' I slid my hand from his and braced myself for the words that needed saying, but how could I even start to say them? 'I can—'

'I still can't believe you got on a plane. You must have been scared on the flight back, huh? How was it, flying alone?'

'I . . . I didn't fly alone. Charlie was with me.'

Joel frowned. 'But I thought he went home.'

'He did, but not for good,' I replied, feeling stifled and overwhelmed. 'We went to a funeral, that's all.'

'Nice.' He scoffed. 'That's his idea of a date is it?'

The first semblance of anger formed in my stomach, jittering in the heat of my stomach acid like a corn kernel ready to pop. 'It was more of a memorial really, for his wife.'

'Christ!' He sighed. 'How long have you known about this?'

'A while.' I sighed. For so many years Joel had been my confidant and so I didn't even think twice before telling him the truth about how Charlie and I met. I told him about the café, about the clock tower, about my phone call with him and his call with Ned two years earlier. It wasn't until I'd finished that I wondered if I should have told him or not.

317

'Wow,' is all he could say. 'No wonder you haven't been around much recently.'

'Listen.' I quickly changed the subject back to what I'd come here to say. 'I realised something tonight that I'm ashamed to say that I haven't really thought about enough before.'

'And what's that?' he asked, his tone and body language hopeful.

'My whole life, I've settled for the time and attention that people felt like giving me. Mum coming back when she had free time, calling me when she felt like it. Popping in and out of my life whenever was convenient and the same can be said about when we were together.'

'I'm not sure I understand,' Joel replied, his brow deeply furrowed.

'We never went anywhere, did anything. You never felt like going out so I just accepted that and stayed in with you.'

'But we spent that time together, even if it was just in that shitty flat.'

'No, we didn't. You'd always be anywhere other than in the room with me. On your PlayStation with that stupid headset on or with your nose in your computer or phone. Paying attention to anything that wasn't me.' I took a breath and steadied myself before carrying on. 'Being with you was like catching smoke in my hand. I thought I had you, but when I opened my fingers, you weren't there. Tonight, I told my mum how much it has hurt over the years to think I had her, convincing myself that she was finally going to choose me and each and every time, watching her walk away. That's exactly what I've been doing to you these past six months. I haven't been fair to you.'

'Hey, I wasn't complaining.' His eyes were strained, almost fearful.

I looked down at my hands and squeezed my eyes shut, the image of Charlie sitting at home in my bed falling into my brain and making my heart ache. 'I understand now how much it hurts, to love someone and to know that they can't love you back. So . . .' I took his hand, turned it over, slipped the ring from my finger and placed it in his palm. 'I need to give this back to you. Because we're not going to be together forever and I think that by me finally letting you go, you'll be able to find the right person for that ring.'

'Nell, please. Don't,' he begged, his face contorting into one I didn't recognise. 'Please. I love you.'

'I know,' I said, on the verge of tears. 'And I'll always love you too, in a way. But not in the way you need me to love you.'

He looked down at the ring in his hand as if it were a death sentence, the black spot etched on his palm.

'I'm sorry, Joel.' I stood, feeling like I needed to leave before I changed my mind. Joel was not what I wanted, but he was easy, safe, familiar and right now, he was the life ring that I felt the need to lunge for. 'I need to go now.'

He was quiet for a moment before a spiteful chuckle left his lips and he looked up at me from under his lashes. 'You're kidding yourself with this Charlie.'

'No, I'm not,' I said.

'You love him?' he asked, silent tears glistening on his cheeks under the glow of the street lamp.

I swallowed the lump in my throat. 'Yes.'

'But he doesn't love you?' I felt his words land like kicks in my solar plexus.

'It's not that he doesn't and more that he won't allow himself to. He's still grieving.'

'Good,' he said, his tone cruel as he spat the words. 'I hope that he's the love of your life and then I hope he breaks your heart on a park bench and tells you that it's what's best for you.'

Something had changed in his eyes. They'd turned cold, unrecognisable.

'Goodbye, Joel,' I said, turning away before he could see me cry.

I swallowed the sobs that were about to burst from my throat and walked under the glow of the street lamp. It wasn't until I was almost out of its beam that I felt something hit me in the back. I turned around as the ring clattered to the pavement and the place where it had hit me began to sing with a gentle sting. I looked back to see him standing on the other side of circle of light, his arms hanging limply at his sides. I was about to bend down to pick up the ring when he spoke again.

'Leave it in the gutter. It's where it belongs now.' And with that, he turned and walked out of the light and into the shadow. I looked at it, glowing orange in the light and then turned and walked away from it. Maybe someone else would find it and love it. Maybe it would mean something more to them than it ever had done to me and not carry the pain with it that it carried for Joel. I was giving Joel and myself a second chance. The ring deserved that too.

Chapter Twenty-Eight

The next morning, I woke with that heavy, stinging feeling in my eyes that always comes after a night of crying. My head throbbed as if I'd necked two bottles of vodka and if that wasn't enough to start the day off badly, I then reached out a hand to find the space beside me empty.

I got up, donned my dressing gown and went down to the kitchen, pausing to endure a scarring mental flashback just before I went through the door. Ned was sat at the dining room table, trying very hard not to look up from his magazine as I walked over to the draining board, took a mug and sat down, not in my usual chair beside him, but opposite. I poured myself a coffee from the cafetière and held it between both hands on the tabletop.

'Where are the others?' I asked.

He stopped reading an article about Elizabeth I's spy network and looked up at me sheepishly, not quite making eye contact, but instead looking just to my left. 'They went on a bonding trip to get some food for dinner. Charlie's making lasagne.'

'What a happy little family we make,' I said sarcastically. 'Do tell me when you want me to start calling you Dad, won't you?'

He sighed and pushed his magazine to the side. 'Look, Nell. Both of us thought very long and hard about acting on any feelings that we had.'

I held up a hand in disgust. 'Please refrain from using words like long and hard. I'm not sure if it's even possible for us to stay friends after seeing your . . . thingy.'

'Come on, Nell, it's only a penis.'

'Yes, but it was *your* penis. Ergo my distress.'

'Penises aside,' he said, frowning a little at his own words, 'I am with you till the end. You are the best, strangest friend I have ever had and nothing is going to tear us apart, not even what you saw last night. Me and your mother have had these feelings for a while now and as I said, we thought long an—'

'Ah!' I shouted and covered my ears.

'Sorry, sorry. We thought very seriously about how to handle them. But in the end, I really like her and just because you're freaking out, doesn't mean I'm not going to see where this goes. I am a man and your mother is an incredibly attractive woman, the likes of which a man can only dream of being with.'

'Oh, sweet Jesus, please stop,' I begged. 'Look, if you and Mum want to date, or whatever it is you two are doing, then that's fine. I just don't want to see it, okay?'

'Deal,' he said reaching over the table with an outstretched hand. 'Does this mean we're friends again?'

'Hmmm.' I pondered. 'We shall see.'

A knock came at the front door and I stood, eager to get away from the conversation and the table, which I was pretty sure I was going to have to take out in the garden and set on fire, and made my way to let the weary shoppers in. But when I opened the door, I wasn't met with the faces I was expecting.

'Rachel?' Joel's mother stood in front of me with a worried look on her face. 'Is everything okay?'

'Nell, is Joel here?' she asked, her eyes darting over my shoulder to see if he was behind me.

'No,' I replied. 'Why?'

'He left the house last night to come and see you, but he never came home. It's not like him to not answer his phone when I call him. I just thought he might be here, seeing as you've been spending time together again recently.'

I saw a flicker of hope in her eyes and the guilt bubbled in my stomach.

'He didn't come back here with me. We met on a bench by the park and had an argument, but I came home alone.'

She raised a hand to her mouth and whimpered into it.

'You don't think something happened to him, do you?'

'I just have a bad feeling,' she said, her eyes moistening with worried tears. My mind was drawn back to that time spent searching the streets for Charlie back in Ireland. The unbridled panic that nothing other than finding him would cure. 'Come in. Would you like some tea?'

She nodded and walked through to the kitchen where Ned was already putting a fresh kettle on.

I called around to some of our mutual friends, mostly people I hadn't talked to since we split up, but whom Joel might have gone to for advice. None of them had seen him and every dead end caused another whimper to escape Rachel's mouth. Charlie and Mum arrived home shortly after I finished making the calls. I rang the hospital to see if he was there, also asking if they had any unidentified people, but all were accounted for. I kept saying that I was sure he was fine, but something about the look in his mother's eyes made me unsure.

'He's been so distant these past few weeks. But I knew that it was all going to be okay because you two were getting back together.'

I frowned and looked to Charlie and Ned who were just as puzzled as I was. 'Did he tell you that?' I asked.

She nodded. 'He said how you two were reconciling and that you just had to end things with someone else before you could get back together, so that you didn't hurt anyone. He was so excited, looking for flats and boxing up his things.' She reached over and placed her hand on mine, a warm smile on her face. 'And after everything he'd been through this year, it made me so happy to know that at least everything was right with the two of you.'

'Rachel, we're not getting back together. We never have been. He knew that,' I said, suddenly a lot more worried. 'The boxes were him bringing my stuff back to me.'

'Oh. That's not what he told me,' she said wringing her fingers. 'Are you sure?'

'I'm sure. What did you mean when you said with everything that had happened this year?'

'With him having to shut his business down and that company that caused all that trouble, threatening that lawsuit because of those details that got out. It's all to do with that GPDR stuff.'

'What, a lawsuit?' I asked, realising that I had only been seeing the tip of the proverbial iceberg with Joel.

'Oh yes, it's been awful. But, dear, I thought you knew.'

It was three before Rachel left. She said she was going to go out and have a look round for him. I promised her I'd do the same and call her if I found him.

'This is nothing to do with you,' Ned said in the hallway as I closed the door. 'With the things he did and said, throwing that ring at you.' He tutted.

'He threw something at you?' Charlie asked, becoming imbued with a sense of masculine protectiveness.

I ignored them both and grabbed my coat and Mum followed me out the front door. We looked for a good while before returning home with nothing to show for it.

We were all sitting in the kitchen, nervous energy forcing us to open a bottle of wine as Charlie's lasagne browned beneath the grill, when my phone rang. It was Rachel.

I picked up and held the phone to my ear. 'Hey, Rachel, did he show up?'

'Nell,' she sobbed.

'What is it?' I asked, standing and putting everyone in the room on high alert.

'I just got in.'

'You only just got in? Rachel, it's almost seven o'clock.'

'I know, but I couldn't just go home and wait for him,' she cried.

'And there was no sign of him?'

'I just went into his room to check it over again and I found a letter on his bed. He must have come home while I was out.' Her voice was broken, distraught.

'What did the letter say?' At this, Charlie stood too.

'I've already called the police, Nell. They're sending a car out to look for him.'

'What did the note say?' I probed.

I heard the sound of crinkling paper and then she began to read. *'Mum, I'm sorry for leaving you. I don't think that anyone other than you will miss me much. Everything I've done with my life so far has failed and I know that I am a financial and emotional burden on you. I thought I saw a way out of it, but I was wrong.*

'Please tell Nell that I am sorry and that I love her. Always have, always will.

'I love you Mum. I'll say hi to Dad for you.

'Joel.'

'Oh my God.' I held my hand to my eyes. This was because of what I'd said last night, wasn't it? I put the idea in his head when I was talking about Charlie.

'Nell, I can't lose my boy too.'

It was me who put the idea in his head.

'Rachel, I think I might know where he is. I'll call you when I'm there.' I hung up the phone and without a word to the others I made for the door.

They called after me but I ignored them, not bothering to put on a coat and just running outside, Charlie on my heels.

'Nell, where is he?' he asked.

'The clock tower,' I said, breathlessly. 'He's at the clock tower.'

Neither of us spoke a word; we just put our heads down and ran. The air was freezing but my skin was hot with anxiety. Charlie was faster than me and so he ploughed

326

on, travelling further ahead but never leaving me too far behind.

When we got there, the window to the fire escape was smashed, a large rock lying beside it.

I dialled Rachel's number as we both took the stairs two at a time. She answered almost immediately.

'Rachel, I think I've found him. Call the police and tell them he's at the town hall. He's on top of the clock tower.' I hung up and grabbed the handrail, pulling myself up faster. Charlie got to the top before me and ran out onto the tower before I even made it to the top step. I heard Charlie's muffled words and I knew that we'd found him. I came to a standstill as I walked through the door. The image of Joel standing on the ledge made my stomach turn.

'I should have known. Wherever she goes, you go too,' Joel said, his eyes red and his mouth pinched in a snarl as he looked over his shoulder at me.

'Joel, please, don't do this,' I begged.

'As if you'd care.' His face crumpled and he let out a sob. 'You don't love me anymore; you said so yourself.'

'Of course I care, Joel.'

'Hey,' Charlie said, stepping forward, his hands outstretched to let Joel know that he wasn't going to come too near. 'I know that I'm probably the last person yer want t'see right now, but I'm probably the only person who knows exactly what yer goin' through here. Yer see, I was standin' exactly where you're stood, literally right there, and not too long ago either.' Joel was looking at him as if every single thing about him was repulsive and he took a micro step back towards the edge. 'I wanted everythin' to stop, I felt like nothin' was worth the struggle anymore and that things were never gonna go my way again. I'd lost the love of my life and I knew that she was never coming back to me.' His own voice broke a little and I thought that he might cry, but he held it together. 'I still feel that pain now. But if I'd gone through with it and stepped off that ledge, then I never would have known what was comin' next. How much better my life would be.'

'Yeah but that's just the point,' Joel said, his voice devoid of emotion. 'The thing that made your life better has ruined mine. Your happiness is my pain, because I still love her.' He pointed to me even though he couldn't bring his eyes to look my way. 'But I don't get to do that anymore – that's your job now.'

'Joel,' I said stepping forward. 'I just got off the phone with your mum. She's in hell thinking that she's gonna lose you.'

'I don't care,' he said, brushing it off with a passive swipe of his hand.

'I know that you're hurting and that I said some things last night that I shouldn't have and I'm sorry for anything I did to hurt you.' I felt myself on the verge of crying and in the distance, I heard the sound of not too far-off sirens. My spirits lifted a little and I took a step closer.

Joel looked from me to Charlie and then back again. 'I can see why you love him, I really can. He's, like, physically perfect and exotic and seems to have his shit together. He's everything I'm not.'

'I wouldn't call Westport, County Mayo, exotic.' Charlie chuckled nervously. 'And believe me, I'm not as together as you seem to think I am. I'm unemployed, widowed, completely lost. The world doesn't give a feck what I'm doin',' he said, holding his arms aloft. 'I have no person in this world who needs me and yet, I decided to stay because I found a glimmer of hope.' The sirens were close now and Joel was beginning to notice them too.

I watched Charlie as he spoke the words. It was as if he was looking at a mirror image, telling himself exactly what he had needed to hear on that night he'd called me. 'You seen *Castaway*?' he asked. 'Tom Hanks. Plane Crash. WILSON!' The sound of sirens was right below us now. From the sound of it, there was more than one car down there.

'Yeah I've seen it,' Joel replied, glancing over his shoulder at the drop and flinching as if filled with a sudden fear.

'Well, there's this bit at the end, where he's been rescued and he's talkin' to his mate about a time when he planned to throw himself from the cliffs instead of be lonely for one more day and he says that he's got to keep breathing because tomorrow the sun will come up, and who knows what the tide will bring along.'

'But what if the tide brings nothing?' Joel asked.

'Then it brings nothing and you ask yourself the same question another day. But for now, you give the tide a chance to come up with somethin'.'

I couldn't help it now. The tears were dripping from my chin onto the bird-mess-spattered floor.

'Please, Joel,' I sobbed and, finally, he turned his eyes to me. 'Please, don't do this. In time you'll see that this was the best thing for both of us. We couldn't have carried on the way we were. I was miserable and so were you.' I swallowed hard and stepped forward. 'Just because it didn't work for us doesn't mean it won't with someone else.'

Joel looked me dead in the eyes, his face draining of emotion, and Charlie inched forward. 'I don't want anyone else.'

His foot moved so slightly that I didn't even see it, as he stepped from the ledge and the bottom fell out of my stomach.

'Joel!' I screamed as he fell. Charlie had moved before Joel had even inched his foot backwards, his hands reaching out and grabbing at his shirt. He flung himself down at the edge, his body flat against the brickwork and the momentum of Joel's weight carrying him towards the edge. I ran forward, flinging myself down onto the floor as well and grabbing Charlie's legs as a counterweight.

'I got him!' Charlie shouted back to me. 'I got him!'

There was a sound behind me as a police officer appeared.

'Hello, miss,' the police officer said. I looked up and saw a young woman's face, round and familiar in some way, although my brain wasn't capable of figuring out from where right now. 'I need you to hold on while the officers get him, okay?' she asked as two police officers moved either side of Charlie and began taking Joel's weight. I listened as she used a calm voice to reassure me, my fingernails still digging into the denim of Charlie's jeans as I felt the physical weight of everything I was holding in my two hands. I held the only two men I had ever loved. I held my future and my past and I didn't want to let go of either of them.

It was midnight before Charlie and I arrived home. Ned and Mum had come to pick us up and, unbeknownst to us, had been waiting at hospital for us for hours. Rachel had gone off with Joel, I assume to check him in to somewhere he couldn't hurt himself. I'd tried to talk to him afterwards, but he didn't want to see me and so Rachel had just told me to go home.

Mum made us tea and tried to force-feed us burned lasagne but we both felt sick and ended up going to bed soon after arriving home. We lay on the bed, on top of the sheets and stared at the ceiling. We didn't say a word to each other and I didn't remember falling asleep, but when I did, I dreamt of falling.

Chapter Twenty-Nine

Joel refused to see me when I turned up at the psychiatric ward after work a couple of days later with a box of his favourite Lindt chocolates. Rachel came instead and took me by the hands, thanking me for finding him in time. She said that Joel didn't want to see me and that I should wait for him to get in contact. I doubted the day would ever come when Joel felt like dropping me a cheery hello, but I think it would be nice, further down the line, to speak to him again.

I'd returned home after the hospital with an exhausted brain and a weary body and Charlie, still unwilling to return home to a flat full of memories, had greeted me with a glass of Pinot Grigio. Ned had left to take Mum to the airport, but I'd decided to give this particular goodbye a miss. I didn't think I was ready yet to see them making out in the drop-off bays.

I sat at the kitchen table with Magnus dozing on my lap and I sipped on the cool, crisp wine as Charlie chopped vegetables and tossed them into a sizzling pan. I wondered if this was what our future looked like? Me arriving home from work and him, the dutiful husband, cooking me dinner and talking non-stop about inane things that filled the silence. I watched his shoulders tense and relax as he worked away at the counter and I thought how strange it was that I hadn't touched him properly yet, had barely kissed him more than a handful of times and yet, I loved him so deeply that it felt like we'd been together for years.

But I knew that it was only me who felt this way. It was like starting a new book before you've finished the last one. Your brain is still engaged with the first story, the new one exciting and distracting, but you have a sense of unease because you never knew how the first story ended. Abi was that story and he still hadn't found the end of it.

'Everyone I've ever made this for has asked me how I always get it to taste so good. Really, I think that the secret's all in the bay leaves,' he said, turning to me and waving his knife in the air to stress the point. 'Wildly underestimated herb.'

'Charlie, I think we need to have a talk.' The words tumbled out of my mouth, making him freeze when they hit him.

'Okay. Should I brace myself? Because nothin' good ever comes after those words,' he said, placing the knife down and coming to sit opposite me, his hands clasped on the table in front of him. I couldn't help but smile at how cute he looked in Ned's old pinny, stained and burned from years of use. 'What about?'

'I think you need to leave.'

He flinched. 'What? Right now? But the bourguignon's not done yet.'

'Not right this second,' I said, reaching out and holding his hand. 'But I just don't think that this is healthy . . . for me to have you staying here and it's not particularly good for you either. Isn't you living in the spare room just another way for you to run away from everything you need to be tackling?'

He looked at me and I had to look down at our hands, clasped together on the table, because I was weak for those eyes. 'I know that we decided that maybe the timing wasn't right for us to make a go of this just yet. But, I'm not going to lie, it's kind of painful to have to see you every day and not be able to be with you in the ways I want to be. To love you and know that you can't love me back, it hurts, Charlie. And there's stuff that both of us need to sort out and I don't think we can do that if we're together, holding each other back.'

He smiled at me sadly, but I could see from his face that he knew I was right.

'You said, when we were up on the clock tower with Joel, that no one needed you, but that wasn't true.'

'You don't need me, Nell. You'd be just fine on your own.'

'I'm not talking about me. I'm talking about Carrick,' I replied. 'I don't think Carrick is as together as you think he is. He misses you and he loves you so much. I think he needs a friend. He needs you.'

'What about you?' he asked, his brows a little downturned at the ends. 'What will you do?'

I shrugged. 'I don't know, but that's the beauty of it I guess.'

He sighed, his thumb stroking my knuckles.

'I wish I could . . . yer know, say *it*.'

'I know.' I smiled and squeezed his hand, all the while, trying not to acknowledge the feeling of my heart cracking in two.

* * *

334

Carrick arrived on the last day of April to help Charlie box up all of his stuff. It was strange having him out of the house and, even though we hadn't been sleeping in the same room since that first night, knowing that he wasn't a wall's width away from me made me feel hollow and achy inside. This was for the best – we both knew it. I hoped that we could have a future, one that wasn't filled with sadness and loose ends of previous loves. But he was going away and taking everything with him, except for Magnus who was now Ned's, body and soul. He was erasing himself from my life, from Birmingham, from the United Kingdom, and knowing that he was going to be so far away gave me the awful feeling that these might be my final days with Charlie.

The night before Charlie was set to leave, we had dinner with Ned and Carrick.

I remained pretty quiet during dinner, which went mostly unnoticed because Carrick filled the quiet with his insatiable need to say whatever came into his head. Magnus dozed on top of the fridge, his long tail trailing down over the front of the door and having to be held up like a bead curtain every time someone needed to get something from inside it.

Ned was about as in love with Magnus as I'd ever seen him with anything, with the exception of my mother. I still shuddered with vomit-inducing recollection every time he casually mentioned her name in conversation. I knew that she'd mentioned finding a non-travelling position within the company so that she could stay home, but I doubted that anything would come of it and Ned would soon learn that Cassandra Coleman was not a woman to pin your hopes and heart on. I assumed that the Ben and Jerry's would be in full flow when that moment came around.

When everyone had finished their meals, Charlie disappeared into the hall, returning with a bottle of whisky and taking four glasses from the cupboard.

'So,' he said, retaking his seat beside me and pulling the cork from the bottle, 'before I go, I just wanted to say a few things.'

'Ah feck, yer not gonna give us a speech are yer?' Carrick teased.

'Will yer shut yer mouth for one bloody minute and let someone else have a chance? Jesus, man.' Charlie chided through a smile. He poured some of the amber liquid into each of the glasses and passed one to each of us. 'I am sittin' here right now, digestin' another one of Ned's culinary triumphs and about to sample this fine whisky because of each and every one of yer.' He looked around at the three of us. 'I don't think many people who sit at the dinner table can say that every one of the people around it has saved their life. But I can and what that proves to me is that I've got some pretty feckin' awesome people in my life. I just wanted to let yer all know that I'm gonna miss yer and that this isn't goodbye.'

He turned to me and smiled.

'Sláinte.' Carrick led the cheers and we all followed.

As I swigged down the burning liquid, I felt a warm tear roll down the side of my face and I wiped it away before anyone could see.

I stood in front of the mirror and washed the make-up from my face. I wasn't tired, quite the opposite. My body was charged with anxiety about tomorrow morning, but sitting downstairs with them all, waiting for the time to come when Charlie would walk out of my life, possibly forever, made me want to do nothing but curl up in bed. I left the bathroom and found Carrick on the landing, leaning against the wall with his thumbs in his pockets, like James Dean.

'Hey, I didn't know you were waiting. Sorry,' I said.

'I was waitin' to talk to yer.' He pushed off from the wall and placed his hands on my shoulders. 'I just wanted to tell yer that there's no need to worry about him when he's over there. He'll be stayin' with me and I'll be lookin' out for him every step of the way. I let him down once already, at the memorial, but I'll do better.'

'I know you will,' I said, drawing him into a hug.

'I know it was your idea for him to come home.' He sighed into the hug and pulled me a little closer. 'You're a selfless lass, I'll give yer that.'

'Not really,' I replied into his greying hair. 'This is for both of us. Just don't let him forget about me,' I whispered, my voice breaking.

'As if he ever could.'

I don't know how long I'd been asleep when I felt something on my cheek. At first, I thought it was one of those fabled spiders that sneak into your mouth while you sleep, but as the panic of that thought brought me round to consciousness, I realised that it wasn't long spindly legs, but soft fingers.

'Hey,' I said, opening my eyes to see Charlie's handsome face illuminated by the warm light of the bedside lamp.

'I'm gonna miss yer, so much,' he whispered, his face so close to mine I could feel his breath on my skin.

I reached up to where his fingers lay on my face and took

them in my hand. 'I'm going to miss you too,' I replied dreamily, the weight of sleep pressing down on me, my eyes straining to keep open.

'Whatever happens I want yer to know that you've changed my life, Nell Coleman. Hell, there wouldn't even have been a life to change if it wasn't for you and Ned. Thank you.'

'You're welcome,' I said, with a sad smile.

His hand pulled free of mine and moved up over my cheekbone, his fingers feeling their way through my hair until his hand came to rest, holding the nape of my neck. His face fell out of focus as he moved closer, his top lip grazing mine and sending a shockwave through me. I raised my hand and rested it on the crown of his head, his hair soft and tousled beneath my fingers, and I gave him the one last push he needed. His lips fell to mine and lingered there for a moment before he pulled away.

'I'd better be going,' he whispered.

'Okay. I'll see you in the morning then,' I said, tears burgeoning in my eyes.

'Ten sharp.' He nodded with a smile and moved to the door. 'Bye, Nell.'

'Bye, Charlie.'

I rolled over in bed and looked at the screen of my phone. It took me a second or two for the time to register in my brain: 9.45 a.m.

My heart thumped, my eyes widened and I flung myself out of bed with a sense of panic. I dressed quickly and tried to make myself look presentable before stumbling my way down the stairs, my brain buzzing with anxiety whilst still being clouded with sleep.

I walked into the kitchen to find Ned sitting in his dressing gown, sipping coffee without a sense of urgency. 'Ned, why didn't you wake me up? And what are you doing? Get dressed. We need to go in, like, five minutes.'

He looked up at me with pity in his eyes and jerked his head towards the counter. I turned to see one of Abi's jars of sea glass sitting by the kettle with an envelope propped up against it.

My heart plummeted down into my stomach and my arms fell limply at my sides. 'He's already gone, hasn't he?'

I placed the jar of sea glass on the bathroom windowsill and ran myself an almost scalding bath, tipping in half a bottle of the bubble bath I'd got for Christmas last year and making sure I was safely ensconced amongst the bubbles before I opened the envelope and pulled out the letter inside. It was short and to-the-point.

Nell,

I thought it would be easier if I just left and I didn't subject you to a long drawn-out goodbye, but I couldn't leave without saying this.

Thank you for giving me something to hope for, something to smile about. For a long time, it seemed like no one cared if I lived or died, until you. I don't know what it is you're planning on using this space and time for, but whatever it is, Nell, I know that, much like you, it's going to be incredible.

I hope the time comes when everything falls into place for us, but for now I think I'm going to leave this one to the fates, seeing as they seem to know so much.

I'm not going to ask you to wait for me, or live your life around the possibility of whether we have a future together. Live your life for you.

Charlie.

P.S. I hope you don't mind, but I took George with me. Don't worry, it won't be the last you see of him. But I couldn't leave without taking something of you with me.

I folded up the note and let it float to the tiles, as I curled myself up inside the bubbles, wrapping my arms around myself in an attempt to keep myself whole. It was clear to me now that the pain I'd been waiting for had finally come. It was nice to dream of a pretty future together where Charlie was whole again and we could be what I'd always wanted us to be, but that's all it was: a dream. Charlie was gone and he'd taken my final scrap of hope with him.

Chapter Thirty

I wish I could say that I flourished in the weeks following Charlie's return to Ireland. That I discovered that I didn't miss him enough to wake up in a sombre mood or that I discovered I valued my freedom more than I valued him, but I didn't. I'd had enough freedom in the last two years and I wanted nothing more now than for him to come back and rid me of this immobilising loneliness.

Charlie being gone made me feel like I was missing half of my head or one of my lungs.

I sat in my swivel chair at work, watching pink clouds drift across the sky when I heard my name being called.

'Nell?' Caleb, the tardy volunteer whose lateness that first night had caused me to be the one to pick up Charlie's call.

'Yeah!' I called back to him, though I couldn't see his face from here over the partition between us. All he was right now was a mop of curly black hair.

'I've got Jackson.'

'I'm open,' I called back. 'Send him over.'

The call appeared on my screen and I accepted it before the second ring.

'Jackson, how's it going?' I asked, putting on a cheerfulness that I didn't quite feel. 'I haven't heard from you in a while.'

'I'm really good actually, Nell,' he replied, his voice so upbeat that it shocked me a little.

'Wow, that's great to hear. What have you been getting up to?'

'I, well, I . . .' He chuckled joyfully. 'I actually got myself a girlfriend.'

'Jackson, that's terrific!' I said. 'I'm so pleased for you.'

'Thanks, thanks. Her name is Audrey and I met her at work. She's a cyclist and we're gonna do this charity bike ride to raise money for you.'

'For me?' I asked, confused.

'Well, not you exactly, the phone line, the charity,' he said, excitedly.

'That's great.'

'Well, you've all been so good to me, no one more than you, and I know that it's your job and I'm not a friend, but it felt like you were, when I needed to believe it the most.'

'I am your friend, Jackson. Just because we've never actually met doesn't change that.'

He chuckled again, emotionally this time. 'If it's okay, when we've raised the money, do you think I could drop it by the office? It'd be so good to put a face to the voice.'

'We don't usually accept walk-ins, but I think that if the rules had to be bent for anyone, it'd be you.' There was a melancholy pause and I had to straighten myself in my chair and take a deep breath to pull myself together. 'So, I guess this means that I won't be hearing much of you from now on?'

342

'I guess not. But I'm sure I'll need to check back in every so often?'

'I'd like that,' I said, glad that I wasn't the only one feeling this separation anxiety.

'Well, ta-ra, Bab.'

'Ta-ra, Jackson.'

Between calls I went into the staff room – i.e. a tiny cordoned-off cubicle with a kettle, a microwave and several itchy chairs – and clicked on the kettle. I was feeling a little lethargic and so I scooped three teaspoons of Kenco Gold into my old mug, the pattern stripped away and destroyed after years of being assaulted by the dishwasher.

I heard the monotone drone of Barry's voice getting louder as he explained to a new volunteer that they were not permitted to take their headset home to use while playing *Call of Duty*.

The volunteer, a girl in her early twenties, with poker-straight hair that turned from blonde at the root to fading teal at the ends, smiled at me when she noticed me standing by the kettle.

Barry opened up a cabinet, from which spilled years of useless crap that had been shoved in there over the years, each time with that quick slam of the door that stops whatever you've just put in from coming straight back out.

'All of this needs sorting,' Barry droned. 'If you think it'll be useful put it back in, if not, chuck it.'

The volunteer got down on her hands and knees as a pot of century-old Berol markers tumbled out and spilled across the floor.

'I'll get you a bin bag,' Barry said, shuffling off.

'You new?' I asked, even though I knew full well that she was. You don't spend five years working in a place without spotting fresh meat in a heartbeat.

'Uh-huh,' she said, turning and smiling. 'Makayla.' We shook hands as the bubbles inside the kettle built to a crescendo and it clicked off.

'Nell,' I replied. 'He seems dull and humourless,' I said nodding in the direction of Barry as he waddled back, barely lifting each foot from the ground as he walked, bin bag in hand. 'But he's a sweetheart really.'

'If you say so.' She pulled out a small cardboard box.

I turned back around and went to the kettle, dousing the mound of coffee granules and watching them disintegrate as the water turned them liquid. I poured in the milk, using the teaspoon to crush the few defiant granules against the side of the mug.

'What do you want doing with these?' Makayla asked Barry as he tossed the bin bag down beside her.

'Let me see,' he said. I turned around to return to my cubicle, taking a mild interest in what she'd found in the depths of the cupboard. 'Oh, these old things.' In his hand he held a spool of stickers for the charity. 'We got these as a sample from a start-up company. We only used them once though because they spelled one of the words wrong.'

I stopped dead in my tracks and turned to Barry.

'Let me see,' I said, placing my coffee down on Dennis's desk and ignoring his snide comment about me invading his personal space. I took the roll from Barry's hands and unfurled a few inches. I let out a disbelieving laugh. There they were, hundreds of the sticker that Charlie had seen on the clock tower, the sticker that had saved his life, twice.

There at the bottom was the same misspelled slogan 'caring for your mental heath'. The only difference was that this one didn't have a movie quote written in Sharpie around the edge.

'Do you want them?' Barry asked.

'Erm, yeah,' I replied. 'You said we only used them once?'

'Yeah.' He chortled. 'How is someone meant to trust us with their mental health when it looks like we can't even spell it?' He looked at Makayla and seemed peeved when he saw she wasn't chuckling along.

'I've seen one of these out in town. Do you remember who put it there?'

'Yeah,' he said, stopping there as if that was enough information on the subject.

'Well?' I prompted, growing impatient.

'Someone came to us a few years back and wanted to volunteer, but we had no spaces and so I offered her the job of putting those stickers around town.'

'Her?' I asked. 'Do you know who she was?'

'I don't recall the name,' he said with an almost pained expression as he tried to regurgitate the memory. 'But I remember she was pretty, real pretty. Redhead. Irish.'

I left work in a sort of trance. Ned hadn't believed it either when I'd told him that Abi had been the one to place the sticker at the top of the tower. Her actions years before her death, saving Charlie's life when he couldn't bear to grieve for her any longer. Charlie had asked me once if I believed in fate and I hadn't been sure at the time, but right now, it seemed pretty real to me.

I know we'd agreed to focus on ourselves, for Charlie to

345

distance himself from me and concentrate on himself for a while, but no matter how hard I'd tried, I'd still been the first to break the pact. I'd sent Charlie a text asking him to call me when he got a moment, but I hadn't heard anything from him as of yet.

I walked towards Cool Beans, my instant caffeine fix not really doing much for me at this point in the day. I entered through the glass door and nodded my usual greeting to the tattooed supervisor before joining the queue.

The first few times I'd visited the café after Charlie had left had been an emotional roller coaster. When I'd walked through the door, my childlike hope would spike at the thought that I might just see him there, sitting at our communal table, ready for me to throw my lunch at him and force him into awkward conversation. Obviously, this hadn't happened, of course, and even though I tried really hard not to let anything to do with Charlie affect how I felt about this place, it did seem somewhat tainted with heartache.

'Any hot drinks?' the supervisor at the till called and I approached with that awkward smile that always comes when you know someone by sight and then speak to them.

'Americano please,' I said and added a brownie to that for good measure. He frowned at me for a moment, which made me wonder what I'd done. He shook the frown away and smiled, gesturing for me to tap my card against the reader. It pinged and I uttered my thanks before walking to the end of the counter to wait for it.

I pulled my phone from my pocket and checked for a response from Charlie, but there was none. I understood that distance was what we both needed right now. But even so, it still stung like abandonment.

I sighed and pushed the phone back into my pocket as a young girl came up to the counter and presented me with my drink. 'Do you want some milk with that?'

'No, thanks,' I replied.

'And, while you're here, would you like to donate to our charity of the month?'

My change was still jangling in my pocket.

'Sure,' I said. She grinned and reached over to a plastic bucket, decorated in glitter and colourful lettering, which I'd somehow missed as I'd been standing there. There was even a string of battery-powered fairy lights wrapped around it to attract maximum attention. 'What's the cause?' I asked.

Her grin widened as the opportunity to bombard me with details came. 'Healthy Minds, have you heard of them? Me and my boyfriend are doing a charity bike ride to raise money for them.'

I frowned and tilted my head to the side as my brain slotted all of that information into place. 'You're not Audrey, are you?' I asked.

'Yeah,' she said uncertainly. 'How'd you know that?'

'Nell?' The supervisor stopped serving the young mother and son at the till, completely abandoning their order as he weaved his way out from behind the counter and stood in front of me with hopeful eyes. 'I thought I recognised your voice when you ordered.'

'No,' I said in disbelief as a smile pulled my mouth up at the corners. 'Jackson?'

He pulled me into a hug and squeezed me so tightly that I could scarcely breathe.

I couldn't believe it.

How many times had I seen him, smiled at him, been

347

inches away from him? And all that time I'd known him, without being aware of it. He'd always seemed perfectly content every time I'd seen him. Sometimes, people's ability to hide their true feelings from the world even surprised me.

I guess I'd been playing into the exact same stereotypes that I always fought against whenever I thought of Jackson. I imagined him as a frightfully thin, very plain man who everyone would always refer to as a boy rather than the adult he was. But Jackson was nothing like my mental image of him. He was tall and broad, buff even, with big wide shoulders and sleeves of tattoos that snaked around toned forearms. His hair was longer than usual, not that that was saying much as it was usually shaved close to his scalp, but I guess that all of his personal choices were changing now that he had a girlfriend.

That had happened with me and Joel. He'd always wanted to keep his hair short but I liked it long, so he'd kept it that way for me. I felt the twinge in my chest that came every time I thought about him and I almost felt myself reach for my phone to call him. But he didn't want to talk to me; he'd told me so himself and I needed to give him time to come around to wanting to speak to me again, if ever.

Jackson pulled away and began explaining to Audrey who I was. She seemed just as overjoyed as he did to finally put a face to the name and hugged me too, once Jackson had let me go.

There was something about this moment that felt like the wrapping up of another loose end. I'd been afraid to leave Healthy Minds because I was worried about Jackson, but now he was moving on and leaving me behind, as he very well should.

The other reason not to leave and pursue old dreams was Ned, but even he was moving on, not from work, but emotionally. The idea of Ned and Mum being together unnerved me, but if that was what made them both happy then who was I to hold them back?

My ties with Joel had been severed and I doubted that he'd ever want to talk to me again. If he needed to, I'd be there, but if he didn't then that was fine too.

Even Charlie had moved on. I'd been so set on sticking around and not moving on for the wellbeing of other people, that I'd somehow fallen behind.

What if I had just been what Charlie had needed during that dark period of his life and what if I'd only needed him to finally move on from Joel? Maybe he didn't need me anymore and maybe I didn't need him. The idea made me feel like I was splitting in two, but I knew that I had to stop waiting around for life to kick me in another direction and tread the path myself. Everyone seemed happy and settled. Except me.

Maybe it was time to move on.

Chapter Thirty-One

One month later

Charlie

For such a tiny person, Kenna sure took up a lot of room. She always had done, sticking out her elbows or leaning at peculiar angles because she was wearing something too fitted that would stop her breathing if she sat like a regular person.

'How's Nell?' she asked, as she absentmindedly twirled a ginger ringlet around her red-gel-tipped finger.

I looked down into the almost empty ice cream tub in my hand and scraped the spoon across the bottom, making patterns on the milky cardboard. 'She was fine last I talked to her.'

'And when was that?' she asked.

'A while ago,' I replied.

I tossed my ice cream pot into the bin beside our bench and looked out at the pale, sunny sky over Clew Bay. Being here brought back the memory of when Nell found me, after I went AWOL at the memorial. How long ago that seemed now.

'She wanted space and I need it too. So, that's exactly what I'm givin' her,' I said.

'It's a shame that yer had to meet her when you did.'

'Yeah,' I agreed, feeling the beginning of an ache inside my ribcage and trying to focus on the water to keep it from growing. 'But the timing was wrong.'

'Do you think you'll go back?' she asked and the words brought instant anxiety with them.

'I don't know. I'm healin' here – I can feel it. I've stopped wakin' up and wishin' the day was over before it's even begun and I know that me bein' here is good for Carrick. I don't know, I just feel like being here is right.' I took a breath of fresh, salty air and I felt the warmth of home fill my chest. 'She saved my life, I can never forget that, but I was a person I've never been before when we were together. Nell never met the old me; she only knew this version. If I get back to normal and then go back, I think I might be a stranger to her.'

She sighed and turned to me, groaning as the waistband of her pencil skirt dug into her torso and pinched her lungs. 'Charlie, you're never gonna be the person you were before. People are always changin'. It doesn't matter who you're with, you're always gonna be different. You pick up on the other person's traits, the way they sit, their ways of thinkin' and in the end you're a mash-up of the two of yer.' She rolled her eyes at me. 'Before all of this, back when you were Abi's version of Charlie, you could be a bit of a shit, not gonna lie, but I still loved yer. When yer went rogue and disappeared on us all, I still loved yer even then. And when you were Nell's version of Charlie, I loved yer all the same.'

'Which version am I now then?' I asked.

'I think that you're just you. You and Abi were together from such a young age that I don't think yer ever had a chance to find out who yer really were on your own. You were always tryin' to impress her and show her that you were worthy of her, flashin' all those fancy clothes and watches around. But she never loved yer for your watches. Honestly, I think I prefer this incarnation of yer.'

'Really? Yer prefer this mopin', miserable eejit?'

'Yeah, I do. I think yer needed a wound or two to size down that big old head of yours. It's just a shame that the wound had to be Abi.'

I felt it again, the lump in my throat, and I instinctively reached my hand inside my pocket and felt around until I found the sea glass with my fingers.

'If only I'd not been distracted, she'd still be here now,' I said, my voice clogging with emotion again.

'What d'yer mean?' Kenna asked and I looked up to see her meticulously pruned brows furrowed and her bottom lip jutting out.

I cleared my throat. I had forgotten that I had never voiced any of this to Kenna before. God knows how she'd react to them. 'Because, if I hadn't gone to make her some tea and then been distracted by the news, I'd have seen that she wasn't well and called the ambulance and she could've been saved.' I braced myself for a slap. I almost turned my face so that she'd have easy access to my cheek. 'If I'd gone back to her sooner, she might have lived.'

'Christ, Charlie, is this what you've been carryin' around

352

with yer all this time? There was no savin' her,' Kenna said with a subtle shake of her head. 'Yer really did just pass it all on to Mammy didn't yer. She died instantly – that's what the coroner said.'

I felt something twang in my chest, like an air lock releasing. 'Instantly?'

'She suffered a massive pulmonary embolism. She died in a couple of seconds.'

Sometime in that hour or so between me leaving the room and returning with her tea, she'd just switched off, like central heating. And this guilt I'd been carrying for so long had never been mine to carry.

'Charlie, breathe. You're turnin' blue,' Kenna said and shook my shoulder.

I gasped air into my lungs. 'So, it wasn't my fault? I'm not the reason she's dead?'

'No, Charlie. It wasn't anyone's fault. It just happened.'

The dry grass was itchy against my legs as I sat facing Abi's tombstone.

Loving daughter, sister, wife and friend, it read, in silver letters.

I rolled the sea glass around in my fingers as I read them over and over again, the faraway sound of passing cars and chirruping birds the only sounds being brought in by the wind.

'So,' I said my voice raspy from my talk with Kenna, 'I found out today that it isn't my fault that you're down there. You'd think that'd make me feel better. And it does, a little, but you're still dead.'

I heard the clang of the gate and looked over my shoulder

to see an old man, flowers in hand, his walking stick making a gentle crunch in the gravel path as he wandered my way. He got to within a few metres before he noticed me and tipped his hat before wandering off to a grave by the wall that separated the graveyard from the road. I wondered if that might be me in forty years, still bringing flowers here, the hurt still sharp enough to sting.

'I met a girl. Her name's Nell. I don't know how you'd feel about that but I just wanted to tell yer. Feels less like I'm cheatin' on yer that way.'

I tossed the orange glass to my other hand and rolled it around between my palms. The feel of it was so familiar now, after carrying it around for so long, that it felt like a part of me. The sea-buffed edges made even smoother after being rolled around for years in anxious hands. 'She called me about a month ago, said that she'd found out who put that sticker up on the tower. I shoulda known you'd have had somethin' to do with it.' I smiled, despite myself. 'So, that musta been when you went through that volunteerin' phase and ended up in the cat shelter where yer got Magnus from?' I looked to the stone, as if waiting for it to answer. 'And writin' that thing from *Castaway* on there, as if you knew I'd need it someday, as if you knew I'd need her.'

I wiped my moistening eyes with my sleeve and sniffed back the emotion. I'd been trying not to 'man up' when the urge to cry came over me. But lately the tears had been coming less often, though the grief behind them was ever present in the background like a thunderstorm one town over that threatened to descend on me.

'I just wanted to come here and tell you, even though I'm pretty sure that I'm just talking to the ground and nothing else, that I love yer and I'm always goin' to love yer. But eventually I'm gonna have to make some room in there to love someone else.' I wiped my cheeks again and exhaled loudly, the air taking with it a weight that I'd felt for far too long. 'I've got a lot of decisions to make. Should I stay or should I go? In the words of The Clash.' I chuckled, knowing that she'd have appreciated that reference with her love of punk rock. 'But whatever I choose, I'm not forgettin' yer and I'm not replacin' yer.'

I took another minute before standing and taking a breath. I reached out a hand and rested it atop the marble stone, thinking how much time Abi and I wasted in those years we hadn't spoken, using our damaged pride as a reason not to act on anything. But there was no changing that now and there was no changing the fact that this stone was here, with her beneath it. I unfurled my hand, the glass clinking a little as it touched the top of the marble. I let my hand linger a moment longer before turning around and walking away to where Steve awaited me in the car park, leaving the piece of orange sea glass where it really belonged.

Chapter Thirty-Two

Four months later

Nell

I walked through the glass-roofed foyer of Aston University and onto the large grassy area out front, which was always speckled with lounging students whenever the weather allowed.

Tom and Marni, the two students in their early twenties who had befriended me in the first week, chattered away beside me as we made our way out into the lazy afternoon sunshine.

We all collapsed down onto the grass amidst the scattered groups of students, all dressed in various forms of blood-spattered shirts and rubber masks. I had completely forgotten that today was Halloween, until I'd walked downstairs and found Ned sitting at the table dressed as Leatherface, the severed arm strapped to his belt making it troublesome for him to sit down.

'Got any plans for the weekend, Nell?' Tom asked, his long brown hair pulled into a tiny little man bun at the crown of his head, that reminded me of a Samurai warrior.

'I have one shift at Healthy Minds tomorrow and then I think my mum is coming to visit for a day or two,' I replied. 'Rock and roll, I know.' I turned my face up to the sorry excuse for sunshine and leaned back on my hands. 'You guys?'

'There's a Halloween party over at Laurie's place if you fancy it?' Tom asked.

'Tom, you should know better,' Marni teased. 'Friday nights are when she and her husband have movie night.'

They'd taken to calling Ned my husband ever since they'd learned about him and the fact that I'd told them he was dating my mother hadn't seemed to deter them.

Lately I'd noticed Tom had started to get a little flirty, touching me more frequently, asking me out for coffee. He was nice enough and good-looking, but there was absolutely no way that I could even contemplate seeing someone right now. Professor Gundersen had approached me after class a couple of weeks ago and told me that the student who was doing a year of study abroad had found out she was pregnant and so was coming home at the end of October. She seemed to think that I would be a good candidate to take her place and had given me a handful of paperwork to think over.

'So,' Tom asked, reading my mind. 'Is New Zealand a go-go or can you simply not deprive yourself of our company for that long?'

'I handed the paperwork in yesterday,' I said with mingled terror and excitement in my gut.

'I can't believe you're abandoning us and your husband for a whole year,' Marni jested.

'Ned will be just fine and so will you guys,' I said, picking at the grass with my nails. 'It's going to be strange, being so far away.'

'Yeah, the flight to Auckland is, like, over twenty-four hours, isn't it?' Tom asked. I gulped audibly. Twenty-four hours, airborne, thousands of miles above the earth. I shook the thought from my head and took a breath. No, I wasn't going to let fear override this chance that had fallen into my lap.

I thought of my last flight, how I'd held on to Charlie's hand so tightly that his fingers had turned blue. I'd have no hand to hold this time, unless I managed to make friends with the person sitting next to me, which, with my verbal diarrhoea, wasn't out of the question. I felt the ache in my chest that came as a by-product of every memory of him and waited. I knew that, like all the other times, it would be only a minute or two until the ache subsided. In his last message to me, Charlie had told me that he was feeling good, working in the family shop, and that living with Carrick was making him feel as if he'd regressed in maturity by about twenty years.

'You okay?' Tom asked, placing his hand on my ankle.

'Yeah,' I replied. 'I'm fine.'

'So,' Marnie said, guessing that the subject needed to be changed. 'Have you decided what you're gonna specialise in when you're out there?' She turned to me, her long purple box-braided hair swinging down in the air like little ropes.

'Pretty sure I want to go into grief and bereavement

counselling.' I looked down at my toes and a small wave of sadness came over me. I gave myself five seconds to feel it before reining it back in and regaining my smile. Yes, my time with Charlie had been beautiful and painful and something that I would always remember with a tinge of regret that it had ended before it had ever really started. But being there for him, helping him through the most devastating event of his life, had helped me to figure out what I was good at and what I wanted to do with the rest of my life. There were millions of broken hearts and grieving people out there and if I could help even one of them, then my time here on this planet was worthwhile.

The second I stepped from the train onto the platform, I felt my phone buzz in my pocket and pulled it out to see that it was a call from Mum.

'*Hola, Madre*,' I said in my best Spanish accent.

'*Buenas Tardes*,' she replied, her accent so much better than mine. 'How was uni?'

'Good. Tom tried to get me to go out with them all tonight, but I passed.'

'Oh, go on, Nelly. From what I hear this Tom has a soft spot for you.' She'd been pushier and pushier ever since my almost love affair with Charlie. I think she was trying to flush the sadness from my system with the possibility of a few meaningless trysts.

'No, Mum. Tom is, like, twelve.'

'There is nothing wrong with a toy boy, Nelly. I've had more than a few in my time.'

I made a gagging sound. 'I thought we agreed that we would never have a conversation about this ever again!'

'Okay. Sorry, love.' She sighed.

'Has he been in touch?' she asked, her tone almost pitiful.

'Can we please talk about something else, before I start crying in the middle of the street?'

'Of course,' she said. 'Have you heard from Joel?'

'Mum! Of all the topics to try and cheer me up you go with Joel?'

'I'm sorry, love, but your life is quite the minefield of conversational topics.'

The last I heard Joel was doing well and they were moving up to Scarborough to be amongst happy memories and Rachel had promised to get in touch when they were both settled.

'There was actually something I wanted to talk to you about,' Mum said.

'And what's that?' I asked, trying to regain some composure as I turned onto my road and saw a couple of street lamps prematurely burst into life in the early evening light.

'I was going to wait and tell you this face-to-face, but I can't wait. I've accepted a permanent job offer in London.'

'You're coming home?' I asked, my mood suddenly lighter. 'Wait, does this mean that you and Ned are a thing, because if you think for one moment that I am ever gonna call that man Dad then you have another thing—'

'No. I'm coming back for you, Nelly. What you said to me in the bathroom that night, well, it hit me pretty hard and I realised that I haven't been the mother to you that I thought I'd been.'

'So, you're coming home, home?'

'Well, I'll be in London. But you're a big girl now. You don't need me hovering around. But I'll be close enough to see you every week or so, if that's something you want. I mean I understand if you don't want me hovering. What fun is it having your mum there when you're trying to have a social life? I've never been a hoverer and I certainly don't expect to start now.'

Christ, was this what I sounded like when I babbled?

'Mum. Firstly, I don't have a social life and secondly, having you at my beck and call is something that I've wanted for at least the last decade of my life. But, as sod's law would have it, I handed my New Zealand paperwork in yesterday.'

'Oh, Nelly. That's great. I'm so proud of you. I think you're going to love it out there.'

'I hope so. But it means that, once again, we're going to be on opposite sides of the globe.' I sighed, wondering for the thousandth time if this was the right thing to do.

'Don't worry about me, Nelly. I'm not going anywhere. Go off and have your long-overdue adventure and when you get back, you'll know exactly where I am.'

I ended the call with Mum the moment I turned into the drive and pushed the phone into my back pocket. I felt slightly drunk with the idea that when I got back, she would finally be here, close enough to call if I needed her and I wouldn't even have to look at my world clock app before doing so. As I reached the doorstep, I heard a sound that I recognised. It was so quiet that it was almost nonexistent, a quiet squeaking. I looked down and a small gasp escaped my lips, because there, sitting in the centre of the step, his head bobbing in the breeze, was George. I bent down so quickly that my knees clicked and I snatched him up. Beneath his feet was a folded-up piece of paper that I almost tore in half trying to open quicker than my trembling hands would allow.

When I finally got it open, I smoothed it out and read the message that simply said:

Coffee? On me.

C x

I'd thought that if this moment ever came, that nothing would be able to hold me back from running headlong in any direction Charlie was in. But right now, I couldn't move.

Charlie was back and if I started now, I could be with him in less than fifteen minutes. But, again, the timing was all wrong. I was leaving, pursuing what I should have long since pursued. Why now?

'So?' The front door swung open and Ned's smirking face popped into sight. 'Are you going or not?'

Charlie

The heat, permeating through the ceramic of the cup was almost painful as it turned my palms red. Little tendrils of steam rose from the surface of the milky tea and brought with it that unmistakable herbal smell.

How different my life was now from when I'd taken refuge here on the day that I'd been heading for the clock tower. I'd been so sure of my plans that, if someone had told me then that I'd be sitting here, months later, waiting on a girl, I'd have laughed in their face and deemed them mentally deranged, but here I was. I lifted the tea to my lips and took a sip.

The sound of the café door opening made me turn around hopefully. My stomach sank when I saw that it was just an employee going outside to fetch some chairs in. I sighed and turned back to my cup. I'd hated being away from Nell and truth be told, I'd even missed Magnus a little. But that's what the therapist that Kenna had found for me had said to do. 'Only by gaining a little distance can we also gain perspective,' she'd said and, in the end, even though it had been almost impossible, I'd distanced myself.

Nell had been right, back when she'd said that the timing had been wrong. Neither of us had been in the right place to fall in love, but that was exactly what we'd done, even though the Abi-shaped wedge between us did its best to keep us apart.

I think, truth be told, Abi was not someone I'd ever be able to get over completely. I had loved her more than anything in this world. All I'd wanted to do was hold her and spend every waking moment in her presence, then all of a sudden, I wasn't able to do any of those things anymore. I don't know if grief ever really goes away completely. It's like a game of pass the bomb: you carry it, never knowing when it will go off, the threat of it terrifying. Until one day, when your time on this planet is up, you exit stage right and pass the grief on to someone else. I guess that death isn't quite as final as people say it is. It remains in this world, until the last person who loved you, is no longer here.

But even though I knew that there would be days to come that would be worse than the others, anniversaries and birthdays where I'd go quiet and reserved, I knew that I wanted Nell by my side through all of them.

I hoped more than anything that she wanted the same, because we had already spent far too long apart.

I heard someone clear their throat behind me and I turned in my seat, almost falling from it with the enthusiasm with which I spun around.

My eyes found the face of the person behind me and my heart sank.

'Excuse me, sir. Would you mind if I just wipe this table down, just so we're ready for when this place turns into boozy housewife central?' the young girl asked with a blushing smile.

'Of course not, go ahead,' I said, lifting up my cup and letting her wipe away the crumbs and coffee rings left by the patrons of the day.

She thanked me, smiled and walked away as I placed my tea back down.

There was no telling if Nell would even come. God knows that I brought a boatload of complications into her life, which had been just fine without me, and in the time that had passed since, maybe she'd realised that the quiet life was what she'd actually wanted all along.

'Excuse me,' a voice came again.

'I didn't spill anything, I swear,' I said, turning with a smile on my lips.

My breath caught in my throat as I was met with the large brown eyes that I'd been craving for months.

Her hair was shorter than it had been all those months ago and she looked happier, more alive than I'd ever seen her before.

Her lips drew up into such a wide smile that my mouth had no choice but to mimic it.

She cleared her throat. 'Excuse me,' she said again, repeating the first words she'd ever said to me. 'Do you mind if I sit here?'

'Be my guest,' I replied.

She sat down nervously, her hands cupping in her lap as she tentatively looked up at me through her lashes.

'It's so good to see you again, Nell.' I almost sighed the words. The relief of being so close to her again was almost overpowering.

'You too,' she responded. She frowned a little, her brows creasing in that adorable way that I remembered so vividly. She looked as though she was trying to figure something out, mulling it over in her brain and weighing up the options.

'What's wrong?' I asked, reaching out a hand and placing it on her arm. It felt strange to touch her again, as if I wasn't sure if I was allowed to anymore.

'Nothing. Nothing's wrong,' she replied, her eyes meeting mine and her brow unfurrowing. 'I just want to ask you a question, is all.'

'And what question is that?' I asked, my heart thumping so loudly that I worried I wouldn't be able to hear her question when the words finally left her mouth. 'Ask me anything.'

Her lips curled into a smile, lighting up her eyes with a sense of excitement that I hadn't seen her wear before. 'Are you up for an adventure?' she asked cryptically.

'I'm up for anything as long as it's with you.'

'Good. Then, how does New Zealand sound?'

From the café, neither Nell or Charlie heard the tolling of the clock tower bell as it struck the hour. The sound ringing out to a town that barely noticed it as it echoed through the sky. Below the lip of the wall, the sticker that had saved a life trembled in the breeze. It had held on through wind and rain, snow and sun, but its time watching over the town from up high was coming to an end. A second gust came and the glue finally gave way, as if peeled away by ghostly fingers, the sticker falling from the brick to which it had clung for so long and fluttering into the evening sky.

Acknowledgements

I have heard people talk about the difficult second book and how they had become unfathomably lost with it, all the while thinking that that would never happen to me, not with all of the ideas I had inside my head. I could not have been more wrong. Getting a second book together has been one of the most frustrating and challenging things I have ever done and I am so happy that I can now breathe a sigh of relief that it is out there in the world, telling the story I always wanted to tell.

At First Sight is the reincarnation of a story I wrote around six years ago and it has always meant so much to me.

Charlie, Carrick and Ned have always had a special place in my heart and the new introduction of Nell has turned *At First Sight* from a beloved idea into what I hope you agree is a beautiful story of the journey to overcome what is holding you back and allowing yourself a second chance.

This story came from inside my brain, but it takes an army to get a book out into the world and I'd like to begin by thanking my agent Elena Langtry, Lisa Moylett and everyone at CMM Agency for their undying and unwavering support. You are always there to help me overcome my doubts and give me the confidence boost I need.

Thank you to Tilda McDonald and Phoebe Morgan for believing in my ideas, no matter how scrambled they start out, and for giving me free rein to run with an idea until it finds its footing. Thank you to Sabah Khan, Ellie Pilcher, Beth Wickington and everyone else at Avon who have been behind me for the past couple of years. Your support and the extremely hard work you all put in during lockdown to help me, and all the other lockdown debut authors, was incredible and I am proud to be part of such a great, award-winning team #imprintoftheyear2020, but we don't like to brag . . . much.

Thank you to Matt Goode for reassuring me that what I'd written wasn't complete garbage and for never moaning about the endless re-readings. Not to mention you putting up with me talking in an Irish accent for the majority of the time I was writing this.

Thank you to Mom for telling anyone who will listen about my books and standing beside them in Waterstones, talking very loudly about how amazing they are to passing customers.

Dad, you don't say a lot, but when you do it is always profound. Thanks for your support and for always knowing what to say, no matter how taciturn your motivational speeches may be.

I would like to give special thanks to Sheila Gibbons for being my virtual guide around Westport and for giving me tons of insider knowledge and facts about the town that I simply couldn't have found anywhere else. Your help was invaluable. I hope I did this beautiful town justice.

I am also thankful to Police Constable D'Arcy Hazlewood

for all the help you've given me, both with this book and in life in general. Thanks Boo.

And my gratitude goes out to Chris Day, who has been so supportive and who owns more copies of my books than anyone else in the world.

Also, to John Howard and Tom Owens. Cheers for letting me write my books during the lulls of my shifts behind the bar at work. I expect my blue plaque to be erected on the Cricket Club walls in due course.

I would also like to let every single one of my readers know how much I appreciate and value your kind words and testimonials. Your word of mouth has helped get my books out there into the world during a very difficult time to be a debut writer and I will always be incredibly grateful for that.

And a final thank you goes out to the workers, doctors, therapists and volunteers, working to help others with their mental health. The work that charities like Samaritans do is incredible and there are so many people out there in the world who are alive and happy because of the work you all do. I am also very grateful for all of the information provided to me by Samaritans to help me do this sensitive topic justice.

In the UK, the highest rate of suicide is in the group of men aged 45–49, but rates among women under 25 has risen by 93.8% in the time between 2012 and 2019.

Depression is something that is often extremely hard to see, so be sympathetic to those around you. Ask a friend how they are and actually pay attention to the answer. Seek out that friend who is slowly withdrawing from the group and make them feel welcome again and above all, be kind, because you never know who is hurting beneath the surface and you might just be the friendly face they need.

If you loved *At First Sight*, don't miss
Hannah Sunderland's stunning debut

Effie's not perfect. Neither is Theo.
But together, they're pretty close . . .

Out now